THE
MEMORY
OF
RUNNING

THE

MEMORY

OF

RUNNING

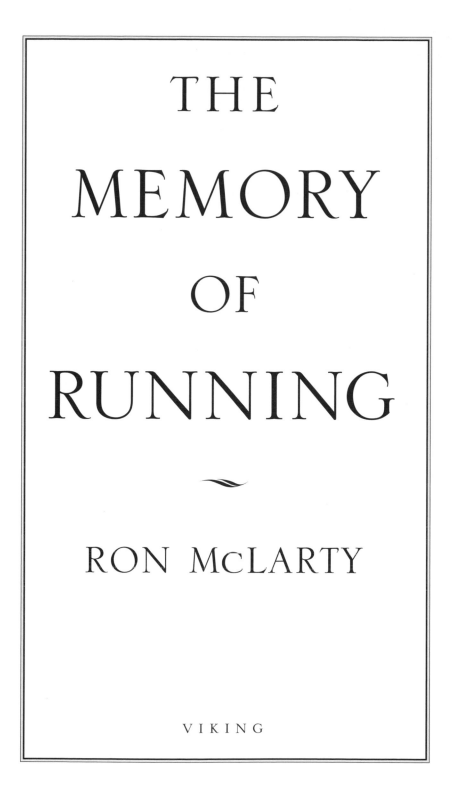

RON McLARTY

VIKING

VIKING
Published by the Penguin Group
Penguin Group (USA) Inc., 375 Hudson Street, New York, New York 10014, USA •
Penguin Group (Canada), 10 Alcorn Avenue, Toronto, Ontario, Canada M4V 3B2 (a
division of Pearson Penguin Canada Inc.) • Penguin Books Ltd, 80 Strand, London
WC2R 0RL, England • Penguin Ireland, 25 St. Stephen's Green, Dublin 2, Ireland (a
division of Penguin Books Ltd) • Penguin Books Australia Ltd, 250 Camberwell Road,
Camberwell, Victoria 3124, Australia (a division of Pearson Australia Group Pty Ltd) •
Penguin Books India Pvt Ltd, 11 Community Centre, Panchsheel Park, New
Delhi–110 017, India • Penguin Group (NZ), Cnr Airborne and Rosedale Roads,
Albany, Auckland 1310, New Zealand (a division of Pearson New Zealand Ltd) •
Penguin Books (South Africa) (Pty) Ltd, 24 Sturdee Avenue, Rosebank, Johannesburg
2196, South Africa

Penguin Books Ltd, Registered Offices:
80 Strand, London WC2R 0RL, England

First published in 2004 by Viking Penguin,
a division of Penguin Group (USA) Inc

10 9 8 7 6 5 4 3 2 1

Copyright © Zaluma, Inc., 2004
All rights reserved

LIBRARY OF CONGRESS CATALOGING-IN-PUBLICATION DATA
McLarty, Ron.
    The memory of running / Ron McLarty.
        p.   cm.
    ISBN 0-670-03363-4
    1. Overweight men—Fiction. 2. Cycling—Fiction. I. Title.
PS3613.C547M46 2005
813'.6—d22   2004049608

This book is printed on acid-free paper. ∞

Printed in the United States of America
Designed by Carla Bolte

In loving memory of Diane Tesitor McLarty,
wife, mother, friend, artist.
Who wrote the books of Zachary, Lucas,
and Matthew. Masterpieces all.

THE
MEMORY
OF
RUNNING

1

My parents' Ford wagon hit a concrete divider on U.S. 95 outside Biddeford, Maine, in August 1990. They'd driven that stretch of highway for maybe thirty years, on the way to Long Lake. Some guy who used to play baseball with Pop had these cabins by the lake and had named them for his children. Jenny. Al. Tyler. Craig. Bugs. Alice and Sam. We always got Alice for two weeks in August, because it had the best waterfront, with a shallow, sandy beach, and Mom and Pop could watch us while they sat in the green Adirondack chairs.

We came up even after Bethany had gone, and after I had become a man with a job. I'd go up and be a son, and then we'd all go back to our places and be regular people.

Long Lake has bass and pickerel and really beautiful yellow perch. You can't convince some people about yellow perch, because perch have a thick, hard lip and are coarse to touch, but they are pretty fish—I think the prettiest—and they taste like red snapper. There are shallow coves all over the lake, where huge turtles live, and at the swampy end, with its high reeds and grass, the bird population is extraordinary. There are two pairs of loons, and one pair always seems to have a baby paddling after it; ducks, too, and Canada geese, and a single heron that stands on one leg and lets people get very close to photograph it. The water is wonderful for swimming, especially in the mornings, when the lake is like a mirror. I used to take all my clothes off and jump in, but I don't do that now.

In 1990 I weighed 279 pounds. My pop would say, "How's that weight, son?" And I would say, "It's holding steady, Pop." I had a forty-six-inch waist, but I was sort of vain and I never bought a pair of pants over forty-two inches—so, of course, I had a terrific hang, with a real water-balloon push. Mom never mentioned my weight, because she liked to cook casseroles, since they were easily prepared ahead of time and were hearty. What she enjoyed asking about was my friends and my girlfriends. Only in 1990 I was a 279-pound forty-three-year-old supervisor at Goddard Toys who spent entire days checking to see that the arms on the action figure SEAL Sam were assembled palms in, and nights at the Tick-Tap Lounge drinking beers and watching sports. I didn't have girlfriends. Or, I suppose, friends, really. I did have drinking friends. We drank hard in a kind of friendly way.

My mom had pictures set up on the piano in the home in East Providence, Rhode Island. Me and Bethany mostly, although Mom's dad was in one, and one had Pop in his Air Corps uniform. Bethany was twenty-two in her big picture. She'd posed with her hands in prayer and looked up at one of her amazing curls. Her pale eyes seemed glossy. I stood in my frame like a stick. My army uniform seemed like a sack, and I couldn't have had more than 125 pounds around the bones. I didn't like to eat then. I didn't like to eat in the army either, but later on, when I came home and Bethany was gone and I moved out to my apartment near Goddard, I didn't have a whole lot to do at night, so I ate, and later I had the beer and the pickled eggs and, of course, the fat pretzels.

My parents pulled their wagon in front of cabin Alice, and I helped load up. They were going to drive home to East Providence on the last Friday of our two weeks, and I would leave on Saturday. That way they could avoid all the Saturday traffic coming up to New Hampshire and Maine. I could do the cleanup and return the rented fishing boat. It was one of those good plans that just make sense. Even Mom, who was worried about what I would eat, had to agree it was a good plan. I told her I would be sure to have a nice sandwich and maybe some soup. What I really was planning was two six-packs of beer and a bag of those crispy Bavarian pretzels. Maybe some different kinds of cheeses. And because I had been limiting my smoking to maybe a pack a day, I planned to fire up a chain-smoke, at least enough to keep the mosquitoes down, and think. Men of a certain weight and certain habits think for a while with a clarity intense and fleeting.

I was sitting in the Adirondack chair, drunk and talking to myself, when a state trooper parked his cruiser next to my old Buick and walked down to the waterfront. Black kid about twenty-six or -seven, wearing the grays like the troopers do, fitted and all, and I turned and stood when I heard him coming.

"Great, isn't it?"

"What?" he asked, like a bass drum.

I had leaned against the chair for support, and it wobbled under my weight and his voice.

"The lake. The outside."

"I'm looking for a Smithson Ide."

"That would be me," I said, a drunk fighting to appear straight.

"Why don't you sit down a second, Mr. Ide."

"I'm not drunk or anything, Officer . . . Trooper. . . . I'm really fine . . . not . . ."

"Mr. Ide, there's been an accident, and your parents are seriously injured. Outside of Portland. Mr. Ide was taken to the head-trauma unit at Portland General, and Mrs. Ide is at the Biddeford Hospital."

"My mom? My pop?" I asked stupidly.

"Why don't you come with me, and I'll get you up there."

"My car . . ."

"You come with me, and we'll get you back, too. You won't have to worry about your car."

"I won't have to worry. Okay. Good."

I changed into a clean pair of shorts and a T-shirt. The trooper tried very hard not to look at me. I was glad, because people tended to form quick opinions of me when I stood there fat and drunk and cigarette-stained in front of them. Even reasonable people go for an immediate response. Drunk. Fat. A smoky-burned aroma.

The trooper, whose name was Alvin Anderson, stopped for two coffees at the bake shop in Bridgton, then took Route 302 into Portland. We didn't talk very much.

"I sure appreciate this."

"Yes, sir."

"Looks like rain."

"I don't know."

Pop had already been admitted when Alvin let me out at Emergency.

"Take a cab over to Biddeford Hospital when you're done here. I'll be by later on."

I watched him drive away. It was about five, and a rain began. A cold rain. My sandals flopped on the blue floor, and I caught my thick reflection stretched against the shorts and T-shirt. My face was purple with beer. The lady at Information directed me to Admitting, where an elderly volunteer directed me to the second-floor trauma unit.

"It's named for L. L. Bean," he said. "Bugger had it, and he gave it. That's the story."

A male nurse at the trauma reception asked me some questions to be sure that this Ide was my Ide.

"White male?"

"Yes."

"Seventy?"

"I . . ."

"About seventy?"

"Yes."

"Artificial valve?"

"Oh, yeah . . . about ten years ago, see. . . . It really made him mad because—"

"Okay. Take this pass and stand on the blue line. That's where the nurse assigned to your father will take you in. There are thirty trauma cells, glass front, usually the curtains are drawn—but some-

4

times they're not. We ask you, when your nurse comes to take you in, to promise not to look into any of the units other than yours."

"I promise," I said solemnly.

I stood on the blue line and waited. I was still drunk. I wished I had put on a baggy sweater and some sweatpants or something, because fat guys are just aware of the way things ride up the crotch, and they've got to always be pulling out the front part of the T-shirt so little breasts don't show through.

The nurse was named Arleen, and she was as round as me. She had on baggy surgical green slacks and an enormous green smock with pockets everywhere. She led me to my pop's cubicle. I didn't look into any of the other ones. I could hear a man saying, "Oh, God. Oh, God," over and over, and crying, but mostly there was a hushed tone, and when the nurses and doctors hurried about, they sounded like leaves on the ground in the fall with kids walking through them. I was very drunk.

Pop lay out on a tall, metal-framed bed. His head, chest, waist, and ankles had heavy straps over them. Except for a sheet, folded to reach from his belly button to his knees, he was naked. When the nurse closed the door, leaving me alone, I remember thinking that this was the quietest room I had ever been in.

I could hear my heart in my head. The bed had an engine that tilted it very slowly. So slowly, really, that even though it moved Pop from side to side, it didn't seem as if he was moving at all, even though he was. I looked under the bed for the engine, but I couldn't see it.

Pop had some bruises around his eyes and the bridge of his nose, and a Band-Aid over a small hole in his forehead that the nurse told me had been bored to relieve some kind of pressure. Pop used to brag about not knowing what a headache felt like, since he'd never had one, so I thought it was odd he needed that little hole.

I put my hand on top of my pop's. It was a little silly, because Pop was not a hand-holder. Pop was a slapper of backs and a shaker of hands. But putting my hand on top of his seemed all right, and felt strange and good. Later on, after I had some time to think about it, I guessed that when these awful kinds of things happen to you, it helps to find a lot of things to feel good about. They don't have to be big-deal things, but more like the hand business or combing Mom's hair, those kinds of things. They add up.

I'd been alone with my pop for twenty minutes when a doctor came in. He was about my age, only trim and sober. He had thick red-gray hair, and for some reason I used my fingers to comb my own thin and shaggy head.

"Mr. Ide?"

"Yes, sir. Thank you."

"I'm Dr. Hoffman."

We shook hands. Then he moved close to Pop's head.

"I put this hole here to relieve the pressure."

"Thank you so much," I said sincerely.

I would have given my car to anyone, right there, if I could have been sober.

"He kept himself pretty good, didn't he?" he said. His little flashlight moved from eye to eye.

"My pop walked and stuff."

Pop swayed imperceptibly on his bed, to the left. The doctor was right. Pop had a great body, and he had a routine to keep it that way. Mom sometimes went up in weight and then got on some diet to lose it, but Pop was really proud of how he kept the old weight at 180, his playing weight.

"Do you know what blood thinners he took for the valve?" Dr. Hoffman asked.

"No. Sorry. It pissed him— He was mad about the heart operation. He worked out, and one day the other doctor said, 'You have to get a new valve in your heart.' But it was because of something that, you know, happened when he was a kid."

"Rheumatic fever."

"That's it. Is it bad? Did it break?"

Was I a huge alcoholic trying to be helpful?

"His heart is fine, and I think under normal circumstances your father probably wouldn't be in bad shape right now, except the blood thinners he took to ensure clot-free flow through the heart chambers, and, of course, through the artificial valve, allowed the blood to hemorrhage violently inside his head when he hit the windshield."

"I see." I nodded again, stupidly.

"Blood is one of the most toxic entities known. When it gets out of the old veins, well . . ."

"I didn't realize that."

"Do you have anyone else in the immediate family I need to talk to?"

"Bethany, but you can't talk to . . . well, no . . . me, I guess."

"Well . . ."

"He really looks good. Just those bruises. He does push-ups, too. Walks and stuff."

"What let's do is this. Why don't we watch what happens tonight, and I'll see you tomorrow, and we'll see."

"That's great, Doctor. And thank you. Thank you so much."

I said good-bye to Pop, went down to the main lobby of the hospital, and took a cab to Mom's hospital in Biddeford. It was about fifteen minutes away. A four-cigarette ride. It was pretty cold by now. Usually I don't mind cold nights, but I did this night, and for some reason my hair hurt.

The hospital in Biddeford was new. It was set in a little forest of fir trees and looked nice, not all big and really nervous-making like Portland General. You got a sense of something bad in Portland. The way it smelled. The way you sounded in the crowded corridors, and the way all those people whispered into the banks of phones. Biddeford Hospital was different. There were plants in the reception area, and the retired volunteers seemed happy to see you. You got this good feeling that everything was going to be all right.

Mom was in the third-floor trauma unit. It was small, and, again unlike Portland, the walls were painted in a hopeful blue-sky color. Portland was green. Old green. Reception had called that I was on my way up, and this pretty black girl met me outside the unit's door. She wore standard green pants bunched around her ankles, and running shoes. Her blouse was white, with happy faces on it.

"Hi," she called out.

"Hi," I said.

"Are you Jan's son?"

"Yes. I'm Smithy Ide."

"I'm Toni, I'm one of her nurses. C'mon."

She didn't tell me about not looking into the rooms, but she didn't have to.

"Jan's in five. She's on a waterbed that tilts."

"My father is, too."

"How's he doing?"

"Well, he takes these blood thinners."

"Aren't you cold?" she asked as we walked.

"I wasn't cold a little while ago."

Mom was amazingly tiny on this big bed. She was tilted away from me, and I walked over so she could see me. Her eyes were half open.

"Hi, Mom," I said very quietly. "I'm here now, Mom."

"We don't think Jan can hear you. She's on a big morphine drip. But we're not sure; maybe some things get through. You can keep talking if you want. Dr. Rosa is Jan's attending physician, but I'm going to give you the rundown, and maybe you can link up with the doctor later."

"Thank you," I said. "Thank you so much."

I pulled the T-shirt away from my sticky breasts and kicked my leg out to loosen my riding-up underwear. I needed a smoke, so I fingered my Winstons.

"There's no smoking, of course," the pretty nurse said.

"Oh, I know that. Sure. It's important. I was just—"

"At first we were going to keep both of your parents together here, but Portland's head unit is state-of-the-art, and, frankly, we were not comfortable moving Jan. Her lungs collapsed, which is why we are inflating them artificially. Later on we'll wean her from the machine. Both hips are broken, multiple crushed ribs, bruised trachea, dislocated right shoulder. The good news is, no head injury."

"That's great," I said.

"Dr. Rosa is Jan's physician."

"Great."

"I'll be at the desk if you need me."

As soon as she left the room, I adjusted my shorts. I sat for about twenty minutes as Mom tilted, and then I got up.

"I'm going now, Mom. What I'm going to do is go back to the camp and pack up the stuff and drive up and get a room or something. I won't be gone long. You rest."

I waited in the lobby for Trooper Anderson, and after a while I figured he was busy—so I took a cab back to Bridgton. It cost seventy-four dollars. My old Buick was already packed with our summer stuff. The folding chairs, coolers, tackle boxes, et cetera. I cleaned the cabin quickly, then paid Pop's friend who owned the cabins, asked him to return the rented boat for me, and drove back to Portland in the deepest Maine dark ever.

2

I was a running boy. That's what our next-door neighbor, Ethel Sunman, called me. I went from one place to another like a duck somebody was shooting at. I made beelines.

In 1958 my pop bought me a new maroon three-speed Raleigh English bike, and I became a running-wheel boy. I would ride every day after school, and on Saturday I usually took a long eleven-miler to Shad Factory in Seekonk, Massachusetts, which is one county over from East Providence, Rhode Island. Even in winter, if the roads were clear, I'd ride to Shad. Nobody ever went with me. Nobody ever went to Shad Factory either—that's why it was my favorite. There were no houses or anything. The Palmer River, on its way to the Atlantic Ocean, formed a lake above the Shad Factory waterfall. The fishing above and below the falls was terrific. Bass and pickerel above the falls, bluegill, perch, and hornpout below in the keep holes formed by the falling water. It looked perfect for trout, but there was always a little salt, just a bit, that backed in from the ocean, so only the tougher fish lived there. They changed in the brackish water. Bluegills got metally looking, and the perch's belly got even deeper orange. I'd fish no matter what time of year, so long as the water wasn't frozen over. In winter I'd take a small path across a footbridge and into the crumbling factory. It used to make metal rims for wagon wheels. I'd build a fire and have a day camp.

When Bethany began posing in places other than our house—those times when she was away from us, and hours would pass, and she didn't come home from school or from one of her friends' houses when she said she would—we'd fan out and look for her. I think that's why Pop got me the Raleigh. I had a pretty good American bike, but it wasn't light and fast, and I'd usually just run, looking, and I'm sure Pop figured that riding a good bike would be faster in a Bethany search.

A lot of the Bethany searches run together in my head, but some of them I remember clearly. These are the ones I think about or talk to myself about. I talk to myself after I have some drinks. It helps to get it all in some order. For a while anyway. I may say, "Jesus, Bethany, c'mon, you're getting Mom and Pop all upset." I always said that when I found her. I'd say, "C'mon, Bethany, stop standing like that. Put your jeans on. C'mon!"

Now, my sister was never a dirty person, or lewd or anything, but this thing inside her would tell her to take off some clothes—and she'd do it, or she'd talk right out loud, like she was answering somebody. It was strange. Crazy, really. Mom and Pop took her to about every doctor there was, but after the Bradley Hospital, Bethany said if they took her any more places, she'd kill herself. She wouldn't, though. My pop wasn't a profound man in the way he talked, but I remember once, right after Bethany was brought home by Winnie Prisco and she had been saying she'd kill herself and stuff, I remember Pop sitting at the kitchen table with Mom, putting his arm around her and saying, "Life expects a lot more out of some people than it does out of others." Then he grabbed Bethany's arm, put her in the Ford wagon, and drove her back to Bradley.

About a week later, we brought her back home. We needed Bethany in our little house. There's always unfinished business when somebody you adore is sick. I can't explain this, but you know what I mean. We had a great four or five days. Then she didn't come home again. My parents drove to the high school and started looking there. Pop's plan was to go to the school, then drive up and down Pawtucket Avenue, which ran from Riverside Terrace to the Seekonk line. My plan was to ride around our plat, yelling "Bethany." I started looking around four in the afternoon, and I heard her crying under the water tower in Kent Heights about seven. I remember it was March, and there was some snow. I dropped the Raleigh and ran to where my sister was crying.

"Bethany?"

"Hook!" she cried, running over and hugging me so hard I couldn't breathe.

"C'mon, huh? You got Mom and Pop all upset."

"Oh, Hook!" she cried again.

She called me "Hook" because she said I never stood up straight, and I was the skinniest human being she ever saw. I didn't like to eat, and I was a runner. It was true.

"C'mon."

"I took all my clothes off. I'm a monster," she said, all slobbery. Bethany looked so beautiful-sad when she was crying. When she didn't cry, she was pretty.

"No, you didn't, Bethany. You've got your clothes on."

Bethany loved kilts. She had a black-and-green plaid one on. I remember her clothes. No one dressed more like she ought to. She was a girl who ought to wear plaids and kilts.

"After school I was going to ride home with Pat Sousa, and I was over at her car. There were a whole lot of kids around, and everybody was being nice, and Bobby Richardson had a new Vespa motor scooter his father bought him, and he was giving people rides and . . . oh, Hook . . . it told me to take all my clothes off. It said it would be good to do it."

"I hate your voice!" I shouted.

"I took my clothes off. I took all my clothes off."

"Did anybody hurt you?"

"Oh, Hook."

"C'mon, Bethany."

"Pat just drove off. Everybody laughed. Everybody laughing at me and pinching me . . ."

"It's all right, Bethany. C'mon."

"Everybody laughing . . ."

Another thing about love that I remember. It's good and bad, but sometimes when you love somebody so much, you just can't forget how they are when they're hurt. When Bethany was hurt, when she cried and hit herself, it was kind of, I guess, complete. All of her hurt. When I got taken to the hospital in Thailand before I got flown to Fitzsimmons in Denver, I saw things. But I never saw things so complete as Bethany's sadness.

"It's not you, Bethany."

"Pinching and . . ."

"C'mon."

She held my hand, and we walked out from under the gray water tower to where I dropped my bike. It had some snow on it, and the lights from the Kent Heights plat looked pretty and clean.

"You can ride the bike, Bethany, I'll run alongside."

"You're a runner, Smithy."

"I guess."

"Don't ever stop running."

"I won't."

"You will, I know it."

She did, and I did.

3

I was staying at the Tidal Motel, pretty much in between Portland General and Biddeford. Goddard gave me an unpaid leave and trusted another guy with the SEAL Sam arms quality control. The night I pulled into the Tidal from Bridgton, I called the hospitals and left my number. It was about two in the morning. I had some beers and some vodka, smoked some cigarettes, and made a list like Mom always did, because I wanted to be sure that, somehow, things were okay.

1. Call Bea Mulvey about picking up the folks' mail. (Bea was our neighbor forever.)
2. Call Mr. Lowrey at Goddard. (He was my supervisor.)
3. Call Aunt Paula and Uncle Count (Mom's sister and her husband).
4. Call Grace Church (their church). (It's what Mom would have done.)

I made one more vodka and orange juice and went to sleep. I dreamed I had just done something wonderful—it wasn't clear what—and a girl I liked in high school kept calling me on the phone because she was in love with me. Bethany was perfect in my dream, and she would say, "Smithson, I think it's Mags on the phone." My pop would say, "Va-va-voom." In my dream I never touch Mags, but I let her tell me how wonderful I am. I've had that dream a lot since then.

Hospitals are hard. Everything is hard, really, but hospitals have a special rockiness about them. I never got used to the ones I was in, even after I'd been in them quite a while. The only way I made it through was by simple ugliness. I was awful to people—especially when they tried to be nice and sympathetic. It surprised me, my nastiness. At least Portland General and Biddeford were more pleasant than the others, even though, as I said, Portland had the feel of dried clay.

My pop died of pneumonia ten days after the accident. It was about ten in the morning when I got there, and some young doctor and the fat nurse intercepted me before I got to his cubicle.

"Well . . ." the doctor said.

"Yes?" I asked quietly. Hospitals are places your instinct tells you to be quiet in. The army hospitals were loud, but that was different. Bethany's hospital, Bradley, was awful loud, too, but Bradley wasn't a real hospital. It was for a different kind of thing. Portland General said "quiet" and meant it.

The young doctor, I forget his name, was a skinny blond guy who talked in a deep voice. It was as if he wanted everything to sound important and serious, so that if he told anyone bad news the words wouldn't leap out like snakes, all over the poor patient. He could say "coffee" with the same weight as "cancer," and "It may snow" with equal importance to "You are going to die."

"My name is Dr. Lapham. I'm the neurologist assigned to your father."

"Thank you. Thank you so much."

"Are you at all familiar with the brain?"

"No, I'm not."

"Well . . . the brain is sort of our command center. Did you see the movie *WarGames*?"

"Uh . . . no, no, I didn't."

"*Hunt for Red October*?"

"No."

"*Star Wars*?"

"I saw *Star Wars*," I said, happy to be helpful.

"I loved that movie," the fat nurse said. "I loved how you always wanted everybody to be all right and not be killed by Darth Vader."

The doctor held his hand up to the nurse but looked at me.

"Do you remember how Darth Vader had a place in the spaceship that ran everything? That was totally in command of everything?"

I nodded yes, but I only remembered how I knew that wasn't really him talking, right off. I didn't remember the other stuff.

"Well, the place on the spaceship where Darth Vader ran everything was, to his space fleet, you see, as your father's brain is to the rest of his body. The heart. The lungs. The stomach and so on."

"Okay."

"Now, do you remember that scene at the end of *Star Wars* when Luke lobbed a photon bomb down the chute and there was a computerized picture of this red blip running all around until it got to Vader's command room?"

"And Han Solo saved him by shooting the emperor's fighters that were sneaking in behind him," the fat nurse added excitedly.

"Yes," the doctor said, "so Luke Skywalker was saved by Han Solo, but what about Vader's command center?"

"It . . . blew up?" I asked, pretty sure I was right.

"Exactly," the doctor said in his deepest voice. He ran his white fingers through his short hair. "Exactly," he said again.

"Darth Vader escaped by jettisoning in the emperor's fighter. He was in the other movies," the nurse volunteered.

"But what good was the fleet without the command room?"

"He could, like, read minds. Maybe he had—"

I could tell that the doctor was getting mad at the nurse.

"The point is, it's the command post that's like Mr. Ide's brain. Once the photon explodes in there, it's very bad."

"My pop's not doing good?"

"The only section of the brain that's showing any electrical activity at all is the brain stem. The brain stem really has one purpose, and that is to regulate breathing. It's a very mechanical thing, breathing."

"But he's breathing."

"Yes, he is. But the command center is gone."

"Gone?" I repeated.

"The photon bomb," added the nurse, as she squeezed my arm.

My pop went about an hour later. The bed had stopped tilting, and most of the big machines were gone. Pop had a lot of congestion, and his breathing was a struggle. I held his hand, and his eyelids fluttered, and then he stopped breathing. I put his hand down, and I was all right, but then I said, so soft I could barely hear myself, "Bye, Pop," and I cried. I didn't let them see me cry. I waited until I had it under control, then splashed some cold water on my eyes and went to the nurses' station.

I called a funeral home in East Providence that Aunt Paula had told me about. I talked to a woman named Polly who said she wanted me to know I wasn't alone. That was part of the service this funeral home offered. She said she would send a man up to Maine for Pop, and we could finalize details tomorrow. I thought it sounded odd that somebody comes and gets somebody and takes them for their funeral. When you think about death, there's really nothing else like it.

I packed up the Buick with some stuff and told the motel guy I was keeping the room but was going to be gone for a while. Then I drove over to Biddeford to fill Mom in on my plans to go back to East Providence for a few days, without telling her that Pop was gone.

"Mom?" I said sitting close and touching her shoulder. "Mom, it's Smithy, Mom. Everything's good, and Pop's doing good and everything, but I have to go back to East Providence for a couple of days. Goddard called and stuff. So I can water plants and things. But Pop's okay. Really."

Mom seemed to be shrinking into her huge bed. I never realized how tiny she was. She always seemed so completely powerful. There's too much history to tell, really, about all of us and how we'd do things like hike and how she loved that I ran so much. There is absolutely too much, because I'm looking to understand the whole thing and not a part of things. Mom was wonderful, and my pop was wonderful, and that's it, really. After Bethany disappeared the final time—that was almost twenty years now—my parents' never-say-die attitude died. I think Mom knew that time that the voice had Bethany, finally, all to itself.

I kissed my mother's forehead, which felt dry on my lips, and walked out of her room. I think she heard me. Her eyes were glassed in haze and half open, but you hear with ears. At least that's what I was always taught.

I had reached my car when Toni from Intensive Care caught me.

"Mr. Ide," she called, "we need you, pronto."

We jogged back to the hospital and up to Mom. I felt a pain in my chest, like a pair of pliers had gotten a hold of something important, and sweat poured through my denim shirt. If it was a big heart attack, it was probably one of the best places to have it. I actually thought that. I actually almost said it out loud. My belly lived like another man, all itself. I followed, that's all, and my heart was an engine that drove both.

An Indian doctor was in with Mom.

"This is Dr. Deni," Toni said.

"Ahhh," he said, all smiley, "the boy."

Dr. Deni was short and wiry, with long white hair. He wore a beautiful suit, double-breasted, I think, and it fit nicely. There was a stethoscope around his neck.

"I am Dr. Deni," he said.

I shook his hand. "Thank you, thank you so much."

He put his hand on my arm and brushed his fingers against me.

"Now Mother is going to God. In her hurried little breaths, you can hear her prayers."

I didn't hear a thing. Her breathing was as tiny as she was. What was he saying? I started to ask something, but the little Indian cut me off.

"We call this the sepsis syndrome, and it is an old enemy of the trauma. Mother was responding, but now sepsis is here for her."

Toni translated for me.

"In a sepsis situation, the brain—or something in the brain; we don't know what—orders the body to begin fighting to stay alive, but that just shoots the temperature sky high, and we can't get it down."

Here is how stupid I could be. Here. "Mom used to give me a tepid bath. Have you guys tried that? Have you tried the tepid bath?"

"Sepsis stops when it wants to. It doesn't want to."

"Mother is going now. Come and sit. Shall I stay?"

I sat. "Uh . . . no . . . I'm okay. Thanks very much."

"We'll be at the nurses' station," Toni said.

Mom looked the same, except, like Dr. Deni told me, I could hear her little breaths. Puffs, really. Her eyes were still open a little, but I knew she couldn't hear me. I pushed her thin hair onto the pillow with my fingers.

"There," I said.

I concentrated on Mom's breathing and told myself that they were small but powerful breaths. Small and powerful, like Mom, and when she got home, I would tell everyone how this Indian doctor had told me she was going to die, but her breathing got more and more powerful, and her body cooled right down, and she lived.

But she stopped breathing. I never felt so stupid. Mom. I went to the nurses' station.

"I think my mom has stopped breathing."

Toni and another nurse, an older man, walked into the room, and I followed them. They closed Mom's eyes, took out the IV, and left. All of the engines and monitors were off. I stood, then sat, then remembered my dead pop and how I had lied to her about him. It was reasonable to lie, because Mom was so tiny and that news was so big, but I have learned you don't want to lie to your mother at the moment of her death. It seems to never stop bothering a person. A lie like that is one of the main reasons I talk out loud when I'm alone. I say, "Mom, Pop died over at Portland General, but everything's still okay."

A person doesn't get over a family.

Sometimes things happen that make a person feel like standing up is just too much. It's the knees then. Legs. Heart. I put my face under Mom's until I could stand up.

4

Norma Mulvey, our neighbor Bea's daughter, was four years younger than me, and because there weren't a lot of kids her age in the plat, she used to always want to play with me. When I was eleven or twelve, I guess it wasn't so bad, but as I grew up and she'd sort of just be everywhere I was, it drove me nutty. Not that Norma wasn't nice when she was a girl. Norma was very nice, and quiet and shy, but still, a sixteen- or seventeen-year-old shouldn't have a kid following him around.

Norma adored Bethany, too. She'd just show up. We'd be having supper, and my pop would have the Red Sox on the radio, and, no knocks or anything, in would walk Norma.

"Hi, Smithy!" she'd shout, and sit next to me, all pigtails and nine and grubby.

"Uh," I'd say.

"Hi, you cutie. Norma Mulvey is my fave," Bethany would say.

My mom was just so nice. "How about a little bowl of macaroni and cheese?"

"Oh, boy! Oh, boy!" Norma would say. "What's the score, Pop?" Norma called Mom "Mom," and Pop "Pop." She kept it simple.

"Five–four, good guys."

"Yayyy!"

Everybody laughed but me. I was thirteen. She made my crew cut itch.

One time I remember, in that clear way that stands out in my memory, there was a puppet show that Norma wanted to have. She'd seen one on *Captain Kangaroo*, and it was all she could talk about and sing about and dream about, so Bethany got this empty refrigerator box and cut out a hole about halfway up for a stage. Bethany came into the house and brought me outside. I was, I think, fourteen then, so Norma would have been ten. It was Bethany's last year at school.

"Look what Norma and I made."

"What is it?"

"It's a puppet show!" Norma screamed.

"We need somebody to be a guy puppet," my sister said, seriously. "Norma wants to do a show about a princess in a tower and a knight rescues her."

"That's stupid," I said.

"Is not!" Norma screamed.

"Careful, Hook," my sister said. "You have to do things like this, or you're gonna end up a fat-ass with no friends."

"I'm gonna be Roxanne," Norma said, oblivious to us. She held up a little girl doll with black hair and eyes that closed when you put her down, and she handed me a boy doll. She had put a little handkerchief around him like a cape.

"I'm not gonna play with dolls."

"They're not dolls, they're puppets. He's Rex. Rex saves Roxanne. I love you so much!" Norma screamed.

"Norma loves Smithy," my sister sang.

"I'm going."

"Rex can't go!" Norma cried.

"You can't go. If you go, you're going to end up a fat-ass like Uncle Count, and you're not going to have any friends."

"That's your stupid voice."

"I don't know what you're talking about."

"I love Smithy this much!" Norma screamed, holding her skinny arms apart.

"Go home, you little creep."

"Careful, Hook."

"Stupid little creep. Stop following me everywhere."

Norma just stood there and started to scream and cry together. Bethany hugged her and glared at me. I glared right back. I was fourteen and had made the ninth-grade basketball team, and I was supposed to play with dolls? Bethany's eyes were lime green.

"All right. If she'll stop that stupid crying."

Norma rubbed her eyes red and said she loved me. I felt so stupid—being Rex, of course, being sort of bullied by my sister. But I rescued Roxanne even though Norma's Roxanne kept kissing Rex with big, stupid, smacking sounds.

5

In 1963 a guy named Wa Ryan bought a used Volkswagen and fixed it up. Wa had almost finished high school in Bethany's class, but he was one of the dumb guys about school. It was cars for Wa. He lived three streets down with his mother, who had emphysema and used to exercise by walking incredibly slow, almost in slow motion, up the main street, holding an unlit cigarette. Wa would always work on the Volks on the front section of his narrow driveway. All the driveways in East Providence are narrow, just like all the houses are small, with two, sometimes three small bedrooms and small yards with, usually, small vegetable gardens. There's a sameness, I guess, that's nice. There's a comfort, I guess, in not beating each other. But Wa, like I said, pulled the bumpers off, raised the body with truck springs, put a simulated Rolls-Royce grille on the front, and removed the mufflers. Then he painted it bloodred.

You could hear Wa coming. He didn't race around like a nut or anything—that's not part of the culture of fixed-up Volkswagens. He drove normally but very loud and very pleased with his creation. He loved people to admire his handiwork, never once stopping to consider that most people thought he was just another guy with a crazy car.

It was the first Saturday in April. I remember that because my pop and I never missed opening day of the Rhode Island trout-fishing season. We always got our stuff ready the night before, loaded up the car with sandwiches and soda and night crawlers and fly rods. Opening day was not a day for flies, even nymphs that bounce low. The trout wanted meat, so we made sure we had on long, light leader and split shot to get the bait down where they were—in the deep, slow pools of Wood River. We always got up real early, sometimes four or four-thirty, so we could get to our spots before sunrise, when the season would officially begin.

I'm not clear about what we caught, but we usually had our limit of six each by noontime, and Pop usually fell in or got water over his boots by ten. I do remember that we ate a couple of tuna sandwiches Pop made. Lousy ones, because he didn't take the time to mix the tuna and mayonnaise good, and then we drove back to East Providence.

When we brought the trout into the kitchen, Mom was sitting at the table crying. She had a way of crying that was so restrained it was truly awful. Pop and I thought the same thing at the same time.

"Where's Bethany?" my father said, holding the stringer of trout.

Mother waited a moment to get herself under control.

"Want some water, Mom?"

"Bethany's at the hospital."

"Oh, Jesus," my father said, closing his eyes tight.

"She's fine," Mom said, "Bethany is fine. It's our little Norma. She was walking to Sunshine Bakery, and she got hit by Wa Ryan's crazy car."

"Oh, Jesus," my father said again. "Was Bethany with her?"

"No, she went to the hospital the second we found out. Poor Bea."

"Oh, Jesus."

I wrapped the trout in waxed paper and put them in the fridge. Pop and I changed clothes. Then we all drove to Providence.

Rhode Island Hospital sits on a small rise and overlooks the little-used Providence Harbor. In 1938, an unbelievable hurricane shot over Block Island into the Connecticut–Rhode Island coast and up the Providence River. A lot of the damage is still there. You could see it out the emergency room's waiting-area windows. We asked for Norma, and they sent us to Intensive Care on the fourth floor of the new hospital wing.

Bethany sat on a window ledge in an alcove that had been set up as a kind of rest area. Bethany ran and hugged Mom and Pop and me.

"Where's Bea?" Mom asked.

"They took her down to the emergency room because she passed out. I was holding her hand, and she just passed out. Oh, Mom! It's so awful. Poor Norma. Poor little Norma." Bethany began crying, and Mom did, too.

My pop lit a cigarette and shook his head. "Oh, Jesus."

Bethany calmed down. "She has pressure behind the ear. She has all these broken bones and cuts. When the doctor told Bea they were going to have to operate to stop all the pressure, Bea just passed out."

· · ·

That's what I was thinking about. Our family at the hospital with little Norma. I don't know why. Maybe it's because we all sat together for a while and concentrated on exactly the same thing. That could be it. Like how everybody becomes one person for a little bit and how the tiniest thing affects everybody in almost the exact same way. A pretty comfortable share, if you absolutely have to share, in a Wa Ryan souped-up-Volkswagen tragedy. But now it was my pop and mom and other hospitals.

I called Polly at the funeral home and told her there would be two in the funeral, and Polly said that at least they were together. I called Aunt Paula and the Count and told her that Mom and Pop had gone, and then I went back to the motel, loaded up the car with the rest of my stuff, and drove to Rhode Island.

I drove right to my parents' home, instead of my apartment near Goddard. Mom's 1971 Karmann Ghia, all rusted out on the front end, was in the garage. It was dark, but I found Pop's spare key on the nail in the garage. It was behind a pile of paint cans. I walked into the screen porch and opened the back door. It smelled like Worcestershire sauce. That was our kitchen smell. We loved Worcestershire sauce. In meat loaves and hamburgers, and you know what else gets this nice tang with Worcestershire sauce? Codfish cakes. It's an all-around sauce. I sat for a little while in the kitchen without turning on any lights and thought of pot roast and turnips and cabbage and even corned beef with shots of Worcestershire. I lit a cigarette and took two beers out of the fridge. I drank them fast and took out a couple more.

I went to the kitchen sink and splashed a little cold water on my face. There was a moon and stars out, and a nice damp, cool night breeze came in when I opened the window above the sink. The Mulveys' house was next door, and there were no lights on, but it was very late. Sometimes I would be at Mom's kitchen window doing the dishes, because when I would drive over from my apartment for dinner, I'd help clean up, and when I stood at the window, I would see Norma, on the side of her window, looking at me, I think. I would, I think, catch her, just looking, and then she'd turn away as if she wasn't looking.

After she had been so hurt with the Volkswagen, we visited the hospital a lot, and when Bea brought her home in that wheelchair, we'd go over, but Norma was so sad and she cried so much and Bethany had started hurting herself with fists and fingernails, so we sort of stopped going over. Sometimes I'd see her getting into the special van the state used to pick up those kids, those hurt kids, to go to the school in Pawtucket that was, I guess, for handicaps. Later on, with Bethany and everything, it was as if little Norma and her little wheelchair were never really there. For us anyway, the family of Bethany. It just gets so hard to go over, and the more you say to yourself to go over and then don't, it actually becomes so hard it seems impossible. So except for that glance at the sink, her sort of peeking out behind Bea's blinds, I guess I hadn't seen Norma, really, for thirty years. I wondered if she saw me—all of me, the weight, the cigarettes, the cases of beer—and knew I wasn't a runner anymore. You think odd things in your parents' house.

I opened two more beers and walked through their house in the dark, into the parlor. Sitting there, on Mom's green couch, I tried to focus on my responsibilities for the next couple of days, tried to order exactly what I should be doing. I smoked a couple more cigarettes, finished the beers, slept on the couch. Too cold to get comfortable, too drunk to get a blanket.

6

You have to learn to look at someone you truly adore through eyes that really aren't your own. It's as if a person has to become another person altogether to be able to take a hard look. Good people protect people they love, even if that means pretending that everything is okay. When the posing and disappearing became a way of life for Bethany, we'd take on this almost casual attitude in our searches. As if we were trying to convince ourselves it was not a bad thing. Even the running into walls had that unintentional fog about it, after it filtered through my parents' conversations. But once Bethany had graduated from high school, her voice began to throw away any subtle signs of self-destruction.

My sister stayed home after school. She'd been accepted at a Catholic girls' college, St. Regina Teachers College in Bristol, Rhode Island, and for a while my parents thought that a perfect situation for her was living at home and commuting the twenty-five miles to Bristol. That way she would still be sort of independent, but Mom and Pop could watch her. My pop bought her a neat little blue used Renault Dauphine. We all had such a wonderful feeling about our college plans. It was euphoric, and this lightness fell all over my parents and, I suppose, me, too, as if there was sun coming out or something.

Bethany had gone through the long summer working at Peoples Drug Store. Her job was a huge success in the Ide house, and Mom and Pop never stopped complimenting her on how nice she was to customers and how hard she worked. I was mowing lawns when I could get the mowing jobs, but mostly I'd get my fish gear and ride the Raleigh to Shad Factory. I was going to be sixteen that fall and already had a driver's permit, but driving wasn't something I thought was so great. As long as I had my bike.

In the summer, especially in August, the lakes would evaporate quite a bit. Streams that fed or were fed by lakes also shriveled. Shad Factory was particularly low the summer of Bethany's senior year, but it had a certain kind of beauty in its black water and how it contrasted with the countryside, which went stick brown.

A fisherman did not have to be an expert to see that catching some good ones had to do with getting the bait down low. I used weighted orange-and-black woolly worms that my pop and I used to tie. They were pretty good for spring trout, which Pop fished for, and absolute killers on the pickerels, bluegills, and fat perch that lay in the holes beneath Shad Factory falls. The bushes on the bank were thick and dry, and even when I took off my sneaks to wade in, a back cast with that big old nine-foot glass fly rod of mine was out of the question. You had to roll the woolly worm or the nymph up above, into the falls, and let the current bounce it into and around the holes and the edges of the big rocks. This is the only way to fish below the falls. I don't have fishing equipment anymore. I don't think I'd remember how to tie that terrific orange-and-black woolly worm, but I'd sure know enough, if I ever found myself up against a falls with nothing but a fly rod, to throw the fly right up into the churning water.

It was about the middle of August. I had gotten up early like I usually did, because a runner almost never sleeps, and anyway I wanted to mow Mrs. Lopes's lawn and still have a full day at Shad. I was sweating like crazy when I got there, what with the yard work and the bike ride, so I took off my clothes and swam a little in the lake, then waded into the stream below, throwing my woolly worm as I went. Casting is hypnotic. The roll cast, the one I used on the flies, is only perfect about once every fifty throws, but by the time you hit that first perfect roll, there's not a thought in your head, so you don't notice that big, round traveling loop.

I caught some beauties, hard and full of colors and, of course, fat, because of all the bugs and minnows that rolled over the falls and into their mouths. I like the perch the best, so I kept a few, cleaned them good, and let pickerel and bluegills go. I always felt successful with a creel of perch. My pop liked to say that not only was I an expert fisherman, but nobody could fry up a perch better than me. He was right. I could catch them and cook them perfectly. The secret, I remember, was, instead of bread crumbs, I used crushed cornflakes.

The best ride home from Shad Factory was past the turkey farms of Rehoboth. It added a few miles onto the trip, but there weren't a lot of cars on these old roads, and the turkey smells that people found so disgusting I thought were kind of nice. It's hard to think their crap smells nice, but what I mean is the turkey itself is so interesting, even beautiful, in its odd way, that you have to get above its smell. Anyway, it made for a satisfying ride home. In the late afternoon, breezes over the small farm ponds cooled everything off, and when I got into an easy pedal, it was like the roll cast. Hypnotic.

Taunton Avenue unofficially divided Rhode Island from Massachusetts. It wasn't a border, or in some spots even close to a border, but the old Taunton–Twin Pike had a sovereignty that you had to live around to understand. I think of it as a kind of asphalt river. I turned onto Taunton Avenue just past the last turkey farm, Amaral Turkey Land, and headed into East Providence. Sometimes on the Seekonk-Rhody border I'd stop for a soda at the Chip 'n' Putt and, if it wasn't too late, play a round alone. There's no other way on the Chip 'n' Putt. I liked it me against me. But this day it was getting dark, so I skipped the soda and the game. I rode past the new bowling alley with the automatic pin boys, the Bay View Drive-In Movie where there were no bay views, and up the big hill where the famous Rendini car crash took place in 1951, when eleven members of the Rendini family from North Providence hit an oil truck from Pennsylvania. My pop played ball with a couple of the Rendini boys. He said they had good arms and were quick to the bag. All dead in '51.

After the Luck Is All Trailer Park at the top of the hill, it was only about ten minutes home. Instead of turning up Pawtucket Avenue for our house, I rode straight on Taunton for the little shopping center where Bethany worked in Peoples Drug.

There were two police cruisers, doors open, engines running, parked outside of Peoples. From my bike I could see a crowd in the back right corner of the store, where Mr. Allenizio, who managed the drugstore, kept a small soda fountain and magazine rack. I got a tightness in my stomach and I realized that the day had turned into gray dark. I smelled autumn even though dust kicked up in the parking lot. I put the kickstand down, dropped my creel over the handlebars, and walked inside.

Mr. Allenizio had stocked a huge supply of summer stuff, and because it was now August and a lot of it hadn't sold, he had moved it up front in two sale aisles. It was a good idea, except it made the store seem cheesy, with plastic floats and cheap sunglasses. But it wasn't a cheesy store. It was actually classy and, I guess, sophisticated in Mr. Allenizio's filing system for prescriptions and credit system for billing. At least Bethany said it was sophisticated, and she had, when it was a good time, a great sense about such things. Now she was pinned on the floor by Bill Poland from the EP Police and another cop.

"Give us some room, folks!" Bill bellowed. He was a big man with a huge signature belly.

There were three or four other customers in the place, and they drifted out of the store. Mr. Allenizio stood over Bethany and the two cops holding her, and hugged himself.

My legs were heavy, but I moved them silently past hair spray and cosmetics to where my sister lay. Bill Poland was looking around as if there were an answer on the walls.

"Call her folks," he said to the other cop.

"Maybe we better just call an ambulance."

"Call her folks," Bill said again. "Ide, on Brightridge Avenue."

The cop went to the phone by the cash register. I couldn't see

Bethany from the waist up, blocked as she was by the great belly of Bill.

"Bethany?" I called softly.

Bill looked away from her and saw me. He'd played ball with Pop for years and sometimes even gave us rides home from the games in the blue cruiser.

"Jesus," he said almost to himself. "Why don't you stay over there. She'll be all right."

"What . . . ?"

"She had a spell. I think it was a spell," volunteered Mr. Allenizio.

"She's all right," Bill said. "Don't worry, kid."

"One minute she's showing a woman a new facial cream, and the next minute she's talking some odd language. She's screaming things. She's saying 'chay' and 'chee' and 'dampers,' and she runs to the back of the store and climbs up on the counter and takes her fingernails—"

"Don't worry, kid," Bill said. "Don't worry. She's a good girl. We're calling your old man."

"Ide?" the cop by the phone yelled.

"Ide! On Brightridge Avenue!" Bill yelled back.

Bethany had been quiet, but now she whispered my name.

"Hook. Oh, Hook." She sobbed quietly, trying to catch her breath.

"I'm here, Bethany," I said, moving toward her.

"Kid, please," Bill said holding up his hand.

"I'm all right," I said.

Bill released his grip on Bethany slowly, then stood up.

"Hook," she sobbed again.

"I'm right here, Bethany," I said, moving to take Bill's place.

I stood over my sister and wobbled. I closed my eyes tightly, then opened them again and felt my head blur. I knelt down next to her and brushed her black hair away from her face, back toward the floor. She opened her eyes and looked up at me. She actually smiled a little smile.

"Hook," she said.

I smiled back to my sister, and that beautiful, sweet face, ripped and torn by her fingernails. The jagged scores bone deep. The amazing quantity of blood such little veins could carry.

"I'm here, Bethany," I said. "Hook's here."

7

Polly Sutter was a small, brown-haired woman, around forty, with two black moles on her temple the size of quarters. She wore a long black jacket that hung almost as low as her black pleated skirt. She smelled exactly like a Camel cigarette.

"How's it going?" she said, nodding a condolence as though she knew what I was going to say.

"Okay."

"Good crowd last night? Good showing? Went well?"

This was the second and last viewing of Mom and Pop at the funeral home of Polly and Dick Sutter. They were brother and sister, offspring of the late Richard Sutter, original owner of Sutter Rest, and grandchildren of Bob Sutter, who had written a book about Virginia ham, called *Salt, Keep Meat Fresh Without Ice.* Polly had had a date the first viewing night and was anxious for news.

"It was fine," I said.

"Tonight? Many?"

"I don't know."

"Life," she said, lighting a cigarette with the last spark of her previous one, "life is a funny thing. We go through ups and downs, winters and summers, but somewhere, sometimes, it's good. I want you to think about all those good times."

Polly coughed, a juicy rumble deep inside.

"Jesus, God." She coughed again and looked at her cigarette. "I got to stop this."

I looked at Polly and wondered if Dick would fix his sister up when it was her time. I wondered if Dick and Polly had fixed up their father.

Aunt Paula and the Count stood next to me at the foot of Mom and Pop, and we shook hands with the people as they filed past. Most of them were friends from school or Masons or church or baseball, but there were some enemies, too, like Mr. Mayeo who kept a kennel of yapping mutts, and Mr. Viera with his accordion, and even the horrible Liz Fox who bumped Mom from Altar Guild to Hymnal Distribution. Everybody came. Everybody comes when you die. Old Jimmy Boylston came.

Jimmy had played with my pop in the early days. He was much older than his teammates, but he had grit, Pop said. You had to respect him. Jimmy lived with his son's family now and was a tremendous burden. He wore a baseball uniform all day, cleats included, and on many occasions, when he felt he had taken a sufficient lead and the pitcher had let his concentration wane, Jimmy Boylston stole kitchen. If you were Jimmy's son, Jimmy Jr., or his son's wife, you would not find the run and slide funny. Baseball was life and death to Jimmy Boylston. It was everything.

What would happen was that Jimmy would be in the TV room watching his soap operas, and something would set him off. He'd slowly get up, take a lead, and crouch. Now, if you caught him in the crouch, he could be talked back to his recliner in front of the TV. But if he had the time to set, you were screwed. When he used to steal for the old Providence Steamrollers, and even later with Pop's Socony club, he was quiet as a mouse until he exploded for second. He'd let out a ferocious "Yaaaaa!" that lasted for fifty or sixty feet. Old age had robbed Jimmy of his speed, stripped that ballsy headfirst, lightning plunge from his arsenal, but time had not eroded the electric "Yaaaaa!" From the TV room, through the living room, and onto the off-white center tile of the kitchen, time turned in on itself.

"Aw, fuck. Well, goddamn it. Now, shit," stammered Jimmy, squeezing my hand with both of his. His gray uniform had thin red stripes. It was baggy and worn but newly laundered. He wore his pants high and his red socks high, too. His head seemed to swim in the blue Steamroller cap.

"Goddamn it to shit. Fuck," he explained softly.

"Thanks for coming, Jimmy. This is my Aunt Paula and Uncle Count."

"Jesus, huh? Fuck, fuck, fuck." He nodded comfortingly.

Jimmy scraped at the rug with his cleats.

"Dad just had to come," Jimmy Jr. said behind him. "We're so sorry about your folks."

"Fuck. Shit. Fuck," Jimmy agreed solemnly.

"C'mon, Dad."

"At least," Jimmy said, "at least, at least, at least. One good thing. One good thing!" Jimmy's eyes welled, and he set his jaw. "At least those fucking Boston Red Sox won't be breaking your father's heart anymore."

"You're right, Jimmy."

"Well . . ." He paused and drew a deep, wheezing breath. "Fuck."

Jimmy and Jimmy Jr. moved on, past Mom and Pop. He looked wonderful in his chess gray home uniform. He didn't take his hat off, but that was okay. He had permission. The big steal was coming soon, and he knew it right down to his cleats. He'd meet Mr. Grim Reaper feetfirst at blazing speed, with those sharpened cleats about chest high. Like my pop said, you just had to respect him.

After about an hour and a half, I took a break. Count had started telling little jokes to his friends, and while me and Aunt Paula were shooting people through the line with just a couple of words, Count stood there like a buddha, holding on to their hands and not letting go until he finished. He'd lean forward, pretend to look around to make sure no one was watching, then let out one of his classics.

"There were these two fags. . . ."

"These fags got into a cab. . . ."

"There was this fag priest. . . ."

"Two fags were in a bar. . . ."

"Four fags were on a boat. . . ."

"Train full of fags going to a convention. . . ."

Count carried something like 300 pounds on his five-foot-eight body. I'm a slob, okay, 279 pounds, five-eleven, can't breathe half the time, a belly with a separate life and everything, but next to Count I was slim. Not slim, okay, but just another fat guy. Count was a higher order of porker. He'd crossed the line that says forget holding in your belly, forget buying smaller clothes, forget everything, baby, and be proud. Count would set those two little feet on the ground, and you knew he wasn't going anywhere. My pop would always laugh and tell Mom that Count would outlive him. He never believed it, though, never. Now Count was seventy-one, 300 pounds, pure New York cheesecake blood, and standing over my pop telling jokes.

"I'm coming? I thought I was going!" Ha, ha, ha.

"I thought it was a corkscrew!" Ha, ha, ha.

"Us? We came on the train!" Ha, ha, ha.

I walked past Polly Sutter out a side door and into the parking lot. The East Providence air was damp but cool, with just a hint of the Rumford Chemical Works one town over. I lit a cigarette, opened the Buick's door, and took a quart of Narragansett Lager out of the small cooler I'd brought. It was very cold, and I drank it right out of the bottle. I finished it quickly, unscrewed another quart, and lit another cigarette. I took another long swallow of Rhode Island's fine lager beer and sat back. It's hard sometimes to think. The cigarette is just a lightness now. My pop said he smoked for the taste. There's a lightness for me, then a little sting, but really no taste to it. I like a lot of beer. Or if not a lot of beer, then beer with maybe some bourbon. I had some small airplane bottles of Ten High I bought on sale at Rose's liquor store. I kept them under the Buick's seat. I don't think a person should drink and drive, and of course say no to drugs. I opened one of the airplane bottles and drank it. Sipped it, really, I sip the bourbon. Beer is more or less drunk; bourbon gets sipped. I sipped it all down, and then I sipped a couple more.

You know how things get quiet when it's an odd time? That's what it was in the parking lot. It was a quiet that was a thing all by itself. I remember the night I got so hurt in the army. Me and this Puerto Rican kid were sitting on a stump at the edge of this swampy place where the company commander had insisted our platoon set up for the night. It was loud, like the bugs had drums and horns. Loud enough that even if you could have fallen asleep—and we never slept out there at night—but even if you could have, you couldn't. So I had to pee and started to pee in such a way that it went into the swampy water, and—this is true—the bugs and the things that were crawling around all over the swamp, not just where we were, went quiet. That exact same quiet that was, like I said, a thing, a solid thing.

The Puerto Rican kid's name was Orlando Cepeda, same as the baseball player. He got shot dead right away, no time for crying or anything. What happened was they heard me peeing. They picked it up, and they all just started firing everything in the general direction of my pee. I got seven different kinds of slugs of the sixteen the doctor took from my thigh and my butt and my chest. I get nervous when it goes very quiet. It's hard to explain, but if I had to sum it up, I'd say that when it gets very quiet, I always feel like I've done something bad.

I put the cigarette out and screwed on the 'Gansett lid. I'd have to pee soon, but I knew I could use Polly and her brother's toilet. That quiet kept coming like a wave. I stepped away from the Buick and looked at Aunt Paula and Count through the window. People kept coming. People kept up the funeral line. My collar was tight, my thoughts weren't clear, and my mouth got so dry. My mouth gets so dry sometimes.

"Smithy," she called, and it scared me. I swung around slowly to where Bethany held a pose in the farthest corner of the parking lot. Her black hair blew gently in the night air. Her arms above her head and fingers splayed to the first stars.

"Smithy," she called again.

"I'm here. Hook's here."

"I'm behind you."

I started to turn, then turned back to Bethany. But Bethany had become the little maple tree in the farthest corner and her black hair blowing, only night leaves. It's true. It happens. I have followed her down rivers and seen her on hospital ceilings. It's the clearness of it that bothers me, and yet it's the clearness that doesn't. I see her. I see her arms and fingers and heavy hair, but it's a ghost that's young and true. Sometimes I watch myself ride my Raleigh to her. Sometimes I watch my own tears in the dark.

"Smithy?"

I turned around. The wheelchair flashed under the light from the funeral home. Norma Mulvey sat with a look of defiance. She had grown into her eyes. They were still pale green but no longer dominated her face, which was lightly freckled. Her red hair was cut short and tight against her head. Norma looked young. Ever see a young person and want to hold your stomach in? I held it in, but it had its life to live, and would live it.

"I'm Norma Mulvey," she said, both hands on her large back wheels.

"I know."

"I'm sorry, Smithy."

"I know."

"Bea's in there," Norma said, gesturing to the funeral home. She always called Bea "Bea," even when she was a kid. I remembered that.

"Bea's paying her respects, but I didn't want to see Mom and Pop in coffins. That okay?"

"Sure. I'm going to light a cigarette, okay?"

"I won't explode," she laughed.

"I meant, you know, smoking and people, sometimes . . ."

"I was kidding."

"I know."

Norma rolled over to a blue van parked sideways across two parking spots.

"This is mine," she said tapping the driver's-side door. "Little lever here opens the door, another lever sends an elevator gizmo down and sets me up to drive. Operate the gas and brakes manually. Manually I'm in good shape. I lift weights. I have good cardiovascular. I really do."

"That's great," I said, the way I say almost everything—stupidly.

"I just wanted you to know."

Norma looked pretty when she was talking. When she talked, she didn't look defiant. I guess a person who's in a wheelchair gets an attitude. I guess the attitude is defiance.

"I do drafting freelance," she said, looking at her van. "Got a facsimile machine, computer linkups, tilt table—the works. Do some magazine layouts, some *Providence Journal*, but mostly, because they can rely on the steadiness of my line, I work on architectural blueprints. It's a skill, you know. I'm very, very good."

"I . . ."

"And because I never see you, I just wanted you to know how it is. I don't want you to think I roll around Bea's house doing nothing. Mostly my days are work. I pay all the bills, I take care of my mother. *Not* the other way around. I have an exercise system set up so I can get a good cardiovascular workout."

Norma still hadn't looked at me. Her arms and shoulders appeared strong, and she sat—it's true—tall in her chair. She had a chesty voice that sounded full and hard. I could feel the bourbon warming me. I started to sweat and needed to pee.

"You get my letters?"

"Letters?" I asked stupidly.

"I wrote you at the hospital."

The hospital was twenty-four years ago.

"I wrote you every day. I sent good thoughts."

"I remember."

"Then how come you never came over to see me? How come? Stupid question. Never mind. I'm sorry. I'm so sorry about Mom and Pop. They were so good. They used to hold hands. I'd look out the window, and they held hands. It was awfully nice. And it wasn't easy for them. Bethany was so beautiful and so nice. But it was hard for them. Do you know where she is now?"

"We don't know. I mean, I don't know."

"Just gone," Norma said. "She would tap on my window, and when I opened it, she would blow me kisses. Or she'd do a pose. Sometimes she'd hold the pose too long. Remember?"

"I remember," I said, not so stupidly.

"She was so beautiful, but it was hard for Mom and Pop. How would a person know what to do when you love someone and they hurt themselves? I'm clean, too. I don't know, I don't know if you've known people who can't move around with their legs. Sometimes you think they can't keep themselves clean. I've got systems for everything. Clean. Very, very mobile. I take care of Bea, you know. There really isn't anything I can't do. You haven't changed."

I moved one hand to my chest. It slid unconsciously to the ridge above my stomach. Down below, the enormous avalanche of guts suspended over my strained belt defying gravity and other laws. My free hand passed unobstructed through the several strands of graying brown hair on my head. I was drunk, but I was used to it.

"I mean," she said as if correcting herself, "you look great."

"I . . . I got to go back in now, Norma. My aunt and uncle . . ."

"Oh, yes, yes, you'd better. I'm so sorry. They were really wonderful, wonderful people."

I walked back into the funeral home. I was numbed from the bourbon and beer, and I kept getting a distracting little pain and racing in my heart, but I could still feel her, it's true, feel her looking at me walk, as if she were behind those venetian blinds in the dark.

42

8

Mom and Pop were at their best when it was worst. There was a kind of calmness, and it would settle over our house. We'd spend so much time waiting for the bad part that it was almost a relief when it came. We didn't have to wait in that edgy, nervous zone, because what we waited for had come, and for a while we were rescued from it. From the waiting, I mean.

I was sixteen when Bethany jumped off the Red Bridge. It was two days after Christmas, and she'd been great. Really. Church was wonderful, and Bethany had helped plan a caroling thing with some of the other choir members. I didn't go because I went to Diamond Hill in Cumberland, Rhode Island. Some kids I knew were going there to ski on the little hill. I didn't ski, but Linda Overson was going, and I just had to go because she was so good-looking, and I wanted her to like me, which she never did. Bethany climbed to the very top of the bridge, which connected East Providence with Providence, adjacent to Swan Point Cemetery, where the Ides go when they die. What I know about it comes mostly from the *Providence Journal*, but some information I got from my pop, who didn't see it, but some of the boys in the Brown crew who were rowing under the bridge at the time told him.

It was snowing and cold, but as long as the oily Providence River was open, the Brown crew rows. They take rowing very seriously, which is good because of the timing of Bethany's jump, but I think it's stupid. But what do I know? I never went to college.

So it was snowing and pretty gray out. It takes a tremendous cold spell to freeze the Providence River because of the oil and dry-cleaning fluid and crap that has poured more or less relentlessly into it for two or three hundred years. This day, while it was cold and snowing, it wasn't part of a prolonged cold and the crews were whipping through their workouts, beginning with a two-mile run from the campus on the east side to the boathouse a half mile up from the Red Bridge.

Bethany had a part-time job at Grace Church working in the thrift shop. The old ladies who volunteered there were members of our church, and the work was pretty easy, so my parents thought it might make a nice transitional situation for Bethany, either to a more real job later on or maybe even another try at college. She also took a dance class at the YMCA, and I think that later, the work she did in that class showed itself in the ever-growing intricacies of her poses. They became amazing, not only in the absolute stillness she made for herself but also in the astounding whirls and leaps. A madness almost forgivable.

My sister drove her little Renault Dauphine out of the church parking lot, through Weybosset Square, and headed home via the Washington Bridge. We never can be sure of what happened exactly, but it seems pretty likely that somewhere between the square and the bridge, Bethany's voice got hold of the car and headed her away from the old Washington Bridge and toward the rust red of the Red Bridge. She parked on the shoulder of the road. The passenger door was open, but for no apparent reason, and Bethany could not give us one either. The trunk was also open. It was a front trunk, as the engine was in the rear of the car, and Bethany had taken off all her clothes and folded them neatly on the spare tire, as if part of the plan was to return to get them.

The coxswain on the Brown crew that was heading toward the bridge was named Sheila Rothenberg. It's the coxswain's job, I found out, to steer the boat and keep a single rhythm going by using a little megaphone. Racing boats aren't set up for the rowers to turn around and glance at what direction they're going in. The rowers' purpose is to row in an enormous stretch and pull, and there is simply no time for worrying where the boat was headed. That was Sheila Rothenberg's job. She was a junior at Pembroke, which was really Brown, but in those days it was considered classy to have a division of the college just for women. At least that's what Sheila Rothenberg told me. Our family saw her maybe six times, because Mom and Pop were trying to figure out what happened. I thought it was enough that it had happened and they should leave it alone, but I surely liked this Sheila Rothenberg, who had the nicest breasts I had ever seen and never wore a bra.

Here it is. The crew had passed under the Washington Bridge, where they did a wide turn before they shot up and away from the Providence Harbor toward the Pawtucket line. These boats fly, and the training for races, which they were doing, consisted of all-out, full-blast rowing until the crew almost died. There were one-man crews, two-man crews, four-man crews, and eight-man crews. Sheila Rothenberg's crew was eight-man, and, as I said, they were flying up the river. Sheila was concentrating on straightening out the heading by directing a stronger pull from her left rowers when she looked up and saw Bethany. At first she thought it was a statue, because she was about two hundred yards from the bridge and Bethany had gone into a pose. It must have been a good one, because Sheila could not see any movement at all except her hair blowing. My sister once tried to explain her poses to me. She said she was always trying to be completely still. More than completely, actually. Bethany told me that if she could stand so even her heart didn't beat against her chest, everything, everywhere, would be all right. But, God, I hated her poses. I hated them.

When Sheila got about seventy-five yards out, she could see it wasn't a statue but my naked sister, and before she could yell, "Stop rowing!" Bethany flew out from the metal girder at the top of the bridge and back-flopped into the icy, oily, polluted, horrible Providence River.

The clippings from the *Providence Journal*, December 28, 1962, say this:

Twenty-Year-Old in Death Leap Saved by Brown University Crew

A twenty-year-old East Providence woman attempted to take her life yesterday afternoon by leaping into the Providence River. Apparently the young woman had removed her clothing, climbed to the top of the old Red Bridge, and hurled herself into the freezing water. Luckily, a crew from Brown University's rowing team pulled the woman to safety.

Then the paper quoted a couple of the guys and made them sound like heroes. The truth was, though, that the crew had hurt her worse than the fall. Sheila had trouble getting out her "stop" command, and when Bethany bobbed to the surface, the boat popped her in the head. It opened a huge gash over her right eye and broke her nose. I'm not saying it was their fault, because they did rescue her, more or less, but they became another link in the chain of nice people who, trying to help, changed my sister's face.

My pop wanted all the facts. He became like a detective. He had to know when. When did she leave the Grace Church Thrift Shop? He had to know why. Why did she make that turn off Weybosset and over to the Red Bridge? All of it. Every night Pop would come home from the tankers, drive Mom to the Bradley Hospital, where Bethany had to go again, and from there start his rounds of investigation. He spoke to each crew member, to the cops at the scene, drove the route to the Red Bridge, parked his car, and walked to the spot where Bethany had started to climb. To say that his beautiful girl was crazy was not enough. There had to be more. There had to be an answer among the embarrassed college kids and the matter-of-fact cops.

Most of the time I went with him. I suppose I was worried about him, but I didn't have to be. Being the detective got him up and moving and pumped a lot of energy into him. Mostly it was really good to see my pop like that. He was a guy who didn't need much of anything—baseball, a few beers—and it was hard for him to be emotional, like it's hard for me, but I think including me in the investigation was his way of saying he loved me and stuff.

The last time we talked to Sheila Rothenberg was at a coffee shop on Thayer Street in Providence. Thayer cuts the Brown campus in half, so it's always packed with smart kids walking around. Sheila was very nice to Pop. She smiled and told him there really wasn't anything to add and that she sure hoped Bethany would be okay. Sheila had on a gray T-shirt that said BRUINS. Her nipples, I remember, were kind of pointing up, and her hair was pulled back in a ponytail. In 1962 all the smart girls at high school wore ponytails, and it was wonderful to see one on this pretty college girl. She was smoking a Marlboro, and the filter had lipstick all over it. I didn't smoke, but when my pop went to the bathroom, I asked her if I could have one. I put it behind my ear, the side that my pop couldn't see, and looked thin and cool. She told me that she understood how concerned Pop was, but she had told him everything she possibly could. Six times. She wouldn't be able to meet with him anymore and would I tell him later on? I said of course. Then I asked her if she'd go out with me. Sheila Rothenberg laughed so hard her coffee came out her nose.

9

Mom and Pop were buried in one grave in Swan Point. My pop had already had their names put on his parents' big marble headstone, so all I had to do was order the dates. Count kept going on about how economical my pop always was, and how much sense it made to use one grave, and what a terrific location my folks had. I kept thinking how odd it was to see the three-hundred-pounder standing over my pop.

The service at Grace Church was nine-thirty that Thursday morning. Then we proceeded to Swan Point for the burial, and then everyone came over to Mom and Pop's house for a sort of informal luncheon and jokefest. Aunt Paula had come to the house and woken me up around five so she could get ready. I had gotten very drunk after the last viewing of Mom and Pop, so I wasn't much help, but Aunt Paula really didn't need much. She'd brought a sliced ham and a sliced roast beef, and a big pile of potato salad, and deviled eggs, and mushroom salad, and macaroni salad, and Swedish meatballs, and pasta salad, and rye bread, and Jell-O with bananas, and her famous light brown butterscotch brownies with almonds instead of walnuts. I drank some beers so I could clear my head for the service.

The Count was master of ceremonies. He'd told everyone at the church and everyone at the cemetery that after the graveside prayers were recited, there was going to be a get-together at the house. Maybe sixty or seventy showed up. Count was beside himself.

"Great turnout," he whispered to me. "Let me get a head count. This is great."

Some members of the Socony local baseball club came. The catcher, Billy Pierce, and Junior Bobian, who was probably the most famous infielder in Rhode Island history. A division of the East Providence Little League was named for him. The Junior Bobian Division. Armando Fecabini came, too. He was my pop's best friend, and it's hard to even think about him, because in New England, and in our home, it was good, very good, to keep things inside. Your emotions were contained. That was why God gave us skin.

But Armando Fecabini's emotions were uncontainable. He was desolate. I can see him sitting in front of my pop's little TV in the kitchen watching old Bilko shows and wailing, while all around him people listened happily to the Count's endless stream of Irish, Portuguese, Italian, black, Puerto Rican, Chinese, women-with-huge-breasts, men-with-twisted-dicks, and girls-that-could-suck-bowling-balls-through-garden-hose jokes.

"Can you get that guy outside?" the Count asked me quietly.

"He's mourning."

"I know he's mourning. I'm mourning, too. Only I'm mourning quietly and not ruining it for everyone else. He's upsetting your aunt."

I knew Armando Fecabini, and his sobbing was not upsetting Aunt Paula. If Count didn't upset her, nothing would. Count looked at me, then pointed to Armando.

"It's too much," he wheezed. Then he turned around to Mr. Almatian, my pop's insurance guy.

"So they put this donkey schlong on this old man in Miami. . . ."

I took Armando outside onto the screen porch.

"How are you holding up?" he asked me.

I stood there, 279 pounds and three six-packs into the party with that damn pinch in the middle of my chest. I lit a smoke. "I'm really, really good."

"I'm going to miss them."

"I know."

"Your father was the best. The best. I don't know."

We stood on the porch, like men do when they talk to each other, looking away at some imaginary horizon. I wondered where Bea and Norma were.

"What do you hear from your sister?"

49

"I don't hear anything from my sister."

When I went back to the party, Bea had arrived alone. Her eyes were still beet red. I went downstairs into the new part of my pop's basement, where he had put linoleum tiles and knotty pine walls, and poured some vodka into my beer glass, because the beer was getting me kind of logy. I sat down on the old pink couch and stretched my legs and drank my drink. I smoked a little, and then I suppose I dozed off, because when I finally stood and went upstairs, most of the guests had gone except for Bea, Armando, Father Fred from Grace Episcopal, and the legendary Junior Bobian. It was almost six when the last one left. I helped clean up, looking out the sink window for signs of Norma. Then Aunt Paula and I loaded up their station wagon with her bowls of leftovers, and the Count piled in for the ride home.

"The big fifty-incher. The color console. Any plans for it?" Count grunted, getting comfortable behind the wheel.

"I don't know. I guess I don't have any plans."

"Well, if you don't want it, I'd take it."

Aunt Paula got a little teary, and then they were gone. And the others were gone, too. Armando Fecabini was the last to leave, and I walked him to his car.

"Me and your father sat on the big rock where the Riverside Nursing Home is now. Then there was nothing, except it was high and you could look out over the beginning of the bay, and me and your father sat on the rock and watched the big hurricane come into East Providence. Riverside first. Our mothers used to push our carriages side by side. I remember stealing cigarettes, me and your father, out of your granddad's shirt pocket."

He sat in his big old boat of a car and rubbed his eyes.

"Well . . ." he said.

"Better hook up your safety belt."

"Yeah. I'm never gonna go anywhere without my belt hooked up."

I walked down the asphalt driveway to the back porch. "Smithy,"

Norma called, rolling out of her driveway, into the street, and into my driveway.

"Hi, Norma."

"Everybody leave?"

"Yes."

"I waited until everybody left. Is that okay?"

"Sure."

"I brought the mail," she said, nodding to her lap and two weeks' worth of Mom and Pop's mail.

"Thanks. Do you . . . want to . . . eat something?"

"Like what?"

"There's lots left. Salads and meat and stuff."

I was still a little drunk, and I was worried that my breath smelled old and stale, so I kept brushing at my mouth. Norma looked at the steps onto the porch.

"I don't let people lift me and my chair. I've got my house arranged so I don't need any help."

"I didn't . . ."

"Ramps and pulleys. I do for myself."

"I could . . . bring something outside. I could . . ."

"I'd let you lift me onto the porch, Smithy."

I suppose I could have pulled her up the stairs, but I was drunk and stupidly bent down and lifted her, chair and all, in a kind of aluminum embrace. I pushed open the screen door with my butt and swung Norma Mulvey onto the porch. It was filled with chairs, and all of Mom's plants were set in a far corner, where Aunt Paula felt they would get sun and be easier for me to care for.

I stood for a moment, maybe longer than a moment, with my arms full of Norma and her chair. Somewhere across the backyards of the side street, a dog barked. I remembered our embrace. I realized that Norma was looking right at my fat face, and I thought of my breath and quickly put her down.

"The porch," she sighed. "I remember helping Pop put the porch on. He gave me a pencil to stick behind my ear for measuring, and he gave me a piece of wood, a hammer and nails, and said, 'Hammer those in, Norma.' And when I finished, he'd give me another piece of wood and more nails."

"I remember," I lied.

"Your mother would put ice cubes in the salad, and sometimes we'd sit out here and have hot dogs and beans and salad and listen to the Red Sox."

I needed to brush my teeth. My old breath was burning me.

"Maybe they're playing now," I said.

"You think so?"

I went into the house. When I turned the corner and was out of Norma's sight, I ran upstairs and brushed. I ran back downstairs, grabbed Pop's radio off the kitchen table, and plugged it in to the porch outlet.

"I follow the Sox," Norma said, rolling to where I fiddled with the dial. "I don't know if they're on tonight. Try 620."

I could barely hear her, because my heart was pounding from running up the stairs, but I got 620, and the game was on. Norma smiled and backed up a foot, as if that would allow her better listening. It was the top of the eighth inning, an afternoon game that ran into the night. Their afternoon games often ran into the night. It's not a put-down to say our Sox have been in a stall, more or less, since 1919.

"Romero takes forever on the mound," Norma said between pitches. "He adds forty minutes to a game. Clemens just throws. One, two, three. I love Clemens."

We listened for a minute. I wasn't the fan I should have been. I knew enough to talk to my pop about the Sox, but after some beers it's all the same. I played the game, too, for Pop, I suppose, but as a distraction mostly, and I was pretty good for a high-school beanpole. I had this real deceptive throw from third base, which was my position. I had the look of a kid who couldn't reach first, but I had real zing on the seed.

"One of the things I'd like to do is go to Fenway and see a game in person. I had a chance to go last year, with the architectural company I was doing some drafting for, but . . . I don't know. I figured it would be a big hassle for them and ruin their Sunday."

"You should have gone, Norma."

"Yeah?"

"Sure. They wouldn't have invited you if they didn't want you to go."

"I don't know."

We sat still for a while and listened to the play-by-play and the crowd murmuring in the background.

"After a while nobody came, Smithy."

I looked at Norma sitting in her chair next to me, looking straight at the radio. Ellis Burks popped to third.

"Sometimes I'd look out the window there—the one you can see from the porch, with the venetian blinds—and I'd see Pop sitting here listening, and I wish he would have come and got me."

Boggs was still with them then. They all loved him, and they all hated him. The announcer described his at-bat. I couldn't take my eyes off Norma. She had on a jogging suit with a huge sweatshirt and hood that hung off her neck and over the back of the chair. Her lips were a little apart, and I could see her teeth.

"You . . . if you asked him, Norma, I'm . . ."

Norma shot out her hand and grabbed my left fat, sweaty paw, so hard it hurt. She held it, and she held her look at the radio. I didn't move, even though I was amazed at how strong she was. I looked at the radio, and when I looked back, a tear was rolling out of her eye. She let my hand go and rubbed it away.

"I've got to go now, Smithy."

I didn't say anything, stupid or otherwise, and lifted her back to the driveway. As soon as she was on the ground, she began to quickly roll away.

"I'm sorry," she said.

"No, I'm . . . I don't . . ."

"Mail's on the table," and she was gone.

It was a warm night, not unusual for the end of August, and when I went back in and shut off Pop's radio, the crickets were already working. I lit a smoke and grabbed some beers out of the fridge and drank. An hour later I was pretty shaky, but I managed to get down to the basement and bring the vodka upstairs to the kitchen table, where I made a big screwdriver. Then I remembered the mail.

I don't enjoy reading as an adult. There's something about it now. But I had read until I fell asleep almost every night in this house, and I read fast, too. Good books that often I would hate to finish because they took me into their lives and let me out of mine, for a while anyway. I thought about what I read then, but these days I read the same page over and over, and of course there's beers. Sometimes I miss reading, but I still don't do it in my adulthood.

So I don't get magazines and things sent through the mail to me. Just some bills, that's about it. But Mom and Pop loved the magazines. They subscribed to *Time*, *U.S. News & World Report*, *Sports Illustrated*, *Field & Stream*, *National Geographic*, the *Sporting News*, and the *Red Sox Quarterly*, which not only had profiles of the ballplayers but included favorite recipes and original poetry. There were two magazines in the batch of mail Norma had dropped off. I separated them and placed them neatly on one section of the kitchen table. Next I put the bills in a separate pile and letters that looked personal in another pile. Most of the mail was junk, so I threw it away.

Wouldn't you think when a person dies there would be a "that's it" kind of thing? I think that. I think that when somebody dies, there ought to be a process where everything about them, like bills and taxes, stops. They don't even slow down. As a matter of fact, they seem to come quicker and louder. In my parents' pile of bills was American Express, two separate phone bills, Mobil gas, Wood's Heating and Oil, Visa, a Travelers Insurance premium, and a pledge card from the East Providence Rescue Squad. They do not stop when you die.

Aunt Paula had set up an appointment with a lawyer she knew who was going to help me sort out my parents' "estate." I love that what they had is called an "estate." Mom particularly would have enjoyed it. The lawyer was going to tell me how to get the bills and things to stop, because Mom and Pop had stopped, so I put a rubber band around the bills and would just give them to whoever the lawyer was when I met him after work on Tuesday. That left only the letters that looked personal. There were two from friends of Mom's who were visiting England with a church tour, one from Pop's rotisserie baseball commissioner, and one from the City of Los Angeles Department of Health. This was the only one I opened. I knew the rotisserie league was to do with his efforts to get Roger Clemens on his fantasy team, and I didn't want to read the letters to Mom. I opened the official-looking one from Los Angeles. It was addressed to Pop:

In response to your letter of the twenty-sixth of July, it is with regret we inform you that Bethany Ide, 51, died from complications of exposure. Her date of death was June 4, and she has since that time been in the Los Angeles Morgue West. The inclusion of Ms. Ide's dental records with your inquiry was extremely helpful in the identification procedure.

I felt a shortness or an absence of breath for a second, and this weird feeling of panic spread out of my chest and covered me. I stood up from the kitchen table and walked out to the porch and air. I found some, and I breathed it. Then I walked back to the kitchen and the Los Angeles letter. I read the first part again, but I was too drunk to finish it, so I folded the letter, put it in my pants pocket, and walked back to the porch. That's when I saw her again. She was in the garage in front of Mom's Karmann Ghia, and she was in her pose. Her hair was longer than before, and the creamy skin caught the last of the sun. My beautiful sister, Bethany. Perfectly still. I opened the screen porch and walked to the garage.

"Bethany. Mom and Pop. They're gone, Bethany. You're gone. What am I gonna do?"

I get tired. I get drunk. I see her. Clearly. Her green eyes. I'm a fool.

I walked into my pop's garage and leaned my big butt against Mom's little blue car.

"Bethany," I said again, almost like a prayer. I lit a cigarette and smoked for a minute.

Pop's garage was about smells. Like Mom's kitchen and Worcestershire sauce, the garage was 3-In-One Oil, citronella candles, kerosene, and latex paint. Good smells. Smells that go on.

I looked around and appreciated Pop's order. I don't have order. Pop had a place for everything. Shelves for paint. Hooks for rope and garden hose. Nails for the rakes and shovels. Above the small window in the back, hanging over Pop's long workbench, was my Raleigh. My Raleigh. I never saw it there.

I was drunk, but that was my Raleigh. I stood on Mom's blue hood and pulled it away from the hooks.

We both crashed onto the roof of the car, me and my Raleigh. The bike pitched again, over me and out the garage door. I lay in the dent of the car roof for a few minutes, then rolled off and walked to the bike.

My Raleigh. My maroon three-speed. I set it on its wheels and popped the kickstand. It still had the light on the front, but there were no batteries inside. It still had my small leather pack hooked onto the back of the seat. I unzipped it.

"The zipper works good," I said out loud.

I threw a leg over, and the bar sat way below my crotch. Had I grown that much? I sat on the seat, keeping balance with my left leg. It was a tight fit, like the blue suit I had on, when I sat down I couldn't keep it buttoned. The tires had no air, so they groaned under the beer and pickled eggs, and the tire rims crunched on the pavement. I lit a cigarette and sat on my bike.

I sat smoking until the cigarette was gone. Then I put up the kickstand with my heel and walked with the bike between my legs, to the end of the driveway. It must have been around eight, because I remember a full moon.

Now, I don't understand this, except I knew there was a Sunoco station at the bottom of our street, and it probably had an air pump, but, as I said, this is a gray area because all of a sudden I gave the Raleigh a few steps, sat ridiculously on the seat, and began to coast on the flat tire rims of my bike, down our little hill.

10

After the Red Bridge Jump, Bethany went into what Pop called a "lull." She was put on a tranquilizer by the doctors at Bradley that lulled the hell out of her. Almost always the bill of goods on these medications is that they are "calming." Bethany was calmed. In fact, my sister pretty much slept through my junior year of high school. She couldn't wake up in the morning and couldn't stay awake when she did. My pop's take on it was almost mystical. He truly believed that during this long rest period, her body and mind were healing.

Sometime around the beginning of May, I realized that Bethany had been cutting down on her dosage. At night, when I was pretending to do homework, I could feel her looking at me. When I would glance up, though, her eyes were closed. I'd talk to her those times, but she'd pretend to be asleep. I had this really bad feeling she was planning something, or at least her goddamn voice was, and it made me nervous. It was one of those things that get inside your head and won't get out. From May on, I had a terrible baseball season. When Coach finally benched me, he told me I had no glove and no bat. That's baseball for being a shitty player. But how can you turn the double play when you're nervous about your sister's goddamn voice?

I did get a date for my junior prom, though. It was going to be at Rhodes on the Pawtuxet, this beautiful old dance place. Mom told me there was a bandstand in the middle and everyone danced around it. That's where her prom was. I was pretty excited. I had never had a date before, and I really didn't think I'd be able to get one, what with not knowing anybody and not having too many friends. Like most things that happen to me, though, getting a date just happened.

I was walking to baseball practice, and the only way you were allowed to go if you had on cleats was through the basement hallway past the music room. You couldn't go the direct route by the science labs on the first floor, because the hall had green linoleum and the cleats would dig it up. So I'm walking by and feeling crappy because I'm not getting to play much for stinking so bad, when I hear this wail. Like a scream, only a little less, and then lots of big crying as if someone's just been hurt. I look into the music room, which is usually empty because it's after school, and there's Jill Fisher and Billy Carrara.

"I'm sorry," Billy says.

"Oh, God! Oh, no, no, oh, no," Jill sobs.

"Look, I'm sorry."

"Oh, no! Oh, God!"

"I'm really sorry. Look, can I have my ring back?"

Suddenly Jill stops crying and looks at Billy like he's just killed her puppy. Her eyes all wet and her teeth kind of pink from where she's chewed her lipstick.

"You want your ring? You want your ring? You want your damn ring?" she screams.

"Yes," he says, and the poor guy is already flinching.

She rips that ring off her finger and snarls at poor Billy Carrara, "There's your ring."

Jill Fisher threw the little gold ring with the red fake ruby and the East Providence townie motto in Greek, VICTORY WITHOUT MERCY, across the long room with all her might.

"Ughhh!" she screamed as she let it go. The ring flew all the way to the percussion section, bounced off the wall, boomed against a brass kettledrum, and slid back across the room, finally stopping at Billy's left foot. He bent down and picked it up.

"Thanks, Jill," he said sincerely.

He slipped it onto his finger, took out a piece of tissue paper that had been folded into a tight ball, and handed it to her. Then Billy left the room.

I watched Jill Fisher from the doorway. She unrolled the tissue, and I noticed it was toilet paper. Her ring was there, and she looked at it. I looked at Jill's big chest. I hadn't noticed it before, and that was

59

strange for me, because big chests were what I was concerned about at that time. I guess I knew she was going out with Billy, or maybe it was because she was in a group that thought I was a piece of shit, but for whatever reason, that day in the music room was the first time I noticed.

Suddenly she threw her own ring and collapsed in tears. There was nothing else to do but get the ring. I picked it up and walked over to Jill.

"Here," I said.

"Thank you," she said.

"I'm going to go to the junior prom."

"You're a junior?"

"Yes."

I felt relaxed and confident. Jill lifted herself off the ground and sat in a metal folding chair. She had to take deep breaths because she was cried out, and when she did, her chest expanded and her red blouse got tight against it.

"Your ring looks okay."

"Thank you."

"It's not one of those cheap rings. It's a good ring."

I was about an inch taller in my cleats, but my practice uniform was baggy. I tried to stick out my chest and stomach, but I didn't have either one.

"I play third base."

"You're on the baseball team?"

"Third base. That's why I'm wearing cleats."

"Thank you for getting me my ring."

"You threw it. . . ."

"Thanks."

"I just . . . picked it up."

I saw Jill's face and realized she was pretty. It was a round face, and she had black eyes, or at least they looked black through her tears.

Also, she had long, straight black hair. Chest men don't notice, I guess, the details. That day, for the first time, I noticed some details.

"I got to go. I got to walk home. Billy was supposed to take me home, but now he's . . ."

She threw her head back and let out one final sob/moan. I forgot about her face. I thought she might just break that red blouse to pieces. She didn't.

We walked to the music-room door and into the hallway.

"Listen, I'm going to my junior prom."

"I know."

"I'm going alone. By myself."

"Why?"

"I want to."

"Oh . . . okay."

This was not good, and I was stupid. We walked to the field door. I was going out, and Jill Fisher was heaving her chest up the stairs.

"You wouldn't want to go. You probably wouldn't like it. You probably would hate to go."

"Where?"

"My junior prom."

"I'm a sophomore."

"That's what I mean."

"I'd have to go with a junior, or I couldn't go."

"Exactly. Some junior would have to ask you, and you'd probably say no."

"I guess."

"Like, if I said, 'Want to go to my junior prom?' you'd say what?"

"I'd say what?"

"Exactly."

"Okay."

"What?"

"I'll go."

And it happened to me in the music room like it almost always did. It just happened. I was a pool ball, really, ricocheting off everybody and everything. So even though my boy life didn't come complete with a specific plan or some logical course of action, it was my own little way of being in the world. Being a part of the whole. But nothing happens anymore. I'm not on the pool table anymore. It wasn't getting hurt, or Bethany, or nothing, really. I just found the TV easier, the beer, the pretzels. You put on the tube, you drink the refreshing lager, you settle in for a good smoke, who needs contemplation?

I didn't talk to Jill for a couple of weeks. Then one day a girl passes me a note in English class with Jill's phone number, and it says to call her. That night I talk to a girl on the phone for the first time.

"Are you mad or something?" she asked me, sort of pissed off.

"No."

"Then what's the story? Are we going to the prom?"

"Sure."

"It's in two weeks."

"I know."

"Well, God! What color cummerbund are you wearing?"

"Cumber— What?"

"God!"

"I mean . . ."

"Look, a cummerbund is a wide belt they wear with tuxedos. They come in different colors. Usually the cummerbund and bow tie are the same color. I want you to get a purple one."

"Okay."

"And . . . have you got some paper?"

"Uh . . . yes."

"Okay, write this. A yellow corsage with some lily in it. Doesn't that sound perfect? I'm so excited. What's your name?"

"Smithy Ide."

"Smithy. Okay. Are you driving?"

"I've got my license."

"Okay. Call me tomorrow night, same time."

"Okay."

"Bye."

"Bye."

It didn't seem like much, but it was a terrific first phone call to a girl. I felt good. I walked downstairs to the kitchen and thought about a bowl of cereal, but I was never hungry and wasn't hungry that night. Bethany came into the kitchen in her robe and slippers and made herself a bologna and cheese sandwich and a coffee milk.

"Want one, Hook?" she yawned.

"No thanks."

She made her sandwich, put the mayonnaise and cheese and bologna in the fridge, and sat down at the table with me. She looked a little ratty.

"I'm feeling icky," she said between chews. "I stopped taking those pills, and I feel clammy."

"You're not supposed to stop taking those pills. C'mon, Bethany. They're good for you."

She looked at me and took a bite of sandwich without looking away.

"C'mon," I said again.

"A lot of times, Hook, not all the time but a lot of times, you can be a real cocksucker."

I hated when she talked like that. Sometimes she could use words that made me actually throw up. I looked away from her and out the window wearing a good hurt face. I heard her take another bite of sandwich, but when I looked back, she was still watching me.

"Asshole," she said, her mouth full of bologna and cheese.

I got up to leave the kitchen, but Bethany grabbed my arm.

"I'm sorry, I'm sorry," she laughed.

"Why do you do that?"

"If I didn't love you, I wouldn't call you names. I heard you're going to the prom. She pretty?"

I sat back down. "Jill Fisher."

"I don't know her."

"She's pretty."

"I went with Bobby Myers to my junior prom."

Her junior prom. The school gym. The parallel bars. The police. Bobby Myers in that Boston hospital.

"Bobby and his friends all wore plaid cummerbunds and plaid bow ties. They looked so dumb."

The stolen car, the first long disappearance.

"I'm wearing purple. And I'm getting Jill a yellow corsage with some lily in it."

"Purple and yellow? Okay. That sounds pretty good."

I watched her finish the sandwich, then rinse off her dish and put it in the sink. Yes, I was nervous because she had taken herself off the pills, and yes, there still was that crummy feeling that something bad was going to happen, but yes, it was more my sister, even looking ratty, than the sleepwalker that had taken her place for three months. She walked to the door that led out of the kitchen.

"I love you, Hook."

"I love you, too."

"Are you ashamed of me? Do you hate me?"

"I love you."

"I know."

"I'm not ashamed of you. I never hate you."

"Good."

Bethany left the kitchen with some energy. I never told my pop about the pills.

11

A fine mist changed over to light rain, and I woke up. I lay on my back, and I could feel uneven grass clumps under my ass. My blue mourning suit was soaked completely through. I could hear ducks quacking overhead and the sound of water falling onto rocks. For a moment, or a minute, or maybe five minutes, I lay still and could form no thoughts whatsoever, only feel the rain washing me, like a dead man or a stroke man.

I tried to stand, but a crackly stiffness and pain wouldn't let me raise my head, clench my fist, or even bend my arm. I lay still again and listened. The falling water was close, very close. I realized that I was cold, only I wasn't sure if it was being wet or on the ground or what. I closed my eyes and opened them and tried to think. The water on the rocks was too much in my mind, and the thick beer and vodka ran all around my body. I could feel my heart pumping. I couldn't think at all, and there was nothing to do under the rain. I closed my eyes and slept.

It was like a blink—only when I opened them again, the rain had stopped and the sun was coming in and out of the clouds. It felt good on my wet body, the parts I could feel. I tried to raise my arm, and this time, even though that deep, dry pain cracked me, I could. I raised it about ten times, each time putting it down gently on the grass, until my shoulder and elbow and fingers felt a part of me; then I did it to the other arm. I pushed myself into a sitting position, but the fullness of the pain, the pulling and tightening, was unbelievable. I lay back down and rolled to my side, and my fat legs plopped over like two sides of beef. I pushed into a kneeling position and tried to stand. It's very hard not being able to stand. There's a helpless, hopeless feeling. I couldn't think, and now I couldn't stand.

I flopped forward and landed with a thump on my stomach. I lay there for a minute until my heart stopped racing, and finally I formed a thought. I have done something to my body, I thought. I have overdone something, like the first day of basic training when we ran and climbed the rope and the next morning our fingers had raised blisters and our arms and shoulders ached. There were pieces of that ache in this ache. I raised my legs and slowly lowered them to the grass, feeling a little more limb each time. I pushed myself up to my knees and slowly stood. I was on my feet. I opened and closed my fingers and took a step and another and another. A mechanical man stiffened in the rain.

The Raleigh was about ten feet from where I slept, and when the sun hit it, sparks bounced off the stainless-steel headlight. I picked it up and set the kickstand down. The tires had lost a little air to a slow leak, but most of the good Sunoco air was still in place. What the hell did I do? What? I rolled down to the gas station and pumped up the tires—then what? And what was this place? I looked back to the grassy mound I had slept on. It looked familiar and the square white cinder-block building next to it looked familiar.

"Pump house," I said. "Shad Factory."

I walked in the direction of the falling water and could see the ivy-covered factory ruins before I saw the falls. They seemed smaller and mysterious in the early, cloudy sun. I stood on the flat cement border of the dam and watched the water roll thinly the twenty or so feet to the river below. It was high summer, and the pump house had been adjusted to allow a minimal flow over the dam, but I could see the same pools below me. A man and a boy were fishing the river. The kid had one of those spin-cast outfits, and I could see a night crawler dangling from his hook. He cast it downstream while the man, who fly-fished sort of heavily, with a slam of the fly on the water, cast across stream. I watched for a while, and I thought about my pools.

"Hey."

The boy looked up at me. He was maybe ten or twelve.

"Throw it up the falls."

"What?"

"Throw your worm up into the falls. The swirls of the falls. It'll go into the pools."

"What pools?"

"There's deep holes up by the falls."

The man kept casting in a whipping, angry way, slapping his big bug on the water, letting it go down about ten yards, then retrieving it so rapidly it made a scary *zzzzz* sound. The boy turned up to the falls and threw his worm.

"Here?"

A long shadow flashed its white belly and pounced like a murderer. At first the boy thought he was wedged under a rock, until the pickerel shot from his pool to another, like a missile.

"Dad!" he screamed. "Daddy!"

"Play him, George," the man said, a little sourly.

The boy's rod bent and straightened and bent again.

"What do I do, Dad?"

"Play him. Play him."

The boy reeled frantically, and the long fish rolled out of the pools toward him.

"I've got him!"

"Play him."

"I'm playing him!"

As suddenly as the fish took the crawler, it was gone. The boy fell back a little at the snap of his line.

"I lost him," the boy said disgustedly.

"You didn't play him."

"I played him."

"You didn't play him right."

"Hey," I called from above. "There's a lot more up there. And the perch are up there, too."

"What was that?"

"That was a pickerel."

The lake itself hadn't changed, but the shore that had been heavy underbrush and small trees gave way now to lawns and homes. The last time I'd been up here was a couple of days before basic training. I was nineteen and working for Horton's Fish Market. Like I said, I never got to college, so I was put into the army, but a couple of days before I went to Fort Dix, I rode my Raleigh up here. I could have taken my pop's car, but I was still a runner then, and I got my fishing gear and the weighted nymphs I tied in the winter and rode up. It was November. Pretty cold, but the fish get harder, stronger in cold water. I remember there was nothing here, not one house.

Now there were houses everywhere. And some had Winnebagos in the yards, and some had boats on trailers, satellite dishes pointing to the stars, dogs, everything.

I felt for my cigarettes, but they weren't in the suit pockets, so I walked back to my Raleigh to see if I had dropped them on the ground. I even tried my seat pouch, but I couldn't find them. I remembered a small store at the top of the lake where I used to stop and get a candy bar. Maybe it was still there. I snapped up the kickstand and sat on the bike. Pain shot from my ass like bullets, and I know bullet pain. I didn't realize how swollen and bruised my poor, fat ass was. My God, I thought. I must have filled up the tires and ridden all the way to Shad Factory in the middle of the night. And I didn't remember anything about it. The memory was stored in my ass, and my legs, and my soft, aching arms.

I walked the bike down the pump-house path to the footbridge and out to the road. I headed away from the houses so I could come up behind that little store, if it was still there. After half an hour, I had to take off my suit jacket because the sun had burned away the clouds. I put it over the seat and walked on.

My memory of Rehoboth was cornfields in the summer, and a lot of time, coming home, I'd steal a few ears of the sweet white ones for us. This August there was still corn, and it was high and beautiful and smelled the way manure and hay make the fields smell. It was wonderful, and I walked slow, which was the only way I could walk, being a porker pushing a bike, but even if I could have gone faster, I believe I wouldn't have.

Another half hour later, the store was there. Still. So while there were houses instead of the dark woods, somewhere there were cornfields and variety food stores. I leaned my bike in the shade and noticed an air pump at the corner of the store. I filled the tires again, brought the bike back to the shade, and walked in.

The store smelled good, like lettuce and coffee, and I was getting hungry. I wondered if they had those thick apple squares with frosting on them. I could have a few of those and some soda. I was dry.

"Cigarettes, too," I said out loud.

"Yes?" a young woman at the checkout stand said.

"I was just . . . uh . . . I guess I need . . . do you know those big apple squares? There's like two in a pack, and they're covered with frosting?"

"I'm not sure."

"I'll look around."

The vegetables looked pretty. I never looked at vegetables, because I didn't eat them anymore, unless it was a potato. Or corn, I'd eat corn. I walked over to the cookie section, and I found the apple squares right away. I picked up four packages. Then I got a quart of root beer. I was very hungry now, and I realized I hadn't eaten anything for a while. Since last night anyway. I put the root beer back and got a quart of Narragansett Lager. I read where beer had lots of nutrients and things. I put the apple squares and the beer on the counter.

"Two packs of Winstons, too."

The girl reached for the cigarettes, and I reached for my money.

"Wait a sec," I said. "I might've left my money . . . crying out loud . . . I might have forgot my money. Just a sec."

I walked out to the bike and went through my suit jacket. I found four quarters. "Jesus Christ."

69

I went back in.

"I got to put the stuff back. I only found a dollar."

She put the Winstons back in the cigarette rack, and I put the beer and the apple squares back.

"Bananas are six for a dollar," she said. "I won't charge any tax."

I hadn't had a banana in years and years.

"Six for a dollar?"

They all smelled good, and I picked the ones that had the least brown spots. I gave her the four quarters, had a long drink of water at the fountain by the door, and then I ate three bananas outside by the Raleigh. Bananas are easy to chew, and they fill you. The air was getting heavier as the night rain evaporated, but it had that sweet summer smell, and the wetness brought up the hay and manure and other things I'd forgotten. A pickup truck came out of a side road cut into the corn and turned onto the pavement. As it went by, I could see Bethany clear, on the back of the flatbed, balanced perfectly in her splayed pose, her hair straight in the breeze, her twenty-year-old skin shining in the sun. And she was gone. I was never alarmed to see Bethany, but I wasn't thinking about her. At least I don't think I was. I reached into my pocket and took out Pop's letter from Los Angeles. I reread the first part again. That she died. That she was fifty-one. That it was exposure, and that it was L.A. I guessed that Pop had sent dental records and inquiries everywhere over the twenty-seven years she'd been gone. My pop was full of energy. I read some more.

The 1931 Cohen/Hughes Act by the California legislature allocates funding for the retaining of the deceased body until implicit instructions are received from next of kin, should they exist. Please advise the details of interment as soon as possible.

Again, the County of Los Angeles extends its sympathy to you and your family.

I folded up the letter and slipped it back in my pocket. I got another drink of water, put the bananas in my suit jacket pocket, and walked off with my Raleigh. I wondered if the big country club was still around here, and the log cabin and the rose farm and the turkey farm. When I got to the top of the hill, I bit my tongue against the pain in my sore ass and coasted toward Taunton Turnpike.

12

By 1961 Bethany had started to go places where we didn't know she'd gone. These were technically not disappearances. Mostly they'd last anywhere from two hours to a day and a night, and even though the Ide family would be frantic, we never panicked and never, ever used the word "disappearance." My pop would do his drive, and I'd do my bike, and Mom would call around to neighbors and friends and eventually the police. Because of the Red Bridge thing, which was the first time her voice had tried to kill her, the Ide family became less concerned about what people might think of Bethany. When she was gone, we just wanted her back. So we rode and biked and called.

Now, this is about her junior prom, so I have to throw in two things that may or may not make it a little clearer. First is Bobby Myers, who was her date. Bobby had gone with Joanie Caveletti, who was to East Providence High School what Brigitte Bardot was to France. She was a hot item, and she was cool. I was still in junior high, but she was a legend. An enormous chest. There it was. That just said it all.

Bobby was not one of the nicest kids in school. He combed his long blond side hairs straight back, and his flattop stood about an inch high and at attention because of thick butch stick. So first impression, even to us little kids, was that he was a punk. He wore a leather jacket, too, but the problem was, he also had one of his EP letters sewed on the back, set against the shiny black leather. We all saw that the girls could not resist, because while Bobby Myers and his pals from the Riverside plat dressed and acted like mondo punks, they were the mainstay of the mighty townie football team, and baseball stars as well. The combination was lethal, and Bobby took full advantage. That was how the lovely and large Joanie Caveletti became his girlfriend. They went together from September of

Bobby's junior year until right before April, when Joanie apparently discovered that Bobby Myers was a dick with ears and dumped him. Bobby was devastated that a girl would abuse him in that way, and he rebounded by asking Bethany to the junior prom. Bethany had been in the back of Bobby's mind since the time she stripped off her clothes in the parking lot. He'd never been with a nut before, and he remembered her nice little breasts and other things.

Bethany had never had a boyfriend before and didn't know how a girlfriend and boyfriend were supposed to behave.

"Meet me at my locker," Bobby would say.

"Okay."

Like that. It was simple. And Bobby would give her a ride home and call her. This was turning into a good Bethany year. She had a couple of girls at school that she liked, and now Bobby Myers—who by the way was an Old Spice man—was her boyfriend.

When Bethany would come home from a Saturday date, usually a movie and a hamburger, Mom would ask casually how the date was.

"Neat."

"What did you do?"

"Movie, you know."

"Is Bobby a nice boy?"

"He's a mondo," I would say.

"He is not. He's very nice."

And he *was* being nice. He'd always open the car door for her and always seemed to be paying tremendous attention to the things she'd say, but I had a suspicion in the cloudy part of my achy brain that old Bobby Myers was planning something. Biding his time. Waiting. I hated him. I hated him, but I worried about him, too, because it was obvious to the Ides that cool Bobby Myers had not met the voice yet.

East Providence had an excellent baseball team that year, and Bobby Myers was certainly heading to his second all-state selection at third base. He had good range, a strong arm, a quick release to turn a double play, and, as much as I hated to admit it, a sweet, natural swing that cannot be taught. He would simply challenge the pitcher to put his best stuff in that strike zone. Bethany went to almost every home game and sometimes even wore a baseball jersey with Bobby's number on it. It was a powerful moment in the life of a high-school baseball player. And while he basked in glory, my junior-high team lost sixteen straight and I was hitless in the last thirteen. But I'm not dwelling on it. No.

Being a gentleman was a strain on the mondo punk from Riverside plat. Sometimes he'd lose his temper and punch one of his friends, which is what they were always doing to one another. Still, anybody could tell he was determined to be a nice boy with my sister, until he made his move. That's what guys like that do. They wait. They're patient. In a lot of ways, they're like good actors. I think that's probably why, as the years went by and I grew out of my life, I never felt completely bad for Bobby Myers. He had made a slick plan but never considered that other things are out there waiting, too.

Bethany's prom was May 11. It's a date I remember. Like April 1 or December 25 or November 22. It's a life date, and there has never been a more—and I know that a brother should not say this—beautiful, amazing prom girl in this whole country. Her dress was black and sleek. And she had blue heels on that clinked on the kitchen floor in a special way. She had silk stockings that caught the light a little and threw it off in sparkles, and her long hair was curled bouncy around her head. Bethany's eyes were made up, too. I had never seen her eyes fixed, and they looked huge and hopeful. She wore Mom's serious pearls and cameo earrings. It was like you couldn't breathe around her; she took the oxygen out of the air.

My pop gave her a big, happy hug and told her she was beautiful. He was careful to hold his lit Camel away from her hair. Mom cried.

"What do you think, Hook?"

"I think you look great."

"You think Bobby will like it?"

74

Bobby Myers was a dog. Bobby Myers was a greasy little shit.

"Yeah, he'll like it."

The doorbell rang, and there was Bobby. Black tuxedo slacks, white dinner jacket, red bow tie and cummerbund, fresh wads of butch stick. He adjusted his crotch and came in. The folks took pictures, and then they left. We watched them get into Bobby's father's Chevy Impala, and they were gone.

We stood on the front lawn in silence, and the clouds came in. My pop lit another Camel.

"She sure looked lovely," Pop said.

"Lovely, lovely, lovely," Mom said.

"Uh-huh," I agreed.

The sun was doing a peekaboo in the high afternoon clouds, and it got cold suddenly. Pop reached over and took Mom's hand and squeezed. I knew that Norma Mulvey would be watching, and I looked over to Bea's house. I wanted to wave, but it was already too late, so I looked off in the direction of Bobby and all his secret plans.

13

After a couple of hours, my ass got numb and the terrible pain went away. My legs were still stiff, but the more I pedaled the Raleigh and sweated, I felt actually soothed. I wasn't ready to stop by the time the turnpike led me into East Providence, so I cut over by the high school, through Six Corners, and crossed the old George Washington Bridge into Providence. I got off 95 on the other side of the bridge and followed the east-side route to Elmwood Avenue. Then, feeling light-headed, I mostly coasted down into Cranston. Cranston is an interesting place. It's loaded with Italians. It makes you wish you were Italian. In Cranston a kid could probably be ashamed not to be Italian. It's good, and I stopped by a ball field and ate another banana and watched some girls play softball. Big girls, throwing fast underhand curves that blurred by. I had another banana.

I got through Warwick about early afternoon. I didn't have a watch, and I didn't miss it, but there's something about time and responsibility. I don't know. Something. The highway always stayed to my right, and for the most part the roads I chose were poorly maintained and poorly traveled.

"A waste of a good road," I said out loud. But on a road where nobody travels, there's a great feeling of not being judged. Does that make any sense at all? When you're 279 pounds and you're wearing a tight blue suit and somebody coming up behind you on your bike could not see the seat, then you think about that. It becomes a distraction. You sweat even more. Your personal chest pain gets even worse. It's another defeat.

I remember quite a bit about this part. The ride part. People I talked to and who were mostly nice and the country. It surprises me how memory goes. I have whole years I can't remember, but this part . . . well, I'm surprised.

I walked my bike up the big Exeter hill and snuck onto Route 95 for a coast down toward Hope Valley. Wood River is in Hope Valley, and Yawgoog, too. That's the Boy Scout camp I went to. The big coast scared me. I was daydreaming, and by the time I realized the air was slapping me so hard I couldn't breathe, I was going about as fast as the cars. Like a jerk I hadn't been checking the tires, and they were almost on the rim again, and they made a high whine against the shoulder of the road. I tried to gently pump the hand brakes, but the tires smoked. I held my breath. My chest hurt, and my fat heart jumped around like a jumping bean.

There did not appear to be a bottom to the big hill, although I do remember one. I coasted on, steadily gaining speed, even though I squeezed the brakes with all my strength. Smoke changed from white to black. I smelled fire.

It is at moments like this, pivotal moments, that I had always failed. Sometimes there are moments when a person has to make a decision, as opposed to letting things just happen. A person then has to happen himself. I had never done this. Life bounced off me, and bounced me, and now it was going to bounce me to death. My fat ass, my blue suit. And so I turned my sizzling Raleigh off the 95 hill onto the Hope Valley exit ramp at approximately sixty-five miles per hour.

My sorry strands of hair stood straight back, and my bike careened into traffic. I headed for the yellow divider, which came over me like color wash. There had been some gas stations and a Howard Johnson's on this route to the Boy Scout camp, but at my speed I simply could not make out signs or landmarks. I zoomed on, and I noticed as I flew through the main intersections of Hope Valley that not only was I not slowing down, I was approaching another hill. This is the way luck goes and goes. My berserk luck. My blindly out-of-control luck. But at least this time I would decide, like I decided to exit into Hope Valley at miraculous speed. What could possibly happen to a load on a sparking Raleigh? For the first time in a long time, life was not just coming at me, I was coming at life. I thought this when I turned the bike toward a small dirt road, and as the tight lines of oaks and maples and fir trees whizzed by, I thought how odd to think this stuff about life. To ruminate at the speed of light.

The dirt road ended in a grassy field. A Little League baseball game was going on, with kids in red shirts up and blue shirts in the field. I exploded onto the field between first base and right. In a split second, I cut between the left and center fielders and charged toward a blurry patch of woods.

"Trees," I said out loud.

Even the slap of birch branches and tiny maples didn't slow me much, so when I began the deep slide down the ravine to where Wood River slowly rolled through Hope Valley, the drop seemed almost nothing. And the water, warmed up by the summer, strangely refreshed me for the instant before I passed out.

Above me, although I didn't know it at the time, the teams and parents of Holy Ghost the Redeemer and Third Reform Baptists ran across the field and down the tricky slope to help. My luck was changing.

The current had apparently rolled me onto my back, and although I did swallow some water, I also swallowed some good, clean Hope Valley air. A Catholic priest, Father Benny Gallo, still wearing his umpire hat, led two burly Baptists waist deep in the river. They reached for me, but because I had picked up speed in a rapid section of the river, they missed me, just before I rolled over the nine-foot Anthony Falls.

My pop and me, on the opening days of the trout season and after sometimes, usually fished a few miles above Hope Valley, where the pools spread out and were a little deeper, but sometimes we'd fish this stretch. It was about twenty-five miles or more from East Providence, and even though it ran right through this little town, you wouldn't know it. I'd like to throw a dry fly into the small rifts, but Pop loved taking a weighted woolly worm and popping it up into the white bubbles of Anthony Falls. He could fish there all day and always did well. Now his fat boy was there, and the tiny bubbles ran over him and kissed him, and the trout had all flipped downstream.

Somehow the thump of the falls shook me awake, or I think I was awake. I remember being in a narrow flume of water and hearing voices around the slam of the waterfall. I was moving again, and I tried to kick my legs, but they were like legs in a dream that aren't really yours. Along the bank I think I glimpsed a man in black who would be the umpire priest, but I can't be sure, because just as I thought of raising my arms for help, I went over Jenner Falls and apparently blacked out again.

It's scary, waking up with a plastic oxygen mask on. In a lot of ways, claustrophobic. Confining. When I got so hurt in the army, I didn't feel it was so scary. One of the other soldiers, Bill Butler, a black guy from St. Louis, leaned me against a tree, took out his little morphine bag we all had with us, stuck the needle into my stomach, and squeezed the whole thing in. I couldn't move, but you know what? I couldn't feel any of those twenty-one holes either. It hurt more being this fat-ass than it hurt then.

"Hello? Hello?" this umpire yelled, kneeling over me while I lay there in the skunk cabbage, by the side of Wood River.

Other faces loomed over me. Two Little League teams, moms and dads, sisters, some grandparents, people from the Hope Valley Rescue Squad. They had cut off my shirt and pants, and I wanted to pretend I was dead rather than spread this blubber out in front of them.

"Thank you," I said quietly to the priest, my words muffled by the oxygen mask. A huge roar went out from the crowd. One of the rescue-squad men made a victory sign, and everyone began to applaud.

They carried me up the slope behind an elementary school,

where I had ended my float, and loaded me into the rescue wagon. Two medics, the umpire, and the two Little League baseball captains climbed in and rode with me to the community hospital.

My clothes were wet and cut, so the hospital gave me a papery pair of pajamas to wear. My nose was broken, and I had a little bruise over my right eye. Also two hip pointers and a bruised kidney. The priest stayed with me. I was embarrassed to be so much trouble, but I was grateful he was there. I gave one of the nurses my name and told her I had insurance, but I wasn't sure what it was. I'd never needed it before. She kept looking up at Father Benny like she didn't believe me.

After about two hours, a young lady doctor with a kind of permanent sneer gave me two prescriptions and an instruction sheet on kidneys. It said to drink lots of water and not to lie on the kidney for a while. Then they released me from the emergency room. I walked with Father Benny, still in my paper pajamas, to the hospital entrance, and we took a cab to Holy Ghost Catholic Church. It was set back from the main street in Hope Valley, and we turned down a narrow paved road to the small white clapboard church.

It was getting dark by now. It might have been six or seven when we walked around the back of the church to an even smaller white cottage. I followed the priest into the house and then into the kitchen. He pulled out a blue kitchen chair for me, and I sat at the table.

"Can I get you a sandwich or anything?" Father Benny Gallo asked.

"A sandwich would be good."

"Tuna," he said. "You'll love this."

I sat in his tiny kitchen while he quickly and expertly put the sandwich together. I had cold bottled water, too.

"Good?"

"Very good. Thank you."

I chewed slowly. Father Benny's tuna salad topped my pop's by about a mile. In fact, since my pop's awful fishing sandwiches, cut too solid with too much mayo, I don't remember the last time I'd had a tuna.

The priest tinkered around the kitchen, so as not to stare at me while I ate. I appreciated that. I could not bear to be watched while I ate. I felt I should apologize for feeding my mountain of flesh.

"You're on the road," he said over his shoulder. "You're on the road like the fifties. Hard times. Bad times, really. But we do go on, don't we? The human spirit. We go on."

I didn't understand, but I nodded at him, even though he was at the sink and his back was turned.

"The emergency-room doctor told me those were bullet wounds— No, sorry, forget that, I promised myself I wouldn't ask."

"Vietnam," I said, with my mouth full of his wonderful sandwich.

"Awful. Horrible."

"No, no, really. This is the best tuna-fish sandwich I have ever had."

"Really?"

"The best."

"I squeeze a little lemon. Not much mayonnaise. Celery. Very healthy."

"Good, too."

"The doctor said there were fourteen wounds . . . holes."

"Twenty-one. I'm fine."

"Horrible."

"No, really."

"Horrible, horrible."

I finished the sandwich and the water.

"Another one?"

Strangely, I was full. Father Benny dried his hands and sat across from me at the small kitchen table.

"Bitterness over such an old war is not good, my friend. It's time to put it behind you."

"I'm not bitter at all. I don't think about it."

The priest looked at me with understanding and smiled sadly.

"Well, if twenty-one bullets didn't pull you into bitterness, then whatever did must have been horrible."

"I'm not bitter."

"Look . . ."

"Smithy," I said, shaking his hand, "Smithy Ide."

"Father Benny Gallo."

"I know."

"Look, Smithy. I'm a little younger than you. You're about what? Fifty? Fifty-five?"

I was forty-three. I ran my fingers over my mouth.

"I know I may seem out of line, but I'd feel remiss if I didn't point out to you that homelessness is not a thing that simply happens. It's a result of a great many factors, and there are many people and agencies that understand this and want to help. I probably could name you twenty different people active in the greater Providence area alone."

"A lot of people are nice," I said.

"They are. They are nice. So before we throw our hands up and go 'on the road,' we should reach out to them."

Father Benny Gallo took my hands in his. They were the hands you'd expect from an outdoor kind of priest who umpired Little League games.

"Don't give up, Smithy Ide. Fight it. Fight it. I have to fight myself, too. Every day. I want to stand up and say, 'I've had it.' But I don't. I go on. I push on through, you see. I push. An archaic church, an unappreciative little town, an empty rectory. I don't know. I had envisioned a kind of pastor-and-flock situation, a Bing Crosby thing. An amazed congregation, but . . . well, I just don't know. Are you Catholic?"

"Sure," I said. Actually not, but they use the word "Catholic" all the time in the Episcopal Church.

"Three," he said, holding up three fingers with an edge in his voice, "count them, three guys made monsignor this year, and every one of them graduated seminary with me and took vows with Bishop Fuget with me, and now they're monsignor. I've had Holy Ghost in Hope Valley for eleven years, and still I'm only an assistant pastor and there's no damn pastor here at all. See? What I'm . . . what I'm trying to say here is, you can't give up."

"Okay."

"Poverty, homelessness, a simple bicycle—"

"My bike," I said. "Is it . . . ?"

"One of the boys said he and his dad would take it home and see if they could fix it. The pitcher, I think. Baptist. And it's not, by the way, that I feel any resentment whatsoever toward the good bishop, but one would have to ask about the blatant effeminacy shared by all three brand-spanking-new monsignors and Queenie Fuget. You see what it is, is the absolute inability of the diocese to forgive and forget."

Father Benny paused and rubbed his forehead with the back of his hand. Suddenly I was as tired as I'd ever been. I could feel my heart slowing.

"Nineteen eighty-six. Nineteen eighty-six. Things were going fine. Great. I was working mass and confession at the Scout camp up the road, maintaining Holy Ghost here. Church school. Commissioner of girls' softball, et cetera, et cetera, et cetera. Then, well . . . I don't know. Well, to be honest, Jeneen Dovrance. Jeneen Dovrance. God!"

Father Benny stood up and slapped his chest. "This was a woman—not, no, not a married woman, no, just a mother of one of the Scouts, and she cornered me after mass at the camp to ask me about her boy's God and Country Award. Jeneen was a divorced mother with two boys and this little beauty spot, here, on her cheek, and violet eyes. I swear to God. Violet. Lashes this long. You know, a priest trains himself to look away. Not unlike a married man, to look away. And I looked away, even though, as I said, the eyes seemed to me almost an aberration of beauty. Violet.

"Later that evening she . . . called again. Providence. East side. Family money and all. She said she needed to ask a couple of questions about the God and Country. The Catholic award is called Ad Altare Dei. I explained that although it's given in conjunction with Scouts, it's not really a Scouting award. It's bestowed by a religious leader. It involves special service and so forth. She was extremely keen on the idea of her Scout earning the award and asked me if I thought her priest, the guy over at Immaculate Conception, was up to helping the boy earn the award."

He paced a little. I felt tired. Sleepy.

"I don't know why, but I said I'd come over and maybe we could set up an independent course of study and he could essentially earn the award independently. Well, it was one of those grand houses. Thayer Street. Actual Tiffany stained glass above the front door. Elegant. It was Saturday afternoon. April. There was a light drizzle, and the damn old Volkswagen of mine with the bald tires . . . I mean . . . I slipped all over the place, but I finally made it. She met me at the front door in these, oh, simple yet stylish yellow linen slacks with a rose-colored blouse. Her hair, her fine brown hair, was pulled high, and a few strands waved carelessly in the breeze of her walk when she took me around to the living room. There was a fire, and it drove the chill completely from the room."

He paused for a moment and remembered. I worked to keep my eyes open. Bethany stood by the watercooler.

"Her son was out, but I sat on this leather couch, and it was cool, and she sat next to me. She smelled like lemons and lilac. This really has nothing to do with anything, but later that evening, in my little sitting room upstairs, I wrote a poem entitled 'Lemons and Lilacs':

A woman resplendent
of smells repentant
to run tormented
on legs cemented.

I can smell the lemons, the lilacs whenever I recite that. It's a prayer. It's a mantra. Jeneen Dovrance had this young skin, pink like a schoolgirl's, even though she was in her mid-thirties, and her lovely full breasts pressed against the rose blouse."

He stopped and bit his lower lip, and his mouth trembled a little. I woke up. Bethany disappeared.

"They pressed against the blouse?" I asked, needing to say something.

"Like they were, somehow, captive. They yearned, actually. I gave her the packet for the Ad Altare Dei, and beside each requirement I noted how other boys had accomplished them, and at the bottom of the set of papers I included my name and address. Jeneen put her hand—her pink, almost translucent hand—onto my knee and thanked me, over and over, for making the trip and being so attentive. I got up, but as I did, my own hand brushed ever so reassuringly on hers. It was a small moment, but of such intensity I can't begin to say. Anyway I . . . called her the very next day under the pretense of concern over the Scouting thing, but I'll say it right out: I simply had to hear her voice and imagine her ensemble. Is that so wrong?"

He looked at me and seemed angry.

"No," I said.

"It's not a human vow. Historically it's not grounded in anything. Property, money, I don't know, but I don't believe that the church can justify it."

He looked out the window at the dark.

"I had sex a few times in high school," he sort of mumbled.

I had been with three women. Been with them in bed, sexually

85

I mean. They were all in-country and prostitutes. I paid them ten dollars in American money, and they were very happy, even though I could feel how much they hated me, months after. Like they put a curse on me so I would remember how they felt. I was the beast Bethany used to say I'd be. My fat ass, my hopeless self. Even when I smiled at a woman, I felt I was inflicting myself into her nice life. Sex.

"They were lovely young girls, but this woman sank into my unconscious. I called her again. And again. And each time she laughed and chatted in her breathless little way."

He took a deep breath and closed his eyes.

"Words," he said. "I just don't know about them. We were on the phone, and I was upstairs in my little bedroom, and I asked about her kid and his progress with Ad Altare Dei, et cetera, and she said . . . she said, 'It's very hot. I'm just going to take this off, just a second.' Well, I'm on the other end thinking, My God, what? What has she taken off? So I ask her casually. I say, 'So . . . what did you have to take off?' and she says, 'Oh, my sweater,' and I say, 'Are you cooler now?' and she says, 'Actually no, I'm still pretty hot,' and there's a pause, and finally I say, I say . . . 'Why don't you, why don't you take off the rest of your clothes so your full, ripe breasts can cool off?' "

He looked at me as if I should say something. But I don't know things. I've always thought they must get hot, but I just don't know. I smiled stupidly.

"Jeneen Dovrance said, 'What?' And I said like a ritual lamb, like a cow in the Chicago stockyards, I said, 'Why don't you slip out of your clothes so I can imagine you there, nude, with your lovely breasts and sweet love box all full and juicy.' She—joke's on me, all right, old celibate Benny Gallo—she hangs up. Know how I can remember what I said word for word? Because Jeneen Dovrance pressed 'record' on her answering machine after I said the word 'breasts' the first time, and Bishop Fuget and his goddamn toadies played it for me, over and over and over during the inquisition. She had transmitted this intensely private conversation to a hierarchy of pansies. You know what they call me behind my back? Shall I tell you? They call me 'old full and juicy.' 'Full and juicy,' ho, ho. Very funny. Assistant pastor. God Almighty."

He put his face into his hands, then went to the sink and splashed some cold water on his eyes.

"So you see how we go on? How we don't give up?"

I saw. I slept on a couch in the rectory, and I dreamed that Bethany was running around our backyard and Norma was chasing her. Laughter dreams good.

14

As soon as he was out of sight of my mom and pop, Bobby Myers lit a Marlboro.

"Open the glove compartment," he said to Bethany.

Inside was a quart bottle of Four Roses Canadian whiskey, which was a favorite of the Riverside mondos.

"That's the good stuff. I stole it from my old man. We're gonna have some fun tonight."

Bethany thought Bobby Myers looked good and cool with the Marlboro in his mouth.

"Did you remember to get the corsage?"

"Oh, shit, I'm glad you reminded me. It's in the trunk. I'll get it when we pick up Sal."

Sal Ruggeri—or Sal the Dago, which he was sometimes called behind his back, way behind his back—was the boy in East Providence High School who, by example, led the Riverside mondos. Without Sal we probably never would have had spot locker checks, for example. Certainly we never would have had the Sal Walk, which all the mondos were required to do. Hands in pockets, as close to your balls as possible, shoulders hunched so the leather jacket rode up around your neck, and a sort of slide step with your hobnail boots. And, of course, you chewed Dubble Bubble. It was their aroma. Sweet-smelling marauders.

Sal's mom and pop were lovely people who both worked for Campenella & Cardi Construction. He operated backhoes, and she did payroll. They went to mass on Wednesdays and Sundays and were active in most of St. Martha's activities. They were pretty typical of the lower-middle-class people in East Providence. They saved for everything they wanted. They worked hard. They were terrific neighbors. And they adored their only child—the evil-minded, pimply-pussed Sal the Dago.

Bobby and Sal were best friends in a way that the mondos were best friends. They'd punch each other on the arms and try to make the other one quit. Friends that way, the mondo way. Sal was taking Debbie Gomes. They weren't boyfriend and girlfriend or anything like that, but she was a tough girl, and she gave hand jobs. At least that's what it said on the wall above the urinal in the first-floor boys' room.

Sal came out of the house on the first honk of the Impala. His tuxedo pants were skintight, and instead of a bow tie, he wore his shirt open so his furry chest could breathe.

"Hey, man," Bobby said coolly. Sal jumped into the backseat.

"Hey, man," Sal said.

Bethany felt a little uncomfortable around Sal. Everybody did. It was a feeling you'd get that was magnetic and repulsive at the same time. Turmoil. But Bethany also felt pretty excited and happy. Bobby was so cool, and she looked great. She knew she did. She felt all her choices were the exact right ones—from her tight curls, which had loosened up enough to bounce, to her sexy blue heels. She had practiced walking in them for weeks and had perfected a natural-looking glide step. It was a very nice package, and she knew it.

Now, I'm not sure about anything, as I've said, but I think generally there's a rhythm to young girls that they don't have to think about. It's not really spontaneous either, because it's always there. It's the big events with gowns and tuxedos and heels that point this up. The girls somehow hear this beat, this rhythm, and that's what the night is like. The boys do not have this rhythm, at least not for an entire night, and that's why the liquor gets into glove compartments.

Bobby steered the big Impala with one hand and reached for the Four Roses with the other. He handed it back to Sal.

"The good stuff. There's cups and orange soda to mix it with. Under the seat."

Sal filled the cups about halfway with the whiskey, then smoothed them out with the orange soda. He handed Bobby his, then Bethany.

"This is fucking great," Sal said. He lit a Marlboro. Bobby took a big swallow and watched Bethany sip a little.

"Great?" Bobby asked.

"Really good," Bethany said.

"Hey," Sal said, "we don't have to pick up Debbie or nothing. She lives next to the car place across from the school. I told her to walk."

It was a warm evening, warmer than usual for Rhode Island. Bobby pulled into the half-full parking lot. Sal climbed over the trunk and walked to the mondos on the grass next to the school gym. Their dates were inside.

"Why don't you go in and stuff. I got to see these guys," Bobby said.

The mondos laughed that Debbie was inside waiting to give Sal his hand job. Sal smiled, grabbed his crotch, and went inside the gym. Bobby followed him. Big Brother Jackson Dees from WICE in Providence spun the records and in between peppered the space with East Providence High School references. He played lots of the Drifters, Elvis, Dion and the Belmonts, and the fabulous Fabian. The girls went back and forth to the girls' room. The boys smoked cigarettes just outside the door to the gym. It was, all in all, a pretty nice prom. At eleven forty-five, Mr. Burke, the principal, flipped the gym lights on and off, signaling last dance, and the formal portion of the evening came to a close.

When Bobby and Bethany reached the car, Debbie was wiping her hands with some Kleenex, and Sal was relaxing with a tall Orange and Roses.

"Weren't the decorations neat?" Bethany gushed, getting into the front seat.

"Real cool." Debbie yawned.

"Yeah, real cool," added Sal.

"It was Sharon Davis's idea to have a Colonial theme. I think Sharon did a real, real neat job."

"How about some drinks up here," said Bobby. He finished his before he started the car.

"Let's go to the beach," Sal said on cue.

"Hey, what a neat idea," said Debbie.

"The beach? Hey, that does sound good."

"But it's past twelve already. I'm supposed to be home," Bethany said. My sister felt awkward and childish, but she wanted to be responsible to Mom and Pop, and maybe even me.

"We'll just go to Barrington. Fifteen, twenty minutes." The big car powered out of the parking lot, up Pawtucket Avenue, through Riverside, and into Barrington. Bethany didn't say anything. Debbie and Sal the Dago had disappeared onto the backseat. Juicy kiss sounds and occasional groans oozed into the front. Bobby finished Bethany's drink as they pulled onto the rise above Barrington Beach. He turned the motor off, and they both sat looking out over the bay. Crickets chirped. The tiniest waves rolled beneath them. Debbie growled quietly, out of sight in the rear darkness. Bobby gently put his arm around Bethany.

"Did I tell you how pretty you look tonight?"

She smiled but felt her body begin to go rigid.

"I thought you were the prettiest girl there."

Bobby leaned over and kissed her cheek, then kissed down her jawline until he reached the lips. He'd kissed her before, and on the lips, too, but not with Sal and Debbie in the backseat, and not quite so differently. She felt his tongue push through her tightened lips and whap at her teeth. In the backseat the slurping of tongues overpowered the waves. Bethany turned her head away.

"I don't know . . ." she said.

"I just like you so much," he whispered. "I just like you so much." Bobby licked at her ears. "Do you remember when you took off your clothes in the school parking lot? All your clothes? I saw your titties. I just like them so much. I like the way you took off all your clothes."

Bethany felt his wet lips on her neck. She remembered the parking lot. She remembered how the other girls had stopped speaking to her and how her skin felt all icy and then like Brillo soap pads, and Smithy finding her underneath the water tower in the snow. And really how her voice had lied then, no matter what it said now, tried to say. How it lied, behind the walls, in the air above her head.

Bobby Myers turned her toward him, and his tongue jumped into her mouth like a lizard. His left hand brushed against her chest, and his finger squeezed where her nipples would be.

"I liked the way you took off all your clothes. I liked the way your titties were all pretty and exciting."

"Oh, God!" Debbie screamed, still out of sight.

"Baby, baby," Sal gushed.

"Titties, titties, titties," uttered Bobby. "Take them off. Take all your clothes off. Please. Please. Please."

Bobby grabbed her right hand and pulled it toward his crotch. "See what you do to me? See how you get me all excited and everything?"

"Don't wipe it on my tuxedo," Sal said from behind them. "I have to take this shit back to the store."

"So what am I supposed to do with it?"

"Rub it on the rug."

"Please," Bobby pushed, "take it off. Take it off so I can see. Please."

"I got this stuff all over my dress," Debbie whined. Her and Sal sat up in the backseat.

"Pass the cups back here," Sal said.

Bobby released the suction on Bethany's neck. "You guys think you could take a walk on the beach or something?"

"We'll close our eyes," Sal snickered.

"We won't watch." Debbie laughed.

"C'mon," Bobby pleaded.

"Shit," said Sal. He climbed on the hood. Debbie followed him.

"Thanks!" yelled Bobby after them. Bethany felt heavy and sleepy and somehow chilled. She watched Sal and Debbie walk toward the water. She felt separated from this place, and the beach, and even the water. It seemed sometimes that the only connection in a world of disconnection was the steadying call of the voice deep in whatever it was she was. She never spoke of the voice, the words, anymore, and she regretted she ever had, because no one could give her the understanding, the sympathy, her private voice required. Indeed, it seemed to anger the people who loved her more and more, until no matter what problems arose, the voice was always assumed to be at the center.

Bethany looked down, and Bobby was removing her panties. He pulled them over the blue heels. She watched his hands run up her thigh and his fingers plunge into her pubic hair. He kissed her lips. She watched herself as if in a mirror.

"Touch me," he breathed. "Touch me now"

She looked away from herself and saw that Bobby had unbuttoned the tuxedo pants and brought his penis into view. He moved her hand to it.

"My dick," he breathed romantically. "My dick, my dick, my dick."

Bethany held the object of his intensity curiously. She moved it left and right like a stick shift.

"No, no, up and down," he drawled.

"I understand it now. Now I get it," she said, removing her hand.

"Get what?"

"I wasn't talking to you"

She looked to where Sal lay humping Debbie on the sand

"I want to take all my clothes off for you," she said shyly, "but I want it to be a surprise, too."

"Why don't you just take them off? I've already seen your thing."

"I just want it to be a surprise. How about this? How about you get in the trunk, and I'll take off all my clothes, and then you can see all of me, with nothing on?"

"And I'll take my clothes off, too. I'll take them off in the trunk."

"And I'll give you a big blow job," she said sweetly.

A blow job? A blow job? Blow job? This was thought about by the Rhode Island mondos to distraction, but none of them ever believed they'd get a girl to actually put her mouth around it and blow! Crazy girls were great. They were crazy, man. Bobby ran around to the rear of the car and unlocked the trunk.

"Give me the keys, quick," she said. "I have to get out of my dress. I have to let my titties out."

Bobby leaped in, and Bethany closed the trunk. She walked around to the driver's side of the car and put her panties on.

"That's enough," she said out loud. "I don't have to do more than that."

The clear water kicked back the three-quarter moon's shape. "I don't want to do more," she said loudly. "Don't tell me to do more. Please."

Sal heard the car engine start and raised his head.

"What?" asked Debbie, beneath him.

"The car started."

They saw the headlights flash on, and the light covered them. Sal jumped up and zipped his pants. He gave the car the finger.

"He's a dick," he said.

Debbie stood, and they brushed sand from each other.

"What's the matter with that jerk?"

"He's a dick," Sal said.

The big car squealed backward and stopped at the far end of the parking lot. It sat revving. An angry rev. A crazy rev. Then the sound fell into the gentle hum of the Chevrolet's eight perfect cylinders.

"What's he doing?" Debbie asked.

"Sshhhh," whispered Sal. He looked behind him. They were about twenty or thirty yards from the water. He didn't know why, but he noted it. He looked back at the idling Impala. Someone was talking in the car, but the voice didn't belong to either Bobby or Bethany. It was cackly and high.

"Who's that?" Debbie whispered.

"I do not have a fucking clue."

Suddenly the car charged across the blacktop, toward the thin wooden barriers separating the parking lot from the cement tidal wall and beach. It ripped apart the barriers and flew off the wall. It seemed to Sal that the Impala actually rose higher before it thudded to the beach, its wheels spewing a tall arc of fine sand. It roared on through the soft granules, but as it closed on Sal and Debbie, the beach became harder packed and the car found new traction.

"Shit!" Sal screamed. He grabbed Debbie's hand and headed toward the water. Behind them the snarl of engine grew louder.

"C'mon, c'mon, c'mon!" Sal urged.

They hit the freezing May Atlantic at a gallop, then frantically dragged their soggy bodies deeper into the bay. The Impala swerved, half in the water, half out, and the closeness of the heavy metal chassis seemed like the end. The engine faded, and they turned their eyes back to land. The car had driven onto the lip of the ocean and was now several hundred yards down the beach. In the distance Warren, Rhode Island, twinkled in its harbor. Sal thought he heard a muffled scream from inside the car; then it turned into the high reeds and disappeared.

15

I lay in bed semi-awake and tried to yawn. My eyes were dry, and I knew a good yawn would activate my tear ducts. Is it like that for everybody? The door to the rectory opened, and Benny Gallo walked in carrying some huge Kmart bags.

"We had a guy in seminary used to sleep late. We called him the 'big sleeper.' "

"What time is it?" I said.

"Almost twelve. You're getting up at the crack of noon."

Benny was wearing sneakers, running shorts, and a blue T-shirt that said PRIESTS DON'T DO IT.

"I wanted to get this stuff before one. There's the regional girls' softball championship and picnic over at Chariho High. I'm umpiring the first game and then judging brownies. Serious stuff."

I sat up and swung my legs to the floor.

"Saturdays are always hectic," he said.

"It's Saturday?"

"If Saturdays don't run like clockwork, I'm lost. I fall behind and never catch up. Mass at six. Jog. Breakfast. AA meeting. Rounds at the nursing home. Coaching or umpiring, there's always something going on. Hospital calls. Knights of Columbus, whatnot. It's a bitch."

But Father Benny was buoyant in his activity-loaded schedule, and the room thumped with his energy.

"I got you some stuff," he said. And he described each of the items as he pulled them from the bags.

"Toothbrush and toothpaste. Got to have this. I got you the soft bristles. Fruit of the Loom. I guessed XXL. Jockeys. Running shorts. Three pairs. Again XXL. See, these are extra stretch in the waist and wide in the leg, so they shouldn't bind on you when you're on the bike. T-shirts and sweatshirts—and look at this baby." Father Benny reverently took out an enormous red-flowered Hawaiian shirt that two of me could have fit in.

"Beautiful, huh? And look at these. Two pairs of Nike trail boots. They're light as sneakers, but they're all-terrain. I got your size out of the shoe you had left. I love mine. Oh, and I got some sweat socks and food. Energy bars and bananas and fruit. And bottled water and stress tablets. These are good. They're special vitamins. I take them, too."

"This stuff is all for me?" I asked.

Father Benny reached into his pocket and pulled out an old telephone-bill envelope. He sat on the edge of the couch and handed it to me. "I wish it could be more."

I opened it up, and inside were three ten-dollar bills. "I'll send it back," I said.

"Sure. Sometime when you're not on the road. Sometime when you have a home."

"I do."

"Sure. Look, Smithy, Mother Mary teaches us that home is what we carry in our hearts. Be strong. Go on."

"I will."

"Don't give up. I'm going over to the nursing home. Your bike's all fixed. It's in the kitchen. If I don't see you, God bless."

"God bless you, too."

Benny Gallo smiled and left the rectory at a jog. I went into the bathroom and brushed my teeth, and he was right. I needed a nice mouth feeling. I took a shower, too; then I put on the clothes he bought me and went to the kitchen. The sneaker boots felt wonderful. My legs and kidney still ached, and my face was purple from the fall, but in the kitchen I took a deep breath, and I didn't remember so much good air getting into me for a long time.

My Raleigh leaned on its kickstand next to the stove. It was oiled and polished, and there were two new tires on it. Also large saddlebags set over the back. Some player and his pop had taken the fat man's bike home and fixed it up and put on red nylon saddlebags. I drank some of the water Benny had given me and had an orange. I ate standing, because even though I was old and fat, I was excited to try a Raleigh that now seemed like a new Raleigh. I took the things Benny bought me and put them in the expanding saddlebags. Then I walked the bike through the door and up to Main Street.

They had raised the seat a little and the handlebars, too, so when I pedaled, my legs extended all the way in a full, natural circle. The bike whirred, and the smoothness of the braking was exhilarating. My bike was the best bike ever.

"Thank you," I said out loud to the player and his pop. Good people were there. There were things for them to do together, and I was somehow a part of that. I felt *easy*, that's the word. It wasn't hard to smile. Also I had bananas and apples and boots in my saddlebags.

I rode under the I-95 overpass and, after an hour or so, picked up Route 1 around Potter Hill. I could smell the salt air and the unmistakable heavy, sweet mountain laurel that grew so strong close to the ocean. I broke into a tremendous sweat, and the parts of my bulky body that had throbbed with pain seemed to become new like my bike. It was as if the pain sweated away with each slow pedal, and I mean slow. I glided down hills. I walked up them. I sucked the air out of entire counties.

When the big houses of Westerly came into view, with their peaks and awnings and widow's walks, I pulled off the road and stopped under a huge elm tree. It was cool this close to the ocean. I took off my blue XXL T-shirt and put on the enormous red Hawaiian shirt. Father Benny knew how to pick clothes. The extra-stretch waist on the shorts had only a moderate amount of gut spillage, and the sneaker boots felt great.

"Thank you, Father Benny," I said.

I got back onto the Raleigh and went through the town. My pop had known some guys here. He knew a ballplayer named Archie Bissette, who played first base for Socony and also had a bait shop in

Westerly where he sold lures and hooks and frozen squid for the tautog, and live eels for the stripers the fishermen would try for off the beaches of Green Hill and Misquamicut and Quonochontaug. I rode around the center of town where their war memorial stood, but I couldn't remember where Archie Bissette's store was, and, really, nothing looked familiar, so I picked up scenic Route 1 again and crossed into Connecticut.

A breeze, moist and constant, blew off the Block Island Sound and got me. There were hawks sitting on the high dead branches of ash trees, and they stared, like I did, at the crazy seagulls and the tight, loud circles they made above us.

I stopped at a picnic grove in Pawcatuck and ate some bananas and an apple and, just because he had taken the time to buy them for me, one of Father Benny's stress tablets.

Now, this is one of those clear things. Where I was. A pretty grove of fir trees. Picnic benches. Bathroom. A pretty place. When you're a kid, place is everything. And when you leave, you're so absolutely aware of departure. I haven't been aware for a while now. Long enough, actually, to not be aware when one place started running into another place, until they were all the same. But on this Saturday, in this cool grove, with kickstand down and my feet feeling wonderful, I had a sense, a real sense, of having left Rhode Island and crossed out of my life. Connecticut felt good, and down the road was Stonington, and past that Mystic, where my pop had taken us to see tall ships and eat clam cakes.

I felt tired and closed my eyes for a while. I must have slept, because I felt good when I opened them. It was getting high afternoon already, and then I remembered my late sleep. I left the grove and rode hard toward Mystic. I had a feeling I would like to see the aquarium there. Then later, in fields near the ocean, I would spend the Connecticut night.

16

The homes in the planned communities that encircle Brickyard Pond and State Park in Barrington, Rhode Island, are really lovely. Big houses, with three and four bedrooms and two-car garages and wonderfully manicured property. The houses on the lake itself, the prime houses, have lawns that slope to the blue-brown water. On the far side of the lake, where the garbage landfill site ruled for almost twenty years, from 1955 on, magnificent white stucco hacienda-type homes spread evenly among new poplars.

I loved to fish the Brickyard. Me and Tony Travanti from across the street would ride down with some night crawlers and clean up. Some trout, bass, pickerel, perch, and—I'm not kidding—bluegill so big we used to think they were a different fish altogether. It was Tony's theory, and I think it's a good one, that a lot of garbage and cans and stuff spilled into the lake from the dump and all this leftover food and medicine and aluminum foil just made a different bluegill. The other parts of the pond were pretty much trees and dirt paths, and when you walked away from the official park, following the bank to fish in the weedy, stumpy sections where the big pickerel were, the underbrush was prehistoric.

Sal the Dago told the police how after the Chevy had tried to murder Miss Gomes and himself, it had driven down the beach and disappeared into the reeds.

"Then it just fucking flew out of the reeds and jumped up the bank back onto the road and took off. I'm eaten alive. I'm eaten by fucking bugs."

"Shut up, greaseball," the crew-cut Barrington police officer said. "Watch your language around this young lady."

"Thank you," Debbie Gomes said, ladylike.

"What did I say?" Sal asked, genuinely confused.

"The officer doesn't want you to offend me," Debbie said.

"I can't offend her, Officer," Sal said sincerely. "She gives me hand jobs."

The punch took the wind out of Sal, and he buckled, then fell on his knees. The policeman easily brought Sal's hands behind his back and handcuffed him, then jerked him to his feet.

"Thank you." Debbie smiled.

The policeman smiled back, then pulled the gasping Sal to the cruiser and leaned him against it. Then he walked back to Debbie.

"He forced himself on you?"

"Kind of, I guess."

It was a cool evening, and the slightest breeze off Narragansett Bay put some real chill in the air.

For the next three days and two nights, the Barrington police, joined by the finest of East Providence and, finally, state troopers from the Bristol barracks, launched an all-out three-state search for Bobby Myers and the young prom date he abducted. They crossed, with permission, into Connecticut and as far as Waltham, Massachusetts, looking for the blond mondo and his father's Chevy Impala. They looked everywhere but the Brickyard, where Bethany's voice had taken them. Not more than three miles from Barrington Beach. They'd driven crazily to the state park entrance, went onto a small playing field and into the thick overgrowth, as far as the car could possibly go. Then my sister had shut off the engine and gone into a three-day, two-night pose. If it wasn't for a fisherman looking for a shortcut to the bass and pickerel, they might be there still. He called to her, but she was frozen and swollen from the heavy mosquito hatches. Then he heard the faintest of whimpers and opened the trunk.

In the weeks after the prom, Bethany was returned once again to Bradley Hospital. My pop found a new psychiatrist through Grace Church, and for a while both he and Mom felt they were moving in the right direction. She became Bethany again, and her bug-ravaged skin returned clear and beautiful. We visited her often, and all of our meetings with Dr. Glenn Golden were upbeat and hopeful.

Bobby Myers didn't make all-state that year. Sal the Dago Ruggeri plea-bargained the sexual-assault charge to simple battery. He was given a one-year suspended sentence. He was also expelled from school.

17

I love penguins. They're not only the silliest bird, I'll bet they're the silliest animal. They walk funny and sound funny and swing their wings like little arms, and then they look right at you with this "what are you looking at?" expression. The penguins were the high point of the Mystic Aquarium, but the porpoise show was pretty amazing, too. And cheap. Oh, and the bathrooms were exceptionally clean and cheerful.

I slept about a mile out of Mystic. It got very black, so I walked into a cornfield and lay down between the rows. I used the sweatshirt for a pillow, and I slept pretty good. In the morning I had more than the usual aches. Complicating the pain of being a fat-ass who hadn't exercised since the army was a terrific sunburn on my arms and legs and head. I stopped at a gas station and bought some aspirin and used the bathroom; then I pedaled for maybe half an hour until I found a little variety store that sold sun lotion. I hadn't worn shorts for twenty or thirty years. I lathered myself up good and ate breakfast. Bananas again. And an apple and the biggest bran muffin I have ever seen for a dollar. But bananas, I want to say, bananas you forget. How else can I explain them? I love them. Everything about the texture and the chewability of bananas is me, but I'd just stopped eating them. I'm happy I found bananas again.

The aspirin worked, and the lotion snuffed the burn, but I still moved slow. I stopped in the middle of the Groton–New London Bridge and saw the coast guard's four-masted training schooner and behind that a nuclear-powered sub as long as a football field. I'd had a tour of the sub base once with the Scouts, but I don't remember when. I thought it was interesting.

I slept on the beach near Old Saybrook that night, and in the morning I called Norma.

"Yes?" she answered on the first ring.

"Norma? I didn't wake you up or anything, did I?"

Norma Mulvey's end of the phone sank into silence.

"Norma? Did I wake you?"

"Smithy? Smithy?" She was crying.

"Don't cry, Norma."

"The garage door was open, the house was open, bills on the table—Bea called the police."

"She called the police?"

"Where are you? Come home. We're . . . Bea's worried sick."

"I'm in Old Saybrook. I'm on my Raleigh. A priest gave me clothes and stress tablets. Norma, I got this letter, one of my pop's letters, really. . . ."

"Pop?"

"From Los Angeles. They found Bethany."

"They found her? They found her?"

"Bethany died, Norma."

Norma's breathing became faster, and her voice dropped. She sniffled.

"They had to . . . they had to identify her through dental records my pop had sent everywhere. Don't cry, Norma."

"I loved her, too." The defiance again, only this time through chokes and sobs. I started to go, too, but I grabbed myself.

"Norma? Would you call Goddard and tell them I'm sick and I'm not coming in for a while?"

"You're sick?"

"No. I'm in Old Saybrook. I'm on my bike. I'm . . . I don't know . . . I think I'm going to Los Angeles."

We hung together with what I just said, in silence, on the line.

"I'll call Goddard. I'll tell them you're sick."

"Thanks, Norma."

"Do you need money?"

"I don't think so . . . well . . . thanks, Norma."

She was quiet, then quieter still. It was hard to believe there wasn't a wild ten-year-old on the other end holding her breath the way she used to when she wanted me to play catch or dolls. Then I remembered her telling me outside the funeral home that she did for herself. That she had these systems for things and important jobs to do.

"Did you hang up, Norma?"

"I've never been held," Norma said like a blow of air over the miles. I didn't say anything. I couldn't think. "Held as a child, I mean, but that's different."

I heard her voice bounce off satellites and flow through the hot wires.

"I . . ."

"I hold myself. I do for myself. I got to go."

I waited for her to hang up the phone, but she didn't. We stayed, without speaking, like kids with tin cans and string.

"I would hold you, Norma," I said after a while, and heard the faintest click. In the east. Near the bay.

18

Frank Malzone was a very good third baseman. He held the spot in the fifties for our Red Sox. I was little when he quit—or, as my pop liked to say, when "they run him out"—but I have fond memories of Pop imitating him in games. Malzone had a big face, and it more or less hung out. He'd take his fielding stance, feet spread, knees bent, forearms balanced on his knees, and his big face actually did just hang out. My pop loved him. "Malzone's up!" he'd yell. "Big face. Big bat." When I was seven, we got a puppy, a mutt with a huge face. We called him Malzone.

Malzone—the dog—had the body of a German shepherd, but he had an auburn color and soft, long hair that tended to knot up when it rained or got hot or snowy. He liked to be near Pop, but really he liked us all. He loved it when you would talk to him like a baby and then rub his belly. When Malzone was three, he got "irritated." That's the word Mom used. He went dog crazy. He would whine and cry at the door for hours, day and night, until somebody let him out. Then he'd leave for days. I'd get frantic. Who knew what could happen to a nice, happy dog out there alone on the streets of East Providence? I remembered this today. I hadn't thought of it for a long, long time. How I came home one Saturday and Malzone was gone.

"Where's Malzone?" I asked Pop in the kitchen.

"Malzone's at the dog hospital. He's fine. He's having a little operation."

My dog? Operated on?

"Malzone's in the hospital?"

Bethany walked into the kitchen. I could tell she'd been crying.

"Just a little operation," Pop said; then he walked out of the room. I looked scared.

"I wanted to hold him. I wanted to comfort him," Bethany said.

"But what do they do to dogs?"

Bethany looked at me a long minute. "They cut off his balls," she said.

"They cut off his balls?"

The screen door opened, and Norma squealed in.

"It was all his yakking and whining," Bethany said.

"Yakking? They cut off his balls for yakking?"

"Don't cry, Smithy!" yelled Norma.

I stepped away, then turned back to my sister. "You can't do that because he gets all excited and yaks. People yak. They wouldn't do it to people, would they?"

I had started to cry, and Bethany hugged me. Norma tried to hug us both.

"Pop wouldn't let me go with him, Hook. But I tried. I wouldn't have been afraid."

"I hate that I'm ten!" I screamed.

"I hate that you're ten, too," Bethany said quietly.

"I'm six!" Norma screamed proudly.

"Just like that," I cried. "Poor Malzone. My poor dog."

"Pop said they had to do it because he was going crazy over girl dogs and he was a runner."

I looked at my sister like she was nutty.

"Of course he's a runner. Malzone's a dog. Dogs run."

"Pop said they have to snip to stop the running."

"Snip, snip!" screamed Norma.

"But Malzone's happy when he runs."

My sister put her hands on her hips. "You are so stupid. You just don't listen. You have Jell-O for brains. When they brought you home from the hospital, we all thought you were retarded."

"Did not!"

"I convinced Mom and Pop to keep you."

"I'd keep you!" Norma screamed.

"They were gonna keep me."

"Maybe." Bethany shrugged.

I sat at the table, and my sister sat across from me. Norma grabbed a chair and pushed it next to me and sat. We were quiet for a minute or two. My pop was having a cigarette in the parlor, and we could smell it.

"Do you think Malzone will be all right?" I asked.

"I think he'll be the same old Malzone."

"But he won't run."

"He'll run. He won't run away."

"I like it when Malzone runs," I said.

"That's because you're a dog, too," Bethany said seriously. "You're a runner, too, Hook. Don't stop, okay? Don't stop or you'll be a fat-ass."

I ignored her. "I like it when Malzone runs."

"I love it when you run!" Norma screamed, trying to grab me. I kept pushing her hands away.

"The animal doctor said that for a while Malzone will think something about it. He'll have a memory of running or something, and after a while he'll forget about the girl dogs and be fat and happy."

"He say 'happy'?"

"Wanna play with puppets, Smithy?" Norma screamed.

I got up and started to walk out of the room. "Get away, Norma, little jerk."

We all picked up Malzone the next day. Mom boiled some chicken legs with rice, which was his absolute favorite food. We had some codfish. We were all together—even Norma screamed over for dessert—and before I had to go to bed, Bethany sang her choir solo from the *Seven Last Words*. It was purely wonderful, and she rubbed Malzone's belly as she sang.

19

Route 1 merges over a bridge just outside New Haven, then heads off on its own again. The walk space is not exactly a sidewalk on this I95 overpass, so I couldn't drive it with the cars shooting by. I walked, pushing my Raleigh next to me. It was late afternoon, and I was pretty tired. See, I made one of those traveling miscalculations that people make when they lose a certain sense of time. I should have stopped earlier, at one of the shore exits, where I might have been able to have a swim and a good sleep, but now I'd have to wait until I got outside the city of New Haven, and I was getting tired.

After I had crossed the New Haven Harbor, I lifted my bike off the main road, onto a grassy slope, and walked it down to the service road. About a hundred yards ahead of me was the New Haven train station. I pushed through the high, ornate doors and walked in. Train stations are amazing. Uncle Count is a train-station buff. Not a train buff, but a station man. It's his theory that when the big stations were built in Boston, Providence, and New York, people must have thought trains would always be the end-all and be-all of travel. Now they seem like museums with newspaper stands, but they are still amazing, with paintings on the ceilings and statues cut into the high walls.

I sat on a long wooden bench that looked exactly like the pews in our church and ate the last of Father Benny's fruit. Then I bought a tuna sandwich at the snack counter and ate that, too. It was 5:40. I didn't think it was anywhere near 5:00. On the opposite wall, the huge information board flipped with each arrival and departure. The next train to New York was at 8:20, and when I bought my ticket, I was instantly sorry I hadn't asked Norma to send some money. The ticket was pretty expensive, and it left me with seventy cents. But my stomach was full of fruit and tuna, and that wasn't too bad a way to wait for my train.

We came into the big Penn Station at 11:00 on the nose. It would have been earlier, but there was some track work going on around Stamford.

I sat on another long, pewlike bench in the New York station and slept until a policeman slammed his nightstick next to me.

I awoke with a start, and my fat heart raced a minute. I watched the young officer walk away, every now and then slapping his nightstick onto the oak benches. The enormous waiting area was filled with exhausted men and women in different stages of sleep. The ones that obviously could get the best rest were the people who'd figured out how to sleep sitting, with their eyes open. I have tried this, but it's a skill I don't have and can't seem to learn. I smelled old pee and sweat. In that big room was sorrow, too. An old woman, who might not have been old at all, talked constantly to something that wasn't there. I have heard that talk. I used to ask my pop if Bethany saw it clear, whatever it was. By then my pop couldn't talk about the voice and didn't. I watched the woman closely, and she turned her head and caught me looking. She didn't stop talking, but she gave me the finger. I smiled like a stupe. Why do I do that?

I sat until the sun came up. Then I got an apple juice out of a machine, went to the dirty toilet, and walked my Raleigh up to Seventh Avenue. It was five-fifteen in the morning, and I had ten cents in my pocket.

"Ten cents," I said out loud, under the Madison Square Garden sign.

"What?"

I turned around.

"You say something?" a young black coffee vendor asked.

"No. I mean, I just said ten cents."

"What ten cents?"

I laughed. "That's all I got."

"Good enough. Cream and sugar?" he said, businesslike.

"Uh . . . yes . . . please."

I gave him my dime and drank the wonderful coffee. By the time I had finished, the street was alive. And the people gave off the same feelings I got when Mrs. Fox took our fourth-grade class to the Narragansett Electric Company. We were studying turbines that made the electricity. This is what I remember. A feeling of energy, of something unbelievably powerful and electric. This is the same feeling I got from the New Yorkers on the street on an early Monday morning. I got onto my bike and pedaled with the traffic.

It was a nervous ride from Pennsylvania Station at Thirty-fourth Street. Everybody screamed at me or honked at me or gave me the finger. Pedestrians, too. I was so frazzled by the time I reached Fourteenth Street that I had forgotten being embarrassed about my fat ass and huge belly. When our family came to New York, we went to Radio City and Mom made us stroll Fifth Avenue. That was New York to me. It was cleaner then. Nobody gave us the finger.

"Where's Fifth Avenue?" I said to a group of kids. They pointed east.

I followed the flow of Fifth Avenue a few blocks and came to a white arch with a crumbling sculpture of George Washington. Behind him was Washington Square Park. In Rhode Island, parks are used occasionally. That's it. It would not be an overstatement to say our parks are not used that much. New York parks are used. They are crammed. They are the magnets, I guess, for interludes. Does that sound right? I sat on a bench facing an empty fountain. Now, this is not by any means a complete list, but in five minutes I saw roller skaters, baby carriages, bikes, skateboards, pogo sticks, stilt walkers, Indians from America in full headdress, Indians from India in full turbans, beautiful girls with large breasts, a group of Spanish kids kicking a soccer ball in a circle, men holding hands with other men, an old man with a ponytail in a black leather jacket that said SPEED on the back, a kid with blond hair who had to be seven feet tall, and, directly in front of me, on her hands and knees, a woman who looked like a hag in one of my nightmares.

She was nearly bald, except for a few wisps of long white hair, and the top of her head was shiny with sweat. She was wearing a pair of baggy overalls, torn and covered with so much paint I couldn't see the denim. She had drawn a circle of blue chalk on the pavement and on the inside had drawn a beautiful blue-and-gold bird. Light— or I guess it was supposed to be light—shot off the head of the bird in silver and orange and red. She worked fast, grunting and groaning, and when the light was wrong off the bird, she would erase the dusty chalk with her bare hands.

"Bad, bad . . . good . . . good," she said.

I leaned forward on my bench. She was putting clouds under and around her shiny bird.

"Art, fat boy. Art. Art. Art," she grunted, not looking up at me. Her hands moved quickly over her sky and through her clouds.

"It's beautiful," I said, and I meant it.

"Notes, that's all. Want to remember it. Want to put it in my noggin. Watch this, fat boy."

She reached across the top of her circle and arced a purple piece of chalk just outside the blue arc.

"That's all, fat boy, that's how you remember. Notes."

She struggled, grunting to her feet, and stood looking down at the bird and the sky.

"I'm eighty-nine," she said, still staring down, "and that bird is always here. There. Up there. That's a bird, and now he's down here, too."

"It's very beautiful," I said again, and, since the purple over the blue, I meant it even more.

After a while she stooped down and dropped the bits of chalk into a canvas sack, then walked to my bench and sat. She was quiet and looked even older sitting next to me, but her eyes lived hard in her head and flew across the park.

"Look," she said, nudging me, "other side of the fountain. Venelli. Venelli the fraud. He sells for hundreds of thousands, and Venelli is a fraud. Maybe that's not Venelli. Wait. No. No, that's not Venelli, but explain this. Paintings of squirrels? Still life with the carcass of a poor squirrel, and Venelli sells it for hundreds of thousands? That is the university painter in a nutshell. I went to Art Students League. Pay what you can, they told me. They were happy to have me. But they taught the tension of preparation. The notes. There. I won't forget my bird. He's there. I won't forget. O'Keeffe was there, too. Of course, that's poster painting."

A bunch of kids with book bags walked by, looking at the picture as they went. They liked it, I could tell.

"That's the real McCoy, children!" she yelled after them. "That's Omega there. That's God's work."

She went quiet again, and we both looked at the bird. When I glanced over at her, she was staring at me.

"Art, fat boy."

"Beautiful."

"People? I don't use them in my notes or my canvas. And when I had just the cardboard, and when I had just the . . . what? Plywood, I don't use them."

A man on those single-line roller skates rolled by. He was wearing a Roman soldier uniform. Sword, too. Nobody seemed to notice him.

"My father would say, 'Art and light, art and light, that's all you ever talk about.' But I knew a secret. People suck the light, they don't give it off. I could get more glow from a tree. Big trees. Chestnuts? Oaks? Oh, yes, fat boy, big oaks, too. I come down from Pennsylvania. Nineteen twenty-seven. My father had hands like this. Big hands, and he would kiss the girls, my father, but even he sucked the light. All people, really. In 1927 I thought Peter Ogilvy might not suck it, but he did, later he did."

A breeze ruffled the leaves and it felt good and comfortable. Pigeons moved together from one end of the park to the other. I realized I wasn't aching very much. I was relaxed and rested, but I still saw Bethany in her hard pose, under the arch. She wore blue like the chalk, and the breeze shimmied her loose dress. A brother sees a sister, then—without the lagers, the pilsner, the occasional pale ale.

"Turned out he loved men and women, which is all right and modern, but, dear God, fat boy, I was twenty-two and in love and had defied my father. There was no going back on that. Running to the big city with the poet Peter Ogilvy. So lovely, lovely, lovely. We made love at night on the train. *On the train.*"

She laughed and coughed and grunted. She slapped her hand against the bench.

"Making love into New York City. I just climbed right over him. Then we were on Union Square, and it wasn't pretty, and it wasn't artistic, and the damn windows were always dirty, and Peter's father gave up on him and stopped the money, and he would cry like a girl. Peter Ogilvy would sob, would weep!

" 'I can't write,' he'd cry. And I would cry, too, and I would say, 'Light, I have to have light. The windows are dirty. I need light to paint.' Then one day Peter Ogilvy comes home, and I think I had done a crow, a blue-black crow that had a face like tar, and I was so happy with it, and he has this young man with him. Did I know him? I'm not sure. 'Here she is,' he says to this other man. I stand covered with paint, gesso. 'Here she is.' I go to kiss him hello, but he turns away. 'Here is this artist,' he says. 'Here she is. She can't find light in people.' They are both drunk, and I see it, and Peter tells me he is a bad poet. I remember him saying over and over, 'I'm a bad poet. I'm a bad poet.' Then he tells me I don't need him and he is going to fuck this other man. I can't believe what he said. So I asked him what he said. He said it again. Dear Peter Ogilvy. I can still hear them in that room while I grabbed all of my paints."

I listened, and I watched my sister float between the columns of the arch.

"On the street. Rain. Cold. Was it April? Above me, my poet and another. I hold my brushes like this. In my fists. My sack of paints and thinners. On the street, in the rain, without love. That! That place, fat boy, is where you must go before you can think of the fact of Art. I'm eighty-nine, and a fuck is not as good as a bird on a branch or a wagon a child has pulled in the afternoon. Light. Light."

She nudged me.

"Is that Foreman by the maple? Could it be that fraud? He sells and sells. They swoon at the galleries in the warehouses. It's shit. Always children in some future pastel. Is that him? Fraud. I'm tired now."

The old woman nudged me again. "What's this?"

"My Raleigh."

She looked hard. My maroon bike. I looked back to the Washington Arch, and Bethany was not there.

"I did a series of six sets of bicycles. Nineteen fifty-two. Flyers and Schwinns. Over there. Across by the college. There were bicycle racks. And no chains. There are chains now that cover the world, but without freedom is there a world to paint? Now? I did the bicycles with Joan Dupree. She worked faster than I did and without the color, but her quick look, that quick-look, I liked the immediacy of it. But . . . I could never love a woman. Sunfeld. That was a man. A lover. An artist who, dear God, made a handsome living. Sunfeld was immediate, contemporary. He knew what they wanted, and he gave them what they wanted. I was thirty and forty and ripe as a plum in the sun. And Sunfeld said that. He would hold these breasts, and he would kiss them, and then he would give them the pastels of children in the park, and he would paint their pets, and he simply sold his art until his art sold him. Killed himself, this happy lover, just here in the head. Dang. And there was the other woman of course, the wife, and there I was in the rain, the wet cement, my brushes all in my little fist. Again."

A small girl in a wheelchair passed us. She was alone, and she labored at the big wheels.

"Norma," I said out loud.

"There was Douglas Owsley," she said, "and there was Chris Lamb, and there was Robert Clavert, and there was that Argentinean who hit me. They were the real item. Not like, over there, by the men's room. Is that Nigel Tranter? I thought he was dead. He would be at least a hundred twenty-five. But he was not the real item. He was a fraud. Once you do a circus elephant, you can put all the Latin names in your title, but it remains circus posters. *You're a fraud, Tranter.*"

I watched the little girl in the wheelchair. Then looked over at my old hag.

"I ought to call my friend Norma."

"I ought to be back at my studio, fat boy. The men across the hall keep my windows clean. Birds and clouds. Look at my notes. It's not a struggle now. It was a struggle before, and the struggle was subject. Now I know it's the birds, because they're the closest to light. It whams, it just whams off them. Once I painted a silver place setting by the window in the sun while Larry Monsanto kissed my naked bottom. Nineteen thirty or 1940. It was a different kind of light."

She grunted to her feet and pulled her sack of chalk over her shoulder. She walked around her bird, and off.

"That's the real McCoy, fat boy. That's Omega there. That's God's work."

The Washington Square Park breeze is like a wheel. I mean, one tree will shake its leaves in the wind and stop, and another one will shake. One at a time. I called Norma from the edge of the park.

"Yes?"

"Norma?"

"Smithy?"

"I watched an old woman draw a circle on the pavement, a blue circle, and then draw this perfect bird with colors and light all shooting off it." I felt silly saying that. Norma couldn't see the bird, and I stopped before I explained about notes that wash away in the rain. But it felt good saying something that somehow seemed important to me. She waited until she was sure I was finished with the bird.

"Where are you, Smithy?"

"I'm in New York City. I'm at the Washington Square Park."

"That's where the hippies used to be."

"There's still some, only they look older. I don't have any money. I was wondering, what do you think is the best way for me to get some money?"

"I can send it."

"But what's the best way?"

"Will you call me back in ten minutes? I can call my bank."

"I have money in my bank. I mean, I can pay you back."

"Oh, Smithy." I could hear her again as if she had to cover the phone with her hand so I wouldn't hear her cry. Me. All disgusting on the other end of the phone, calling collect. She came back on. "Ten minutes," she said, hanging up.

Ten minutes later I called her back.

"Smithy? Okay. I called my banker. Find a Chemical Bank, tell them you're having money wired from the Old Stone Bank in Providence."

"Chemical?"

"Chemical."

She had energy and defiance, even in her voice. I could see her sitting tall. I could imagine all of her work spread out in front of her.

"I'll pay you back."

"Oh, Smithy. Oh . . ." She sounded like she might cover the phone again, but she didn't. "I'm looking at a picture. I'm holding Bethany's hand, and I'm grabbing at your sleeve, and Pop is in his Socony base-ball uniform. I remember Mom taking the picture I just love . . . I just get happy seeing this picture."

"I . . . see Bethany sometimes, Norma. I see her really clearly and when I do, she's dancing or she's in a pose. Do you think it's all right for me to see her?"

I felt her in Rhode Island. I felt how fierce she could be when she wanted to.

"I think it's perfect," she said.

"Well . . ." I said after a bit.

"I suppose . . ." she said, and her voice drifted off into the park.

We held the phone, I guess, Norma and I. We held each other quietly to our ears.

"Thanks, Norma."

"Smithy, I'm sorry I said all that about not being held and making you feel bad so you had to say you'd hold me."

"I didn't feel bad, Norma. I'd hold you."

We hung for a minute in the air, and then she said, "Bye, Smithy."

"Bye, Norma."

20

Dr. Glenn Golden had been recommended by several members of Grace Episcopal as a caring physician with a warm, outgoing personality. He could talk to Mom and Pop and even occasionally me about Bethany's profound psychosis as if he were talking about some slight outbreak of teenage acne. His process was loosely like this: He would visit Bethany at Bradley on Tuesdays and Thursdays (when she came home, he added Saturday) and then schedule a weekly chat with Mom and Pop, usually on Mondays. The financial arrangement, again loosely, was that Pop agreed never to take another vacation for the rest of his life and to give all the money to Glenn. My pop thought this was actually a fair deal, because it coincided with my sister's voice hiding out for a while—and he was all too happy to give credit to the warm and outgoing Glenn Golden.

"What do we do when the voice comes back?" I asked one Monday, sitting with Mom and Pop in the Thayer Street Medical Building.

"Say hi," the doctor joked, smiling his warm smile.

Mom and Pop smiled also, but I kept the question on my skinny face.

"Well, you know, Bethany's voice is not something that's really there. It's not something she really hears."

"Yes she does," I said.

He smiled warmly "No, what I meant was, she gets a feeling, maybe, but she doesn't actually hear a voice."

"Yes she does."

"Shhhh," Mom whispered.

"You see, the voice she hears is sort of intuitive. It's really not correct clinically to call it a voice at all."

"But she hears it. She really, actually hears it, and she really, actually talks to it. Sometimes I've heard it, when she's in her room alone. It says things, and what it says is crazy."

"Lots of people talk to themselves," he said, less warmly.

"This is not talking to yourself or anything. This is real, like, conversations."

"Let's remember Bethany first," he said. "Let's remember that she comes first."

I didn't understand what he meant, but he got up and walked over to the door. "We're counting progress minute by minute. I'm very encouraged."

We left the doctor and drove home. Bethany had cooked for us, but she seemed distant, as if she were thinking of something she shouldn't have been thinking. That, I would say, is the hardest of all. Knowing that something called her, from God knows where.

21

At first they wouldn't give me the money. I really didn't blame them. My reason for not having any identification must have seemed crazy. How I took the exit ramp too fast and how my brakes weren't adjusted properly, causing me to crash through the trees and fly into Wood River. The bank officers kept saying, "Just a second," and they'd get another officer to hear the story, then another, until all the Chemical Bank officers at Fifth and Fourteenth knew my story. If it weren't for Norma, who had driven to the Old Stone Bank and was sitting right there with her banker, I never would have been able to take the money she wired.

It was almost noontime when I walked out of the bank. The money felt very nice in my shorts pocket. I kept feeling it. Money is nice. I don't mean it's wonderful like a river or anything; and, as they say, it can't buy happiness, but it's comfortable in your pocket. And it's a real pleasure to know you can fill up your bike's saddlebags with bananas and apples, and even those huge juice oranges, anytime you want. Which I did on Sixteenth Street. Right next to the fruit stand was a clothing store, and in the window was a serious answer to my porkiness. A huge XXL, twelve-pocketed, khaki fishing vest. The store dummy had camera gear in his vest, but I figured the pockets were a bonus. The vest could cover my Europe-size hips and Mount McKinley ass. Especially on the road. This doesn't mean anything, but I thought I looked okay in it. Twenty-five bucks. So I was getting set. I was sort of taking some control. I stopped at a bookstore and bought a pocket map of the United States and a paperback novel at the checkout line. The novel was called *Iggy*, and I didn't know what it was about, but, like money, it felt good zipped into my vest pocket.

It was afternoon, and I was ready to ride. Where? I needed to go somewhere. Denver. I spread my map, and I saw it. I felt something, and I think it was determination. People looked clear on the street. I had a book, for God's sake, in one of my pockets. An older man in shorts and a New York Yankees T-shirt jogged in place next to me waiting for the light to change.

"Excuse me, sir, what's the best way to get out of the city?"

"Out of the city?" he said.

"Yes, sir."

"You don't get out of the city. Nobody does." After he jogged off, I asked a young woman.

"Where to?"

"Denver."

"That's west."

"I guess."

"PATH tubes."

"PATH tubes?"

"Fourteenth, Sixth."

"Thank you."

"Then Jersey Transit."

"Thank you."

"West."

"Thanks."

I walked my bike to Fourteenth and Sixth, and everybody helped me west. Out of New York from under a river, I got on a train heading toward a place I recognized from my map of New Jersey. Montclair. I got off the train with my Raleigh, and nobody said boo about a fat guy with a bike in the aisle. I bought a tuna sandwich and some apple juice and took it to a little park and ate and marked up my map. Denver didn't look that far. I walked across the space between New Jersey and Denver with my fingers. A dog ran across the green of the park, and I thought of Malzone. I began *Iggy*, there in that park. Reading is a lot like riding a bike. Once you get back to it, it's easy, it's natural. But at first—like the deep, deep, stab in your legs and hips and stomach and chest from the Raleigh—the sentences twist your head. I read eleven pages that afternoon before my brain said, "Wait." I found out that Iggy was black, was a cowboy, and that 70 to 80 percent of the true cowboys in the Old West were black. Eleven pages. Headache.

I ate some bananas, and when it got dark, I pushed the bike under a pine tree and lay near it on the grass. In the very early morning, I was cold and damp, and I dreamed it had rained all night. I made a mental note, in a part of my huge head that Iggy hadn't banged up, to get a sleeping bag and a raincoat; then I pumped off in the general direction of Pennsylvania.

22

So I picked up Jill Fisher at six o'clock in my pop's Ford wagon. She looked nice in a sort of off-white long dress that made her appear taller than she was but didn't show how big her chest was. I gave her the corsage, which was expensive but just what she wanted, with yellow somethings and lilies. Her mother made a big fuss about how nice we looked together. I could tell that Jill had been crying, because her eyes were all red.

"I wish your father could see his little girl," Mrs. Fisher gushed. Jack Fisher had gone to school with my pop and had bought it in Italy on the last day of the Big War. Pop always thought some wop had got him, but Mom said it was most likely a leftover kraut. Whatever, I was glad I didn't have to deal with another parent. I don't mean that like it sounds.

I opened the door to the Ford, and she got in and folded her long dress in with her.

"Listen, Jill," I said, "we have to stop at my house for five minutes. My mom wants pictures and stuff."

Jill Fisher was quiet for a few blocks. Then she said, "Look, no big deal, but Billy is going to the prom, too, and we're probably going to run into him."

"That's okay," I said.

"He's going with Cheryl Adams. It's no big deal."

We drove for a minute, and then she started to cry. I didn't know what to say. I didn't know why she would cry for somebody who didn't want to be with her. I guess I don't get that part of it.

"Don't cry, Jill."

"Cheryl Adams," she sniffed, "honest to God."

When I pulled into our driveway, Mom and Pop came out. We posed for pictures, and Jill did that girl thing that girls do so good. Made it all seem natural and happy. I looked around for Bethany and finally saw her looking out her bedroom window. She waved at me with a small wave, and I waved back. I knew Norma was watching, too. I almost walked next door to show her my tuxedo, which was all black with the purple tie and purple cummerbund, but there were too many years now. I'd let them pile up, like a coward. I could feel her venetian blinds bend and snap behind me.

A bunch of us were going to Chip Santos's house before heading to Rhodes on the Pawtuxet for the dance. I liked Chip, and I thought his mother and father and sisters were terrific. Mrs. Santos had the rec room all decorated and lots of food and soda and stuff, and Mr. Santos came down and told Chip that if the gang wanted to go to their summer home in Bristol for a late party after the prom, that was okay. He made a big deal about giving Chip the key. It was this thing that Mr. Santos could do for his boy. It was just so nice.

Jill found some of her girlfriends and went over to them immediately, and I went upstairs and watched some Red Sox with Mr. and Mrs. Santos.

"Radatz has no snap in his arm," Mr. Santos said to no one in particular.

"That's not good," his wife said.

"No snap at all."

After a while I went back downstairs and got some soda and went over to stand around sort of close to Jill. I assumed that was my assignment. Her friends, I guess, didn't like me, because some of them acted as though they had to protect her from me. That was really getting someone wrong. Nobody in the world ever had to be protected from me. I never even fired my weapon in-country. Ever.

Anyway, I stood there; then we all left in a kind of caravan to Rhodes on the Pawtuxet. Jill was very quiet, and she squnched against her door as if at any second I was going to reach out and grab her. Well, here is the truth. Here is my dilemma. I do not like to touch, and I cannot stand being touched. Not that I wouldn't like to have sex with a girl or touch her in wonderful places, and not that I

125

don't think about it, or used to think about it, but I suppose I really, really would have to love that girl, and I haven't done that yet. The stuff I told you about those prostitutes was awful. I couldn't bear it. I don't know why I did it. I understand why they hated me so very much. Yes.

Todd Sanderson and his swing band—a piano, a trumpet, a saxophone, and a bass, with Naomi Lesko from Warwick, Rhode Island, on vocals—performed arrangements of Dion & The Belmonts, Fats Domino, and Elvis, as well as some outstanding movie themes. The bandstand was in the middle of the dance floor, so of course you danced around it. Like standing near Jill in Chip's basement, I wanted to try to get the assignment right.

"May I have this dance?" I said, as cute as I could.

"I . . . have to go to the girls' room."

"Okay," I said, and Jill walked away. This was going better than I thought. I had imagined there might have been some social or cultural rituals to proms that I didn't know about, and I wasn't prepared for any surprises. The girls' room was something I guessed might happen.

I stood around for an hour or so, and then I figured I better find Jill and go stand near her. I thought I saw her by the parking-lot door, but as I walked over, somebody grabbed my arm.

"Where you going?"

I turned around, and Dick Marshall stood there, not letting go of me. Like all really dumb guys, Dick had a group that did everything together. Billy Carrara, who was usually a pretty good guy, was also part of this group. Actually, Jill was part of it and Billy sort of joined up. I shook off his hand.

"So where you going?"

"Outside."

"Stay inside."

"What do you mean, 'stay inside'?"

His girlfriend, for as long as I remembered, even in grade school, was Barbie Zinowitz. I see her now sometimes, when I go to the big movie complex in Sekonk. She's bigger than me, and I pretend I don't know her.

"Stay away, that's all. Jill and Billy are talking," Barbie snarled.

"Yeah," added Dick.

"Why don't you dance with Cheryl Adams or something," Barbie said. Her group laughed.

I saw Cheryl across the dance floor, moving in place, snapping her fingers by her side. She didn't seem sad or anything, so I walked over. I enjoyed walking in my tuxedo. It hung on me nicely, and I looked heavier in it. I put my hand in my pocket and swung the other arm coolly and evenly.

"Hello," I said.

"Hi."

She continued dancing in place, and I looked at her from the side. She was a short girl, with a nice face and brown hair that she wore in the way that Dutch Boy, on the paint can, wears his. Her dress was light blue and tight and reached the top of her toes. She looked more Portuguese than most of the Rhode Island Adamses, and she had, I guess, a more or less normal chest.

"I like this band," I said casually.

"I don't like them," she said, not looking at me.

"I mean, for a band that's a bunch of older guys, I mean, I don't really like them either, but . . ."

"You mean they're not good but the beat is okay."

"That's it," I said. "I like the beat."

"I'd give it a seventy," she said, moving gracefully.

"Absolutely."

I started to move a little, too. You wouldn't call it dancing, but maybe a beat move or step. Maybe. I didn't think Todd Sanderson and Miss Lesko did a bad job at all with "Jailhouse Rock" and made a neat transition into "Throw Momma from the Train."

When the song ended, I asked Cheryl if she'd like some punch, and I got her some. Then we danced again, like before, kind of side to side and separate. This was okay. I could do this. I looked around, and I guessed I must be having as good a time as anybody else. I mean, nobody looked particularly happy except during the bunny hop, which Cheryl and I just watched.

"Where's your date?" she asked.

"She's somewhere. I'm not sure."

"Who is she?"

"Jill Fisher."

Cheryl stopped dancing and turned and for the first time that evening looked right at me.

"You?"

"Me."

"But Billy said he had to go and protect her from you."

"Huh?"

"You're so jealous and you grab her and stuff."

I looked around to make sure people weren't looking at me and hearing things about me I didn't know myself.

"I'm jealous? I grab her?"

"That's what she told Billy. He went off to protect her."

When I was sixteen years old, I had grown to my full height of five foot eleven. I weighed 121 pounds. I took my hands out of my pockets and let them dangle at the ends of my arms. My butch cut had grown out about a quarter of an inch and lay flat on my big head. Cheryl looked me over. I started to sweat a little.

"Why do you grab her?"

I shrugged and looked around. I wanted to be in the Ford.

I wanted to stop, all by myself, at the A&W in Riverside and get a cheeseburger and onion rings and a big root beer in a frosty mug and eat it alone. I didn't want to hurt Cheryl's feelings, and I figured I could if I told her that Billy Carrara was a liar and a guy who gave rings back in toilet paper.

"How long have you been Billy's girlfriend?"

"I'm not his girlfriend."

"You're not?"

"We're just at the prom together. He's just a nice guy."

"So he's not, like, your boyfriend or anything."

"No, he's not my boyfriend."

"Oh, well, he's a big liar, then. I mean, Jill's not my girlfriend either. I'm not jealous. I don't grab anybody. I didn't want to hurt your feelings or anything, but since you're not his girlfriend, he's out in the parking lot with Jill."

Cheryl Adams's hair went limp.

"What?" she yelled so loud that Naomi Lesko, in the middle of Pat Boone's "April Love," looked over to us.

"Want some more punch?" I asked hopefully, but by then Cheryl was rushing toward the parking lot with tears of rage splashing over her mascara.

I went to the bathroom and had a Marlboro with the other guys, and then I walked back to the spot where I had stood with Cheryl. Some of the dancers had made a circle and were clapping to the music, and inside the circle dancing and twirling was Lewis Rand, a senior man about campus, and Carol Robey in her wheelchair. Carol was the president of our junior class, and Lewis was her boyfriend. I felt good to see her always so happy, and I felt bad about a littler girl behind her blinds. I watched them twirl for a while; then I went back and had another smoke.

Carol Robey became the principal of East Providence High School some years later, and people still love her and like to see her happy. Lewis Rand went to Carnegie Mellon's School of Drama and died of AIDS maybe five years ago. Carol named the high school stage after him. Love dies hard.

I waited until most everybody had gone, but I couldn't find Cheryl or Jill or Billy. I drove back to East Providence, but the A&W was closed.

23

On Tuesday I rode an hour before the sun had technically come up. I stopped for breakfast at a diner that promised country brown eggs, and I had them poached. Poached eggs are a treat, because they don't back up on you like fried eggs and they have a form on the toast that makes them look like a face. It was like breakfast at Mom's. There were truck drivers and guys in suits, and just everybody was friendly. I used the bathroom and took a sort of sink shower and felt really good. Like usual, after I woke up and rode and walked a little, the pain and stiffness in my body seemed to go away.

I pushed pretty hard for another couple of hours—hard for me anyway. I mean, I still walked up the hills and coasted when I had the opportunity. I picked Route 10 from my little road guide, and at Florham Park, New Jersey, picked up 510. After a while you get into a bike trance and don't have to think too much about pedaling. At least, because I was going so slow, I didn't, and I could look around at where I was. This was new for me. The whole idea of a place, I mean. And away from the big interstate road system—which you couldn't use if you didn't have an engine—New Jersey was, I suppose, gorgeous. In Rhode Island the words "New Jersey" were interchangeable with "dog shit," but it's amazing to see how many perfect farms and groves and forests there are. And the rivers and streams are great. Around Ralston I walked my bike off the road and sat by the Raritan River. Beautiful. I had a couple of bananas and splashed some of that good water over my face and hair. I had a beard coming up, and the cool water stayed around my stubble, taking away the itch. Every stop has a purpose. I was learning, I suppose, about refreshment.

I stopped at a small sporting goods store with a sign in the window that said UNDER NEW MANAGEMENT and treated myself to a ground cloth, a waterproof sleeping bag, a small tent, and a knapsack to keep the stuff in. The new owners, a young guy and his wife, came out to look at my bike and measured me for my bag and made a real effort to get me good, lightweight supplies.

"You're getting a lot of sun," the wife said as I paid her.

"Yes."

She reached behind her to a counter hat rack and took down a modified baseball cap with a sunglass visor.

"These are new. Maximum protection."

"I'll take it."

"One size fits all."

"I'll take it."

When the sun got a little low, I pulled off the road and into a field. There were some mosquitoes, but it wasn't too bad, because the day was cooling toward night, but I made another little promise to myself to get repellent. Then I drank a bottled water, had another banana and a juice orange, and read a little more *Iggy*.

The book was a western, but it really wasn't a western in that the cowboy part was not as important as him starting to feel good about his place in the world. The world of the Old West.

I read about fifteen pages, slowly, still getting into reading shape. Iggy never knew his father, who abandoned his mother when he was freed after the Civil War. Iggy's mother was a kind but powerful woman named Esther Booklook. She had gotten her last name from her father, who got it from his father, who got it from the nine-year-old daughter of a plantation owner because he liked to look at books. Iggy didn't like the name Booklook. Nothing against his mother, but he changed his last name to Hannibal after the hero from Carthage, because his mother used to tell stories about Hannibal to her children and told them they were related to him. Iggy changed his name in 1878, the year he headed west. He was fourteen, and I felt my reading headache coming on. I spread out my gear, everything except the tent, and after an apple I slept the sleep of the just.

By Wednesday afternoon I had zigzagged onto Route 645 to 614, cut through the deep valley of the Musconetcong Mountains, and crossed the Delaware River into Pennsylvania. Here is what I discovered over a tuna sandwich: Even walking uphill and not killing myself on the straightaways, I could make between fifty and seventy miles a day. It had to do with consistency.

I picked up Penn. 212 down to Quakertown, and ten miles later, outside Pennsburg, I had the Quaker Meat Loaf Special at the Quaker Restaurant. The baked potato was still in its foil, and the iced coffee was really perked and not freeze-dried. I wasn't a great diner man. I had become a volume guy, I guess, what with Burger King and those big hoagies they make in a second. Uncle Count had the dual aptitude for mass food of quality. He could sit—and I am not kidding, and I don't use this often—I swear to God, he could sit in a restaurant and sniff and tell not only what was choicest among the foodstuffs but also what had been prepared in great quantities. I was understanding my uncle. A little anyway. For me, though, the slice of meat loaf and the baked potato were plenty. What is it? Medical? The more you do, the less you need? I don't get it. I had Jell-O with grapes, too.

Pennsylvania is also beautiful. Big hills, though. Just when I figured I was going to average that 50 or so miles, I got beaten up by the hills. I had estimated that from Durham, where I entered Pennsylvania, to Wayne Heights, where I would get into the tip of Maryland, was less than two hundred miles and I could do it in three or four days, but even though the weather was nice and dry I didn't get to Gettysburg, which was forty or so miles from Maryland, until Sunday.

I checked into a Howard Johnson's and parked the Raleigh in my room. It was pretty early—three in the afternoon, I think—and as much as I wanted a shower and a bed, I wanted to do everything on my mental list first. I crossed the street to a shopping center and bought some shaving supplies and fruit and bottled water. Back inside the room, I laid out my new purchases on the TV set. I spread the sleeping bag over the clothes rack and generally laid out the rest of my stuff to dry. I wanted a beer and a cigarette. I don't know why. Probably because hotel rooms always required an activity. Television, cigarettes, beer. I sat there and looked at my stuff all around the little blue room, and it was very comforting to be there with my bike and my stuff. I thought I would eat an orange, maybe, and then stretch out on the bed for a while before I found a good place to eat. I was very tired, and the bed and pillows looked perfect. I fell asleep in the chair thinking about them.

24

In 1966 three things happened that I would call events, in the sense that you couldn't under any circumstances forget them. I got drafted; Charlie Love, trying to score from third base, got struck by lightning; and my sister, Bethany, disappeared again.

Most of the kids I graduated with went to college or business school. They went, really, because their parents were afraid of the Russians. That's the short reason. When the Soviet Union flew *Sputnik*, it looked as though they were doing better than we were in the brain department, and somehow we had to catch up or they'd kill us. That's how I understood it anyway.

East Providence roared into action. First they separated the kids by how smart they were. They formed divisions, and all the divisions together were called ROXY SUMAC-GL. If you were an accelerated person, you were placed in R and O, and it was hoped you'd go to Ivy League schools and lose your accent. X, Y, and S were, I guess, college preparatory; U, M, A, and C were business stuff about being secretaries and typists; and G and L were shop, auto mechanics. The R and O divisions were kept pretty separate from the other kids and were given special lunchtimes and up-to-date science labs and stuff. The divisions all dressed different, too, with chinos and plaid shirts favored by the accelerates and college preps, blue and gray by the business kids, and blue jeans and leather jackets by the mondos in auto shop.

We all knew, but weren't supposed to say, that our school now had four groups arranged by letters. We had very smart, pretty smart, could learn to hold a job, dumb. I was in pretty smart, but I should have been in dumb. I got C's, and no college wanted me, even Springfield College in Massachusetts, where they train gym teachers and people who work at the Y and they had classes in the fundamentals of badminton. College did not want me. Mom thought I should go to junior college, and I was thinking about it when I got my notice to go into the army. But I'm not complaining. If I wanted to go to college and study bowling or table tennis, I should have applied myself better in high school. I didn't. You get what you deserve.

Sometimes, I mean. Sometimes you get what you deserve. Charlie Love—my pop's shortstop and leadoff hitter who unloaded oil with Pop and had the locker next to his—did not get what he deserved. He deserved more.

A month before I got my draft notice, Pop's team made the Metropolitan Rhode Island Playoffs. This was huge. Everybody suspected that this might be Pop's last year, and the Socony Red Sox's slow start in April, where they stood sixth in their division, put him into a real slump. He gave up nine homers, he made three errors in the field, and for the first time in twenty-one years with the Sox, his average dipped below .300.

One morning at breakfast, when he was getting ready to go to the oil plant, he said, "You know what it could be? It could be that a ballplayer should just play ball. This working, I don't know. What does this working all the time have to do with being a ballplayer?"

Bethany had had an excellent summer, and the Ides were basking in the false confidence we clung to. She was lifeguarding at the Crestwood Country Club and had an Indian tan. She buttered her toast and listened to Pop.

"Getting the old stick around . . . well, I think all the lifting and pulling of the oil hoses, my swing just seems a step off. I don't know."

Pop drank some coffee, and we were all pretty quiet. We were a family that had placed a pretty high premium on Pop's natural swing, and now he was baffled.

"I just don't know."

Bethany didn't look up from her toast.

"You got a hitch, Pop, that's for sure. Course, this new stance makes it hard for me to tell."

"What new stance?" Pop said, putting his coffee down.

"It's Pop's same old stance," I laughed.

"Nope."

"Bethany," Mom said, "your father's stance is the same one he had in American Legion ball. Eat your toast."

Bethany got up and took one of Pop's bats out of the umbrella basket. "Here's Pop's stance. Right? Right?"

"Yeah," I said, getting bored.

"Now you take your stance, Pop."

"C'mon . . ." I whined.

Pop shrugged and took the bat from Bethany and got into his stance. Bethany stayed in hers.

"That's my stance," he said.

"That's it," Mom said admiringly.

"No," said Bethany, "that's not your stance. I'm doing your stance. See, my front heel is off the ground, and your front heel is flat."

Mom's hand covered her mouth. I stared in astonishment. Pop about fainted.

"Right," he said. "Yes, yes, yes."

That night, against the Pawtucket Penguins, Pop started in left field. He hit a homer, a triple, a double, and a single for the cycle, and even though going into the ninth they were down 4–3, we all felt that a win was in the cards—especially since Charlie Love singled, then stole second with one out. Charlie Love was a complicated man for East Providence. He was short and a little fat—in the hips and butt, I mean—but he had pretty good speed for a man in his forties. He was balding like one of those monks, so he never took off his baseball cap, and he always had his uniform laundered before each game. He also was the only bachelor on the club, and although Charlie would tell a continuous line of dirty stories about his many girlfriends, it was pretty clear that Charlie was very womanly. I guess, effeminate. One game I remember in particular, because it was the only game that a downright free-for-all broke out, was against that

Irish mob, the Riverside Rollers. They were a lousy team, but, God, could they get on a player. This one night they were on Charlie hard. He hit a home run and played excellent shortstop for the Sox, and after a second base hit, one of the Rollers yelled "Fag," and then they all started yelling about "the little fag," "homo," "fruitcake," and making sucking sounds. After ten minutes of this stuff, my pop called time and asked the coach of the Rollers to have his guys knock it off because there were kids around, but the coach, who had been drinking 'Gansetts all night and was probably not much of a strategist anyway, gave Pop the finger, which Pop took and bent back to the coach's wrist. This cleared the benches, and these old guys stood there bombing each other with punches.

So anyway, Charlie's on second and looking for a sacrifice or a hit to score, and Pop steps up. Something was going to happen, you could feel it. He took a strike. Then three balls. The pitcher had given Pop all the respect he possibly could, but everybody knew what was coming—three and one. Pop cracked that fastball and sent it to deepest center. Back, back, looked like it was going, but the center fielder caught it backpedaling and hit his cutoff man. Charlie had tagged up the instant the ball entered the glove and sprinted toward third. The cutoff man whirled and fired for home, which by now Charlie Love was charging for like a steam engine.

Now, it's important not to forget that this was the Metropolitan Playoffs and Pop had got his heel up thanks to my sister. It was inevitable that this afternoon would get burned into memory even without that one lonely dark cloud in an otherwise sunny sky. I can see them all, another of my clear memories, standing tense and screaming for Charlie to slide. I can see him go into his crouch and start to spring out, as if it were in slow motion and I was watching it again and again.

I think he became illuminated for a fraction of a second, but it's the one thing that's not clear, so perhaps he didn't. Before he could complete the slide and while he was still on his feet, the lightning found him. It popped into his head on entry and found the earth out of his left leg. The bolt flipped his hat off and set it on fire and, for some reason, set his belt on fire, too. He landed facedown in his slide position, two arms extended, but stopped about one inch from home plate.

For a moment everyone was still, stunned by the electricity that leaped from that one small cloud and struck Charlie out. The relay would have been late anyway. The cutoff man threw wild, and the ball sailed over the catcher's head and rested against the backstop. The players and fans approached the prone, unmoving Charlie Love, almost as if he still had the electricity in him. Then Hy Cramer, the chiropractor, broke through the circle of people and took charge.

"Jesus," said Hy, kneeling by Charlie's head. He reached over and picked up his hat by its bill. Everyone looked at the flames. "This goddamn hat is actually burning," marveled Hy.

My pop knelt down, too, and so did the catcher, who brushed the ball against Charlie's outstretched hand to seal the play.

"Fried dead," said Hy.

That turned out to be Pop's last game. I was drafted the next month, September, and told to report in November. I got a little job frying clam cakes at Horton's Fish Market and fished the Shad Factory whenever I could. Then, in October, Bethany walked off.

I still say that, don't I? Notice that? She "disappeared" or she "walked off." We all talked like that, even to each other, because it tends to soften the actuality of it. And the actuality of it is that her voice took her. I never spoke to Mom or Pop about my fears—they had enough of their own, and probably we all had the same ones— but in August, about the time when Charlie Love burned up, I was afraid that Bethany's voice was becoming bigger and stronger than we were.

I came home from work around five and immediately sensed a feeling in the house of action. The tension, the wait, was gone. Mom was on the phone to the police, to her friends, to people at church. Pop had his road atlas spread over the kitchen table and was making some marks with a red crayon.

"Maybe she's just with some friends. Maybe she's at the beach," I said.

Pop took a note out of his pocket and handed it to me. The penmanship was crazy, and most of the words were printed as a child might print them.

Gone, I am gone
Babalask and gone
The sun, shit, shit

I read the words and felt cold. I gave the note back to Pop.

"This time we'll have to commit. This time," he uttered. My pop was mumbling to himself and crying, but only a little.

I rode the Raleigh around Kent Heights and into Riverside, but I had a feeling she wasn't close by. Her note upset me a lot. I would call her name and feel the anger in my voice. Maybe anger wasn't the word. Maybe fear. Pop drove his usual route, and we linked up at home around nine-fifteen. Mom told us a police cruiser stopped by, and there were no leads. At times like this, the Ide kitchen was more a command central than a family room.

Pop leaned on the table and nodded at Mom's news. It was a small room, our kitchen, like all the rooms in our house, but that night we were small, too. We fit nicely. I even remember a steady breeze through the window over the sink and Mom's fine brown hair waving in it. I knew that Norma watched, too, behind those fluttering venetian blinds, watched the movement in the kitchen and the long shadows we threw. I thought about Norma that night and how we all had stopped going over, little by little, until for everybody it was too late.

"Okay. I'm going to call Al Prisco at the plant and tell him I can't work for a few days. We'll get a good night's sleep, then start in Barrington. Did you try the water tower?"

"Yes, sir," I said. It was the only time I called my pop "sir."

"Okay. All right. Let's get some rest."

Mom and Pop didn't sleep well. In the morning they looked old. That was the look they had in Bethany searches. Old. After a while I managed to fall asleep. I dreamed I was me but wasn't me, and when horrible things started happening to me, I could watch it happen from some safe place. I was set on fire, and nobody helped me. Even me watching from that safe place couldn't help. Or wouldn't help. And because it was my darling sister who put a torch to me, what I watched were her eyes. It wasn't bad, because I could see that they weren't her eyes but almost purple, like the bottom of a lake, or a bruise.

In the morning, and for three weeks of mornings, we got out of bed strong. By afternoon we fell back hard under the weight of our own failure, until finally, when we found her, we had no energy for each other.

25

Monday Night

(Couple of rings.)

Norma: Hello?

Me: Norma?

(I hear a catch of breath and a pause, as if she is determined not to say what she needs to. It comes anyway.)

Norma: I'm not gonna jump up and down, Smithy, you have to know that. I'm not Norma, little next-door Norma that you can pat, just pat, pat on the head. I've got, I've got . . . I've got responsibility. I do. I take care, is all—Bea, the architects I draw for, layouts, prints, and I even write articles and things about being kids and being in wheelchairs, and these things I do make me . . . make me necessary. I'm a necessary person. Woman. And if you think I wait by the phone, if I have to wait by the phone because you call and then you don't call and don't call and there are . . . there are . . . and . . . bicycles and . . . and . . .

(I hear the phone fall on the table or desk, and I hear crying over it. I wait, but the tears are away and steady. I'm that skinny kid in the kitchen window all over again. I'm the thing that just stopped going over. I wait, and she's back.)

Norma: And I'm . . . I'm crying about something that doesn't concern you. I have a life, you know. I have friends. I could have gone . . . could have gone to that Red Sox game . . . but . . . but . . . I have this big responsibility. Bea raised me, and now I'm taking care because I'm crucial. Because I'm a crucial, necessary person. And you think that you can call and don't call because Norma's always, always . . . here.

(I listen to her sniffles, because she doesn't put the receiver on the desk. I listen to her and wait.)

Me: Norma?

Norma: Uh-huh.

Me: I'm in a Howard Johnson's. I treated myself because I needed a shower and I had to get organized.

(I am hearing a real quiet, even miles away, hundreds of miles, Norma pushes the quiet from East Providence to Gettysburg.)

Me: I'm in Gettysburg.

Norma: You're in Pennsylvania? It's a lot on a bike.

Me: Howard Johnson's. Mostly I've slept in fields. I got a little tent and sleeping bag and stuff. I saw a whole herd of deer. Some of them had babies.

(I try a phony laugh. Norma is quiet for a moment.)

Norma: Los Angeles is too far. I've looked at a map. Goddard said this week will count as your vacation.

Me: You know what I do at Goddard, Norma? I walk up and down this aisle next to a long table and I make sure the hands of SEAL Sam face inward. Are right. I never thought about my job.

Norma: I never feel sorry for myself.

Me: I don't . . .

Norma: Even in the morning, when it takes all the energy in the world to get up and get going, I never feel sorry for myself. Because they fall down, I know, they one day can't get themselves up early, then later can't get up until ten, then eleven, and all the time saying how hard it is with the chair and . . . and . . . and you have to be . . . you . . . I don't . . .

(I wait, but she doesn't finish. Her breathing may be angry, may have tears, I'm not sure. But, Jesus Christ, I wished I had gone over every day. I wished I had played dolls or puppets or anything this necessary little girl wanted. Bethany looks in my second-floor window and shakes her head. I turn my face to the wall.)

Me: Gettysburg . . . is beautiful. I'm going to leave tomorrow. I stayed another day and walked around the battlefields. I tried . . . I tried to imagine, like Mom was always trying to get us to use our imagination, and . . .

Norma: You have a wonderful imagination.

(I am the phone quiet this time, because Norma is wrong.)

Me: Anyway . . . I imagined what it would be like to be one of those men.

Norma: You don't have to imagine, Smithy. They almost killed you.

Me: Well . . .

Norma: You were shot.

Me: I thought about how minty the fields smelled, and the big sassafras trees have a kind of root beer smell. I mean, fighting and all these good smells. And I took a huge tuna-fish sandwich with me and leaned against this rock in the middle of a field where thirty-five thousand men died in fifteen minutes. I thought how I never wanted anything bad enough to hurt someone.

Norma: I have.

Me: I don't know.

Norma: I just told you. I made myself, Smithy. I am a sophisticated, useful woman. But I think there's something I'd be uncivilized for.

(I wait but can't ask. I hear some rain against the window.)

Me: It's raining outside, Norma. I'm glad I stayed. It's just that all the dead men—I never thought about it.

(A heavy rain, and I imagine the boys all soaked and muddy and chapped.)

I never told anybody. I mean, Mom and Pop, and now I'm old—

Norma: You're not!

Me: —but, Norma, I didn't really mind being hurt in the army, because I was so afraid all the time. I was a big coward in the army. I never . . . I never told my pop, anybody   I . . . cried sometimes just being . . . away.

(I think in the quiet. I never thought about it before. That's why those big pickled eggs and hard pretzels work at night. That's what the tall glasses of beer do. They take me away from that skinny boy. They take me so far away.)

Norma: I cry, too.

143

(Lightning, thunder.)

But I don't feel sorry for myself. I'm sorry I said that about not calling. You don't have to call. I don't feel sorry for me, you don't feel sorry for me. I just . . . I just wanted you to know I'm strong. I do. I make it. I go on.

Me: I know you do, Norma. I know. I'm very sorry I never came over. After a while it got too hard. I mean . . .

Norma: I looked through the windows. I hated Pop and Mom too, but when I saw Bethany sometime, I looked away. I guess I wouldn't have come over for Bethany. Her eyes . . .

Me: I know.

(Her anger tightens my hands on the phone.)

Norma: You don't know. You don't know anything. You don't come over, that's all. You thought my legs are all there is.

Me: I don't . . .

Norma: You want to hang up. You never call me like you don't come over, and I love you.

(I am so disgusting. My stomach oozes over my shorts, and I stand—as if I can escape myself. My body aches, my fat chins, my empty hairless head. A dog. An old mutt wishing he were dead. I cannot speak. Now I am sorry for her, in her necessary, useful, and crucial life. I think of the dead here, and I am so utterly ashamed. All that good life gone, and mine still going. My fat ass, my huge belly, my battlefield sogged down with Marlboro butts and 'Gansett.)

Me: It's raining hard now.

Norma: I got to go. Listen, what I said was something called transposition. I transposed because I was thinking about someone else. That happens. It's not you. Not you.

(I wait for a while. Cowards don't think of things to say. Cowards wait. I hear it all the way here, and it's a click, made with her finger.)

144

26

"It's an offer of sorts," Dr. Glenn Golden said to us, from behind his mahogany desk. "It's an offer of release. Your release. And it's given with love. That's the way I would view it, if Bethany were my daughter. Or my sister."

Glenn Golden lounged back in his swivel chair and watched us absorb his assessment. He watched us the way he watched his voice-hearing, sign-seeking, compulsion-heaped patients. I watched my pop. His neck veins were pulsing against the starched white shirt.

"What are you saying?" Pop asked quietly.

"I think she loves you all very much," said Glenn.

"We know she loves us. You don't have to tell us she loves us. We want to get her back so we can take care of her."

Mom started crying. Pop put his arm around her. I sat against the back wall in a sticky leather chair. The army loomed. I was missing work at the fish market. No Shad Factory.

"In any delusionary state, a patient often formulates some type of bizarre plan to make everything right. To be a cure-all, if you will, for any problems they may have caused, past or present. Most likely Bethany has such a plan."

"What about her voice?" I asked, looking at my feet.

Dr. Golden turned to me in my back corner and sighed the sigh of a man the voice has hidden from.

"Bethany's problems are certainly complex, involving both emotional stress and some imbalance, but her actions are in the range of compulsive, that's compulsive behaviors, and the idea of some inner thing—a voice, whatever—guiding her is, I'm sorry, absurd."

"Look," my father said, "all we're trying to do is a little detective work. She's been gone now more than two weeks. We're frantic. You can see we're frantic. If there's anything you can tell us that might help . . ."

"I don't have a clue." Glenn Golden shrugged, and that shithead told the truth.

We went home. Pop went back to the maps, and I spread my Raleigh search out past Kent Heights all the way to the Riverside plat. The army was less than a month away, but then it wasn't like college or anything. It was just "put all your clothes in that Goodwill bin and cough," so I really didn't need to prepare, I guess.

Ide action had turned to sorrow. We ate pretty quiet, and we all went to bed early. People who saw us then will never know how fast me and my pop were or how Mom was in the middle of our family. People who saw us then agreed my sister had killed us. Now that's absurd, Dr. Golden. I remember lying in my bed reading *The Nick Adams Stories*, because Nick could throw a beautiful fly and tied his own. I got as far as this story about Nick going with his father to deliver an Indian couple's baby. The Indian woman cried so much in childbirth, and the Indian man felt so sorry for her he killed himself. I couldn't read any more. Sad story just to be sad, and, of course, including a doctor.

Two days after visiting Golden, we got a letter from Rockville, Rhode Island, which is next to Hope Valley and my old Boy Scout camp. It was a very nice letter from a girl named Priscilla, who explained that she had gotten our address from the front of Bethany's overnight bag. Priscilla told, to whom it may concern, that she was a member of a group dedicated to living life in peace and abiding friendship with the world of man and nature. Man, it seemed, had overdone its part of the balance, and that was why there was the Vietnam War. At least I think that's what she said. Bethany had heard about them through Grace Episcopal Church's Young People's Fellowship, which supported anything that was disgusted with America of the 1960s. Priscilla wrote that while Bethany had been a real asset to the People's Way (their group), it now appeared that some disturbing little trends had developed in my sister that included screaming at herself in a voice that seemed not of this earth and pulling out her hair. Priscilla gave their address in huge block letters.

"Hippie commune," Pop said, folding the letter and putting it in his shirt pocket.

"Hippies?" Mom asked.

"Jesus, Mary, and Joseph. Call Golden."

Glenn Golden was irritated when he got on the phone. It was early afternoon, and he wanted to get away for some golf.

"Golden," said my pop. "We know where she is."

"Who?"

"Bethany. Bethany Ide."

"Oh . . . that's wonderful. Can you bring her in, say . . . a week from tomorrow?"

"A week from— Listen, I'm not calling to make a goddamn appointment. I want to know what do we do? What? Jesus, Mary, and Joseph."

"Well, first of all you don't yell at me," whined Golden.

Pop took a deep breath, and I watched his hand roll into a hard fist, then relax. "Right. Sorry. What?"

"Do you know what state she's in?"

"Rhode Island."

"Mental state."

"She's talking to herself. She's pulling out her hair."

"Agitated, then?"

My pop would have liked to kill him. Another deep breath. Another fist clench. "Yes. Agitated."

"Agitated. Agitated. It's strange, this hair-pulling stuff. I had a boy once who used to pluck out his eyebrows in a rage. Bizarre."

"Look, Dr. Golden, I was hoping you could go with us. This is the longest she's been gone. She obviously hasn't been taking her medicine."

"Go with you?"

147

"Yes?"

"Go with you to actually retrieve her?"

"Yes, retrieve."

"This is, I'm going to say, irregular."

"Yes."

"Highly irregular. Actually going with you . . . well . . . I'm going to have to look at my schedule, and the . . . well . . . I mean, you aren't actually thinking of a . . . uh . . . forcible retrieval?"

Pop let the phone hang by his side and rubbed his eyes. He raised it to talk but at the last second hung up. He dialed Bradley Hospital and told them he'd be bringing Bethany in as soon as he could. At least Bradley was a constant. A real starting point. Or stopping point. Then we all got into the car and drove to Rockville.

"Rockville's next to Yawgoog," I said, wanting to say something. Pop nodded. Mom turned around and smiled.

Rockville, on the border of Connecticut, was not much more than a post office and a cluster of old houses. At one time there was a rope-and-twine factory, but it burned down, so of course nobody really worked in Rockville. My pop pulled in front of the post office and walked in.

"I'm looking for the hippies," he said to a woman in a blue, official-looking hat.

"Hippies? Well, there's three sets of them."

"The People's Way."

"Know what they did? They think they could put nutrients into the soil by putting their own poop into it. I'm not kidding. Their own poop! I wouldn't eat one of their squashes if my life depended on it."

"Where?"

"End of that road. Old Methodist church they live in, dirty buggers."

We drove down to the church and parked. Pop helped Mother out of the car; then the three of us walked past an unattended vegetable stand that sold oversize zucchini and summer squash, and into the old white church. Most of the pews, except four or five rows, had been removed, and five lines of folding metal beds had taken their place. Each line had seven beds, and each bed was neatly made up with a different color blanket and had a suitcase under it. There were no crosses inside or anything to do with the Methodist Church—instead a large quilt showing many different kinds of vegetables on a white background hung against a stained-glass window behind what once was the Protestant altar.

"Vegetable is Lord," a confident, priestly voice said behind us.

We turned around, and there was this young man, a little fat and short, with long, bushy red hair caked down his neck. He had on a white pair of coveralls that were pretty played out. I guess I had expected robes.

"Hi, welcome. I'm Thomas."

Thomas walked forward and shook all our hands.

"I'm Thomas for Thomas Jefferson. What we've done is take names that we can associate with the time when the country was working toward an agricultural standard. What's your name?"

We told him our names.

"Neat," he said. "Do you want to buy some vegetables?"

"No thanks," Pop said. "We're looking for someone."

Thomas smiled all-knowingly. He sighed heavily and motioned to one of the pews. "Please, sit."

We did. Thomas confidently ascended three stairs that led to the sermon podium. He put both hands on it and leaned back onto his right leg.

"In . . . 1751 a man from Germany by the name of Casper Muller and a hardy band of agro-dreamers left Europe to establish in this fair land a new, nitrogen-rich, self-encapsulating ethnic enclave in complete accord with concepts of Pennsylvania Dutchdom.

"Passion, weather, barbarism—all combined to deprive the soil of these heroes, but instead the heroes prevailed. We owe so much—so very much—to them. This is the mantle the People's Way has taken up. A process by which we put a portion of our actual selves back into the earth."

"Jesus," Pop sighed.

"Other families have come to claim their children, and the People of the Way understand the fears and uncertainties, but please understand that our love and attachments are strong also, and we will struggle passionately to retain any member of our circle."

"Where's Bethany?" Pop said evenly.

"Bethany? Out back. I'll help you get her stuff into your car."

We left Thomas Jefferson at Bethany's bed, pushing her belongings into a blue suitcase, and walked through the kitchen into the backyard. The growing field of the People's Way extended right up against the back steps and looked as if it had been turned by hand. It was late afternoon, and the field was in shade, but the smell was unmistakable and one I didn't smell again until the army. Two small foreign cars were parked under a tree, and grass grew up underneath them. Several men and women whacked at the ground with hoes and rakes; still others were hanging wash on a line. I didn't see my sister. A girl bounced over to us.

"Hi, I'm Countess Minelli. I brought oregano to this country in 1784."

I could see her breasts point up against a man's denim work shirt. They were not large, but I imagined they were lovely. They were as happy as she was.

"We're looking for Bethany Ide," Mom said sweetly.

"Bethany is Princess Wincek. She was a Narragansett Indian who taught the first Europeans how to roast corn in its own husk. At first they thought it was too bitter. I think corn is bitter."

She had a huge smile that looked like it hurt to stretch her mouth that much. When she shifted weight from her left to her right leg, small hips pointed against her baggy pants and her pretty breasts shifted, left to right.

"Well, we would like to see her," Mom said.

Countess Minelli turned and walked into the field. We followed, carefully watching where we stepped. We passed several outbuildings that looked unused and ready to fall down. Old grapevines completely covered one. Countess Minelli stopped and pointed to the far side of the field, where rows of tomatoes stood staked with sticks. There was a scarecrow in the middle of this portion of field, and Princess Wincek was the scarecrow. She wore a long summer dress that seemed more brown than blue, and her hair fell only on the right side of her head—the rest was bald and scabby where she had torn at it. Her face also had the familiar scars of a few summers ago. Her pose was purely Bethany-perfect, with the left arm up and slanted and fingers splayed up to God. A small breeze puffed dirt at her feet and ruffled the cotton dress but did not touch her stillness.

"Dear Christ," my pop said.

We did not run to her across the shit-filled field. We stepped like people not in a hurry to get where we had to go.

It wasn't that we didn't want to comfort her, to tell her it was again all right, but, really, like everyone who traces their steps and so themselves, we moved slowly, hoping to somehow awake. So "repeat," then, is pain. A sort of SEAL Sam assembly line that never shuts down and just sucks out your life. We stood around her, and Mom and Pop began cooing to her between their tears. I had never seen Bethany rip herself so utterly and completely before. For a second I could see her beneath the scabs and empty patches, where her amazing hair had been, and her half-open eyes seemed only reflected, like a sunken moon under the blue ocean.

She had stiffened into her pose and didn't hear my parents. Sun had hardened and seared her wounds. Her quiet, like quiet will, filled the awful field. I watched her behind Pop. I studied her and in studying became removed from the subject. This is really the only way to push off the world of the people you love and save yourself. She stayed stiff and burned.

Mom kept whispering cheerily about her friends and church, and Pop talked baseball. She didn't move. That deep inside stillness, the perfect stillness her voice demanded, formed her against the staked tomatoes. Staked herself. Standing so close to him then, I could not imagine my pop ever having thrown the no-hitter in '53 or hit those four home runs against the Warwick Despots in '61. All that he was filled the small space between himself and his darling Bethany. I might have hated her right then. I guess I'm not sure.

"It's no good, Bethany," I said. "I can see the air going in and out of your nose. I can see your nostrils going."

"Shhhh!" Mom whispered angrily.

"It's true, Mom. Look. Everything else is perfect, but that's not. Not her nose. It's no good. She might as well quit it now. It's no good, Bethany."

The only thing that my folks could see was that I was not with them. I did not coo with them. I did not whisper a life lie with them.

"Why don't you wait in the car," Pop said.

"Pop, she's—"

"Right," Bethany sighed from the deepest part of her chest. "You're right. You're right. You're right."

I reached up and brought her extended arm down onto my shoulder, and I kissed her disfigured cheek.

"I want!" she cried. "I want . . . I want . . ."

I scooped her up, one scarecrow picking up another, and began walking back to the church and our car.

"I want . . ."

"I know, Bethany. I know."

We took her back to Bradley Hospital in the morning. Pop thought we should drive directly there from Rockville, but Mom held her tight in the backseat and would not hear of it.

That night I went to bed early. I could hear Mom rocking in the chair next to Bethany in my sister's room. She was singing "In

Dublin's Fair City," and she was singing it as slow as she could. I imagined she stroked Bethany's hair and wondered how something this familiar seemed so unfamiliar. I felt as though the things I had here weren't mine anymore, or that I didn't want them. I suppose I was going away then, and not waiting for the bus to Fort Dix to make it official.

27

The rain had gone the other way, east from where I had come, and the roll-down—out of Pennsylvania, into Maryland, and on up through West Virginia—was warm and dry. My little road map showed Route 50 to be the longest somewhat-connected smaller road that eventually dropped into the Los Angeles area, so I followed Route 11 until I picked it up.

Plans just happen, I have found out. I was someone who'd never had a plan, so it shook me up to see how simple they were to make and how often they just made themselves. First I found myself checking my tires every fifty or so miles, and then I realized I was essentially eating the same thing all the time and actually taking Father Benny's stress tablets, and finally, each evening after I set my tent off the road, I would read some *Iggy*. Maybe that's not a plan, maybe that's a habit. Whatever—it was comfortable and gave me a feeling I sort of knew what I was doing.

I finished *Iggy* in Hoagland, Ohio, eight days after I left the Gettysburg Motel. I had a wonderful day on the road. It was easier, a lot easier, for me to ride, and I had what I call a "Shad Factory feeling." A kind of tingle to get going every morning. The only difference, really, was, I'd known that the pickerel and perch were in their riffs waiting for me at Shad, and now I didn't know anything, which was, like I said, wonderful. Every morning I had an orange and a banana, then a big tuna sandwich for lunch, and more apples and bananas for dinner.

Anyway, *Iggy*. So good I was sorry I finished it. It was his whole life right until he was an old black man eating an apple under a Colorado cottonwood. Everybody would think that he was just another old black man, but all of us who had read the book knew that he was a giant. A great man at the end of his life. It was a tender kind of a secret, and I loved knowing it.

In Hoagland that night, it thundered and flashed enough to light the cornfield that my little tent was nestled against. I finished *Iggy* just as it started to rain. I brought my saddlebags into the tent, then stretched out and listened to the rain ping all around me. I began to think, and I guess the thoughts took me away. I was thinking about Norma, and in my head I kissed her and felt her hands go around my back, and it was a powerful squeeze. We kept our lips together, and I returned her squeeze and picked her out of that chair and lay down with her in the long, warm, dewy grass of Ohio. I guess it was a love dream, or thought, and I don't have many of them. A dream, maybe a hope, I don't know.

And I don't know about other things. Whenever I'd felt a thought or something like an idea or a desire creeping through my ice-cold Narragansett beers and tall screwdrivers, I could always turn on the television and get away from me. In Scouts, before the beers and the seventy channels on the TV, I'd lie in my tent, awake all night with hopes of happy grapefruit breasts and worries about tomorrow. They're here again. The breasts, the worries, the hopefulness. How strange it is to feel a child's feelings again. This man full of holes. This bicycle-pushing, knapsacked old man. I felt my face, the thickness of my beard. I traced the lines of it over my cheeks and lips. Maybe I could trim this. Maybe I could shave my neck. Maybe if I combed this high hair back. Maybe the dog that's howling outside in the rain is hurt. Maybe it's laughing or crying. But that was a country howl there in the dark. A big mutt, somewhere. God, I love those big, sloppy mutts. Why don't I have one? A big, sloppy friend who would shake himself apart for me. He howls again, and I am satisfied it's a good howl and he's not hurt. But this is how I think, away from the tall drinks and remote control.

28

I weighed 121 pounds when I stood for my induction physical. A marine doctor was doing the examining at the draft center and was convinced I had tried to starve myself to avoid the war.

"Not gonna work, little man," he snarled.

"What's not gonna work?"

"I'm just gonna write down one hundred thirty-one pounds. Got a problem with that, little man?"

Anyway, here it is. I did basic training at Fort Dix, went to Quartermaster School, Fort Lee—that's Virginia—and after eight weeks I had demonstrated I could pass out supplies and mark ten sheets of paper each time I did. Then they sent me to Vietnam in the infantry. I replaced a guy who was killed in advanced infantry training. During some exercise he had wandered onto the mortar range. I didn't know any of the guys, and really I only got to know Bill Butler pretty good because he had the bunk under me. Everybody called me "Slim." I didn't tell anybody it was Smithy.

One night after dinner, we were reading the posted orders. Our company was going to the war. We were told to get our shit "short, straight, and clean," which meant pack up neat. They lifted us up from Fort Lewis in Washington (state), and before we knew anything, we were in the Alpha Base about twenty-five miles from Saigon and maybe one mile from a village called Hee Ho. This was sort of our village, where Alpha would spend time and drink and stuff. And, as I said, there were a lot of prostitutes. In America, from what I've seen in movies and magazines, it's not hard to tell an American prostitute. They have a certain way, a certain talk, like that. In-country prostitutes were like any of the other women. Also, you didn't get a sense that the other women blamed them. For ten months of my eleven-month tour, I did not see—let alone shoot at—any enemy troops, so my real memories are of Hee Ho and especially the three times I was with a woman. And, of course, of Bill Butler, who knew my name and saved my life.

Bill was the blackest human I had ever seen. His skin was like a ripe eggplant. He had the slightest mustache and short, flat hair. He was a little taller than me, maybe six foot, and was a really muscular 180, 190 pounds. He was very mature for being only a year older than me, and he called himself "hep to the jive." Everybody liked him. He was cool and tough in the way some people are cool and tough and never have to prove it.

"Ya understand the shit I am laying down?" he said under his sunglasses, relaxing on his cot.

"Sure," I said.

"Ya understand, see, that the women have the need, too. You see the muthafucks say, 'Shit, jack, bitch don't need shit!' See that? Oh, she need shit—she don't need *your* shit."

Bill threw back his square head and laughed and laughed. Bill loved to laugh at himself, at how funny he could make the world look.

"Now you, Slim man, you got to pop it here or you may never. I say Bill find you some fine young thing. I'm saying we all probably gonna die."

I laughed. Some of the other guys laughed. Anybody could die but us. Orlando Cepeda laughed. From our tent we could hear music drifting over the tall grass from Hee Ho. The music was Smokey Robinson and the Miracles. Every now and then Bill threw back his head and sang a high accompanying scream. We laughed. It was beyond hot outside, and we pulled our tent flap down tight to escape a breeze that was actually hotter than the stilled air. Even in the heat, Bill jumped up and danced with the backbeat. Sweat popped and dribbled and pressed through his olive T-shirt.

"Got to move. We got to move, baby. Bill gonna find all the fine young things."

Bill glided across the plywood-hinged flooring with an imaginary girl we could almost see. He smiled at her tenderly.

"You with Bill now, baby. There we go. Oooooh, look at how pretty you look. You fine, baby. You Bill's fine girl."

The music stopped, and Bill lay back down, sweating, on his cot. I was writing to my family, only I had nothing to say. I knew they were worried, and it bothered me. So I kept writing them pretty much the same thing. I was fine. I was safe. What an interesting jungle this was.

We would go on perimeter patrols about every third day. We'd go for about three hours. Most of the time, we'd stay in the tent or play softball. At night we'd walk over to Hee Ho. That's where I had my early beers and vodka, only it never tasted perfect until after Bethany had gone and I discovered the pretzels and fresh orange juice. The village was filled with bars. Our noncoms all had a piece of one bar or another, so they were pretty much the same except for the Sandy Beach and the East St. Louis. The Sandy Beach was a bar where the Vietnamese women were really men. A lot of soldiers went there. Bill and I never did.

"It's their thing," Bill would say, "it's their thing, that's all. But Jeeeee-sus. Man. Shit."

The East St. Louis was a black bar. There was a sign outside—two signs, actually—and they both said NO WHITES ALLOWED. If I was with Bill, which I usually was, I would wait outside while he went in.

"Got to see the brothers."

"Oh, sure."

"Ya know."

"Sure."

"See what goin' down."

"Sure."

"Uh-huh."

One night—I remember it was a cool night—Bill and I went to this bar, and we were standing in a corner drinking something, because the place was packed and the seats were taken. I was kind of unsteady.

"You swayin'," Bill laughed.

"I don't know," I laughed.

"You one drunk muthafucka."

A very little girl came over and nuzzled Bill. She was maybe eighteen or twenty, but she was so little her face didn't go with the rest of her.

"How you doin', baby? Smith man, this is Faye. Don't she look like Faye Dunaway?"

She looked over to me and smiled. I couldn't tell who she looked like. I smiled back. I made a stupid face, and she giggled.

"Hello, Faye," I said.

"This is my man, Slim."

"Hello, my man Slim," she said in imitation of Bill.

"Faye's gonna come to America one day. Be an actress."

"That's great."

"She's gonna be a big star."

"That's great."

"San Diego," Faye said.

"I've never been there," I said stupidly.

"San Diego," she said again.

Bill slipped his hand onto her shoulder and gave her a squeeze.

"So, Faye, want to pop Slim's cherry?"

"Oh, sure." Faye smiled at me. "Sucky, fucky. Come on."

She grabbed my arm and started to pull me toward the door. I looked at Bill, and I knew my face was ridiculous because he laughed and shook his head. Outside were empty oil drums stacked two high, arranged to create a maze of little rooms. Each room was covered with canvas or oilcloth. You could hear other people in other rooms, their voices and noises made louder by the hollow metal walls. An echo chamber where private sounds bounced around the barrels. The floor was packed dirt, but there were sleeping bags spread around it. Faye pulled her little brown dress over her head, and she was naked except for her sneakers.

"This is a . . . a . . . interesting room," I said.

"Pussy," she said pointing to herself.

"It's very . . . pretty. . . . We don't . . ."

Faye unbuttoned my belt and pulled down my pants in one motion. She pulled down my shorts. My penis was shrinking. It wasn't Faye's fault. It was actually going back up inside me. I was afraid it would just disappear.

"Where cock go?" she asked me, concerned.

"Well, I never . . ."

Faye took my hands and put them over her breasts. "Tits," she said.

Now, you know what's clear about this time? This first time? Clear enough so I can recall it exactly? Nipples. They went from brown, wide, and flat to pointy little erasers. It was wonderful to feel them change under my hands.

"Ooooh," she said. "Mr. Cock come back."

And okay, it was silly and only lasted about a minute, and afterward, when I paid her, she had that look of nausea or something at having been with me—hate, too. But I still see it clear. Me and Faye Dunaway under the oil barrels.

There's a girl on the Goddard assembly line, working doll-eyes quality control. She looks like Faye. She's little, too, and her hair is the same, but she speaks perfect English and might be Japanese. I just don't know. What I do know is that I've seen her working and chatting with her friends and laughing out loud when one of the guys tells a joke, and I wish I had been shot before I used a girl that looked like her. The way we did. I did. Money being what it was.

I just don't know.

29

I had never heard of Lovella Loveland, which wasn't a surprise, because *Iggy* was the first book I'd read in years. But there were her books arranged on a spin rack at a little grocery store on the Ohio-Indiana border. She'd written a lot. I counted forty titles. *Savage and Silk, Señor Sundown, Orbs and Opus.* Like that. Each cover had a drawing of a beautiful woman, her full breasts ripping and pushing to escape her shirt fabric, and standing over her was a man, a bulging, hearty sort of man. In the picture, it was clear, the woman was going to be okay. The cover of one particular book had a woman kind of sprawled on the ground with a lot of her bottom showing, a big V of flesh between her enormous breasts, and Norma's face. Hair, too. It was called *The Incidental Iconoclast* and—I'm not kidding—the girl looked like red-haired, high-cheeked, dark-eyed Norma, right down to that defiant face she makes. I didn't look like the Iconoclast or whatever standing over her, but I put the book with my bananas and grapes and water and bought it.

The sun was out after four full days and nights of rain, so I was very careful to spread my sunblock thick and wear my hat. My clothes also seemed to be stretching from all the moisture in the air, because they seemed too big, and my neat Father Benny's shorts slipped down when I walked.

I pedaled an easy rhythm over flat country that day. I made real progress and, for the first time ever, didn't stop for lunch. I had my bananas and water while I rode. I had some crackers. I sang some songs I remembered from Yawgoog, the Boy Scout camp. I talked to myself. I saw Bethany under a huge tree and on top of a horse trailer. I saw her on the water of a small pond and in the shape of a cloud. "Hook's here," I would say. "Hook's coming." And I would say those things without sadness, because I was not sad with the poses she showed me and the long smiles she threw.

Between Hartford and Dillsboro, Indiana, I slowed and stopped. It was getting night, and I hadn't even noticed. It was my best bike day yet. I thought of Norma and wished I'd called her earlier, because there was no phone around, only a huge field of sunflowers. All the flowers faced the setting sun. All the rows of flowers waved in a warm breeze. I had never slept in a flower field before, and I said out loud, "What a lucky man Hook is."

That's when Carl Greenleaf's pickup truck hit me from behind.

30

Bill Butler was the only person—besides my family, the doctors, and Norma—I'd told about Bethany. My Aunt Paula knew, of course, and Count and Bea and our priest at Grace Episcopal, but I never talked to them about her. I mean, I wasn't ashamed, but a person couldn't explain it—and even if a person could explain it, it would probably come out as some kind of apology or something. I didn't have to apologize for my sister.

Bill never got much mail, so one day while I was reading a letter from my sister, one of the few she sent, he sat down next to me.

"Good news?"

"Just my sister."

"She fine?"

"I guess."

"Pretty?"

"Oh, yeah."

"What she say?"

It was raining outside our tent, and I remember how much it felt like Boy Scout camp. That was the war to me. I didn't get it. I just didn't know. Small, muddy ponds formed in Alpha Base, and streams flowed under our plywood floorboards.

"My sister writes sort of strange."

"What?"

Bill lit a cigarette and gave me one. Marlboros. Marlboro Country. I took a drag and looked back at the letter.

"Well, Bethany, that's my sister, she says she knows a lot of secrets, and one of them is that when her voice tells her to scratch and claw at her face or pull out her hair, it's a stage she must go through to get to a better Bethany. Also she knows where God lives, and sometimes at church she knows she could float around if she wanted to, but she doesn't want to scare anybody."

Bill nodded and inhaled.

"She says my folks are good but my pop is always watching her, and one day she might take a steak knife and cut her own head off. She says he'll stop watching then. Also, she thinks I'm going to die over here."

Bill inhaled again. "I got two sisters. I got Tanya and I got Dorothy. Tanya is black, and Dorothy is brown. Same daddy, too. Tanya got a mouth. Girl can throw it. Yap, yap, yap. Dorothy like a mouse."

"They pretty?"

"Tanya fine. Dorothy shit. She nice, though."

"That's good, too," I said. We finished our cigarettes silently, thirty seconds of smoky breath. The rain continued. Bill took out two more Marlboros and gave me one.

"She crazy, then?"

Out of our tent flap, across the mesh rubber walkway that connected us all, in a white prom gown, stood Bethany in her pose. It was one of the first times I had seen her clear. She stood in the rain but stood dry. Her smile, her hair, her eyes bounced sun where there was no sun.

"Yes," I said.

Bill nodded and didn't say anything else. After a while he got up and lay down on his bed. I just kept watching the rain until Bethany was gone.

31

He came around the edge of the front fender and stood, both hands on the hood, looking at me. At my bike. He was crying.

"Oh," he said. "Oh, no."

I was sitting with my legs out and I'm sure the dumbest look on my face the man had ever seen. I swayed from side to side.

"Raleigh," I said.

"I can't get to it," he said. "If I got to it, I couldn't pick it up."

Some birds swirled over us, and I could see, maybe, mist on another field, in the shape of a cloud. We were silent. I could feel blood under my hands that held me sitting.

"Bike," I said finally.

He looked past me to the pieces of my maroon childhood.

"No more bike. Are you going to die?"

Bill Butler had asked me the same thing when they shot me. I was pretty sure I was, but I didn't.

"No."

"Can you get in my car?"

"Can I get in your car?"

We both waited, and he came clear, slowly. Bone-thin arms leaned flat against the car. Baggy jeans and a gray sweatshirt that covered him like a tent. Long, fine brown hair hung sweaty to his ears, and where no beard covered his milk-colored face, I saw large, square red blotches that looked ready to give way to spurts of blood. This is what I thought while we looked at each other: I thought how odd the lake in Maine ran in currents cool and warm. Mom counting by twos when I held my breath and clung underwater to rocks. I thought about a huge rock only inches from the surface and my pop and Bethany and me swimming out with yellow buoys and tying them fast to the underside of the rock so the motorboats wouldn't crash into it. The red canoe. The mother ducks showing off their babies, begging for food in the breeze of the late-summer afternoon.

His crying took me back from Maine.

"I am so sorry," he said still leaning on the hood of the pickup. It was blue. No, it was green. It was a green pickup.

"You have to get to my truck. I don't think I can let go of it. I'm sick. I'm very sick."

"You look sick," I said. "My Raleigh . . ."

"The bike is gone."

My bike, my bananas. That good, clear spring water in the good, clear plastic bottles.

"You have to get in my truck."

"Your green truck?"

"Yes."

The sun hung utterly red, a red ball with yellow fringe, inches above the tall sunflowers.

"Come to my truck on your hands and knees."

I held my hands up to him and the corner of the pickup. "Blood," I said.

"Oh, God!" he sobbed. "Hands and knees, hands and knees."

I rolled onto my hands and knees and faced the truck like a bloodhound.

"C'mon now. C'mon now. You can do it."

I could do it. I didn't feel any pain. I remembered flying, but not landing. Hands and knees. Hands and knees. My paws left their bloody prints. Some cars slowed but did not stop. He pushed himself, a shuffle at a time, hands on the metal, to the passenger side and opened the door.

"Jesus," he gasped in exhaustion.

I crawled into the cab of the pickup, lay on my side, then pushed up to a sitting position. He closed the door. In the time he took to work his way around the hood to the driver's side, the sun had gone down completely. He pulled himself in, and we moved away from my Raleigh.

"Clarion Mercy Hospital," he said.

Five minutes later he said, "The Mennonites administer Clarion Mercy Hospital. I go there sometimes."

I put my hands on the dashboard. I held myself that way. As long as you sit up, you can't die.

"Breasts," I said sort of casually. "Titties, she said, but afterward pointing pussy. And how sorry, of course, and embarrassed. Pickerel."

The sick and skinny man stepped on the gas.

We pulled onto the half circle drive of the emergency-room entrance. He got out of the pickup and made his way, in slow motion, to the passenger side.

"I'm coming," he gasped, "don't worry."

He had just put his hand on the door handle when two uniformed emergency medical workers, a black man and a huge woman in orange and green, firmly eased him into a wheelchair.

He tried to speak, but the woman pivoted the wheelchair and began to push him up a ramp toward double doors.

"We'll get him comfortable." The black man nodded at me reassuringly.

I nodded back.

I watched them disappear through the light blue doors. I glanced about me. My eyes were cold, and I could feel the blood hardening on my arm and my back. I took a good, deep breath and fell asleep.

I thought of Faye Dunaway, and I dreamed Norma watched us in the barrels.

"I'm sorry, Norma," I said, opening my eyes.

"Listen, you have to move this. You can't block this entrance."

My eyes darted about until I found the black attendant leaning in the driver's window.

"You have to move this."

I slid over, turned the ignition, and pulled around into Parking Lot B. I didn't see Parking Lot A.

I had no idea how long I'd been asleep. Not long, I guess, but the moon was out and three-quarters bright, the way it is in the country. I got out of the truck and walked to the emergency room. There was no one at the admitting desk, so I went into the men's room. I had a headache, and my balls hurt. I pulled my shirt over my head. The blood down my arm came from a slice just below the back of my neck. I wet a paper towel, two towels, and washed it down. I washed my arms. The caked blood ran blackish. My ass was pretty cut, small cuts, but my underwear was soaked with blood. I threw them in the trash and washed myself with more towels. I put my shorts back on without undies. I washed the black-red parts of my legs. I turned my blue T-shirt inside out, but it was ruined, so I threw it away. I left the men's room in shorts and sneaks. I like underwear. I do not feel great without that support, and the dark brown shorts, even with the strings tightened, felt as if they could slip off in a second.

There were a few people in the waiting room. A little girl crying, an old man with his arm in a sling made of what looked like a really used handkerchief, a young black guy holding his head. There still wasn't anybody at the admitting desk. I went into one of the examining rooms, but no one was there either. Every cabinet in the room had been marked in huge red letters. HEART. TRAUMA. WOUNDS. I opened WOUNDS. I took some white cream marked ANTIBACTERIAL and rubbed it onto my back slice, my arm cuts, and my ass, then covered them with huge Band-Aids. I found some aspirin, too. I took four, then put on a long green paper shirt and walked back to admitting.

The huge woman emergency worker in the green-and-orange uniform was walking by. She recognized me from the pickup. She linked her muscular arm with mine, and I walked with her down the blue corridor.

"Carl's in number six. What we've done is got some fluid going, sugar and water. B_I shot, for what it's worth. Carl has to be better aware of secondary infections. He hasn't taken his AZT. You know it's not fair of Carl to have it and not take it. There's people all over the world waiting for it."

We walked into number six. This was where everybody had gone. There was a female doctor with a blond ponytail and horn-rimmed glasses, and a tall male doctor with a gray ponytail. Four nurses crowded in beside the gurney where Carl lay. One of them gave me a mask.

"Carl! Now, Jesus Christ!" the male doctor shouted.

"Look," the lady doctor said to me, "we've got about a half hour more here; then he can go home, but I'm going to want to talk to both of you. Wait in the waiting room."

The huge woman gently pulled me out of Carl's room and pushed me into the waiting area. I sat in the corner on a red molded plastic chair and fell asleep. I started to dream a good Norma dream, but it didn't go anywhere, because some little boy with a gash over his nose stuck his thumb in my ear.

"Jarrod, get your damned little thumb out of there!" an old woman yelled.

"Ear," he said.

"Jarrod!"

I didn't know what to say. I didn't want Jarrod to get in trouble, and I didn't want the old lady to get all mad.

"Balls," I said reasonably. "As long as he doesn't whack my balls. They hurt."

I smiled. I felt stupid, but again, like Bill Butler had told me, keep talking and don't die.

It was a lot longer than half an hour before they pushed the wheelchair, with Carl in it, down the blue corridor to the waiting room. The lady doctor walked alongside and spoke as she went. Bethany drifted on the other side, her arm punched up, her wonderful eyes half closed. Behind her lips the tiniest teeth. She left me when the doctor called out.

"One problem child ready to go home."

My balls really ached. I remembered I had been hit and I had flown. I stood up and walked over to Carl and the doctor.

"You've got your hands full," she chuckled. "Seriously, though, if Carl didn't assure us you could take good care of him, we wouldn't release him. He speaks very highly of you."

I looked at Carl. He looked away from me.

"Lots, I mean *lots,* of liquids. Soup. Juice, soda, I don't care. And protein. Lots and lots." She looked at me quietly. "Are you all right?"

"Am I all right?"

"Mr. . . ."

"Smith . . . y."

"Smith."

"Ide."

"Ide?"

"Smith Ide."

"Smith Ide?"

"Smithy Ide. There's a *y.* Sorry."

"Are you all right? You look . . ."

Carl looked at me. I knew I had to talk. Talk or die.

"My balls hurt. That's all. They're just . . . well . . . you know . . . aching balls. I've had bad balls . . . before . . . before your . . . see . . . your balls get like an egg, ostrich egg, and even if air gets on them . . . it's . . . I mean . . . you know."

She looked at me, paused for a moment, and spoke to Carl. "Where's Renny?"

"Renny had to get back to New York."

"Just like that?"

"The Big Apple. Top of the heap."

"God."

"This is the way the world ends."

She looked at me again, then back to Carl. "Let me admit you, Carl. It's time now, honey."

It probably took three-quarters of all his strength, but Carl wheeled away. "No. Not here. Not in a hospital. I'm afraid enough."

The doctor went and put her arms around him. "Okay, honey, okay. I'm here, you know."

"I know."

She stood up tall and looked back at me.

"You better take care, Mr. . . ."

"Ide," Carl said.

"Okay," I said.

I brought the truck around, but it wasn't easy. I tripped getting into the driver's side, fell out completely onto the pavement, and couldn't get back on my feet. Finally I crawled into position. The huge woman and the black man gently eased Carl into the passenger side, and I pulled out into the Indiana moon.

"Go left here . . . right here. We stay on this about ten miles. I'm in Providence."

I took the left and right. "I'm from East Providence, Rhode Island."

Roger Williams thought of all his good luck when he named the Providence River and the little town on it. I thought if I concentrated and talked, I'd be all right.

"Roger Williams named Providence . . . Rhode Island."

"Almost there. There's a big mailbox . . . there. . . . Now turn onto the dirt road."

The headlights passed through trees into a large field of flowers. Across the road from the flowers was a greenhouse in a Quonset hut design. A new log cabin, one of those nice kits, stood in three levels by the greenhouse. It looked like the cover of a brochure. A red metal roof looked pretty over yellowing logs.

"Here."

I parked the pickup next to the porch stairs.

Carl looked at the property. He didn't move. "Could you step into the greenhouse? If you get a warmish, clammy feeling, that's good. If it seems cold or too hot, I'll tell you what to do."

I eased down to the ground. I could feel my feet. I was getting better. The greenhouse gave me the warm, clammy skin he said, so I walked to the passenger side holding thumbs up and opened the door.

"Warmish," I said. "Clammy."

I concentrated on not letting go of the feeling of feet underneath me. Carl concentrated, too. He put both hands onto my shoulders and stepped slowly behind. We both edged up the stairs, the railing becoming a life support. Carl fumbled at the lock, got the key in but couldn't turn it. I turned it and stepped inside. He reached past the doorframe and switched the lights on.

There was no hall in Carl's house, only a gigantic, three-story open room and, in the back of the room, an iron circular staircase leading to a landing and, on that, another staircase to another landing. The room was oak and pine varnished clear, and it smelled better than any room I had ever been in, like fresh wood shavings or new cedar. A large glass light fixture of many different colors was suspended over a square arrangement of stuffed chairs. A new-looking rough wood coffee table of, maybe, oak or, again, pine was squarely in the center. A stone fireplace, also three stories, was the entire left side of the house.

I looked at Carl, and he was admiring it also. I realized then that Carl wasn't an old man, although he moved old. His skin was tight on his face, but it wasn't a wrinkled one. His lips were dry. His eyes were green, so green that his light brown hair seemed kind of greenish, too.

"I built this myself."

I looked at him stupidly and said stupidly, "You built this yourself."

"Myself and Renny Kurtz. Designed. Built. Staired. Furnished. Lived. Sixteen years."

"It smells wonderful," I said, "and it's beautiful."

"I moved downstairs two weeks ago. Two weeks ago I knew I wouldn't be able to climb the stairs. There."

He shuffled toward a bed in the corner where two huge bookcases, filled with books, connected.

"Bathroom is behind the bookcase."

He pulled the case lightly, and it opened. He walked in and closed the case. I walked to the arrangement of chairs and sat. I sat for about an hour; then I walked back to the bookcase and asked the books, "Are you all right?"

"I'm all right. Runs."

I sat back down, and about fifteen or twenty minutes later, Carl came into the room.

He had on red plaid pajamas that were, of course, much too big. I got up and stood by the bed like a servant. Only, I mean, you know, not like it was a bad thing. I pulled the covers back, which were loosely made up, and he sat down and then lay out in his bed.

"Just the sheet," he said quietly.

I pulled the two blankets all the way down and covered him with the sheet.

"Would you get me some water? Kitchen is there."

The kitchen was open, set off by peach-colored tile. I thought how Mom would have loved the kitchen. A big butcher-block table with knives on the side and oak stools around it, and a gas range and grill right in the center of the room. I found a glass and filled it with tap water.

Carl leaned up and took the water. He had a tiny drink, then set the glass on his night table. He took some Vaseline and smeared it all over his lips.

"All the things, all things, and still I hate most the dry lips, the dry and cracked lips."

He lay back down, his bony head sinking almost out of sight into a blue feather pillow.

"I built," he said, drifting.

"It smells wonderful," I said stupidly.

I watched him until I knew he was sleeping. Then I turned on a small table lamp and switched off the glass fixture overhead. I went to the bathroom, peed, and checked my cuts. I walked into the kitchen and got a nice drink of water. I realized that probably I should have been hungry, but I suppose that the accident and flying through the air pretty well finished my hunger for the day. I just wanted to sleep. The phone rang, and I picked it up next to the refrigerator.

"Carl's house," I said.

A woman's voice. Clipped. Impatient. "Where is he?"

"He's sleeping."

"Did he take his medicine?"

"He was in the bathroom a long time."

"He has to take his medicine tomorrow, and I wasn't kidding about the fluids and the protein."

"I wasn't kidding when I listened to you."

I had done it again in my stupid way. I had taken words away from her. I never try to do that, but it happens.

"Look . . . uh . . . what's the name?"

"Smithy Ide."

"Look, let's put it out there, okay? You're some sort of derelict, right? I'm sorry if that sounds insensitive, but really, all in all, that's tough fucking shit. I'm Carl's physician, and I'm not about to let some scumbag cocksucker rob that dear man blind. You understand? Now, he's had one treatment at the hospital, and I'm coming out to-morrow, and take this to the bank, Mr. Smith or whatever the fuck you call yourself: If he's not comfortable, with plenty of fluids and protein in him, I'll ream you a new asshole. Got it?"

"Yes, ma'am," I said. And she hung up.

32

So anyway, I peed into the swampy water. What was stupid was not the actual peeing, really, because who knew that all the critters in the swamp would go quiet and all the guns would start firing? You'd have to be a mind reader to know that in advance. No, what was incredibly stupid was that I didn't take enough care. It happened in the tenth month, and you only had to stay for eleven months. When you get "short," that means you don't have long to stay, so the closer you're getting to home, the more caring you're supposed to be. If I didn't explain it right, that's my fault, but it's completely true.

Like I said, that nice boy, Orlando Cepeda, who was standing behind me when I peed, got shot dead. One clean bullet. Just a little wound, too, which was odd. Clean. Clear. Now, I got hit a million times big rips, dirty and all that—but I suppose I was lucky. As a matter of fact, I'm pretty sure only luck can explain it. And Bill Butler. But it's lucky he was there, too. He looked at Orlando Cepeda and spit. Then he squeezed my morphine pack into my left arm, Orlando's morphine pack into my right arm, and his own into my belly. I watched him do it. I watched myself. I saw Bethany above the swamp.

"Hook's here," I said, drooling.

"You gonna die?" Bill asked.

"I don't know."

"Okay."

"Hook's here."

I don't remember anything else, except Bethany's floating up to tree level. She was dressed casual in one of her kilts, and she looked like every Sears ad in the world. Young and happy in a silent, arm-raised pose, floating above.

Then I was in Japan. I don't remember anything else. I woke up in Japan seven weeks later. And it seemed I went from Bethany at tree level to the U.S. hospital outside of Tokyo in a minute. No dreams. I had a tube for breathing and one for peeing. I remembered peeing. I remembered Orlando Cepeda.

I was bad in the hospital. I was feeling very sorry for myself, and when I found out that everyone else felt sorry for me and wasn't going to get mad at me no matter what, I started to say cruel things and do cruel things.

I said:

"I hate this fucking food."

"I peed myself, and it was your fault."

"You're a fat slob for a doctor."

"I hate this fucking hospital."

I turned over my bedpan on purpose . . . twice. I gave the finger to the Catholic chaplain, a nice white-haired chaplain in uniform, who surely didn't deserve it.

So I was bad, but it took my mind off of myself for a while. Norma says she wrote every day to me, but I don't remember that. I got some letters from her, but I don't remember them. Of course, now I wish I had them so I could read them over and over in the fields and places.

After another six weeks, they put me in a wheelchair and airlifted about two hundred of us to Fitzsimmons Army Hospital in Denver. Before we left for the airport, I looked out the bus window at the Tokyo hospital and saw the chaplain. He wore camo fatigues and held his Bible. He looked exhausted. I guess it's really an impossible job. He saw me, too. He gave me the finger.

33

In the morning I could hear rain pelting the red metal roof. I rolled onto my back, but the cut above my shoulder blades put me back onto my side. I had fallen asleep in one of the stuffed square chairs in the center of the big room and somehow made my way to the floor, where I spent the night. I looked over to the bookcase corner. Carl was still asleep—or at least amazingly still.

It was day outside, and some of that gray light spilled onto my head from a large bay window. As I became more awake—and it was hard, because I slept solid and didn't even dream—I could sense an ache that pinched all over me like a lot of tiny pins. My hands and arms were black and blue. I looked at my chest and my stomach and the rest of me, curled, swollen, and discolored. Using the square chairs, I stood, feeling as if I were balanced on a ball. It was a high-wire shuffle to the bathroom, where I ran a hot-hot bath and soaked in it until at least the little pins disappeared. My shorts had a big hole in the thigh part and the heel of my Father Benny sneaks had been ripped clean off. I pulled on my clothes and my paper shirt. I took four more aspirin.

When I pushed open the bookshelves and walked out of the bathroom, Carl was sitting up in bed. He had brushed his damp hair back with a brush from his night table. Even in his illness, he looked young, almost like a child. I felt embarrassed in my green paper shirt.

"You're all messed up," he said quietly, pushing out the words in a kind of puff.

"I don't know."

"You are. God. Look at what I did."

"No, no. I shouldn't have been stopped there."

"You were on the grass. You were twenty feet off the road." Carl raised his arms and dropped them. His fingers were pink skeleton fingers. "I was out of it at the hospital."

"That's okay."

"I'm out of it. Even my doctor says I'm out of it."

I remembered something about the doctor but not much. Ponytail. Protein. Food.

"Food," I said.

"Check the fridge. There's food. I'd eat."

I made things I could make. I could make scrambled eggs and toast and tea and pour apple juice.

"I can't drink apple juice," Carl said when I put the tray on his lap. "I drink it and actually piss it out as apple juice. Right away. I'm out of it."

I pushed one of the square chairs over and ate, too. Eggs have a lot of protein, but for some reason I only ate a little.

"Good," he said, chewing. He put some egg on the corner of his toast and said it again. "Good."

We were quiet while he ate. My family was quiet while we ate, too. Some families have loud meals, and food is only a part of the loudness. My family was quiet with food. Respectful, really. Almost as if our meal was a ceremony we had just learned and were trying to get it right.

After a while Carl laid his utensils down and leaned his head back. He made a little gurgle sound and closed his eyes.

"Finished?" I asked.

He nodded slowly, and I took his tray back into the kitchen.

"It's raining," I said, wanting to say something.

"Oh, it rains," he puffed. "It rains and rains."

I brought Carl a fresh glass of water and sat back down in the big square chair I had pushed over to the side of his bed. The aspirin and the eggs helped me. The aches were less.

Carl sipped the water and then laid his head back down again. He closed his eyes and was very still. He is the only person who ever reminded me of my sister's poses. Nothing moved. When he spoke like this, his head back, his eyes fastened, the puffs of words barely moved his lips.

"I am the 'capable dreamer,' " he said out into the room. "In high school, my yearbook—'Carl Everett Greenleaf, swimming 2-3, cross-country 1-2-3, chorus 1-2-3'—it said, 'Carl is our capable dreamer.' That was in '75. And it was true."

The gray light had become a blaze of bright sun through the bay window and the small row of glass above the bookcase, but the rain oddly continued on the roof.

"I want to talk out loud. I want to say things, but it's not fair. I almost killed you."

"That's okay."

"You shouldn't have to listen to my shit."

"I'm a good listener. Maybe I'm better at listening than anything else."

Carl might have smiled at that. He rolled his head a touch. "I don't feel sorry for myself. That's one thing. That's because I was raised a farm boy, right down the road. The Greenleaf Dairy Farm. Farm boys don't feel sorry for themselves, even the flitty ones, even the silly ones. There's just no time. And I believe we are what God made us, and that's that. My father is Carl Everett Greenleaf, too. Oh, he's a big man. A respected man. But he knew who I was and more or less pushed away from me, although we worked together and he would just whitewash the fences where other boys scribbled 'Carl the Swish' and 'Carl's a fag.' Mommy loves me, of course. Brother is angry at me. I think it's your obligation—no, it's your biology—to love and understand your family and to be kind and just . . . nice to them. I'm sad about my brother, because he would always throw the ball with me in the yard. And he would play horseshoes with me. And I was his best man, and then he talked to some people and stopped talking to me. But the truth is, it's against your biology not to love your brother no matter what.

"I liked the cows. I liked the process of the cows. It's commerce, but it's life. Only farm people know that. But I liked my garden best. It made sense. I had a vegetable stand all late summer and fall. Squash, pumpkins, corn. Eggplants and tomatoes. Herbs. One year I grew flats of African violets. Now that made sense. Flowers are understandable. They're in the rhythm of the world, and the colors and textures are a gift. They simply give out to the world. The next growing season, I raised my beds, altered my fertilizer, and planted gloxinia, dahlias, pasqueflowers, primroses, fuchsia in hanging pots, and I'm not exaggerating to say I sold and sold and sold. Once, for the adventure of it, I arranged to sell at a farmers' market in New York. I'd sold in Indianapolis, Dayton, Columbus. You're a gypsy, really. You're a vagabond selling with your people. Farmers. My people are farmers. This New York market was in Union Square, and I drove fourteen straight hours. It was wonderful. Oh, God. Breads and jams and apples and cider and everything. And my peonies and chrysanthemums and arrangements of white plum. Nice arrangements. Not 'special' or 'cutesy,' but fine and nice. You let the flowers do the display. You can't add to the grandeur of flowers, so don't try. That's all. Don't try.

"Here comes a browser in Union Square, and the browser became Renny Kurtz, who had a small shop on Twenty-eighth Street. That's New York's flower district. We talked and talked. He bought muffins and coffee and brought them to my truck. We discussed compositions of flowers. Of stalks and stems and petals and pods. We could have been talking classical art, which the natural state of flowers was to us. Simpatico. Understanding. Conclusions. We bought here, so close to the dairy, because Indiana is flower-friendly. There's ash in the soil. There's volcanic power. We did well. We did so well. And things would frighten Renny, because he wasn't a farm boy. He wasn't fearless like we are, but that was all right, to be frightened. Hard weather. Storms. I would tell him that that is where soil comes from. And it's true. The soil smells like mint leaves in a storm. But my bad luck, my sickness, frightened him most, and he became ashamed of being frightened and finally couldn't move out of his fear. He would sit in the greenhouse and pretend to cut flowers, but he was waiting for me to sleep. And it was okay. I wasn't mad. I wrote him a note and made him an offer for his part, and one day he was gone. New York. I think, I really think, that people who love each other should never let anything interfere with that strange emotion. But I'm not angry. I'm sad. I'm disappointed."

The rain had stopped. Strips of white sunlight cut into the room from everywhere.

"Rain's stopped," I said.

"It's a general disappointment. A general sadness. Could I have some water?"

I handed him his water.

"I grow, is what I want to say. I sink my hands into our black soil, and I understand variety. What is good for what. Nutrients. So I'm a little sad. But did I say I'm not angry?"

"Yes."

"Because I'm not. I have to go to the bathroom."

I helped Carl move his legs to the floor. I never had felt anything quite like that before. Even through the heavy plaid pajamas, it was as if I had plastic pipe in my hand. I pulled him to his feet and led him to the bookcase/door of the bathroom. While I waited for him, I filled his water glass and shook out his damp sheets. He stayed in the bathroom about an hour.

"You okay in there?"

"I'm okay."

"Okay."

"Runs."

"Okay."

Carl got back in bed and fell immediately asleep. I neatened up his covers, then went into the kitchen and called Norma.

"Hello?"

"It's early. It's too early, isn't it?"

"Smithy! Smithy! Smithy Ide!" she hollered into the phone.

"It's not too early?"

Norma was crying hard. I didn't know if they were the good kind of cries or the bad kind.

"I'm sorry I was mad. I'm sorry I was mad. I'm sorry I was mad."

"You weren't mad, Norma."

"When you called me, I was mad, and I was mad at you, and then you didn't call me anymore. You didn't call me."

"I wanted—"

"Please call me. Oh, please call me."

"I'll call, Norma, and I didn't not call because you were mad. It's okay to be mad at me."

She was quiet for a minute. East Providence paused and sniffled. "You have to call me."

"I do. I know. I been calling you in my mind."

"You have?"

"Norma, I swear to God. And it's nice, it's wonderful."

"Oh, Smithy."

"And I'm in Indiana. Providence, Indiana."

"No!"

"Really! We're from East Providence, Rhode Island, and here I am in Providence, Indiana."

"Here it is. I've got it. I've got my map out."

"Providence, Indiana."

"I've got it. Wow."

"Yesterday I had a beautiful ride, and guess where I was going to sleep? You can't guess."

"A field."

"What kind of field?"

"Cornfield."

"Sunflower field. More sunflowers than you could imagine, and every beautiful sunflower faced in the same direction. I was going to park my Raleigh in from the road and make a space right there in the flowers to sleep, but Carl Everett Greenleaf hit me with his pickup truck and broke my bike."

"Smithy!"

"And he's awfully sick and sleeping in the other room, and I don't know. I just don't know."

"Wait a minute. Wait a minute. Tell me again exactly what happened."

I told her.

"And the doctors wouldn't look at you?"

"They were so busy. Carl is so sick. I've taken a hot bath and some aspirins."

"They can upset your stomach."

"Yesterday a busload of kids went by and waved. People are just better than I thought."

"Sometimes they're good."

We were quiet again, like we get on the phone, only this time it was a nice quiet, a really hopeful kind of quiet. And I could see her as clearly as I saw Bethany. Tall and powerful in her chair. A complete human being surrounded by the tools of her life.

"Smithy?" Norma said after a while.

"I'm still here, Norma."

"I meant what I said. I didn't mean somebody else. I meant . . . I meant you, me."

"Okay."

"Okay."

I enjoy our quiet, our pauses, when they're these kind. I'm not great on the phone. I would say that I have no phone skills. I always hold the receiver with both hands and lean my body against something, because I'm sure, somewhere along in my conversation, there'll be bad news. Horrible news. This time I didn't feel this.

"I got to go now, Norma, I got to watch Carl."

"He's very sick."

"It's terrible . . . but maybe not, maybe I'm wrong. All I—"

Someone pulled the receiver out of my hand and slammed it onto the counter. Both of my arms seemed to fly behind my back in one smooth motion, and I could feel plastic handcuff strips tightening over my wrists. I was whirled around facing into the kitchen. The doctor, the woman doctor who was at the hospital, was standing about ten feet away. A policeman in a light green uniform stood to the side of me, tilting my handcuffed wrists up so that it felt as if my shoulders would break up over my ears.

"Norma, I was—" Stupid me.

"Shut up," the big blond cop ordered, raising my arms again.

"Oww!"

"Just a sample, pal."

"I warned you," the doctor said. "I warned you not to take advantage of the situation."

"What situation?"

The cop raised my arms so high I fell on my knees.

"Tommy, don't hurt him."

"This doesn't hurt," he said.

"I went to school with Carl," she said angrily. "Carl has been a friend of mine for twenty-five years. If you think I'm going to allow some bum, some fucking drifter, to clean him out—"

"C'mon, asshole," the cop said ripping me to my feet. "You're hitting the road."

The cop pushed me to the door and the doctor walked into Carl's library bedroom.

We stepped onto the porch, and he closed the door behind me. He kicked me hard in my ass, and I lurched forward, lost my balance, and fell down the eight or ten steps to the walk. Carl had done a nice job with his yard. The lawn was thick, and the variety of healthy-looking trees was amazing. At the bottom of the stairs, my face bounced next to a pink azalea, and I could imagine, at that inappropriate moment, a healthy Carl preparing the Indiana dirt for his plants.

The big cop pulled me to my feet almost gently and unsnapped the plastic handcuffs. I was swaying a little, and the more I tried not to sway, the more I swayed.

"Hope you enjoyed Providence," he said happily. "Oh, by the way. . . ."

Tommy's kidney punch felt as if he had broken me in two fat pieces. I fell. I peed in my pants. I got to my feet and tried to move to the end of the walk. I threw up.

"Jesus," Tommy said disgustedly.

I fell again, got up, fell, got up. My head felt worse than when Carl's truck hit me. I could feel flows of things crashing up my neck, rolling to the front of my head.

"Tommy, Tommy, wait, wait! It's a mistake! We made a terrible mistake! I just talked to Carl!"

I turned, facing the porch. The doctor came onto the landing. She let out a breath I could hear when she saw me. Tommy seemed nonchalant.

"What do you mean, 'we' made a mistake? You told me to scare this creep off."

"I didn't tell you to hit him."

"This is how we scare creeps off, and so help me God, on the graves of my mother and father, I never laid a hand on him."

I threw up again and pitched forward onto an American Beauty rose.

34

I let Pop take pictures. Me. Me in my uniform. Me with my Purple Heart. Me and Mom, Me and Pop. Then Me, Mom, and Pop with the camera timer on. Then we went onto the back porch, and I asked them where my sister was. It's not important that you know this. But I knew she was gone, and I had to ask, because I had to lead them to talk. I know it all sounds like I think I'm so damn important, leading Mom and Pop, but I feel and felt as common as always. They needed the tears. I sat opposite them in our old chaise lounge while my parents wept.

I think they wept that I was all right, too. I was part of it, I know, because Mom saw me with my shirt off before I went to bed, and she cried again. What's wrong with a man who lets his mother see him and all his new holes? I could have run headfirst into a door-knob. I could have poked one of my eyes. I disgust myself. My poor mom. Me. But on the porch they cried the tears of loss and release. I walked over and sort of stooped down so I could hug them both at the same time. I could touch Mom and Pop. I didn't feel bad about touching them the way I did about other people. Bethany could touch me, too, of course, because I loved her. Love her.

My pop stood up and brushed his tears away. He didn't cry much.

"Gone," he said, looking past me out into the dark backyard. "She took the money she saved from her job with the church and packed up and left."

"She'll come home soon," Mom said.

"She will," I said.

My pop kept looking out through the porch screen, and Mom sat crying into her hands. This was before my lagers, my pretzels.

I stood skinny and unsure. I didn't have the legs for my family. She was gone.

"Such a beautiful, such a beautiful, beautiful girl," Pop said.

"You could hear her singing in her room, and you would just not believe . . ."

We were there in the September night. Bugs hit at the screen, swarmed near the lights.

"She will come back," Mom said.

"She will, Mom," I said.

Mom and Pop had come out to Fitzsimmons Hospital in Denver when I first was flown there. Bethany came, too. I think the time in Denver, as far at least as her looks, was Bethany's best period. The guys in my ward could only stare. I was so proud of her. She wore a different kilt each time she visited. I felt so bad for Mom and Pop. I felt so damn bad. Stupid, really. On top of Bethany's voice, I had to go pee in that swamp and get slaughtered like that. Then this really handsome kid next to me, who had been wounded in the chest, too, and who looked a whole lot healthier than me, had the bullets shift near his heart or something and just died with a huge groan, and with my pop and mom standing right there. They didn't need that.

I stayed in Denver for four months and then flew to Providence and our porch.

"Three months now. About," Pop said.

"Has it been three months?" Mom asked.

"About."

Somewhere crickets rubbed their legs together. I was happy at least that that night our backyard crackled into the night and left silence behind. We sat and listened to the evening. I thought about Norma, and I had a feeling she was watching. I will never understand, really, why the Ides left our little Norma there. It seems too easy to put it on Bethany. To say we didn't have any more to give or be for anyone else, even our Norma behind venetian blinds, is not enough. I will never understand.

"Uncle Count had a heart attack," Mom said.

"Another one?" I asked.

"Too much meat," Pop said.

We stopped talking for a while, and then I said, to be saying some-thing, "How many is this?"

"This was number twenty-eight," Mom said.

"Twenty-eight," I said.

"They count all the little ones," Pop said. "They count all the tiny ones. It wasn't twenty-eight big ones."

Mom nodded. "Eight big ones."

"Or nine," my pop said.

Crickets.

35

I had walked back up the porch stairs and into the house under my own power, although I don't remember it at all. I went upstairs to the guest bedroom, a large blue room with Indian pictures all over it, and got into a bed. I don't remember doing that either. It was night outside when I woke up. Bugs were working loud, and because I lay still, only moving my eyes a little, they seemed even louder than they actually were. I listened to the bugs. I heard the buzzsawing mosquitoes. I heard the whap and bang of the moths on the screens trying for the table lamp someone had switched on. I wanted to switch it off and save them.

I had to pee, but I lay there a long time and thought about it, and thought maybe the urge to let go of the water would just go away, but it didn't.

"Kidneys," I said.

The bedroom had its own bathroom. I pulled my bed covers down and stood. Oddly, I didn't feel all that bad. Nana used to tell us whenever we got sick that there was nothing wrong with us a good night's sleep couldn't fix. I had made it into the bathroom and was standing over the toilet when I realized that I was naked. For the first time, I remembered the doctor. I felt sorry for her. A person could go blind, seeing me naked. I peed.

I peed in spurts, and each spurt brought a terrific pinch of pain, but my pee was pee, and even though I looked closely for the blood that had seeped into my pee at Father Benny's, I didn't see any.

I smiled to myself, and then I laughed, and then I said out loud that the big blond cop Tommy couldn't punch worth a shit. Although he could. And he did.

I needed to brush my teeth, so I looked in Carl's medicine cabinet for a guest toothbrush like Mom used to have around. I couldn't find one, and I squeezed some toothpaste onto my finger and rubbed my teeth good. In Carl's medicine cabinet was a large box of Epsom salts. Epsom salts works. It helps you. I started a hot bath and poured the whole box in.

"Epsom salts," I said. "It really helps you." I soaked for fifteen or twenty minutes, and I did little stretches and shoulder shrugs to keep myself clear and loose. I feel childish in a hot tub. I keep expecting Mom or Nana to come in and wash my hair and give me those hard rubs on my back with a facecloth. I closed my eyes and smiled stupidly to myself, but I would be four again if I could have those heavy rubs.

"You're awake."

I put both hands over my private parts and sat up in the tub. The doctor had come into the bathroom. She hadn't even knocked or anything.

"Did you urinate okay?" she asked.

I nodded.

"Blood? Discoloration?"

"Uh-uh."

"Oh, that's good. Oh, that is so, so good."

She knelt down on the bathroom rug, put her hands on the rim of the tub, and leaned in close to me.

"I'm Donna Trivitch, Dr. Trivitch from the ER, and I am so embarrassed and so ashamed and so sorry about everything."

"I'm Smithy Ide."

"When Carl told me how he hit you and how he took you to the hospital and you ended up taking care of him . . . well, I am just so . . . sorry."

"I don't have any clothes on."

"Just a sec."

Dr. Trivitch left the bathroom and came back a minute later carrying a red terry-cloth bathrobe and a towel.

"I'll leave these right here. This is Carl's. I have to go down to Carl now."

"How is he?"

"Carl's going to die tonight. I'm going to be here all night with him."

She wasn't teary or solemn or anything. I wanted to get out of the tub, but not with her standing there.

"We went to school together," she said. I noticed how tired she looked and probably older than she really was, but it was a sweet face, and I would call it pretty. She had on chino pants and a plain white T-shirt. Her breasts were smallish, and I don't mean that in a way that evaluates them—it's just that I do notice breasts. Smallish, but I'd bet very pretty. Red-brown hair, tall.

Dr. Trivitch started to leave the bathroom but turned back.

"I had the wildest crush on Carl, and maybe I still do. He's very gay. I'm pretty dumb, huh?"

"I used to think . . . I used to think I loved my sister, and now she's dead."

Dr. Trivitch looked at me with an empty face and left the bathroom. I dried off, put on Carl's red robe, and went down quietly to the kitchen. In the bookshelf corner, Carl lay on his side and Donna Trivitch lay with him. She rubbed his back and sang a song I didn't know. Carl's eyes were open. He lifted his hand a touch and tried to speak, but only a wet mumble came. She put her hand over his.

"I know. I know, Carl. I know."

36

The Young People's Fellowship at Grace Church gave me a service award because I got wounded, and they displayed my Purple Heart in the chapel entrance on Westminster Street. After the award I stood with the rector while people shook my hand. It was nice of them to do this, but I hated it very much. My pop circulated among the kids with a small notepad, asking questions about Bethany. This was not her group. They were much younger than my sister, and I tried to tell Pop that, but the detective work was part of him now and stayed a part. On that last visit to Maine, Pop brought up his Bethany File, and a day never went by when he didn't add to it.

"That Carlson girl knows something," Pop said on the ride home. "She kept staring down at her feet. It's a giveaway. She knows something."

"I don't know," I said.

"Well, I'm telling you."

Pop followed every lead, real and imagined. I stayed around the house, still recovering. I had a little limp. I was taking some vodka for it. One night I was drinking some vodka at the kitchen table—Mom and Pop had gone up to bed, so I guess it was around twelve or one—and the phone rang.

"Hello," I said.

I always sound sort of anxious on the telephone, or sort of like I'm out to please everyone. It's one of those subservient hellos that really say "I'll do anything for you," but of course I don't really feel that way and I won't do anything for you.

"Hello. Hello."

I could hear something on the other end like teeth sliding over other teeth. It wasn't loud, but it was a grating noise, enough to make me wrinkle up my face.

"I can't hear you," I said.

The teeth noise stopped, and there was nothing.

"Hello?"

Nothing.

"I can't hear you. Maybe it's a bad connection. I'll hang up, and you can call back."

"Fuck," something rasped.

"I . . ."

"F–U–U–U–C–K, fuck!" something screamed.

"I don't . . . I . . ."

"They killed. They fucking . . . fuck. Fuuuuck."

It was the voice of an old man. Like an old man would sound yelling at you. Older than that. A very old man with a cheese grater of a voice.

"Who killed . . . ?"

"THEY KILLED YOU! THEY KILLED YOU!"

"Bethany?"

"All those holes. I knew they'd kill you."

The old man screamed into the phone from some deep part of Bethany's stomach. "F–U–U–U–U–C–K!"

"They didn't kill me, Bethany. I'm here. Hook's here. Where are you?"

"Sometimes I'm all dirty."

"Where are you? Mom . . . and . . . and Pop—"

"Say I'm away."

"We know you're away. We want you to come home."

"Fat-ass. Watch out."

I waited. The old voice coughed and faded. I waited longer, my heart rumbling into my ear.

"Hook?" The voice was soft. Bethany again.

"I'm here, Bethany. Where are you?"

"Oh, Hook, I'm all disgusting. I'm all dirty and disgusting."

"We love you, Bethany. Where are you? I'll come get you. We miss you."

"I miss you. I miss my room."

"Where are you?"

The light in Mom's kitchen seemed dull. It might have been the vodka.

"Where?" I asked again.

"Providence. I'm at church. I'm across the street now at a telephone booth, but now I'm going to go to church."

The connection held, but I heard the receiver hit against the base of the phone booth and knew she had dropped it.

I grabbed Pop's keys to the old Ford. Drove down past Woody's gas station and took 95 over the Old George Washington Bridge into Providence. No cars were at the church this time of night, and I parked directly in front of the main entrance. Across the street and to my left was the phone booth she had called from, and the receiver still hung free. I limped around the front of the car and up the concrete stairs. The heavy, ornate wooden doors were locked. Like the jerk that I am, I pounded on them a little and shouted her name.

I limped to the Westminster Chapel entrance, and it was open, even this late. Occasionally the sexton would have to drive some old bum out of the back pews, where he'd be trying to bed down for the night, but mostly then, in the late sixties, doors could still be open without asking for something awful to happen.

I walked into the church, past the side chapel, and stopped in front of the choir stalls.

"Bethany?"

I stood very still. A dim light fell on the main altar, and moonlight peeked in through the beautiful stained-glass windows. Grace Church's windows on the moon side of the building depicted Christ's seven last words. They seemed eerie in the semidarkness.

"I'm so happy you called, Bethany. I missed you so much."

I walked up to the choir stalls and began to look up and down each row. I started with the soprano row, of course.

"I'm limping a little. See how I'm limping? Bethany? See? But all that's wrong is the limp, and it's going away. Pretty soon I won't even be limping. That's all."

I thought I saw something at the end of the baritone row, but it turned out to be a stack of hymnals. I took one and carried it up the ten steps to the marble sermon mount.

"All my friends . . . all those other soldiers you saw in Denver? They all thought you were so beautiful. I mean it. Bethany?"

My favorite thought, still, about Grace Church, was how I felt when I looked over the old church with its columns and arches and carvings, from up here on the marble sermon mount. I used to sneak up here after choir practice when no one was around. You could just feel you had things to say standing here. Important words for all the congregation. And they would listen and even sometimes nod their heads and turn to their wives and things when you said something that could particularly make everything clear for them. Of course, I never had anything to say. Clear anyway.

"Remember . . . remember how Dr. Homer would take so long to get up here and how he would get himself angry during his sermons and start yelling? Remember, Bethany?"

I listened. My head hurt.

"And no matter how loud old Dr. Homer kept yelling and shouting and how loud he kept banging on the podium, Pop would go right on snoring."

"And Mom would poke him."

"Bethany?"

"Oh, Hook, and then we'd go get doughnuts to bring home, and we'd throw the ball with Pop."

"Bethany."

My eyes strained in the direction of her voice. I saw her under the stained glass of Jesus being fed a sponge of vinegar by the centurion. She was by the baptismal font. No. No. She was *in* the baptismal font. I walked down the stairs to the church floor and over to her. She sat on the edge of the font, and she was splashing water over herself. Slowly.

"I'm being baptized. I'm baptizing myself. I'm going to be all right now. Right? Hook? I'm going to be all right? I can be Bethany?"

"Yes," I said.

I wanted to look away, but I wanted to look at her, too. That was how I was with her, and she knew it, and I knew she knew it, and if there was one thing right now, thinking so hard about my sister, one thing I would change, I would never, ever let myself want to look away.

Bethany solemnly dripped water onto the top of her head. Her mouth was open enough so I could see that several teeth were missing in front, and her lips were cut and scabby. Her nose seemed puffy, as if she'd been punched, her eyes unclear and set somehow deeper than before.

"I baptize thee Bethany Adele Ide, in the Name of the Father, and of the Son, and of the Holy Ghost."

She looked at me, and for a moment I thought her eyes were shining. "Amen," I said, wanting to do anything for my beaten Bethany, scrunched and squatting on the marble baptismal.

"Amen," she said. "That's all I know about how they baptize. Do you think that's enough, Hook?"

I stepped to her. "I think that's beautiful, Bethany. C'mon."

I picked her off the baptismal and set her down on the ground. She wasn't wearing shoes, and she smelled of urine and shit and dampness. I hugged her, and she squeezed me so tight and for so long I thought she might have gone into a pose, but she released her grip and looked at me.

"I want to die now, Hook. I think that's best."

I started crying. I never cried in-country, but her words tumbled, like those small rolling slugs that hit me sideways and ran around inside me. Only hers were hot. Hers were hotter. The only thing I wanted right then was for her never to talk again. I took her hand, and we walked out of the cold stone church onto Westminster Street. It had begun to drizzle, but it felt good. I put Bethany into the car, then walked around to the driver's side. I turned and for a second or two stared at the phone hanging in the red booth across the street. I walked over, hung it up; then I drove my Bethany directly to Bradley Hospital.

37

Me: Norma? Are you busy? If you're busy, I can—

Norma: What happened?

Me: I know it's been five days, but . . .

Norma: We were talking, and then we were not talking.

Me: Everything's been so crazy, but I wanted to call earlier. . . . It's so weird. I wrote you a letter, but I didn't send it.

Norma: You wrote me a letter?

Me: Honest to God. I've got it right here.

Norma: Read it.

Me: I don't know.

Norma: Please read it to me.

(I was in the middle of Indiana now. A pay phone in a drugstore. I opened my letter to Norma.)

Me: Okay. "Dear Norma. Carl is dead. He was a very nice man, and even though I did not get to know him very well, I think of him as a friend, kind of." . . . That sounds stupid.

Norma: No, it doesn't . . . dead?

Me: I'm so stupid sometimes.

Norma: Read. Read.

Me: "Why I didn't call you before is because Carl dying caused some problems. First I had to take care of Carl, and then Dr. Donna Trivitch, Carl's friend from the hospital, came to the house with a policeman and he beat me up."

Norma: Smithy!

Me: I'm all right now, Norma. Honest to God. Should I keep reading?

Norma: Please read, Smithy. It's my letter.

Me: "After I got beat up, Carl told the doctor that I was not a bum, and she put me to bed on the second floor of Carl's really beautiful, beautiful house." Oh—I didn't write this, but Norma, Carl grew flowers for a living, and his house is surrounded, absolutely surrounded with roses and flowers. Every color in the world. You would love it.

Norma: I would. I would love it. Read, Smithy.

Me: And his house was truly beautiful. All wood and smelling like wood.

Norma: Ooooh. Read.

Me: Okay . . . "After a while I felt better, so I went downstairs, and Carl died. It was actually all right, that part, his dying, I mean. Dr. Donna Trivitch, his friend, sort of held him until he stopped breathing. It was peaceful, but then the doctor started crying and couldn't stop. There was a letter Carl had given her with stuff he needed done, when he couldn't do it anymore, but she was crying and she gave the letter to me and said I had to do it because she couldn't. I felt funny reading Carl's letter. He had about ten names, and next to each name was a phone number and what he wanted to say. Most of it was okay, but some of it was awful, and I didn't want to do it, but I did do it. I saved the three awful calls for last. Awful is not fair. Hard is fair. They were hard things, and I knew that if Carl asked Dr. Donna Trivitch to make these calls, then she should. When I told her they were hard, she started crying again. I had to call his brother, father, and a man named Renny Kurtz in New York. All his brother kept doing was shouting at me over the phone. He kept saying, 'Who the hell are you? Who the hell are you?' and then he said, 'Are you   ?' " Norma?

Norma: Read. I'm here.

Me: I know, but it was easier to write some of this than speak it.

Norma: It's all right. What did he say?

Me: " 'Are you some old faggot, is that what you are?' "

Norma: No!

Me: Well, yes he did. He said that. Carl was homosexual.

Norma: Oh.

Me: So he figured I must be homosexual. Carl was his brother. Jeez.

Norma: Read.

Me: Let's see . . . "Every time I tried to read to Carl's brother, he kept calling me names. Carl was saying things about how much he loved him and how he set up something to give money to his brother's kids, and his brother kept saying to me, 'You faggot. You old queen' . . . like that."

Norma: That bastard . . . that bastard.

Me: "So I told him what Carl wanted me to tell him, and I called his father. I probably shouldn't have, but who else would? And Dr. Donna Trivitch was still crying hard, only now she had gone out onto the porch. I told his father that Carl had died. He said thank you and hung up."

Norma: Bastard.

Me: "I wanted to call him back, but I would let the doctor do that later. There was something that seemed to be urgent about the calls. Is death urgent? I don't know. Maybe it just gives a feeling that things have to be done quickly. Calls have to be made. My last call was to this Renny Kurtz."

Norma: Who was Renny Kurtz?

Me: He used to be in Carl's business.

Norma: Where was he now?

Me: He was in New York now.

Norma: What did he say?

Me: Let me see . . . okay . . . "My last call was to this Renny Kurtz. I had to try three or four times, but finally I got him. I told him. For some reason—I don't know why—it was a lot harder telling Renny Kurtz than anybody else. I didn't hear anything on the other end of the phone, so I read what Carl had written. Except for things Carl was giving to his family, he was giving everything else to Renny Kurtz. Renny Kurtz made a sound I had never heard before and never wanted to hear again. Then he started screaming. He was screaming Carl's name. I thought he would stop, but after a few minutes, I sort of gently put the receiver down. Dr. Donna Trivitch had Carl taken to an undertaker and took me to get some clothes. I had no clothes because of when Carl hit me with his truck, but I wasn't passing blood so I was all right. I bought—or she bought for me, because she felt bad she had me beaten up—some new shorts and socks and sneakers and knapsack and hat and sunglasses and chino pants and a belt and two sweaters and underwear and water and some fruit and stress tablets and a brand-new English ten-speed touring bike, and the guy adjusted the seat and handlebars perfectly. Also new nylon saddlebags. She bought me a little cassette player with earphones, and she gave me some tapes, and I bought a book. I bought a book called *Ringo* by the same guy who wrote *Iggy*." . . . Then . . . then I say . . . I say, "Good-bye, Smithy."

Norma: That's a nice letter. That's a sad letter. . . . You say good-bye?

(I look out through the glass door of the phone booth where I sit holding Norma to my ear. A red-haired girl is pushing a stroller up the aisle toward me. When did I become so turned in on myself that I swallow feelings like fast food and everything tastes the same salty way? She's waiting. I feel her patience and power. Jesus, I want to be more. I want to be more than I am. The baby is reaching at the passing shelves. The girl smiles, and they wheel away. I'm the one without legs.)

Me: I say . . . I say . . . you know, "Love, Smithy."

Norma: I love you, Smithy.

Me: So . . . so I left Providence, Indiana, on my new bike, and I went through . . . oh, Seymour and North Vernon and Bedford. . . . I'm still on Route 50. And I'm in Huron, Indiana, now. I've got a beard.

Norma: A beard? Wow. I'd love to see you in a beard.

Me: I don't know.

Norma: I bet you look great.

Me: I don't look great. . . . Well, I should go so I can put up my little tent. . . . She bought me a tent.

Norma: I love you.

Me: Hey, Norma?

Norma: Yes, Smithy?

Me: Did I get fired from Goddard?

Norma: Yes.

Me: Bye, Norma.

Norma: Bye, Smithy.

38

We never found out where Bethany had been those months before I came back. I suppose she might not have known herself. I did know it wasn't a gentle place, because some teeth were knocked out, and Bradley Hospital, on top of her madness, found a cracked thighbone and a broken rib. Bethany stayed in Bradley for two weeks while they adjusted and then readjusted her medicine. Pop had gotten her a new psychiatrist, too. A woman named Georgina Glass. Dr. Glass was one of the most beautiful women I had ever seen. She probably had the thickest black hair in the world, and she was tall, and she had gigantic breasts. They gave Dr. Glass an aura, I guess. I really respected her, and whenever Bethany had an appointment at her office on Blackstone Boulevard in Providence, I would go with her.

Dr. Glass was divorced. I knew this because she told Bethany everything. She told her everything, and she expected Bethany to tell her everything, too. She had a couple of boyfriends—a doctor, of course, and a football coach at Brown University. She was lovely, and to see her with my sister was a sort of miracle. She would let all of Bethany's great things out. They would hug after every session.

I had started my job at Goddard. I was on the SEAL Sam line. I hadn't gotten up to supervisor yet, and so most of my day was spent in assembly. Assembly is easy, but after a while it becomes hard. I never got angry, when I was a supervisor, if one of the line people put a leg on where an arm should be. I understood from working the line for seven and a half years that by eleven-thirty in the morning, the arms and the legs looked the same.

On days that Bethany would see Dr. Glass, I would race home—I was still at home then—and take off my red Goddard jumpsuit with the SEAL Sam face on the back and dress up in my charcoal suit from Anderson Little and Co. I was gaining weight by then, and my forty-long jacket wouldn't button, but if I left it unbuttoned, it didn't look too bad. Also, I always put on my Purple Heart pin.

"You like driving me to the doctor's, don't you?" Bethany said, as I drove Pop's car across the old George Washington.

"I guess."

"Why?"

"No reason."

Bethany was quiet for about a minute. She stared out over the black Providence River. "I'm going to go back to work in the thrift shop," she said, sort of matter-of-fact.

"Good."

"Old people come in. Sometimes people that are bums. It's hard to tell if they are, but I can pretty much tell. They want shoes and warm coats. Sometimes they want them and they don't have any money at all."

I turned onto Waterman Avenue and cut over toward Blackstone Boulevard. "What do you do if they want some shoes and they don't have any money?"

"I give them to them."

"Nobody minds?"

"Schnibe," she muttered. "Schnibe, callop, disper."

"What?"

"What?"

"You just said something."

"No I didn't."

" 'Schnibe' or something."

"No I didn't."

Dr. Glass's office was in her brick home near the Brown University campus. The football field was above it, and I parked alongside the concrete bleachers.

"Callop," she said louder.

"What?"

"It's the football field. One of Dr. Glass's boyfriends is a football coach."

"I know," I said. I pretended I wasn't interested, but I was. I liked Dr. Georgina Glass. I liked her name. She was the only Georgina I had ever met. Every time I saw her in the office with Bethany, it was like the first time, because she never remembered me, and so she would always stick out her hand and say, "Hi, I'm Georgina Glass." She was, of course, a lot older than me, but I found her very attractive.

"She gives him blow jobs," Bethany said.

"C'mon," I said. "Quit it."

"Really. She told me before they have sex he likes her to give him blow jobs. Her doctor boyfriend just wants to have the sex."

We walked up the steps to the office portion of her house. I put all that stuff out of my head. I didn't understand why Bethany felt she had to throw all these lies at me, why she had to try to make me feel bad at the expense of Georgina Glass.

Dr. Glass met us at the red mahogany door. She looked amazing, framed by red. I stood to the back right of Bethany, my Purple Heart pin just over my sister's shoulder.

"Hi," Dr. Glass said, and hugged Bethany. She extended her hand to me. "Georgina Glass," she said.

"Smithson Ide," I said in my loudest voice. I followed them, as usual, into the hall, picked up an *Outdoor Life* from a magazine rack, and sat in the small waiting alcove. They walked into the office.

In the doorway Bethany stopped and turned to Dr. Glass. "Oh, I almost forgot."

"What, honey?"

"Tell him," she said, pointing to me. "Tell him you give blow jobs to the coach."

Georgina Glass laughed and threw up her hands. "Bethany, you knock me out." Then, still laughing, she looked over at me. "I give blow jobs to the coach."

"Schnibe," my sister said, looking at me. "Schnibe, callop, disper."

39

Two days after I read my letter to Norma, I rode the new Moto touring bike across the Wabash and into Illinois. I still had a few residual pains from the cop Tommy and from Carl's pickup, but my breathing was easier and the new clothes gave me a sort of clean feeling. It was good to be fresh and on the road. Route 50 still did not disappoint me. It moved through pure farm country until just outside of East St. Louis. I loved the smell of the road. The hay and manure, and pollen from the corn, and even the hard smells of pigs. They were like living smells. I know it sounds stupid, but they were smells with muscles. Each morning the smells were crispy and separated from each other, but as I pedaled into the afternoon, the wet heat of the Midwest mixed all the odors together. Both times of day were wonderful.

The new tent Dr. Trivitch had bought for me was actually quite a bit better than the old one. It was easier to pitch and kept the rain out. The truth was, all the stuff was better than what I'd had. Dr. Donna Trivitch took me to the best outfitter, so that the people who worked there could fit me up for my needs. Two things, though, that shocked me. First, in my new clothes, my belly didn't hang very much, only a little; and second, the Moto bike. See, I didn't notice my belly getting smaller until I put on biking shorts. It was like it just happened. Don't get me wrong, I was still a porker in biking shorts, but I was getting curious to see what I weighed from the 279 that first rolled those flat Raleigh tires down Brightridge Avenue.

The Moto bike was another thing altogether. When did this happen? When did bikes become things like this? This was a jet plane of bikes! This was a happy dream of bikes! It was dark blue, and it looked so solid you would think it weighed a hundred pounds, but you could literally pick it off the ground with one finger. The seat was padded with lamb's wool, and the handlebars curved wide and down and had a soft foam cover. It was a bike that could make me forget my Raleigh (but I would never forget my Raleigh).

I slept exclusively in cornfields while I rode Illinois. Because it was hot during the day, I stayed pretty much to cold tuna sandwiches for lunch and dinner, and lots of apples and bottled water, although in Ryan, Illinois, I treated myself to a steak dinner at Angie's on Main Street. What I did was clean up at a gas station, trimmed my beard, and changed into the chino pants. It was nice to be around folks. There was a couple who sort of reminded me of my mom and my pop, but they had a table full of grandkids with them, and, of course, me and Bethany never had any kids. At night I read *Ringo*. I didn't have to get in reading shape or anything since *Iggy*. I enjoyed *Ringo* very much. Like *Iggy* it was the story of a guy who has a good and interesting life despite all the odds that are stacked against him. Ringo was a cowboy in 1900 Wyoming who had lost his left leg and right arm in an accident. Even though some of the other cowboys made fun of him, he relearned to ride as well as anybody and fell in love with an Indian girl named Doris Redleaf who had gone to Carlyle Indian College in Pennsylvania and had come back to Wyoming to teach little Indians English. It was, I guess, a heartwarming story. I wondered, if I were Ringo, could I have taken all he did? I thought about this through most of Illinois.

I also was thinking hard about Bill Butler. Not about how he propped me up and gave me those three morphine shots and saved me, but I was thinking about Bill and East St. Louis. I knew he was from there, because I used to think he said St. Louis and he was always correcting me.

"Not St. Louis, muthafucka. *East* St. Louis." And East St. Louis was straight on Route 50. I used a pay phone in Mascoutah, Illinois, to call information. There were no Bill Butlers in East St. Louis, but there was one William Butler III on Landham Street. I let the phone ring eight times, then got on my bike and headed into the city.

Now, this is important. I do not feel sorry for myself, and if there was any way to tell about the East St. Louis part of the Bethany trip without having me in it, I would. But there isn't any way that can happen. I even thought maybe I wouldn't tell this part, but I'm going to because it happened, and Bill Butler happened, too.

It was late afternoon when I flew through Fairview Heights and into East St. Louis. East St. Louis happens slowly. Cut fences. Buildings spray-painted with numbers and names. Bags of garbage left even on road islands. Pretty soon you see that the little stores are boarded up and things—everything—looks like they were burned up. Or at least touched by a lot of heat.

There's a scorched feel about the wide sidewalks and metal-clamped stores. It was September 17. I had been riding for twenty-one days, and even though the sky had a soft sun going into blue and the weather was very comfortable, I was feeling discouraged for the first time. For the stretch of a mile past the vacant stores, I didn't see anyone. A dog chased me for about a hundred yards or so—that's it. At the next intersection, I found a self-serve gas station and stopped to use the phone. The attendant sat in a concrete bunker with eye slots made of thick Plexiglas. There was a drop for money for the gas machines, which he could operate from inside. One sign read EXACT CHANGE REQUIRED. Another sign read ANYONE MESSING WITH PUMPS WILL BE SHOT BY ATTENDANT. I spoke into the little voice box.

"Hi," I said.

The attendant's eyes stared out at me.

"Listen, I'm trying to find a pay phone."

The eyes kept staring at me. They seemed more concrete than the little square building he was in.

"Pay phone," I said, mimicking dialing.

After a few more seconds, I walked to my bike and pedaled on. About ten minutes later, I found a small variety store in the middle of an abandoned block. Its signs were in both English and some Asian language. There were some young black kids, boys and girls, standing around on the sidewalk. I asked them if there was a pay phone around, and a girl pointed to the store.

An elderly Oriental man sat on a rocking chair in front of a display of Campbell's Soup, and a young woman, also Oriental, stood waiting behind the counter.

"Pay phone?" I asked.

"There." She pointed.

"I'm going to buy something, too. I'm just gonna use the pay phone first."

A woman picked up on the second ring.

"Uh-huh."

"Yes. Yes. I'm trying to reach Bill Butler. I guess William Butler."

"You tryin' for Bill Butler?"

"Yes. I'm Smithy Ide."

"You Ide?"

"Yes."

There was a long silence, and it wasn't good and it wasn't bad. It was a nothing kind of silence.

"Is this the Bill Butler that was in Vietnam?"

"He was in Vietnam. Uh-huh. Who this?"

"This is Smithy Ide. Ide. Bill saved my life."

"He never said nothin' 'bout savin' anything."

"Is he there?"

She laughed.

"Will he be around later? I'm in East St. Louis, and—"

"Where?"

"Where am I?" I yelled over to the standing woman.

"You are in Great-Full Sunrise Food store."

"Great-Full Sunrise Food store," I said into the phone.

"Chink store?"

"Uhhh . . . okay."

"Go two blocks more into the city, and on the corner they be a bunch of brick buildings. Each building got a number. Butler number be eleven. We be apartment 417."

"Number eleven. Number 417. Okay."

"Uh-huh," she said, and hung up.

I bought some chewing gum at Great-Full Sunrise Food store. I probably should have bought more, because I promised and everything, but I wasn't hungry at all, having eaten four bananas for lunch.

I found number eleven, and then I stood outside door 417. I thought about my sister. I thought hard about her, because, besides being the most filthy, dirty place I had ever stood, even in-country, the halls smelled like Bethany's hippie commune, where they used their own fertilizer. It was that awful. How could people live here? What could they do to make it all right? It's true, then—people can take anything.

"You Ide?"

"Yes."

She was an enormous human being with straightened hair dyed a sort of yellow-orange. The skin was brown and smooth, but there was clearly a lot more of it than a person should have.

"I'm Theresa. Where you parked?"

"I'm on a bike. It's downstairs by the elevator."

"Don't use the elevator. Didn't I tell you that?"

"No."

"Get your bike and bring it up here."

I went back down by the stairs and got my bike. I didn't want to take it back up the stairs because it smelled actually worse than the rest of the building. She held the door open so I could wheel my bike in.

Inside, Theresa's house was perfect. A nice smell of sudsy ammonia came from the kitchen floor. Yellow curtains hung gracefully, covering the window bars. A rug of great beauty, light brown, with a ring of woven blackbirds, lay under a blond dining-room table. A piano was in the living room, an old upright that shined under a coat of blue lacquer. The living room had a maroon wall-to-wall carpet, a curved green corduroy couch, a recliner with a side stick control, and a black John F. Kennedy rocking chair with green cushions. A large TV was turned on, and a little boy, maybe four, watched a Tom and Jerry cartoon.

"I never seen a white man here. Never. Thirty-two years. My mama's place, now mine. Never seen one. Even send the black police. You police?"

"No, ma'am. I'm Smithy Ide. Bill saved my life."

She threw her head back and laughed again. A high and complete laugh.

"That Bill, oh, yes, that Bill. He save lives. He don't say nothin'."

I saw Bill's picture. He was in his uniform, and he smiled out of the glass set on the piano. Next to him was an arrangement of different black people in different periods of an American time.

"This Bill," she said, pointing and smiling, so that her beautiful teeth shined out of her mouth.

"And this Bill's father, Bill, and this Bill's boy Bill."

"Your boy?"

"Uh-huh," she said seriously.

"And Moona, that's what we all called him. Our gramps."

A man with close-cropped hair, comfortable in a World War I uniform, sergeant stripes on his sleeve, stared into the room importantly.

"And this Bill's boy Alvin."

"Yours, too," I said happily.

"Uh-uh," she said, shaking her head. "And my mama, and Bill's mama, who died a young girl, and my girl, Lorraine, who not Bill's, and Grandma Butler, who wrote a history book and was a dentist. I'm not foolin'. She go out of St. Louis in 1921, and she come home from Boston, and we got the papers. She had her office on Brookmayer, and Bill's gramps and his grams lived by the mayor's. That's true."

"I believe you."

"Sit."

I did.

"Bill saved your life?"

I told her. Theresa was silent for a little bit. Tom and Jerry music played in the background, but her difficult breathing pretty much drowned it out. She straightened some things on the upright and sat down on the piano bench. She wasn't old. She couldn't have been much more than forty, but she was as tired as anyone I had ever seen, and it made her seem old. Very old.

"Bill, he just fill up a place with Bill. He so happy and so . . . filling, you understand. He always, never ever not, happy. He think he win with that smile and that laugh and the way he touch people, and I mean even the ladies, which sometime make me cry, but it nice to see how he get everybody laughing and such. That big smile. His big face. And he good. That thing that good about folks, so big in Bill. Big. Dancin' and singin' and laughin'. Too bad, too bad. That Bill's thing. That what Bill does. He pick up people. He get people up. I'm not surprised he save you. You understand? He savin' them all with that laugh and that smile, but nobody miss it till they push him away. And till he have to make Bill laugh himself. Bill dance for himself. Wine do that. More and more of that dancin' for himself."

Theresa looked into the room at the little boy. "You put that lower, hear!" she shouted.

"Bill sometime come, but not for a long time. He out there. You seen them. He a wine man now. Bill a wine man."

Theresa stopped talking. She looked at me passively, a matter-of-fact look, but something happened in that big body and that flat face. She began to cry. I reached over to touch her hand, but she pulled away as if I were something hot.

"That it. Nothin' more. If I ever see him again, I say the man who you save be here. If I see him."

Theresa didn't have to tell me that she didn't feel very good about having me in her house, her apartment. I said thank you and went over to my bike. I had turned it facing the door, when it opened and a young man, nineteen or twenty, walked in. I never say things like this, but I promise you he looked more like Bill than Bill did. We stared at each other.

"I'm Smithy Ide," I said.

"He know Bill. He know your father," Theresa said, almost apologetically.

"Your father saved my life."

"He Bill's boy Bill," Theresa said wearily.

I reached out my hand. In one fluid motion, as fast as I imagined the old gunfighters were, Bill slapped my hand away and brought a small blue metal handgun up to my face. Theresa let out a scream and fell onto her knees praying to God. The little boy ran in and stood next to his enormous mother. My mouth went dry. I felt dizzy.

"He gonna be shot, Bill?" the little boy asked.

Bill took a deep breath and seemed to suck all the energy from the room. His torso expanded out as if challenging the world.

"Sure I'm gonna shoot him. Shit. The white man know the drunk. He know the drunk."

Theresa's prayers and exhortations for mercy for me had dropped to a soft, sobbing mumble.

"He know the drunk piss himself. He know the down drunk. He know the clown drunk. The clown drunk save his white ass."

"Baby, no, baby, baby," sobbed Theresa, crawling, really crawling on her hands and knees, to her son.

"Mama, stop! Mama, get up! Charles, get your mama out of here."

"I can't get Mama anywhere, Bill. Mama too big."

"Baby, no. Baby boy, no."

"Stop!"

Bill's eyes were wet at the sight of his mother prone in front of him. What had happened between him and my Bill, or white people or anything for that matter, didn't seem important. I could feel the barrel now pushed into my left eye. Theresa was grasping at his pants.

"Please. Oh, God of the righteous, please save my boy. Render his heart . . . oh, baby. Oh God, please."

Bill turned from his mother and glared at me. Tears were now pouring down his black face. The wet lines of rage shone, and his terrible hand shook. Slowly he lowered the gun.

"White man," he groaned at me. "White, white man."

He looked down at his mother. I could feel some blood flowing into my legs. I pushed my Moto out of the apartment and ran down the stairs. There were lots of young black men in the dirt front yard. No one seemed older than thirty. There were no women either. I walked my bike past them. The sun was sinking red.

"Red sky at night, sailor's delight," I said stupidly, stupidly, stupidly.

I couldn't take a full breath. I got onto the bike, and for the first time since my pop ran around behind me while I tried to balance without training wheels, I had to concentrate on the act of pedaling. I turned onto the first street I came to, then took another turn, convinced that young Bill just might change his mind.

INTERLUDE

Dear Smithy,

This is my own letter to you, only I won't send it. I'm writing this by a window in my room, and the window is open. Outside, the maple in your yard is fluttering, and I'm just going to let that breeze carry this to you, because it can and because I truly believe that words can float.

I have done everything, or started everything, right here. My things comfort me, my work sustains me, my reading informs me, the music I've gone in and around with colors me and adds texture to it all. So it was not only good to savor or learn to savor what's mine but somehow right to arrange things so I wouldn't be broken by my experience. Do you understand that? Not *can* you, but *do* you? I know you can understand everything because I see you still bringing her back again and again, whispering to her, books in your back pocket. You.

And I know you stopped understanding, because it was easier, only you can't anymore. You're needed, and you have to arrive. And I have to arrive, too. Because I'm needed. You tell me over and over that you don't know, but you do. As much as anybody can know. It's all pretend, Smithy Ide. It's all how we construct the world. I refuse to believe that you don't see that. We have to get through, and if we're really lucky, we can find somebody to get through with. To share the map. To make the good choices and the bad choices.

Maybe I have been a fool. I don't think so, but I don't care if I was. The sky and my dreams all mix together. For so long I couldn't get back to me. I couldn't sense if it was warm or cold or snowy or anything. And it wasn't my body, which in so many ways hasn't failed me. Has been there in its incompleteness and at the same time made me complete. Yes, I know you can understand that, too. Maybe you shake your head and say you don't know, but that just won't work anymore. You need more, and people need more than a head shake.

I'm cold now. My arms are getting goose bumps, and my breath is fogging. I'd better close the window. I'd better finish the draft of the yacht and move on to the new Fleet Banking Center I'm doing the drawing of. But before I close it, I have to throw one more thing into the wind. When I was twenty-two, I cut my foot somehow and, of course, couldn't feel it. Didn't notice it until it started to swell, and I had to get it drained at the hospital. They almost took it off. Yes, they almost did. I cried and cried, and they didn't understand that. They said my feet were just in the way. They honest-to-God said that. Because of the infection and the medication and really because I hadn't yet started to work out and take responsibility for myself, I sort of went into a five-day, hospital-room dream. And in that dream I walked with a boy all around East Providence. Everywhere I remembered. We walked holding hands, and we both wore our hair long, and it kept bouncing onto our shoulders. And then we were walking in other places. Past rivers with mountains in the distance and flowers in high meadows. Indian paintbrushes and mountain lupine and asters and columbines. And he said, "I hope you will think of me." I dreamed that. But I believe it happened. And I believe that boy was true and very beautiful.

I'm closing the window,
Norma

40

I sat in my pop's den looking at the phone. I wanted to call Bethany's new doctor, Georgina Glass. If I called, I could say, "I'd like to come over, maybe discuss Bethany's progress, maybe take a walk while we talk, maybe you could tell me about those blow jobs." I know. I look at things, always look at things, wrong. I'd just like a date. I could say something like, "Hi, I'm not sure you remember me, but I'm Smithson Ide, war hero, scars all over the place, and not yet all turned to shit, and I was wondering if maybe you'd like to go out with a young guy." But there was the coach, and there was the doctor, and I'm fresh from the SEAL Sam assembly line. Why couldn't she just call me? *Hello? Is this Mr. Ide? May I call you Smithson? Do you think my breasts are too large or just about right? Could you come right over so we could discuss it?* I wish things would happen like that.

Calls not made. Opportunities missed. I don't want to dwell on that right now.

Bethany.

I picked Bethany up at the Thrift Center at Grace Church. She came out still wearing her apron. She was now seeing Dr. Glass, Georgina, every Tuesday and Thursday. We were all still pretty psychiatrist-shy at the Ide house, but we had to admit that Dr. Glass was a definite step up from "the golfer," as my pop had taken to calling Glenn Golden, who still refused to even consider the reality of Bethany's voice and insisted instead that she was just sort of a nutty girl.

I had bought a 1968 VW Beetle. It was gray and ran good. I don't think I could squeeze into one of them now, but then it was easy. My sister got into the passenger side.

"Drive slow," she said.

"I always drive slow," I said. "How was work?"

"It's not work. It's not really work. Don't be a fuckoff."

I was quiet. I guess work was not good. I watched the road. She watched me.

"Fucking asshole," she said.

"Stop, jeez."

"Stop, jeez," she said, mimicking me.

I didn't say anything. I took the fastest route to the east side of Providence. We took the Red Bridge.

"I jumped off this bridge. I almost died. I ruined everything. Thanks a fucking lot. Thanks for reminding me. Maybe I ought to do it again. Maybe then you'll be happy. I hate you."

I didn't look at her. The Red Bridge. I took it without thinking. Maybe I deserved this.

"Maybe you ought to die. Maybe you ought to jump off the bridge. Maybe I ought to grab the steering wheel and put us both out of our misery."

Bethany punched me in the arm.

"I'm not kidding," she said.

"Stop."

"Stop," she mimicked.

I turned onto Waterman Avenue, then onto Blackstone Boulevard, and parked near the Brown Stadium. Bethany didn't speak at all as we walked down the sidewalk to Dr. Glass. She met us at the door. She had on a blue skirt—pleated and hanging just an inch or two below her knees—a silky white blouse, and a string of large pearls that rested happily on her chest.

"Hey, sweetie," Dr. Glass said, giving Bethany a kiss on the cheek.

"Hi," bubbled my sister.

I would have felt a lot more comfortable if the name-caller had shown up for Dr. Glass, but I had the feeling Mr. Voice was too smart for that and was getting smarter.

"Hello, Mr. Ide," she said, shaking my hand.

She remembered my name! She knew now that I was connected to her patient.

"Hello, Dr. Glass," I said. I felt she may have held my handshake a split second longer than was necessary, but I couldn't be sure.

Bethany and Dr. Glass went into the office, and I read, as usual, in the waiting alcove. I read an old *Outdoor Life*, I remember, until a shaken Georgina Glass came out about fifteen minutes later.

"Mr. Ide?" she whispered urgently. "Can you come in for a second?"

I knew immediately what had upset Dr. Glass. She was always so light and airy with us all, it was obvious she had never seen the things the voice could do. The poses. The stillness. There, by the corner of the doctor's delicate black antique desk, Bethany had thrown out her left arm, brought her shoulders into a hunch, and frozen.

"She is not moving. She is not moving," Dr. Glass said anxiously but softly. "Even, even . . . is she breathing? Can she not be breathing?"

"No, she's breathing. It's happened enough so I know she's breathing."

We stood next to Bethany and watched her closely. There is another thing about the pose. It's mesmerizing, hypnotizing. It's terrible because it seems so utterly unnatural, but at the same time it is amazing and beautiful.

"I've never seen anything like it. Can she hear us?"

"I think the voice hears us."

"The 'voice'?"

I looked at the doctor and stepped away from my frozen sister.

"There's something inside of Bethany. Always has been. It ruins things. It tells her things and tells her to do things, and she does them. I hate it."

"She hears voices?" Dr. Glass asked, very surprised.

"She hears a voice, the voice. I tried to tell the other doctor . . . Glenn Golden. . . ."

"I know Glenn. . . ."

"He wasn't interested. He didn't believe it. That was before I had

219

to go to Vietnam, where I was wounded and became a sort of hero and came home without a girlfriend or anything."

"You went to Vietnam? You poor boy."

"Well . . . you know . . . I'm a lot older than I look."

She stared again at my motionless sister. "Why wasn't I told about any of this? Why wasn't any of this in her case report?"

Dr. Glass had none of that formal sort of pleasant stiffness that she had when she'd meet us at the door. She was so put off by Bethany that she had dropped the doctor stuff. She moved more sensually, if that's the word, as plain old Georgina Glass. I took a deep breath.

"Well, Georgina, you told me and Mom and my pop that you wanted to get all the dope from my sister herself. And a lot of the stuff, the voice stuff, wouldn't be in any reports, because Dr. Golden didn't believe it. I wasn't around long enough while he was treating her, because I had to go to Vietnam, where I was wounded eighteen or twenty times and won the Purple Heart."

"You won the Purple Heart?"

Now, some people might think I was being a little prick talking about myself with Bethany stuck right there in her pose, her still life, but there is comfort in knowing where she was at any given time. Sometimes, especially when I was younger, I used to wish there was a way she could live forever in a pose, so we would always know the voice couldn't take her away.

"Listen," I said, "I know this looks like a stupid time to ask, but—"

"How old are you?"

"How old am I? Now?"

"Yes."

I was gaining weight. I was working a job. I was twenty . . . soon I'd be twenty-one.

"I'm twenty . . . six."

"You look younger."

"A lot of people tell me I look younger, too."

"I'm thirty-nine."

She smelled, and I will not lie about this, like peaches. Really. Peaches. The skin on her cheeks and forehead was moist. Her breasts easily supported the hang of pearls around her neck.

"What do you think about thirty-nine?" she said, watching my eyes.

"I think thirty-nine is wonderful. I think there's something about thirty-nine that's fantastic."

She laughed. "I said thirty-nine, not sixty-nine."

Sixty-nine? Did she say that? Did she?

"So what do we do? Do you call an ambulance? How long does it last? Are you sure she can't hear us?"

I called my pop, and he drove over with the station wagon. We put the backseat down and spread some blankets and laid Bethany inside.

"Will she be all right? Will it last long? Maybe we should take her to the hospital."

I told Georgina that she'd sleep in her room and tomorrow she'd be fine. We made another appointment for Bethany to make up for this lost one, and I followed Pop home in my Volks. I felt pretty good about myself, I will admit. I felt I had put my best foot forward with Dr. Georgina Glass and in the very near future I would, maybe, be out with her. And maybe I'd take her to the Grist Mill in Rehoboth and get a table near the waterfall and order a nice wine with my earnings from the SEAL Sam assembly line. I was very hopeful.

But in the morning Bethany did not wake out of her pose, or the next morning, and by the weekend we had to get her back to Bradley Hospital for liquid food. Something new was happening, and we knew it.

We never talked about it, but we knew it.

41

The longer you wait and put off the nice things you should do on a regular basis, the harder it is to do them, until finally you have to force yourself to be nice, to be thoughtful, and it isn't easy, because you're embarrassed about not having done those easy, nice things in a natural kind of way. Also, the people who you're nice to come to expect your regular niceness. That's it in a nutshell.

It was raining hard in the middle of Missouri. An autumn rain, and cool. I had given up trying to stay dry. It was the fifth straight day of hard rain. The cornfields had gotten so muddy I was sleeping only in rest areas and small-town parks. My gear was so soaked that for the last two nights I hadn't even bothered setting up my tent. What was the point? Man, I was feeling sorry for myself. Thinking about things. Talking out loud. I'd go along on that wonderful bike, those touring tires firm on the slippery road, and I'd just talk.

". . . and you're a genius, too. You get on a Raleigh, and your fat ass all hangs out of the seat, and Shad Factory and people all laughing at you. Who's gonna visit the graves? Why are you on the bike? I hate you, you goddamn slob. . . ."

I talked for hundreds of miles and ate bananas in the rain. Now I had gotten myself sick, right here, in the middle of a Missouri monsoon. I had lost my energy, and I had a terrible headache and even the runs, which I hate in the rain especially. I had to walk the Moto maybe the last fifteen miles to this rest area. There was a restroom, a soda machine, and a phone bank with six phones. Some truckers had pulled in and, I'd say, fifteen or twenty cars, to sleep until daylight. It was past one in the morning. I used the toilet and a forest of paper towels. I rummaged for change, but if I had any, it was at the bottom of my pack, so I settled for water and, of course, a banana. When I leaned my bike against the phone bank and picked up the receiver, I was shivering so hard I had to push the number four separate times until I got it right. Even at this hour, she answered on the first ring.

"Hello."

"Hello, Norma."

I tried to sound relaxed and comfortable, but an arctic wind blew my words to East Providence.

"You're shivering! You're sick, aren't you? Aren't you?"

"Norma, Norma, I'm sorry, I'm sorry about not calling. I'm—"

"You're all shivering!"

"I'm always screwing things up, and who's gonna visit them, I was thinking, who's gonna, I don't know, put the flowers and—"

"Smithy . . ."

"—prayers and stuff. It's just raining and raining. I feel—"

"Smithy, don't . . ."

"I feel so . . . old all of a sudden."

That was it. That was what I felt. I was so tired and so old. My long hair made the bald spot much clearer, and my beard came in with heavy strips of gray. But what was wrong with a guy crying to poor Norma?

"Smithy. Will you listen? Will you listen? If you don't think enough of me to listen, then tell me so and I'll hang up! Now!"

Norma never had one emotion working alone. Never. It was as if some mad scientist mixed all of the feelings into different combinations. Norma was very complex. But she always said what she felt.

"Don't hang up, Norma," I whispered, probably in a voice as pathetic as had ever traveled fifteen hundred miles. I heard Norma fill her lungs and exhale.

"I won't hang up, Smithy. I'll never hang up on you."

The rain sheeted down heavier than before and drummed onto the metal roof of the phone bank.

"Is that the rain?" she asked.

"Uh-huh, listen." I held the phone stupidly in the direction of the metal roof. "Can you hear that?"

"It's a heavy rain."

"It's been raining for five days. I'm so wet I don't even pitch my tent anymore."

"You should pitch your tent. I want you to."

"I wanted to call. I . . ."

"It's okay."

"No, it's not okay, because I wanted to talk to you about Bill and Bill's boy. I got saved in the army. Did you know that? And now Bill is one of those homeless people, and his son wanted to kill me."

Norma didn't say anything, so I leaned against the rain and told her everything. And telling everything made me feel good and less ashamed.

"That's so sad. Poor Bill and poor Theresa, and even though he had that gun, poor Bill's son."

"I know."

"I wish we could help them."

"I know."

"Do you think we could?"

"I think, I think later on, I'm going to try. I don't know. I know a nice priest who has ideas about being strong. I don't know."

The rain had lightened into a mere downpour, but it still pinged loudly against the phone bank.

"You know what I've been working on, Smithy? I've got it spread out right here on my drafting table. I've been working on the blue-prints of a new yacht that Blount Shipyard is building. It's going to try to race in the America's Cup."

"I bet it's beautiful."

"It's like a rocket ship on water. Do you need money?"

"I'm all right."

"If you need money . . ."

"I'm hardly spending anything. I've got about two hundred dollars. Really."

"Would you tell me if you needed money?"

"I would."

"I love you, Smithy."

Another truck pulled into the rest stop, a couple more cars. I wonder what they thought about me, in the rain, on the phone.

"What's your room like, Norma? Is it . . . do you have all your favorite stuff around? I mean . . ."

"I spend most of my time here, working and all, so really it's my domain, I guess. Let's see, I bought a new, very good Persian rug in Providence, and it covers all but about a foot around the edges. It's red and gold, very intricate design. Soft. I've got my business things on either side of the drafting table. My table is blue, usually the drafting tables are brown or blond, but I had them put a nice robin's-egg lacquer on it. . . . There's my fax machine and two computers with design capability and CD-ROM and things, and the phone and printer and rolling side table that I keep my pens and paper on. I've got a Mary Cassatt print of a mom and her daughter. I've got an autographed picture of Teddy Ballgame—"

"Ted Williams? Really?"

"Pop gave it to me. It was Pop's."

"I remember."

"I miss them, Smithy. I miss them so much. Pop . . ."

Through bad weather all across the states, Norma fought off her tears. I liked that she missed them. I missed them. Sometimes now, when I see Bethany in a field or a cloud, I see Mom and Pop, too. Pop always has his uniform on. He always has his baseball bat.

"There . . . there's my library, too. . . . I call it my library. I have one whole wall filled with books. Reference books, novels . . . and then I have my big old brass bed. I have it on the corner of the rug next to the bookshelves. It's a huge bed. It was made in 1844. I bought it at an estate sale in Barrington."

My headache was not going away, and now my ear, my right ear, was hurting, but it was better than aspirin to hear Norma describe her dry, sweet room.

"If you were here, I'd put you to bed and keep you warm all night. I'd just hold you and hold you and, and . . . and you could . . ."

"I could hold you, too, Norma."

Somewhere between the middle of Missouri and East Providence, Rhode Island, were our words. And the words hung on the line like soft pajamas. And we hung, too, even in the rain.

After a while Norma said, "Pitch your tent."

"Okay."

"Promise?"

"Okay."

"Okay . . . go do it now so you can get out of the rain."

"Okay . . . bye, Norma."

"I love you so much. . . . Bye."

I pitched the tent next to the picnic table. I didn't use my wet sleeping bag for anything more than a pillow, but I managed to sleep some. I woke up to sun and spread all my things out over the picnic table to dry. I had the rest of my fruit—two bananas and a pear—went to the bathroom, and waited for my clothes to dry. I read my book, *Ringo*. My ear didn't hurt.

42

I put people off. I must. When I got back home from the Denver hospital, I realized I had nobody my own age in East Providence I was friendly with. I knew some people, sure, to nod to if I saw them in Stop & Shop or the drugstore, but as people I could, say, call up at night or go to a movie with . . . well, I wasn't connected in that way. It's a very New Englandy thing, this being alone even though you don't want to be. It proves, I guess, that you're above being lonely and can take or leave friendship. So, then, I was a loner who wished not to be alone. It's something I have thought about and thought about, and I now feel that at any given time there are a lot of lonely loners out there. We just don't understand the process of making some friends. The complicated format of friendship. It's not easy.

I was spending a lot of time at Bradley Hospital with Mom and Pop. Bethany was just not making the kind of progress she used to make. She wasn't responding to anything, and for the very first time, her voice made no bones about being in there. It was demanding and loud and awful. It screamed at us when we were alone with Bethany. It called us horrible names in that dry, cracking desert of a voice. But it was madness, and they knew madness at Bradley, so the staff was understanding toward Bethany and comforting to us.

It still hurt, though. It still made us wince and hold ourselves up by thinking about something else. I'm sure, when she was truly horrible, Mom and Pop thought about all the nice things our family was and what a sweet human being my sister was at the center, her poor center. I thought about the certain roundness and neatness and push of Dr. Georgina Glass's wonderful chest. I thought about how nice her hair fell and how blossoming her smells, but mostly what turned me away from Bethany's vicious accusations and loud curses were the doctor's imagined breasts and hoped-for . . . well, nipples. Because I did notice these things. It was, in a way, my awareness of the world, my connection. And it wasn't lurid or creepy either. It was a notice and then a thought. A sort of daydream with flesh. But what I'm saying is, it wasn't a preoccupation. It was an introduction to liking someone, say, in the way a girl's eyes or skin or lips make you want a date. That's all. It was essentially healthy, this breast thing.

One afternoon that week, late afternoon after work, I met the folks at Bradley. After an hour or so of Mr. Voice, I went into the hall for a smoke. Dr. Glass was at the nurses' station and waved.

"Hi, Dr. Glass," I said as I walked over.

"Hello, Mr. Ide. Our girl is being pretty tough, huh? I changed her medication, but short of something that'll knock her out, it doesn't seem to be slowing her down."

She had on gray slacks and a light blue sweater. This time the pearls hung between her mounds. I looked at my cigarette so I wouldn't stare at them.

"How are your parents?"

"They're, you know, used to it."

"How are you doing?"

"I'm used to it, too."

"And the war and coming home and whatnot? Are you adjusting?"

It has always bothered people that I didn't have to go through some kind of adjustment. Actually, I was adjusting so many times from since I can remember, five or so, that if I did have to adjust, I didn't notice it.

"Yes," I said.

She said something to one of the nurses behind the desk. I put out my cigarette. "Bethany has an appointment on Thursday, Mr. Ide. And of course she won't be making it, but why don't you come by yourself, same time, and maybe you can give me a better insight into your sister."

She wrote something on a nurse's chart, speaking to me casually but not looking up.

"A little one-to-one," she said.

One-to-one, I thought. Oh, yes, Dr. Glass. Smithy Ide one-to-one with Georgina Glass.

"Uhhh," I said thoughtfully. "Okay."

The day and a half until Thursday dragged the bottom of the oily Providence River. It trudged along like a grandfather. Thursday itself moved even slower, and the assembly line went on forever. If there were arms and legs on the wrong sides of SEAL Sam, I was too distracted to notice. At four I punched out for my one-to-one.

Georgina met me at the door in jeans and a Brown University sweatshirt. "Hi, c'mon in."

I followed her into her office. She gestured to a blue-and-red wing chair opposite her desk. "Want some coffee or a soft drink?"

"No thanks."

She sat down at her desk. "I saw your sister about ten this morning. She wasn't growling or anything like that."

"Yeah, the last day it's gone back in there."

"Who?"

"It. The . . . you know . . ."

"The voice?"

"Yup."

"Ah." Georgina wrote something down. "Did you kill anyone in Vietnam?"

"Huh?"

"In the army. Did you have to kill anyone?"

"No, I didn't kill anybody. I never even discharged my weapon."

"But you got wounded."

"I got wounded all right," I said. "I really got wounded. I got the Purple Heart."

"And now you're home. Living at home?" Dr. Glass shifted in her seat, and the Brown University crest fell slightly between the outlined points. Did I live at home?

"Well . . . you know . . . I'm helping my folks out with Bethany. It's just until I'm sure they can handle things. I'm . . . you know . . . I got the Purple Heart and everything."

Dr. Glass smiled at me, and it was a very pretty and, I would say, girlish smile. But maybe not. "It's all right to live at home. I lived with my parents after medical school until I got married."

"I would want my daughter to live with me until she got married, too," I said, like someone with his high-school diploma posted on his forehead.

"And Bethany lives at home because . . . ?"

"Because of the voice. It's a different situation with Bethany. She's beautiful, but there's that voice, and it does things that mess her up. It's hard to explain. I like the way you've done your hair."

"My hair?"

"Yeah. It's nice. That's a ponytail kind of thing."

"Not really, it's just longish in the back."

"Longish. That's what I meant."

"You think it's an entirely different personality, from the perspective of, say, a division of selves? That far?"

"Uhh . . . it's just, I don't know. I like it."

"What?"

"Your hair."

"I was talking about Bethany's voice."

"Oh, of course. Well, yes, yes, a . . . of selves."

"You're very close to your sister, aren't you, Mr. Ide?"

"Yes, and it's okay to call me Smithy."

"Smithy. How close?"

"Well, she's my big sister. Sometimes she gave me good advice about stuff, and I was always helping find her, and she's got a wonderful beautiful voice—singing voice I mean, not the bad voice—and we talk about stuff."

Dr. Glass wrote down some quick thoughts on a small pile of index cards she had stacked on her desk. She leaned back on her chair. Her breasts shifted ever so slightly to the left. She didn't speak for a while, so I did.

"We'd . . . you know . . . well, we were interested in Pop's baseball—he played with Socony—and we'd go and be together and talk and stuff."

A big cat curled up on a corner of her desk.

"That's Mitsi. She's a good girl. You're a good girl, aren't you, Mitsi?"

Mitsi yawned and closed her eyes.

"What about sex? Have much in the army? High school?"

"Huh?"

"Intercourse."

"Well, I . . . I guess, for sure. I mean . . ."

"I'm sorry, I didn't mean to shoot that question out of nowhere, but I'm curious, frankly, from all I've observed of Bethany, to know the extent of your relationship."

My blank face may have stayed blank—I'm not sure—but the raw endings of my nerves twitched me in that chair.

"For example, Bethany at one point told me that you often showed her your penis as a boy."

My mouth was open, but the words were not there. I might have made a slight sound like a cry a million miles away.

"And that often you would touch her and finally you would have sex with her."

My upper palate had no moisture. My mouth was sand dry. My lips stuck together.

"She . . . she . . . what? What?"

I was absolutely at my Purple Heart point of tears, but my small brain warned me not to let them out.

"She said . . ."

"I heard."

I stood on wobbly legs and walked behind my chair. Oh, Bethany, I thought. Did that goddamn voice really make you believe that? I'm Hook. I'll always be Hook.

Dr. Glass watched me calmly, but I felt a little touch of hostility. Maybe. "Bethany told me—and I must say, in the kind of detail that might stretch a fictional account—that your fucking her became a daily routine. Almost a way of life."

To answer something that the mind's picture of is so revolting, so past anything ugly I ever imagined, seemed beyond me.

"She told me she knew how wrong it was, but you were so insistent and then violent. She's showed me pictures. Pictures of her face all scratched and bruised. You just had her over and over until her mind was broken, didn't you? Tell me. At least tell me the truth so we can start healing that poor little girl." With those words Dr. Glass threw down four photos that Bethany had kept from the four major "accidents" the voice had caused. The pharmacy, the Red Bridge, the hippie commune, and the prom. I recognized each one. There were three taken by the police and one by a plastic surgeon. I knew she saved them. I never knew why. I looked at them and arranged them slowly, chronologically, on the desk. I was crying now. I was crying for my sister. The events of each terrible day roared over me. Of course, Dr. Glass took it all as the remorse of the pervert Smithy Ide.

"It's all the proof I need to go to the police, Mr. Ide, and by God I'm going to."

She pointed to the pharmacy photo.

"Remember this one? You beat her over and over, until she finally gave in." She pointed to the Red Bridge photo. The one used in the follow-up story by the *Providence Journal*. "And this one?"

There was no mistaking Dr. Glass's vengeful anger now. "How you threw her into your swimming pool and wouldn't let her up to get to your mother's cabana. You just kicked and pushed until she acquiesced. And this?"

Dr. Georgina Glass slammed her fist down on the photo of the prom, where we had found my sister mosquito bitten and scratched. I sobbed to think of her, alone, in that swamp. My poor, poor sister. "Look at what you did, Mr. Ide, when you scratched her over and over while you kept her tied in the basement. What kind of a person does such a thing to his own sister? Answer me, goddamn it."

For the first time, I looked up from the pictures and directly at Dr. Glass. She stepped back from her desk.

"People know I'm here with you. Don't try anything. I've got all the dates and the times. For your own sake, come clean. You have to end this cycle. You're as sick as your sister. You have to act fast to re-activate your soul."

Her tone softened. Her fists unclenched. She took a deep breath.

"Look, I know you must suffer horribly over your actions. Remember last Thanksgiving?"

Last Thanksgiving my lungs collapsed in Denver. Last Thanksgiving they stuck tubes in my chest and inflated me like a cartoon character.

"You told your folks you were going to go to the family lodge in Vail for a little relaxation. You only did that because you knew that Bethany was already there."

"Last Thanksgiving?" I asked through my sniffles.

"Don't play dumb. It's time to start healing yourself. Bethany. Look . . . I know how you kept her a virtual prisoner in Vail and then Aspen, and I won't even get into the Paris thing."

"The Paris thing?"

"Okay, have it your way. You're a terribly sick individual, Mr. Ide. Terribly sick. And like most sick people, you have affected the well-being of everyone around you. And I'm not surprised your parents have failed to protect Bethany. Maybe they didn't know, maybe they did, or maybe the rich just live differently than we do."

"The rich?"

"Nevertheless I'm going to the authorities with this. Bethany gave me permission."

"Dr. Glass . . ."

"Good-bye, Mr. Ide."

I walked to the door of her office. My eyes ached and threw short, incredibly sharp stabs of pain back at my brain. I put my hand on the doorknob and talked to the door.

"We don't have a swimming pool," I mumbled.

"Did you say something?" she said.

I turned around. Dr. Georgina Glass stood behind her desk with her hands on her hips. Her feet were spread apart. I have seen pictures of matadors standing next to dead bulls that did not give off anywhere near her sense of victory. "I said, we don't have a swimming pool."

"Well, that—"

"No pool. None, and we don't ski at all, let alone have a place in . . . where?"

"You don't have a place in Vail?"

"No."

"Aspen?"

"No, we don't. That . . . that first picture . . . that one on the left . . . your right . . . East Providence police took that at the drugstore she worked at. The next one, the swimming pool one, is when she jumped off the Red Bridge."

"She . . . jumped off the Red Bridge?"

"Yes, she did."

Dr. Glass narrowed her eyes and thought hard. She didn't look nice. She looked old, at least to me. If she lifted up her sweatshirt, I would have closed my wet eyes before I would look at those previously interesting breasts. "I suppose you have an explanation for last Thanksgiving."

"No."

"I thought not."

"I asked the doctors why my lungs just collapsed in the army hospital in Denver and why Thanksgiving Day they had to stick tubes in my chest to pump me up, but they said that it just happened. They couldn't give me any explanation. No."

"Oh," she said.

I walked out of her office, and then I walked out the front door and down the steps. By the time I turned onto the sidewalk, she was at the door.

"Sorry," she called.

43

I finished reading *Ringo* in Colorado. I had now read two books by Harold Becker, the author. Here is what he would say about Smithy Ide:

Page one. "*He sailed across the open plains like a jayhawk. Blown high and wide and away from everyone. He felt that Kansas was the most beautiful of places, until he saw the push of the Rockies outside of Goodland. But maybe this Smithy Ide was a plainsman. Maybe that would be his legacy. A momentum of bike and body blown high and wide through the history of jayhawkers.*"

That's the style. A little flowery, but this Becker guy could take a common person and describe him like a knight, or a hero, even if the odds were stacked so high. Iggy, with all the prejudice and stuff that went along with being black in 1878, never felt sorry for himself at all. And Ringo, with one arm and one leg, sat taller in the saddle than anyone. It just took him a lot longer to get up there. I didn't have anything to overcome, except maybe my fat ass, which dropped off somewhere in Missouri—or, at least, part of it did. Even the clothes that the doctor in Indiana had bought for me hung loose.

This October—I can say for certain because it was October—the American plains swayed orange and gold. The days were Rhode Island crisp, and the nights and early mornings were freezing. I rode hard, one day even going three four-hour jaunts. Twelve hours. Blew a tire outside of Oakley, Kansas. Fixed my tire at Ray's Bike Shop, had a pile of fried chicken, and then found a sweet, flat field about two hundred yards off the road to set up my tent and even build a fire out of scrub wood.

In the morning, cows looked in my tent, and their heavy tails swished against the nylon material. I lay wide awake in my warm sleeping bag, feeling particularly secure. I suppose that comes from the toasty bag in the middle of the freezing field. I ran my fingers along the sides of my chest. I could feel my ribs. I mean, I knew they were there—people have ribs—but I hadn't felt my ribs under the layers of me for maybe twenty years. I felt the cavity the bottom of my ribs formed around my stomach. "Losing weight," I said out loud.

That afternoon in Keana, Kansas, a town that was a gas station, I weighed myself for a nickel. Two hundred twenty-eight pounds. I stepped off the machine, put in another nickel, and weighed myself again. Two hundred twenty-eight.

Possible?

I stood on the machine, looking stupidly at the meter.

"That means . . . that means I've lost fifty-one pounds," I said, again, out loud.

Possible?

I made numbers in my head. Had I been gone thirty-three or thirty-four days? Fifty-one pounds?

"Norma?"

"Smithy. Hi. Hold on one second. I have to put my screen saver up on the computer."

"Do what you have to. I can wait."

"I have a Mac. There."

"Macs are supposed to be good."

"It's got a lot of capabilities. Do you have one?"

Oh, my God, this girl. There was a huge world out there, and she wasn't afraid of it one bit.

"Why?"

"People can have fun with them."

"I don't think I could learn how to use one."

"They're easy. I'll teach. I'm going to teach you, Smithy." Another Smithy-Norma pause. A nice pause. A moment filled up and not at all uncomfortable.

"Norma. I lost weight."

"You don't have to lose weight," she said, as if she were defending my right to be a load. "I like you just the way you are."

"I'm in Kansas. Kansas is beautiful."

"Oh, Smithy. Kansas. You've taken your bike to Kansas. I'm looking at my map. Kansas is ridiculously big."

"Big and flat."

I told her about the cows and the weather and the way I get almost hypnotized by the road after a while. She said, "I love you, Smithy."

And for a second I saw Norma in Pop's baseball hat, with a hot cocoa, and the Red Sox filling up our porch. I think it was that spirit, and then the metal chair was just nothing to her. I saw her in it outside the funeral home. I saw her tall and almost angrily proud, and I missed her. I hadn't really seen her more than forty-five minutes total in thirty years, but I missed her so much my stomach ached.

"I . . . I miss you, Norma. I really miss you."

Another good silence. Another wonderful, filled-up, forty-some years of silence.

"Oh, Smithy . . ."

More silence. More long Kansas wheat-and-cow pause. Sun-dipping pause.

"Bye, Norma."

"Bye, Smithy."

So much is Kansas, then. So much room and so many rolls of the earth. That writer, that Harold Becker, would say in that Iggy way, in that one-arm, one-leg Ringo way, he'd say, *"Sometimes in the afternoon, when you squint the glare away, you can't tell if that old girl Kansas is the sky or the sky is the earth. It turns you around so."*

44

I wasn't mad at Bethany. I figured that the damn voice was doing the terrible lying to Dr. Glass. I wasn't mad, but I never went with her again to the doctor's office. How could I?

Bethany got better—that was the important thing. She got out of her cloud and healed nicely, except for a narrow rip scar from the corner of her eye to her temple. But it was a real small scar, and unless you were looking for it, you wouldn't notice it. She cut her thick hair short and began wearing eye makeup that made her eyes look enormous. It was a pretty look, maybe beautiful—at least that's what Jeffrey Greene of Attleboro, Massachusetts, thought.

Jeff Greene was twenty-seven when he met my sister. His mom had to go to Bradley because she kept having mental problems. Jeff told me "mental problems." I don't know any specifics, and, really, I don't think anybody else but loved ones should know certain things. That's what I think, but I don't know. Jeff would visit his mom, then go sit in the patient park for a smoke, and one day he met Bethany.

Jeff used to visit his mom once a week, because he didn't think she knew he was there at all, but after he got to talking to Bethany, he began coming every day. They would sit and talk for hours and hours, and Dr. Glass told Mom and my pop that Jeff should get a lot of the credit for Bethany's snapping out of it. He even brought Bethany home on Sunday afternoons when she was allowed out, and finally, when she was released, he decorated his car with signs saying BETHANY IS GOING HOME, and he took her.

I was, I guess, a little jealous of Jeff. I was usually the one looking after her, but now it was Jeff, and, really, he was very good at it. I had moved into my apartment in Pawtucket, near Goddard, so it was good she had Jeff, but I worried. You know what I mean? I'm a worrier. Anyway, Jeff had what I thought was a great job. He was the manager of Benny's Home and Auto Store on Newport Avenue in

Pawtucket, and lived, like I said, in Attleboro, in a nice house he had just bought. Jeff Greene was a guy that had things falling into place. And he deserved good things. Not only because he was in love with Bethany, but because he was one of those genuine hardworking people my father admired, even if he was Jewish.

"As long as he's good to Bethany," my father would say.

"I just don't know," my mother would say.

But after a while we all found we liked Jeff very much. He was tall and heavyset and walked a little flat-footed, which was why he didn't have to get drafted, but he had so much energy, and when he was around, which seemed like all the time, we had energy also.

The change in Bethany was so complete, love and all, that the joy popped back into Mom and Pop's house. Pop went back to the base-ball field as a third-base coach for the Socony Sox, and we'd all go to the games when we could. It was a wonderful time, although I was having trouble meeting people, and work was boring, and the tall lagers were filling up my nights, and while Bethany was returning to normal, I had begun to lose my face in a storm of food and alcohol. Still, it was great to see her so happy and herself.

Jeff now accompanied her to her visits to Dr. Glass. Bethany had started working as an assistant librarian at Ann Ide Fuller Branch, under the East Providence water tower, and whenever he could, Jeff Greene would drop in and visit. When I think of Jeff, I think of this guy waiting to say hello to Bethany and give her a little kiss and then be happy just to stand next to her. I understand this. It would be great to get to a place where there's comfort all around in just being somewhere.

One Sunday afternoon, after the snow had melted and the early spring flowers and grass were pushing up all over the place, Jeff picked Bethany up and drove to Colts Drive in Bristol, Rhode Island. It's a long walk built along the ocean, and it is pretty amazing and pretty beautiful. People from all over like to stroll around and look out to sea. It's nice to see people like that. Looking. Thinking.

Jeff looked out to sea, too. He stuttered, tried to say something, stopped, looked out to sea again, and stuttered.

"What, honey?" Bethany said, squeezing his arm. She had on a turtleneck Irish fisherman's sweater and a Red Sox baseball cap.

"I was wondering. . . ."

"What?"

Poor Jeff Greene. There's this good guy not being able to speak.

"You know. . . ." He reached into his pocket and handed her a small blue snap box. There was a ring inside, and inside the ring he'd had a jeweler write BETHANY AND JEFF, 1972. Bethany held the ring in her hand and stared at it with her mouth open.

"I love you, and I want to marry you," Jeff said, nice and stupidly.

"Oh, Jeffrey," said Bethany, a waterfall bobbing out of her eyes.

"Will you?"

"Oh, yes. Oh, I will. I love you, too."

45

Okay. Be me. You're speaking to Norma from a phone booth, and you have to tell this story. Tell me how I tell this story. Oh, and it's cold. It's got to be cold enough so that if it starts to rain, you know it will be snow.

The story.

Kansas spoiled me. Even though I understand there was a gradual incline and the altitude was always rising, the key word was "gradual." Colorado, after the high-plains part, from where I entered at Holly, still on U.S. 50, through Rocky Ford, where I got off 50 and onto Colorado Route 10, and on into Walsenburg, was fine—until I slipped onto Route 160 and up into the mountains. I felt like I was just starting. If there was enough air, it surely hadn't settled around me. I wasn't putting in twelve hours, or ten, or, after Walsenburg, even eight. I biked and walked like a snail, six or seven hours a day, and barely had the energy to pitch my tent, which I had to do because it was now seriously cold.

The stretch between Fort Garland and Alamosa across that high valley took me two whole days, and it probably was only forty miles. I was pretty discouraged, although I did tour Fort Garland, where Kit Carson used to be the commander. I was the only one on the tour. A little old guy in a cowboy hat gave the tour and spoke for maybe twenty-five straight minutes and didn't look at me once, except when I raised my hand.

"Question there?" he said looking at me.

"Where did he get killed?"

"Carson?"

"Yes."

"No idea."

Alamosa was a kind of old and new American town, with the new outskirts and the heavy old main street. I liked it, but I was too cold to enjoy it. I stopped at Wal-Mart and got ready for the Rocky Mountains. Wool socks, longjohns, a space age alpaca sweater, good gloves, jeans with a red flannel lining, a blue wool cap, and insulated work boots. I had to pay just over a hundred dollars. After I stopped at the grocery store for bananas and water and oatmeal cookies, I had less than fifty dollars left. I put my other clothes, except the shorts and sweatsuit and sneakers, in a Goodwill bin.

I slept that night at the most beautiful rest area I had ever seen. It was in Del Norte, and it was maybe a half mile off 160. It had a clean bathroom and a neat mowed field where I could set my tent over soft grass. I slept great, and in the morning the sun blazed down on that valley so bright you'd have thought it was August. What a day! It had to be around sixty degrees. I started riding in my sweats, but after an hour or so, I switched to shorts and a T-shirt. It was that warm. Really.

Route 160 outside Del Norte takes a dip into South Fork, making the ride easy, and the mountains, near and far, made it beautiful. I was so mesmerized by the beauty of it I took the wrong turnoff. Instead of staying on 160 for the climb into Durango, Colorado, I veered right across the clear headwaters of the Rio Grande River and into Mineral County.

I followed fifteen miles of wide fly-fishing water on a narrow road that cut through rock slides, lava flows, and cottonwoods. The road grew narrower and narrower until it came to a small settlement called Wagon Wheel Gap, then immediately opened into a long, curving valley of river and grass bordered by amazing mountains and foothills

I was, I guess, reenergized. By now I had figured out that the road I was on was not Colorado 160, but the ride was level and warm, and fishermen were throwing flies at every other bend. At a point where the road was closest to the river, I pulled off onto a dirt jeep trail and rode down to the riverbank.

I had seen pictures of rivers like this. You know, long, grassy banks easing gently down into crystal-clear, pebble-bottomed water, rapid and powerful, then settling into perfect deep holes and pools, each one holding hundreds of river trout and rainbow trout and, just maybe, cutthroat trout. I had assumed that the pictures I had seen had to be some sort of trick photography. But sitting on the bank of the Upper Rio Grande eating a banana, the sun falling on me, I have to say that there are rivers like this. True.

I spread my map on the dry grass. Here was South Fork, and here, right here, was where I'd screwed up. I went right. If I stayed on this road for about eight or nine miles, I would come to Creede, Colorado. From there this new road simply disappeared into the mountains. I was not discouraged. I would relax a little, have another good banana, and go back to 160. I suppose I could have felt stupid about missing the road. It's not like I'm a bus or a car or something traveling so fast it's understandable not to see a sign. But I didn't feel stupid. Actually I felt wonderful to have spent a moment with this river. The water over stones made a kind of hum. I lay back on the grass and closed my eyes. I fell asleep.

It must have been hiding just over the mountains behind me. Friendly-looking mountains with a narrow tree line and rounded tops. Soft-looking mountains, really, but behind them was a storm ready to get me. The temperature must have fallen quickly—but not so quickly that it woke me. The snow, too. It must have been just a puff of snow at first, because when I finally opened my eyes, I was lightly covered with wet snow, and a swirl was just beginning. It came unbelievably quick. I could see nothing, and my body felt stiff and, I suppose, like frozen food.

I felt for my bike. I reached out in every direction, not daring to stand up, because I honestly felt that the wind, the power of the snowstorm, could have lifted me into the river. The bike! I felt down to the saddlebags. It seemed incredibly stupid to do, a waste of time, maybe impossible, but I pulled the tent out, felt for the metal stakes, staked it, and pushed up the fiberglass poles until they mounded the nylon. I unsnapped the saddlebags from the metal bike frame and pushed them into the tent. It rocked into a right angle. It would rip out the stakes unless I added my weight. Inside was dark and cold. I sat huddled in the center of the tent concentrating on holding it to the earth. That's when I heard the cry.

At first it was a small sound, like an angry crow in the distance, but as I listened, I heard this little voice yelling "Help," yelling "Help me." And the squeak of tears. I knew that frightened sound. My heart was pounding in the high, cold air. I crawled out of the tent.

"Oh, please don't blow away," I said out loud.

I am not brave. I don't have to tell you that. Not by now. I would always like to help, but there's a lot of, I guess, unsure stuff working in me.

I stood in front of the tent and leaned into the wind for balance. I listened hard. The wet snow pinched at my face, and then I heard it again. The cry for help. A sob.

"Stand still and keep talking!" I screamed.

"I'm afraid!" it screamed.

"Stand still and keep talking! I'm coming!"

"My name is Kenny. My name is Kenny. My name . . ."

"Don't stop!" I screamed. I was closer now. I wanted to go in a pretty constant line, so I had at least a chance to get back to the tent.

"My . . . my name . . ." He started crying. Great, huge cries. Louder than he could talk. I sensed him directly in front of me and grabbed at air until my fingers closed on his T-shirt. He was small, and I picked him up and slung him over my shoulder.

"My name is Kenny! My name is Kenny!"

"You can stop now."

"My name is Kenny!"

I walked in what I prayed was the direction I had come in. I walked until I was at the river's edge. I had missed the tent. Panic started in my feet and knees. It always starts there for me. Panic weighted me into the already calf-deep plop of snow. I moved away from the bank and, in a side-slide sort of way, I felt in every direction with each slide of my freezing feet. I hit something and reached down hopefully. My tent. I ran my hand around it, feeling for the entrance. When I extended my arms, I couldn't see my hands. Snow like that seems beyond belief. A waterfall of snow. Cold. Whipping. The tent flap.

I fell on my knees, folded Kenny inside the tent, and crawled in after him. He was whimpering a little and shivering. I couldn't tell for sure if he was shivering because of the cold or from fright, but he was wearing only sneakers, T-shirt, and shorts, so cold was a good bet. It was black inside the snow-piled tent. I took my flashlight and pulled out my sleeping bag.

"Take off all your wet clothes," I told Kenny.

He was nervous about taking off any clothes in front of someone.

"I'll turn my back. Take off the sneaks and stuff and get in the bag."

I counted to fifty, so he had a lot of time. When I turned around, there was a little square head with a blond crew cut, maybe ten years old, sticking out of my bag.

I pulled my longjohns, wool socks, and lined jeans out of the pack.

"Your turn to turn around," I told him.

I changed into the heavy, warm clothes and shoved the others back into my knapsack. Outside, the wind made sounds like a lot of rockets taking off. I imagined the trees shooting out of the ground. The tent rocked but held. Snow weighted it like a little igloo.

"You're Kenny, huh?"

"Uh-huh."

Suddenly I had an image of more Kennys out there.

"Were you alone?"

"Yes."

"Good. I'm Smithy."

I held my hand out for a shake. He took it. His teeth chattered.

He put his hand back into the bag and lay on his side facing me. I put the saddlebags at the end of the tent and laid my head against it. We listened to the wind.

"Are you hurt anywhere?"

"I don't think so."

"Good."

"I live in Creede. I skipped school."

"You skipped school? That's not good."

"I went fishing."

The wind and the snow rocked us hard for a second but subsided, and for the first time since I woke to the snow, I could hear the rush of the river.

"Catch anything?"

46

The weeks following Bethany's engagement to Jeff Greene were happy ones for the Ides and, I have to say, especially for Mom. It was so sweet to see her sitting at the kitchen table with my sister, planning and laughing and even talking about her own wedding, although it had been sort of different, as Pop was getting ready to ship out for the war and they didn't even have a honeymoon—but, of course, a bride's memories are always shining. I think. I hope so.

Bethany and Jeff's plans were roughly this:

A June 11 wedding in an ecumenical setting with one of the Episcopal priests from Grace Church and Jeff's rabbi, who he hadn't seen since he was thirteen but who he liked. They were going to honeymoon for one week in Nags Head, North Carolina, on the beach and then live in Attleboro, where Bethany could work at the Benny's Home and Auto with Jeff, until they felt the time was right for little Greenes.

This was the sort of news I loved. There was order to it. I mean, you knew the old ABCs of what was happening, and the chance of you getting all screwed up was pretty limited. You make the plans, write it down, easy. Mrs. Alivera, who was a friend of Mom's from the neighborhood, took Mom's wedding dress and altered it to exactly the style and fit Bethany wanted. So that was perfect, too. Mom's only daughter would be married in her heirloom, fixed up though it may be. It was a good time. It was one of the really good times. Getting ready and all.

47

Roger eased my bike into the back of his pickup, and Kenny hopped into the middle of the front seat.

"We'll be back fiveish," Roger said to his wife, Kate.

"You drive safe."

"I will."

Kate kissed me on the cheek and gave a hard hug that lasted as long as a little prayer. "Thank you, thank you, thank you."

"Thank you, Kate. And Roger and Kenny. Thanks for everything."

Roger and I got into the truck, crossed Bachelor Creek, and rolled out of Creede toward Durango. I had stayed with Kenny and his folks for two days. They wanted to do something nice for me because of getting Kenny out of the storm. It was all a little embarrassing, that I would be rewarded for doing what a human being should do, but I suppose it was good for them to say a loud thank-you.

The storm had lasted into the night, slowing down, then driving forward, so that by early morning twenty-six inches of snow had fallen, and the drifts on either side of the tent formed a natural sound barrier.

Kenny was sleeping—snoring, really—when I pushed out from the tent opening. The snow seemed packed, and my hands got wet from the water content. It was a heavy snow, and there was great difficulty in reaching the top, but I did, one hand first, then the other, until slowly I had created a sort of tunnel opening. I stood. The snow in drift came easily to my waist. For a moment the reflection of the first light blinded me, and I had to close my eyes until the sensation of red went away. When I opened them again, I saw one of those sights almost too beautiful to be real. A valley as utterly white as a cotton ball and through it a zigzag of river so blue it seemed to be ink. It was warm, and I was sweating under the heavy clothes I had put on. Then I heard the engines. I looked to the road, but no plows had been through to open the valley. The engines grew louder. I concentrated on the sound, but in the valley it bounced off trees and hills and seemed to come from everywhere. I looked out over an amazingly loud field of white.

I saw them all at the same time. Three skimobiles, white and orange, zooming in a wide parallel through the valley. One on the road, one in the center of the field, and one on the ridge above the river. I waved and shouted. They all got to me at about the same time. There was a pretty young woman and a fat-faced redheaded guy both wearing green police jackets, and a man with a red checkered jacket and camouflage pants. Red Check was frantic.

"Seen a kid? Seen a kid?" he screamed as he drove up.

"In the tent!" I yelled over the engine.

"What tent?" the redheaded cop asked.

I looked at the snow behind me. The tent was totally buried.

"In there," I said, pointing to the hole I had crawled out of. Red Check dove in headfirst and emerged pulling my sleeping bag with Kenny inside it.

The policewoman stepped through the waist-high snow to Kenny. The other policeman kept his eyes on me.

"How long you had the boy?"

"I'm not sure. You know . . . how long did it snow?"

"Don't be a wise-ass. Answer the question."

"I'm not sure how long he was in the tent."

"Where'd you take him from? Where'd you get him? What'd you do to the boy?"

You know how when you get so angry it kind of gets beyond anger and you want to kill the thing that makes you angry? I don't get like that. I drop them. It's as if I can't see them or hear them anymore. Especially after Dr. Georgina Glass. I turned away and looked at Kenny, his little head looking at the other two, his living, unfrozen, going-on little head.

"Answer me, shithead!"

I high-stepped to Kenny and the others. Red Check was crying, and it was relief I heard in his sobs. I spoke to the young woman in the police uniform.

"I was on my bike, and I pulled off for a nap by the river. When I woke up, it was snowing, so even though I thought it was stupid, I set up my tent. Now I'm glad I did, because it got worse and worse, and then I heard Kenny. I was just lucky to even get him. He was wearing these summer clothes, and they were wet, so I got him into the bag, and I got my warm stuff on. We were lucky."

"What's that son of a bitch saying?" the other policeman roared from ten feet away.

"Thank you! Thank you!" cried Red Check.

"He's a lucky boy," the young woman said.

"I asked that pervert a question! I asked him a goddamn question!" screamed the other one over the roar of his skimobile.

"Kenny says you saved him. Thank you," the weeping Red Check said again.

The young woman smiled at me. She tried to take a step forward but stumbled and began to fall. I reached for her quickly, for her waist to stop her from tumbling into the tent, and the fat-faced, red-headed guy shot me.

48

With Bethany's wedding about a month away, Jeff Greene was spending an awful lot of time at our little house in East Providence. May was a great time in Rhode Island. Everything pretty much blooms and blossoms, and people take walks, and old Italian men sit in their tiny backyards—stuff like that. It was an easy time, and the Ides felt easy.

One of those evenings I remember, I came over from my apartment near Goddard Toys for dinner. Mom had made codfish cakes and boiled potatoes and a salad with ice cubes in it. It was European, I guess, to put ice cubes on your lettuce and cucumbers, but it was wonderful. After dinner Bethany and Mom stayed giggling in the kitchen, cleaning up, and me, Jeff Greene, and my pop went into the parlor to watch Curt Gowdy call a Red Sox game. I never knew for sure, but I think Jeff hated baseball. Hated the whole activity, but he knew we believed it could save you, so he'd watch and sort of try to get excited.

Around the fourth inning, with Cleveland up at bat, I heard something in the driveway, or thought I did. I got up and peered through the venetian blinds, but I couldn't see what it was, so I went out to the back porch. Some light was coming off the porch, and right before the light went black, on the edge of the asphalt drive, sat Norma in her chair. She looked up at me with such pain and loss I can't even see it in my mind's eye, because it was so terrible. For a few seconds I just stared as if I were captured by her agony. She reached for her back wheels and pulled out of the throw of light. I could only see her feet and the sparkle of chair.

"Hi, Norma," I said, as if I didn't have years to be ashamed of. As if I hadn't seen her face. Seen her eyes.

She said nothing at first. Silence that starts awkward, then moves to self-conscious, and finally lays out like another defeat.

"They didn't kill you," she said, when I couldn't stand our pause a second longer.

"I'm fine."

"I'm a dog," she said. "I'm a dog and a cat and a rat. I'm nothing."

There is courage a man—well, anybody—should show. A resolve. A goodness. A heroism that puts away all the things you're unsure about and sends you off the porch, arms out, heart open, holding, embracing. I remember 1972 as the year of my cowardice. I said nothing. I let her sorrow float through me.

"I'm . . . I'm nothing, Smithy," she said again.

I knew she was crying because of her breathing and sniffling. Quietly, absolutely, and alone.

"Nothing," she cried again, even softer.

Bethany nearly pushed me down, shoving past me to the screen door. She rushed down the steps and flung her arms around Norma. Mom was behind her, and the two held her completely, as if holding a child against a storm.

"What is it?" Pop said, coming out onto the porch.

"It's Norma," I said quietly.

"It's Norma? It's my Norma?" And Pop was there, with them, an almost total hold of Ide. Even Jeff Greene oddly walked down the steps to be with them and away from the Sox.

I stood in the porch door. For the first time, I felt air escaping through my wounds. I felt altered. I felt changed. I was something else, and I remained it a long time, and I saw it reflected in Norma's stainless chair as surely as in her eyes, just out of the light.

49

Red Check was named Roger, and he was Kenny's father. The bullet had grazed my neck, turned me around, and sent me into the snow-filled Upper Rio Grande. It was rivers again. Rivers and bullets and the crazy people that we've all become. Not me. I really and truly thought, as I bobbed up from the icy trout pool, that no matter what, I would never, ever live a suspicious life. A silly life, sure. Ridiculous, maybe, but not looking for lousy things everywhere. I mean it.

The river was high and rising quickly with the fast-melting snow. I swirled dazed in a crystal whirlpool, then was wedged hard under the overhanging bank. I remember seeing Roger then, only we were out of the water and lying in the snow and shouting and engines and then Bethany. Our backyard. She might have been twelve or thir-teen, and she had had her hair cut boy-short for the summer. She was walking on her hands, and her legs were straight up and down. Norma and I sat at a picnic bench, although I don't remember a pic-nic bench in any of our yards.

My pop had on his baseball uniform, and Mom had made the big tuna-salad sandwiches that were, of course, much, much better than my pop would make, because he never had the patience to break up the clumps of tuna and cut the onion into small pieces or mix the mayo smoothly into one nice spread. Norma had her arms around me and was dressed like a six-year-old, except with way-too-big bib overalls, but I didn't push her away or anything. I have always felt bad about the ten-year-old me. I was pretty mean to Norma. I guess, when I think about it, there wasn't much niceness to go around after Bethany had taken it all.

They put me in an ambulance that drove behind a county snow-plow. They took me to a small medical center in Creede. The wound, it turned out, was just a nick, but I had a little shock from the force of it whizzing so close. They gave me a couple of Tylenols and cleaned and dressed the wound.

Kenny's father and the lady policeman stayed while the doctor worked on me. I was embarrassed. Kenny's dad, Roger, was embarrassed for all his crying over Kenny. The lady was embarrassed because her partner had shot me. We were all just embarrassed. Here I was, back in the hospital, in a paper dress, with my ass all hanging out.

"Your blood pressure is great for a big guy," the doctor said.

In East Providence at last year's Goddard blood-pressure screening test, where you got an extra hour's pay if you participated, my blood pressure was 170 over 115.

The doctor removed the blood pressure strap from my biceps.

"It's a hundred over sixty-five."

"If it's good, it's lots of bananas," I said, going stupid again.

We walked out of the hospital, the four of us, and rode to Roger and Kenny's house.

"What about my stuff?"

"Brian—that's the officer who . . . Brian is getting all of that. The snowmobiles, too," the policewoman said.

"But my bike . . ."

"We'll get your bike, don't worry," Roger said.

We came to a low gray house with a blue-shingled roof, set on a rise over an old silver mine. It was easy to see that whoever had built this place originally had something to do with the mine. A zigzag set of wooden stairs made its way to the opening of the shaft.

"Want me to come in?" the policewoman asked.

"You don't have to, Marjorie. Thanks. Sorry about   "

"Hey, it's your kid, you got a right."

A tall, round-faced, very pretty woman came running from the house and scooped up Kenny in strong arms. Her long, curly hair fell onto her shoulders in brown and gray. She had on khaki slacks and a blue-jean shirt. She wore beads that looked like Kenny had made them for her in school. Roger had called from the hospital to say

255

we'd found the boy. From what I'd heard in the ambulance, she had gone with another search party in another direction. Her relief was sweet to see. She squeezed Kenny and cried. Crying is good. The idea of a little boy in that snow by that river is, I guess, unbearable. She put him down, walked over to me, took my hand, and led me into the kitchen. She sat me at the table, a long oak table, old, with lots of wonderful meals in its past, and ladled squash barley soup into my bowl.

"I'm Kate," she said.

"Hi," I said, slurping my soup. Eating with other people will always trouble me. I am not a comfortable man. Even in the army, when my body said I never ate enough, I always felt I was being watched and that I was eating too much or not eating right. Later on, when I actually didn't eat right and food and I collided, it became impossible to eat with people. I felt comfortable at Kate's table. And I felt good. I sipped in some barley, some tender yellow squash.

"Mmm."

"We're vegetarians," Kate said.

"Although sometimes I'll eat some meat," Roger said.

"Roger doesn't eat much meat. We like Kenny to see we eat healthy. See that we can grow strong on legumes and veggies and really good breads."

"I like bread!" yelled Kenny.

We went quiet for a minute. They watched me dip my bread into Kate's amazing vegetable soup, and I didn't care. But I wanted them to be comfortable, and I knew they were not, and I knew why.

"This is the best soup I have ever eaten."

Kate looked embarrassed.

I looked up at Roger and smiled. He smiled back.

"Kenny's a really brave kid. He did everything right. Remember, Kenny?"

Kenny smiled and started to yell. "My name is KENNY! MY NAME IS KENNY!"

"He kept saying that in the snowstorm until I got to him."

"We can't thank you en—"

"You don't have to thank me," I said, interrupting Kate. "It's good for me. It's a good feeling. Look . . . uhh . . . look, at the hospital I guess you saw me with my shirt off, and I was in the field with a bike, and maybe you think I'm a bum or something or—"

"We don't."

"No . . ."

"But it's okay if you thought that. I might think that, but I'm . . . I'm not homeless or a bum or anything. I want you to know all the holes I got were from the war—"

"Vietnam?" asked Kate.

"Yeah. No big deal, but I'm not . . . you know . . . like, look, I know what we could do. I would be so thankful if you'd do this. Would you call Norma? She's my friend."

"She's your friend?"

"It would be nice to call Norma. She'd love to talk to somebody. She'd tell you about me, and I guess I want you to know. I don't know why, but I want you to know."

Kate brought the phone to me, and I dialed Norma's number.

I stopped before I finished the whole number and looked at Kate. "Don't tell Norma he shot me."

"That idiot!" Roger said, clenching his fist.

"Okay? Don't tell her?"

I finished Norma's number and handed the phone to Kate, who took the receiver into a corner of the kitchen.

I couldn't hear the conversation, but every now and then Kate would look over to me and then turn back into the corner. I went with Roger, and he showed me the rest of his home and told me about his family. Roger and Kate had been married for twenty-five years—and for fifteen of those years, while his business in Oklahoma City was growing, his family was not. They couldn't have a baby. They tried everything and finally adopted Kenny. That's why they moved to this little town in the mountains. To give Kenny every chance to be closer to real life. That's what Roger said, how he put it. Real life.

I loved that some people could talk to other people like that. I was bursting that Roger would include me in the telling of his story.

They didn't know what they would do or how they would make a living, but they knew they had to come here. Now Roger is a roofer and jack-of-all-trades, and Kate has gone back to her weaving. Kate made rugs.

"And we're gonna have another kid," Roger said in the living room.

"That's great," I said.

"A Hispanic kid or something. We told them we don't care."

Kate's rugs were everywhere, and a closed-in porch held a pile of material and a large loom.

"Kate's really an artist," Roger said.

"Her rugs are beautiful."

"They are."

Roger had done over the house himself. One room at a time. It was originally built for the wife of prospector George Ryan of Denver, who discovered silver in this slope. He married a Denver teacher in 1881 and moved her here. She became a famous hostess, and he became more and more of a nutty millionaire miner, who liked to sleep in the tunnels. Sometimes he'd stay in the tunnels for days at a time. Once he was gone for a month, and when he came up to ground level, his skin was white as a sheet, but he had mined a thousand pounds of silver. Sometime in the night, he murdered his wife, put the silver back in the mine, and disappeared. Now Roger and Kate live here, and Kenny, and pretty soon their new child, whatever kind doesn't matter.

"I'm still looking for his silver," Roger said seriously.

When we had circled back to the kitchen, Kate's conversation with Norma had turned tearful. But they were the good kind of tears, at which I was becoming an expert, and I knew that Norma had them, too.

"... but he reached out and caught him. He caught him as if he were falling off a cliff. He put him in the tent, and now we've got him back. . . . Uh-huh . . . oh, he is. . . . Yes, I know you do. . . . I'm going to put him on, because I'm going to start all blubbering again. . . . Remember, it's definite . . . as soon as you can. . . . Bye, honey. . . ."

Kate held the receiver out to me, then put her arms around Roger. "Poor Bethany," she said.

"Who?"

I felt Norma in my hand. Is that possible? "Hello, Norma?"

"Smithy. Oh, Smithy. I want to hold you. I want to be there with Kate and you and everybody. You saved that little boy."

"It really wasn't—"

"I . . . told Kate all about Bethany. Are you mad?"

"I wanted you to, Norma, that's why I asked her to call. I kinda look like a bum, and I—"

"You don't! You couldn't! You're beautiful."

"I'm not beautiful, but I'm not a bum or anything. See, I've got a beard, and my hair is kind of long where I have hair, and I'm on a bike and things."

"I told Kate you were beautiful. I told her I'm in a chair and what I do, and I told her about Bethany and Mom and Pop and why you're riding your bike, and she told me things."

"Why am I on the bike, Norma?"

I felt her silence. I imagined her giving me the quiet, and knowing the quiet also. Through the kitchen window, snow gleamed, and I had to stop myself from worrying about my bike. I suppose what Mom always said was true. Everything is relative. She said it, and now I got it. Other people worry about big things, I worry about my bike. Or something.

"I think you're on a quest."

259

There were still gold leaves on the aspen. Up on a ridge, I saw some horsemen in a line.

"You think I'm on a quest?"

"I know it sounds silly, but every now and then great men have gone on quests to find answers to the big questions. There have been books written about men who search the whole world for answers."

"But what if I don't know the question?"

"You know the question."

The horsemen drifted over a ridge and out of sight. Bethany leaped from the top of the aspens. She turned once on the tallest tree and followed the horsemen.

"I love you, Smithy."

"I'm tired all of a sudden."

"I want to come out. I want to take care of you."

"I'm so tired. Jeez. I'd better . . . I'll call you tomorrow."

"I'll dream about you, Smithy."

"Bye, Norma."

Tired. Oh, God, tired. "Sleep," said my mom. "Sleep," said my nana.

"Bye, Smithy. My Smithy Ide."

50

Aunt Paula gave the wedding shower for Bethany. It was at her house in East Greenwich, and Uncle Count had the homestead standing tall. He had the neighborhood kids working on the yard and bushes ten full hours on Saturday, while he rubbed down the brass fixtures inside. Uncle Count loved brass. He had a brass wedding ring. Honest to God. Uncle Count had worked out all the arrangements with Aunt Paula. Because he wasn't invited to the shower, because he was a man, he would confine himself to the general areas of the house and yard. That way the Count would be able to carry out his unofficial duties as family host, while still allowing a thin separation of men and women.

"Hello, sweetheart," he would say in his inimitable style to every female who rang the front doorbell, whether he knew her or not.

"You look yummy. You look good enough to eat. Listen, there were these two homos in Belgium. . . ."

About twenty-five women, ranging in age from twenty (our neighbor Adella, who was retarded) to eighty-two (Ethel Sunman from church), were greeted in like fashion.

"Baby, you're the greatest."

"Va-va-voom."

"Tell me it's a mirage."

and

"Couple of queens go to a bar. . . ."

"Five queer guys are shooting baskets. . . ."

"I got nothing against homos, but eighty-five of them are on a bus. . . ."

When they all were finally gathered around my sister in the living room, Count did a silent head count.

"Twenty-five, counting you, Paula."

"That's everybody. Thanks, Count."

"There was a football stadium filled with fags. Iowa. Cornfields and everything, but this one big stadium, and this guy who was not a fag wanders into the place. He buys a hot dog. . . ." The girls all smiled politely as the master of ceremonies presented his exit routine; then they turned back into the room and my beautiful, beautiful sister. It was late May and unseasonably warm, and the girls all sported casual spring ensembles. They all looked lovely, especially Bethany, who, as Mom said, had a radiance about her. She wore a peasant's dress of light blue and a kind of Indian band around her head. The band was red and beaded and went with her eyes. I could see that Jeff Greene must have thought he'd struck gold. She was such an honest-to-God nice human being, 99 percent of the time.

Paula and Count's beagle, Wiggy, jumped around in the pile of gift wrap and gave little-guy barks every time one of the girls crinkled up the paper. He would jump from lap to lap and end up on Bethany's, who sat on the floor surrounded by her stuff. She put a big blue ribbon around his neck, and everybody called him "Blue-Ribbon-Winner Wiggy."

My sister got sweaters and soap and lingerie. Rhode Island didn't have the dirty lingerie, the naughty kind, where you could see nipples and things, but they had these short little satiny, shiny nighties that were very sexy, and this is what Bethany got. I prefer the dirty kind, but I never knew anybody who would go with it, except maybe Dr. Georgina Glass, and by then I never wanted to see her again, dressed or partly clothed in one of those blackish net things that let almost everything out with her large breasts squeezed against the little silky squares of net all sweaty and sexy and everything. I mean. You know. Maybe. I don't know.

Aunt Paula was a fantastic cook who loved to experiment with food. In Uncle Count she had the most appreciative and encouraging partner a great cook could have. She would sit in the TV room while he watched a show, and she would read her cookbooks. Every now and then, she'd say, "I'm thinking of trying something new. How does a sirloin steak, lightly seasoned with pepper and garlic, braised only slightly, then simmered for a few minutes in a mild chili sauce, which is then served over the accompanying rice, sound?" Count would turn to her, make a bold gesture of turning off the TV, stand, and say, "You make me happy, baby. Va-va-voom." It was common ground. It was a meeting of the minds. As long as Aunt Paula used her kitchen utensils like magic wands, she would never, ever be taken for granted.

For my sister's shower, Aunt Paula turned to Francis Gerard, whose previous cookbooks had been among her favorites and whose latest one, *Fun, Food, and Fantasy*, she absolutely loved. From its pages she chose a unique luncheon consommé (aux profiteroles), saddle of lamb (Prince Orloff), sautéed tomatoes, a delicate dish of flageolets, and a Gruyère soufflé. She even had Mogen David wine, which was sweet and which was Count's favorite, even though he was confined to a different part of the house. The girls thought this was the fanciest, nicest luncheon they had ever had—except for Ethel Sunman, who fell asleep and missed it.

The party broke up slowly, and there were lots of tears and kisses. Mom probably held Bethany's hand as one by one the girls filed past her tall and wonderful child. When it was all clear, Count came into his TV room with his tray of leftovers, and Mom, Paula, and Bethany cleaned up.

It was always nice at Paula's. Count was unique and funny and, really, I guess, a very kind man. He could be blunt and sort of odd in a usually inappropriate way, but, as my pop always said, "That guy would give you the shirt off his back." And he would. After a while everybody kissed good-bye, and Mom and Bethany drove back to East Providence.

Count had two more servings of the lamb and questioned Aunt Paula extensively about this guy Prince Orloff; then they watched TV.

It wasn't for about two hours that something in the back of Count's head told him that wherever Wiggy was, he was being aw-fully quiet.

51

The guy who shot me found my great bike after all. We put it in Roger's workroom, and he and Kenny polished it and oiled it. I ate lots of vegetables and rice and juice stuff, while my things dried in the high mountain sun. I spent a whole afternoon watching Kate at her loom and talking about my sister and folks and Norma. It's true that I'm a man who has a hard time talking about anything, but it was easy with Kate, and I found myself saying my feelings in ways I never had been able to before. Like Bethany. God knows I loved my sister, but in some ways, probably because I never really stood up to her voice, I hated her a little, too. Hate is hard to admit. Somehow, with Kate building a rug in the middle of that sunny room, it seemed at least all right to know it. Somehow.

Kate called Norma again that night and told me she thought they could be real friends. Good friends. I thought so, too. In some silly way, I thought I had done this really wonderful thing for Norma. At least I was glad to have helped friendship.

So Roger and Kenny drove me and my bike and stuff to Durango. It was a pretty day, sun and clouds and chilly, but I was dressed for the weather, even prepared a little. I felt encouraged when I looked at my road map. I had come more miles than I had left to Los Angeles. Just knowing that made me feel great. And vegetables also. Roger taught me stretching exercises, which I added to my vitamins and bananas and spring water and other things I was learning about. I had a new book, too. Kate had given it to me and said it was an appropriate book for me. It was called *Suzanne of the Aspens*. It was a fat book, and I hoped I would like it.

I said good-bye to Roger and Kenny and pedaled across the San Juan River down toward New Mexico. My route would take me through the Navajo Reservation. Kate told me that the reservation is the size of New England. Now, that's large. Almost too large for me to think about. I like things, or I'm finding out I'm liking things, better when I see all their little parts first. That's good. I knew that if I saw some of the little parts, I'd understand better, and understanding has been a problem area for me.

By nightfall I had gone sixty-five miles, which, considering I got a late start out of Durango, was pretty good. In those sixty-five miles, the country changed completely. It was as if you came off a mountain and at the bottom of the mountain was a desert. It just spread out there in the semiflatness. Wind cut out of nowhere. I pulled off the road, lifted my bike over a fence, and walked in maybe fifty yards from the road. Far enough that the whiz of trucks and cars wouldn't rattle my sleep. I staked out the tent and pushed my saddlebags inside. I spread out the sleeping bag. After I had a quick supper of cold rice and beans, water, and of course a banana, I snuggled into my bag and began *Suzanne of the Aspens* by flashlight.

This was the true story of Suzanne Bowen who left Boston, Massachusetts, with her husband, Captain John Bowen, who had fought in the Civil War, and her young son, John Jr., and had gone across the country on horse and foot and wagon to settle in California. When they got to the Rocky Mountains, Captain John got very sick. The three of them were forced to leave their wagon train, because the other travelers were concerned it might be smallpox. That night, with no one around, in the middle of nowhere, Captain John died. His symptoms were a sore throat. If only they'd had penicillin, everything would be all right. The next morning Suzanne and John Jr. buried the captain, then started back to where the wagon train had gone. But by nightfall not only were they lost but John Jr. was terribly sick, too. When he died in the morning, I closed up the book and shut off my flashlight.

52

Aunt Paula called Mom a few days after the shower. Wiggy had not returned. Uncle Count was inconsolable. She took the call in the den.

Pop, Jeff Greene, Bethany, and me were in the living room watching the Red Sox. The Yankees were at Fenway, and they were a hated team, and my pop was the biggest Yankee hater of all.

"Concentrate," he would mutter to every Bosox batter.

Bethany sat curled up with Jeff on the couch. "We got to get a new catcher, Pop," she said with determination.

"Give the kid a chance," Pop said, waving her off.

"He's thirty-five years old."

"That's not old," chimed in Jeff.

Bethany patted his hand. "It is for a catcher, sweetie."

Mom had finished her phone conversation and came back to the Red Sox.

"Find Wiggy?" Pop asked, his eyes glued to Harry Peterson and his full count.

"He's run off. Poor Count."

The Yankees called time with two out and the full count going. The manager dragged his ass to the mound.

Mom looked over to Bethany. "He was there when we were opening gifts, wasn't he?"

"Who?"

"Wiggy."

"Oh, yeah. He was jumping all around in the paper."

"Well, he's just run off."

"Probably a girl dog," Jeff said.

"Jumping all around like that. Jumping on my presents."

I looked at Bethany then, but she just smiled and pointed to the TV. "Here we go," she said.

53

Two days later I made Gallup, New Mexico. I would have done it sooner, but the ride was a true crow's flight. Those few miles in New Mexico were the most peaceful of my trip. The air was sweet with sage (as Kate said it would be), and the cool, sunny air became like fuel. I had gone through Farmington and saw this thing on the horizon. The man who cooked my poached eggs at El Pollo's restaurant told me it was Shiprock. It looked like a ship, and the eggs were excellent. At the tiny town of Naschitti, I met a Navajo who was just sitting by the side of the road. We had a banana together and some of my water.

"I'm Smithy," I said.

"Good banana," he said.

"What's your name?"

"Ronald."

"I knew a Navajo in the army."

"I knew some white guys in the marines."

I remembered the Navajo in the army. His name was Jesse, and he thought the training was absolutely stupid. When our drill sergeant would scream at us and we'd all jump up, Jesse would take his time. It wasn't defiance either. It was a sort of denial.

Later on, on the road to Gallup, some guys who looked like Navajos ran me off the road and into a ditch. I wasn't hurt or anything, but I kept thinking how strange a human being can be. They can be Jesse, or Ronald, or they can drive trucks and try to scare you—or, like that policeman, shoot you.

But this did not get in the way of how wonderful the feeling of New Mexico was, and after three nights on the zigzaggy road, I rolled my bike into the Gallup bus station and slept on a warm bench. No one bothered me.

Early the next morning, I ate my last banana and drank my last bottle of water. I sat on my bench and counted my change. There was a little more than twenty-four dollars. So there it is, I remember thinking. Twenty-five dollars, a bike, and my stuff. I cannot describe to you how perfectly wonderful I felt all over as I pushed out of the bus station and into the very early New Mexico sun. Across the street in a parking lot, three trucks, old pickups, were unloading goods for a farmers' market. There were half a dozen long tables set up, and the men unloaded, and the women arranged a display of food. Some little kids ran around the trucks and under the tables. I walked the bike across the street and bought a large cup of Mexican coffee. One of the women put a cinnamon stick in it and handed me a puffy piece of dough covered in powdered sugar. It cost a dollar and was wonderful. I leaned against one of the trucks, ate my dough, and watched the kids run around.

"They left yet?" a voice called.

I looked past the kids at two men. They stood straddling tall English racing bikes and wore fancy headgear and tight-fitting uniforms of blue and black.

"Huh?" I asked brilliantly.

"The road club. They gone yet?"

"There they are," the other one said, pointing to another lot. I turned and saw perhaps three hundred bicycles and their riders milling around a platform truck.

"We're not late. Great! C'mon."

The two men pedaled off. I swallowed my coffee and watched them.

He turned and yelled back at me, "C'mon."

I got on my bike and followed. All of the men and women, and it seemed equally divided, had on beautiful tight outfits of various colors and designs. It was obvious that they were all from different teams or clubs. They all seemed to be different ages too. I spotted what looked like a young family with their grandparents. A large banner over the truck read GALLUP ROAD CLUB AND SESWAN BICYCLES RIDE TO

THE DESERT. A pretty little teenage girl in a purple suit came up to me with a clipboard in her hand.

"It's twenty dollars for the three nights, room and board. Gallup to Winslow, Winslow to Williams, Williams to Kingman. Kingman is technically the desert."

"Twenty dollars?" I said.

"Seswan Bikes are picking up room and board. We're responsible for the two rescue vans that are going to be with us. That's the twenty."

"I'm not with a team or anything."

"No teams. These are all clubs. Independents can go, too. It's not a contest or anything. You could be a club of one."

"Okay," I said stupidly. I say stupidly, because I'm old and a little fat and I'm going. I took out my money and counted out twenty dollars.

"You're number 307," she said officially, pinning the paper number to the back of my sweatshirt.

"Thanks."

"So what do you want me to call your club?"

"I told you I'm not in a club."

"Yeah, but now you're a club of one. What should I call it?"

I thought for a second, but I couldn't come up with anything original. "Norma," I said.

"Club Norma," she said, writing it down. Then she walked off into the crowd of people and wheels. Suddenly I had an awful feeling. What if where I had paid twenty dollars to go wasn't where I needed to go? I now had five dollars in my saddlebags. I took out my road map and looked for Kingman. I heard someone testing the speakers on the truck.

"Testing. Testing. Can y'all hear me okay?"

Kingman. Damn. I couldn't find it. How about Winslow?

"I'm Bob Eastman, president of the Gallup Road Club, and I

want to welcome y'all to our big event. Gallup Road Club and Seswan Bicycles Ride to the Desert."

It was so frustrating. I mean, I've been a Boy Scout. It was astounding how I couldn't find where I was on a map.

"Every year we have more and more folks joining us on the beautiful route, and this year we have more than three hundred. I kid you not. Three hundred."

Winslow! There it is. And there's Kingman. Perfect. Right through most of Arizona and just above Los Angeles. I began to stretch out my poor old body.

"Now, everything is clearly marked, and we've got spotters along the route, and you'll find the hundred twenty-five miles to Winslow a flat ride. Don't race. It's not a race. There's the Rocky Mountain Roadsters, and they'll be taking off first, but don't try to keep up, because they're training for the nationals. Just try a steady pace. Make sure to get your official— Can y'all see what I'm holding up? This is the official Seswan Bicycle Lunch Pack. Fits on the frame. Comes with sandwiches and juice and energy bar. It's free, so get the pack before you head out. And remember, safety, safety, safety. See y'all in Winslow."

Some of the riders didn't listen to Bob Eastman. They grabbed the Seswan Lunch Packs and pedaled madly after the Rocky Mountain team, but most everyone else set a reasonable pace through the high desert air. The lunch pack wrapped nicely around the bar of my bike and attached with Velcro. I pushed off from the parking lot into the main body of bikers and, after a few miles of getting used to riding in a crowd, let my mind drift over everything. That's really the best way to do it. It sort of lets your thoughts do the biking, and your body with its little aches and stuff sort of becomes detached. Sometimes, not always, but sometimes, if my thoughts are free enough and truly take me away, my body becomes almost a portion of the bike itself. It's weird and nice.

People passed me, I passed people. My good bike sat sweet on the road. Three very pretty girls, maybe twenty-five or so, passed, then slowed a bit, and I fell into a similar pace. It was nice, thinking away, and also watching their round little bottoms sitting so strongly on those leather seats. They wore blue-and-gold uniforms and they were numbers 78, 79, and 80. I could have watched them for twenty miles. I did. We passed into Arizona at Lupton, traveling in a happy, raggedy line down through the great reservation. Some of the riders were getting tired by now, perhaps having misjudged the ride. There were trucks trailing behind, of course, so no one would get stranded out here. I felt bad for the riders who had pulled over. I remembered what the seven-mile ride to Shad Factory had done to me. I was glad, though, that the three friends with the nice little bottoms seemed strong.

After a couple of hours, one of the rescue trucks casually passed us, and I saw my sister, first on the top of it, in her spectacular pose, then looking out from the back window. She was waving to me and smiling, and her hair had been braided. I didn't want to lose this vision of Bethany, so I increased my speed slightly and pulled away from the pretty bottoms. For the next hour or so, I followed my sister closely and admired her beautiful stillness, even if it was in my mind. Finally, as we entered the Petrified Forest at Adamans, Arizona, she turned skyward, changed into a lonely cloud, then disappeared into blue.

I stopped a little off the road to have my Seswan lunch, added a banana to it, and headed out again at an easy pace. I'd had to change into my shorts and red T-shirt, because even though there was a little brace to the air, the ride was hard work and my temperature was warming up. That's the thing that has happened to me. When I'm getting something, hot or cold or whatever, I'm aware of it. I never was before. It's okay to be aware.

By late afternoon several trucks began to pass, carrying riders and their bikes who had fallen out. I saw the grandparents and one of the kids. It would be hard for a grandparent, I guess. By five o'clock I passed a sign saying WINSLOW 8 MILES, and twenty minutes later I followed big makeshift signs to the Winslow Fairgrounds, where the Arizona National Guard had set up tents for the event. There were maybe sixty people already there. I looked around for 78, 79, and 80 but didn't see them. I parked my bike in a rack, checked my tires—because part of the deal here was that if your tires failed, old Seswan Bicycles would fix them—then got in line for a big spaghetti dinner. I took my dinner alone by my bike, then carried my saddlebags and sleeping bag over to one of the rows of army cots.

"What do I do?" I asked an official-looking older woman in a blue dress.

"Are you a participant?"

"Yes, I am. I'm number 307."

"Okay. It's coed. First come, first served. Rest facilities are on either side of the tent."

I put my stuff on one of the cots and went to a restroom. They had two trailers set up on each side of the tent. Men and women. I was glad the restrooms were not coed. I washed up in a sink bath and paper-toweled off. I was getting good at a sink bath. I walked back to my cot, grabbed my sweatsuit, and returned to the restroom to put it on. It would be cold, and I wanted to remember to do the things I needed to do to make myself the most comfortable. Being clean was one. The sweats were another.

When I got back to my cot, the tent had still not filled up very noticeably. It was a good time to lay out my things and repack them. Kate had a great idea for keeping my socks and underwear dry. She bought these big plastic food bags, and what I did was put my clothes in the bags. I put on clean, dry socks and put the old ones in my dirty-sock bag. I was getting efficient. That was something Mom and Pop admired in people and something I never got the hang of until

I broke it all down to a bike and saddlebag. I stretched out on the cot using my sleeping bag for a pillow. It was time for *Suzanne of the Aspens*.

So young John Bowen died too, just like his father, the captain, and so, for the second time in three days, Suzanne Bowen had to bury a loved one. It was clear from the very pretty and precise way that Rosalind Clarkson, who wrote the big book, described this burial scene, that it drove poor delicate Suzanne Bowen of Boston absolutely crazy. She sprawled over the grave of her boy and froze up and could not move, so great was her sorrow. For several days and bitter-cold nights, Suzanne lay over her son talking at the mound of dirt, as though she could bring him back by the sheer force of her wish to see him again, running and playing the way he did in the fields and woods around Boston. But finally, with the wagon horses starving and thirsty, she raised her head and realized that John Jr. was not coming back. She led the horses to a grassy hill and let them graze and drink from a pond. She wanted to just die, because her family had died, but something inside her that she never knew was there made her begin to do the things she would need to do to live out in that hard and beautiful part of the Colorado Rockies.

She hitched up the horses and rode until she came to a gentle rise nestled against a larger hill where below, a small stream rolled down to the valley. She brought her wagon up snug against a large rock on the rise and placed rocks on the wooden spokes to stop them from rolling and began to prepare for some way to get through the winter.

"Good book?"

I hadn't noticed the tent filling up or that 78, 79, and 80 were spreading out their things on the adjacent cots. They all had sweaty dark hair. Two were very hard-looking and athletic. They were shorter than the third one, who was also a little softer-looking. It was this one who asked about the book.

"I think it is, but I've just started it, really."

"Cool," she said.

They looked pretty tired. Exhausted, maybe. Riding in the cold takes something out of you, although I had to admit I felt great, with a belly full of spaghetti and all. They picked up their bathroom stuff and some clothes and walked off, chatting away. I liked that these three girls were friends and were doing something odd, with hundreds of other odd people. About halfway through the tent, the one that had asked me about the book, 80, turned and waved to me as if she knew I'd be watching.

Anyway, Suzanne Bowen anchored her wagon and then made a crude but effective corral out of dead branches and wood she found on the ground. She assembled the Franklin stove her husband had brought with them for California, and she bent its pipes out the front opening of the covered wagon so the wagon wouldn't burn. She collected a huge stack of firewood and even planned how she would ration food for herself to get through this winter, which was obviously almost upon her. Suzanne did not have any idea why she did all this, because she had such a longing to be with her husband and her boy, yet something inside her, deep inside her, insisted on what she called "saving grace."

"That's gotta be great. I mean, you're really into that."

It was 80 again. The other two weren't back yet. I saw that 80 had changed into a long, heavy green plaid nightshirt, buttoned to the neck, that seemed as big as a sleeping bag itself. Her thick hair was swept back and had comb marks on it. She had very white skin, and the rose in her cheeks from the wind looked painted on.

"A friend of mine gave me the book. She said it was really about me, but I don't know."

"Girlfriend?"

"Huh?"

"The friend who gave you the book."

"Oh . . . no, no. She's married and everything. She makes rugs."

"Cool. I'm Chris."

"I'm Smithy."

"That's a funny name. Nickname?"

"Smithson, really."

"Smithson. Cool."

"My pop named me after Robert Smithson, who was a shortstop on the Cincinnati Redlegs in 1884. He turned the first double play."

"Cool."

One day I woke up and twenty years or so had gone by, and I realized I never spoke comfortably to anyone unless I had a buzz on. And even then it was always about nothing. So here is another thing. I speak now. I'm interested in people now. I want to know things.

"We were just talking about how you ride. You ride great for an older guy."

I got red. I couldn't talk. I mean . . . compliments.

"I mean, older guys are cool. I mean . . . am I dumb or what? You ride great."

"You ride great, too."

Her friends came back, and I met them both, and they were named Rosie and Joanie. They had a day-care center they owned and operated in Boulder, Colorado. It was called The Company of Three. After a while they shut the big light off, and except for a scattering of flashlights, most of the tent settled in for the night. We'd be off at six forty-five the next morning, and sleep was like food, really. The girls whispered good night to each other. Before Chris got into her sleeping bag, she knelt down at the side of my cot and kissed my fat, balding, scraggy face right on its mouth.

"Good night, Smithson," she whispered.

"Uh-huh," I choked, like an idiot in a bag.

54

Georgina Glass picked up the phone on the second ring. It was night, and I had borrowed the number from Bethany's private address book.

"Hello."

"Dr. Glass? It's Smithson Ide," I said deeply and formally.

There was a slight pause on the Glass end. "How did you get this number?"

"I got it from my sister."

"Bethany gave it to you?"

"No, I looked in her address book."

"So then it's not only a violation of my privacy, but it's a violation of your sister's as well."

It's true that I was in the early stages of my dissipation, but I was not drunk—in fact, I had not had a drink. Still, being sober could not make my words come any smoother or easier in this difficult challenge of human communication.

"Wiggy's gone. I think . . . I think . . . Could my sister start hurting things, Dr. Glass?"

Another pause. This time I didn't feel anything. Anger or anything.

"Who is Wiggy?"

"Wiggy is Uncle Count's dog. He's a beagle. Whenever you go over there, he's always jumping around. He never gets tired and stuff. Aunt Paula gave Bethany a shower, and Wiggy was all jumping around and things, and after everybody left, Count couldn't find him."

"Maybe he ran away."

"Count said in dog years he's fifty-five. I don't think old dogs run away."

"No, you think your sister murders old dogs."

Now it was my turn to go silent. I remembered how I would call for a bedpan in the army hospital and the orderly telling me that I didn't really need one because he wanted to finish his smoke.

"I'm just scared that maybe—"

"Look, Mr. Ide," she said, sternly cutting me off, "if there is one thing you should know about that lovely and, yes, disturbed young woman you call your sister, it is that she would be incapable of doing anything harmful to anyone or anything."

"Good," I said. Georgina Glass had made me cry again, but she didn't know it.

"More important, this telephone number is my private number, and only individuals whom I have given this number are free to call it. I have not given this number to you. Do you understand my meaning?"

I had driven to Woody's Gas Station to call from a corner phone booth, because I didn't want any of the Ides to know I called. I was cold, and every time a car or truck whizzed by, the wet evening got wetter. I needed to have something to drink.

"Yes," I said, "I understand your meaning."

Dr. Georgina Glass hung the phone up immediately.

After I had peed myself, the orderly got so angry he made me lie in it for two hours before he changed my sheets. By then I was chapped raw.

55

Twenty-three miles out of Winslow, the promised flat road became a hill and then a mountain. The road club had gotten permission, for this big event, to use Interstate 40. Besides the hills and mountains, the hurricane-like truck winds made for a treacherous approach into Flagstaff. Sometimes I could feel the drivers trying to get too close. I don't know. It was a feeling. But it was another very pretty day and I stayed with 78, 79, and 80 until I saw Bethany on top of a slow-moving oil tanker, and I pushed close behind it as we struggled up one of the steeper climbs. The altitude no longer affected my breathing. It's a curious thing, as my mom would say, but after you get used to it, the thin, high air gives your whole body a lighter sensation.

I took my lunch at a Marriott hotel. I pulled off the road, walked my bike into the courtyard pool area, and just sat at a table. No one was outside, because, unless you were moving, it was pretty cold. The Seswan representatives had happily restocked our lunch packs with juice, cookies, and huge hoagie sandwiches. I added the banana, of course. It was good sitting there at a white metal table with the cold pool water, smooth as a morning lake. I had made good time from Winslow to Flagstaff, and Williams was probably only another forty miles or so. I closed my eyes a minute and listened to my easy heart. Sometimes these few silent, eyes-closed moments gave back more than a night's sleep. I followed the beat of my heart away from my chest and into my head, then down to my sloping shoulders and into each arm. By the time I had moved the beat down to my feet and into the ground, I felt a sort of release. Being away from myself, but being closer at the same time. I'm probably not saying it right. I'm not a lousy packed suitcase anymore, I guess is what I mean. I'm only taking what I need.

When I opened my eyes, the sun had peeked behind a perfect round cloud for the first time all day, and the pool water, so placid a second ago, now bristled in the breeze. Bethany stood on it, and the lumps of wave licked her feet. She was eighteen, and her prom dress and Mom's jewelry made her look even younger. She glided at first, as if on skates, and then, turning, she rose above the pool and shimmered in the cooling air.

"Bethany," I said evenly and slowly. The word felt good to say, and I said it again.

56

The ease with which Georgina Glass could upset me was astounding. When I think about it now, years later, I think that Dr. Glass knew exactly what she was doing. I was a cipher, sort of, in a medical career that was specializing in something that, with all her training, she knew nothing about at all. I think she knew I felt that about psychiatrists, and why not? So she always made a beeline for my tear ducts, no matter how important the subject or how desperate I sounded. I understand her, then, but I don't understand her. So what else is new?

I hung up the phone and left Woody's Gas Station and drove directly to Bovi's Tavern. Some of the guys I had gone to high school with were usually there, the ones who you always assumed would be there. I sat at the least crowded corner of the bar and ordered some Narragansett. I had four quick glasses, then switched to screwdrivers. I had six or seven, then drove to my apartment on Newport Avenue. I hated this place for the whole twenty-something years I lived there, but I hated it the most those first few months. I never put up a picture or bought furniture that I liked or anything. I always hoped that pretty soon I'd be out of there.

I fixed myself another screwdriver and loosened my belt and pants because, I guess, of the Bovi's Tavern beer and pretzels. I sat down at one end of the old sofa Pop had let me have from the basement. I wanted to call someone. I wanted to talk to someone. Not about Bethany or anything, just a conversation where one person says something and you listen and then you say something and that person listens.

The phone rang, and I picked it up on the second ring.

"Hello?" I said.

I thought I heard some breathing, but I couldn't be sure. Then the phone buzzed. I hung it up and sat back down. A few minutes later, it rang again, and I picked it up again on the second ring.

"Hello," I said, as pleasantly as a drunken man can.

This time I did hear something. Maybe breathing. The phone was connected. No buzz, only an uncomfortable pause.

"Hello. Hello," I said.

In all that silence, I felt some kind of distance, as though this particular call could have been from Russia or Australia or Vietnam. When it spoke, I couldn't tell if it was a man's voice or a woman's voice. It was like a croak from a lily pad or a yell from an escape tunnel.

"Bow-wow," it said. "Bow-wow. Bow-wow. Bow-wow."

57

For Suzanne of the Aspens, the coming of that first great Rocky Mountain winter brought amazing hardships. Snows that drove on day after day, herds of elk that actually ate part of her firewood store. If it weren't for this "state of grace" she claimed she found herself in, there was no way this Boston woman could have survived. Yet every day she trudged out of her wagon dressed in layers of her husband's clothing and brushed the snow from the wagon's sagging canvas top. She added to her firewood by pulling down the dry branches of fir and aspen. She boiled the snow to drink. Above her, Indians as strange and fearsome as anything she could have imagined, wearing deer hide and heavily armed, sat watching her. Suzanne Bowen showed no fear. Instead, every day she would walk through the heavy drifts of snow with a small sack of oats, or corn, or dried beans and, without looking up, would leave the sack in plain view. In the morning the offering was always gone. Often in its place was a feather.

I twined my fingers under my head, leaned back onto my bunched-up sleeping bag, and closed my eyes for a second. Outside Flagstaff, the road seemed to rise in a constant ascent. It wasn't like I was riding anymore. I was a mountain climber. By Bellemont I had hit the cusp of Bill Williams Mountain, which was ninety-two hundred feet high and seemed to be placed there by rival bicycle clubs. This was a kind of low point for me.

Many younger riders didn't seem to have the trouble I was having. At one distinct point, I was balanced on my bike but I couldn't move it forward as nine or ten happy, orange-and-black-clothed kids shot by. I solved the problem by walking it up the great hill. The twenty-nine miles between Bellemont and Williams were a repeat of my mountain strategy. Walk up. Coast down. It was dark when I glided into Williams and followed the signs to the tennis club where we'd stay the night. The nets had been taken down, with the same deal going that we had in the tent. In fact, the men's and ladies' rooms, the trucks parked at either side of the tennis club, were the same ones as in Winslow. I washed up, ate an enormous chicken casserole and salad at my bike, and walked into the court to pick a cot.

"Smithson! Smithson!"

I looked in the direction of my name, and Chris, number 80, was frantically waving.

"We saved you a place! Come on!"

I made my way through the lines of cots. I noticed there seemed to be fewer people than last night. Chris was standing with her hands on her hips and a big smile. She had on bib overalls with a green sweatshirt underneath. Her hair was combed sort of to the side with a green ribbon bunching a handful of it together. She looked very young and not at all exhausted, which the ride had made me.

"Hi," she said, bounding over to me and standing about one inch away from my sweaty old person.

"Hi," I said, trying to sound, you know, young.

Then she kissed me. Like last night. Quickly. And happily sat on the edge of one of the cots. I could taste her lipstick, and it lingered in my beard. She tasted like apples.

"Sit," she said, patting the space of cot next to her.

I put my saddlebags down and sat. I didn't know what to do, so I started taking my stuff out of the bags.

"Know how many people made it?" she asked.

"Made what?"

"Made it over Bill Williams Mountain? Without help, I mean. Fifty-two. That's it."

"Fifty-two? That's not many."

"We stopped at the rest area where the spring comes out under the picnic table. Know the one?"

"Yeah. About halfway up the mountain."

"We stopped, had the rest of our lunch, and just couldn't get going again. Took one of the vans into Williams."

"I think that it's smart to know when to stop something."

"Cool."

Chris leaned on her elbows and threw her head back. Her small apple breasts held on to my eyes. They were happy breasts. They were the Golden Delicious of breasts. I turned away and pretended to be looking for something in my bag.

"You made it. You're in great shape," she said.

"I'm tired. I'm very tired, I think."

"Yeah, but you made it. How old are you?"

I looked at my forearms as if I had to consider my age. Actually, I had just noticed I could see veins in my arms and a certain shape to myself.

"I'm forty-three," I said, still looking at my arms.

"You're in great shape."

There was a pause, and I knew it was my turn to fill it, but I didn't, or I couldn't. After a few more seconds, she said, "Are you married or anything?"

"I'm not married."

"You don't seem gay or anything."

"I'm not."

"You're just out here. You made it over the mountain. It's so cool."

Bethany stood posed on a cot several rows over. Her eyes were on me. She wore the kilt and the hair of the beautiful girl who had visited me in the Denver hospital. I would have liked to have said her name again, but I didn't.

"Do you live in Gallup?"

"No, I'm not from around here."

"Colorado?"

Chris wanted to know, I guess.

"East Providence, Rhode Island."

"Rhode Island! You came out from Rhode Island? For this?"

Across the room Bethany danced above her cot and smiled at me.

"I didn't know you had these things. No, I saw everybody and sort of joined up. I started riding one night, and here I am. I'm going to Los Angeles. I'm going for my sister."

I watched Bethany fold into another woman and disappear. Chris was just staring at me. I shrugged.

"You rode from Rhode Island?"

"Yes."

And I told her. In the middle of my story, I excused myself to go to the men's room, but Chris just walked with me and waited by the truck. It didn't make me uncomfortable at all that this lovely and, as I say, apple-breasted young woman linked her arm in mine and clung to me and my words. She cried easily. The Red Bridge. Carl. Bill. Norma. I liked that these things could bring up tears in her. In people. I felt kind of right. I didn't feel as if I had to apologize. I think the only part of my story she didn't believe was the 279-pound part. The big part. That it was me and my gasp for air and smoke and booze. I miss nothing, but I miss it all. I told her that, too. It was a lot like listening to my heart at poolside. It was good, and it made me refreshed.

When we got back to the cot, her friends Joanie and Rosie were there, already in their flannel longjohns. They were so pretty and regular in a way that I suppose I never thought girls could be. Of course, they weren't girls. They were women with a business and everything. Partners, really. But I felt, somehow, easy with them. We all talked for a while. Not about me, because I think that Chris liked the idea that I shared that with just her, like a secret, even though it wasn't a secret. After a while I lay on my cot and read more *Suzanne*. Kate was right. I think I was enjoying this book the most.

When the overhead lights went out, some flashlights popped on here and there. I spread out my bag and got in. It was warm inside the tennis club. I slipped off my sweatpants and sweatshirt and slept in my undies. Man, I was pooped. The second I curled up, I was out cold.

I'm not sure how much longer I slept or what exactly woke me, but when I opened my eyes into the darkness, I felt her body against me. She was sleeping, so she must have been there for a while. I reached my arms over slowly, and my fingers realized she was naked. Her face was between my chin and my chest. I could feel her apples pressing against my T-shirt, expanding with each breath. She threw her top leg around me and raised her head up to my eyes.

"Hi," she whispered, "I just unzipped you and climbed in."

When she kissed me, I felt my heart race out of its area and into my lips. She licked my cheek, my nose. She pushed away for a fuller look at my astonishment, and her breasts, her beautiful orchard (I really felt that), popped away from my chest and pointed up at me. I made no bones about it. I liked them. I looked at them. After a moment I touched them. She closed her eyes and smiled. The back of her hand brushed the front of my shorts, and I guess my excitement began to rise.

"I just climbed in with you," she whispered. "I don't want to bother you."

"You . . . bother . . . no bother . . . no . . . uhh . . ."

"I just . . ."

She pushed me over and was on top of me. A bag of man and woman. A hard and a soft bag. She moved against me. Her smoothness. Her amazing body that couldn't climb the mountain, on me. She pulled at my T-shirt. We took it off. Me and this young and beautiful woman, taking off my T-shirt. I remembered then that we were in cot city. Some flashlights still glinted on and off in the distance. My hands ran down the muscles of her back and followed her spine up to her shoulders once more. One of her friends rolled in her sleep, and I turned, startled, to her cot. Bethany lay still, her curls falling sideways on the pillow. Her twelve-year-old eyes wide and flat. I turned away, but when I looked again, she still watched me. A sad watch. A sad little girl. I put my hands down to my sides.

"Smithson?" Chris whispered. "What?"

I looked from my fragile sister to Chris above me in a way that would never leave me and be in my thoughts maybe always. Her mouth a bit open. Her eyes a lot green. Her black hair pressed down over the milky forehead. My God, I thought, I love the girls so much.

"What?" she asked again.

I couldn't explain how I had lifted that heavy wheelchair. How I couldn't look at those closed venetian blinds after the visits stopped. How the letters came every day to Smithy Ide in many pieces. Letters I never read.

"It's not you," I said finally. "You're so wonderful. You're so beautiful. It's me, really. It's me, Chris, that's all."

She looked at my eyes and then looked away. A tiny sigh, and when she turned back, she had a smile.

"I don't usually do this, you know."

"I know."

"I don't, really."

"I know you don't."

She rolled off me and sat on the side of my cot, facing away. Her hair still to one side. Her naked body catching goose bumps from the stale tennis-court air. I wanted to touch her, let my hand rest on her, anywhere on her, but I knew that wasn't possible. She stood and walked softly to her cot. I should have closed my eyes, I think, but I would keep this picture of beautiful Chris. She pulled on her green plaid nightshirt and then her white athletic socks. She got into her sleeping bag and rolled onto her side. Dim fluorescent night lights on either side of the tennis club lit us like the moon.

"Good night," I said finally. Tortured. Stupid.

She pulled the bag up to her ears.

58

The big day for Bethany and Jeff Greene was less than a week away. I
had made the decision to forget about the "bow-wow" call. After all,
Dr. Glass had assured me that Bethany was perfectly harmless, and, in
truth, her behavior, in this particularly tense time in a girl's life, was
the picture of calm. Now, Mom, on the other hand, was the one
causing problems. Once she got it into her head that Bethany should
have a wedding train, nothing could stop her from pushing the idea.
Bethany held firm to her hopes of "simplicity." She said, "Mom, I
don't want a wedding train. I really don't." And Mom would say,
"Please." And "Please" and "Oh, please," until, finally and maturely,
Bethany gave in. It was this kind of compromise that helped me put
Wiggy in perspective for a while.

Jeff's best man, Dave Stone, his college roommate, came down
from Nashua, New Hampshire, to help him with the stuff a guy
needs help with when he's getting married. Jeff's dad was dead, and
his mom had become a more or less permanent resident at Bradley
Hospital. Dave also had come down to plan and execute the all-
important bachelor party. I didn't like Dave. He didn't like me either,
but we'd smile and pretend we did for everybody's sake. But now I
can say that Dave Stone had an attitude that he was much smarter
and cooler than you. When he said something, I always had the feeling that you were supposed to consider his words and nod and agree.
What really pissed me was how wonderful he felt the Baltimore Ori-
oles were. I mean, it's true they had a couple of great players, but he
was from New Hampshire. What about the Red Sox?

Dave scheduled the bachelor party at the F.E.I. Club in Pawtucket.
It was a striptease place where bad old comedians introduced old
dancers who would dance and take their clothes off all the way down
to a kind of shiny bikini. I had been to strip places when I was in the
army where the dancers would have actual sex with themselves on

the stage. The F.E.I. Club was tame stuff, I guess. I was glad, because of course my pop was going to go, and I didn't think Dave was the kind of guy to take the older men into consideration. Anyway, we all met up there, and we brought silly gifts. They put us at two tables down at the end of an elevated runway bar. The place smelled of old beer and a sour mop. Dave ordered pitchers of beer. There were fourteen of us. Dave and Jeff's pals, and me, my pop and the Count. Pop and Count had on their Sunday suits. I had on a sports jacket that wouldn't button.

"I hope everybody's heart is good, because these girls are hot!" yelled Dave over the loud three-piece orchestra.

"I could go any second!" yelled Count.

"What?" yelled Dave.

"My ticker's shot. I could go like that." Count snapped his fingers. My pop shook his head and chuckled.

"You'll outlive me, Count."

"Only if you get hit by a truck," Count guffawed.

The beer arrived, served by dancers from a later show, and the drumbeat pounded a slow, dirty introduction to Brigitte Bardoni, the opening salvo of entertainment. A checkered-suited man with a bad toupee did the honors.

"Ladies and gentlemen. Won't you meet and greet a young lady who has brought modern dance to a new high. All the way from Florence, Italy, the one, the only, Miss Brigitte Bardoni." It's been a while, but I'm guessing Brigitte was somewhere in her forties. She wore a sparkly white fancy dress that cut over her large chest at the nipples and flowed bumpily to the ground. The high heels made it difficult for much modern dancing, but that was okay, because she seemed too drunk to even balance on them. She had her blond-white hair piled high onto her head, and she wore a benign, knowing snarl, which she shared with everyone. After a tentative strut from one end of the runway to the other, she did a little kick and nimbly tore off one of her long black gloves. She twirled it at the faces of the men barside and snarled again. Then the other glove. With a flourish she tossed them into a safe pile behind the bar.

My pop looked around the room, pretending to be interested in anything except Miss Bardoni, who by now had unzipped the side of her gown and was attempting to shimmy it to the ground. I know for sure that Pop was embarrassed because he was there with his son. I respected that. I was embarrassed also.

Miss Bardoni's dress bunched up at her knees. Apparently some of the sparkles had gotten tangled up in her stockings.

She struggled to undo them for a second, then lost her balance and crashed to the floor. "Fuck!" she said, to the heavy backbeat of the drum. Brigitte Bardoni rolled over into a sitting position and sensually detached the dress. She stood triumphantly and snarled at the room in general. She resumed her strut. Our tables at the south end of the runway watched in a relative silence. Maybe the whole table had picked up on Pop's discomfort, I'm not sure. She pulled her slip over her head and twirled that also. Brigitte Bardoni was now down to the essence of the F.E.I. strip: a too-small, sky blue, shiny bikini set of underwear with black stockings attached by a garter belt. It had been a struggle for her, but she had taken her clothes off.

"Take it off, baby!" Count yelled.

Everybody looked at my uncle with a kind of shock and disbelief.

"Take it all off!" he yelled again. Count drained his beer and poured another.

"Va-va-voom," he said, shaking his hand at Miss Bardoni as if she were something that had just burned his fingers.

"Settle down, old-timer," Dave said in that squirrelly voice I still remember. "They'll throw us out."

"This is neat," said Jeff. What a nice person he was. That was his way of telling his best man to leave Count alone. Count ignored them both. Brigitte Bardoni was strutting down to the south end.

"Va-va-voom," he said again at each heavy stride.

This time the dancer did not snarl. Her face softened, and her eyes

291

became sort of kind. She had bluish liner all around her eyes. In a snarl, it made them seem dangerous, but without the snarl they became like Mrs. Harry's eyes, who was my kindergarten teacher and was probably the kindest person I had ever met. Anyway, Brigitte's snarl left, and she focused in on the supportive Count. She stopped in front of him and, elevated there on the runway, pushed her pelvis out and around to the annoying beat.

"Yeah!" yelled Count.

"Hey," countered Dave.

"Baby, you're the greatest!" Count yelled, holding up his beer to Miss Bardoni in a toast. Dave was coming unhinged. He had delivered a direct command to my Uncle Count, and he was being ignored.

"That's enough, goddamn it," Dave said, standing up.

My pop stood up, too, and got between the asshole and my uncle, who saw only Brigitte and heard only the downbeat.

"Ahhhoooooooooh!" he howled in his best wolf call.

"You better knock it off!" screamed Dave.

Now, if we had all drawn guns and begun shooting each other, the other patrons would continue to sip their beverages and Miss Bardoni would finish her number. This essential fact of the F.E.I. was lost on Dave. He had planned the event but somehow had skewed the reality of honest down-and-dirty, with fraternity-house down-and-dirty. Dave was the complete jerk. No college diploma could change that.

"He's not bothering anyone," said Pop kindly.

"Sit down, Dave," said Jeff. "This is neat."

"Oh, baby! You know what I like!" yelled Count.

"Stop shouting," Dave commanded.

But Count was not under orders, and Brigitte Bardoni had made the decision to cross the Pawtucket fire code. In an instant she had stripped off the top of her underwear, exposing her impossible, unmanageable breasts. She bent at the waist and happily held them out to Count.

"Hubba, hubba, hubba!" yelled my uncle, who by now was clapping like a seal.

They were water balloons about to burst. They were liquid gold, and I stared with an open mouth.

"I'm disgusted!" cried Dave. "Look at him! Look at him clapping!"

"Beautiful, baby, beautiful!" yelled Count squeezing his fingers into thin air.

"Ugh!" cried Dave.

"This is neat," said Jeff, his face fire-engine red under the heavy balls of flesh hanging inches above his head. "This is really, really neat."

"You're not supposed to have your breasts exposed!" Dave screamed at Brigitte. She reached down and pulled the front of her panties a touch, so that a great tuft of pubic hair became exposed.

"She's not supposed to do that!" Dave cried, pleading to Jeff.

"Va-va-va-voom!" Count countered.

"Maybe you boys ought to take off. I'll stay here with Count," Pop coolly said.

"But then the bachelor party would be ruined!" Dave cried, by now hysterical. Everywhere he looked, the sky was blocked by breasts.

"No, really. Let's go over to my place. Watch the Celtics," Jeff said.

Jeff stood up and joined the reluctant Dave. His loyal celebrants also rose, although I knew that most of them would rather stand in the rain than go with Dave. Jeff shook hands with Pop, and they filed past us and out the door.

"They are the best!" Count yelled, pointing to Brigitte's peaks. "They are the very best!"

Pop turned to me and said, "Smithy, you don't have to stay with us."

293

"I want to."

"I figured."

Count had started accentuating the drummer's downbeat on the wooden tabletop. Pop looked at him for a long moment. Like me, he wore the concerns of his life in deep, sad, heavy eyes that could have been the Narragansett Bay on a hot August night.

"Pop," I called from across the table.

He turned and saw me and smiled.

"Bethany will sure be a beautiful bride, huh?"

Pop kept smiling and nodded, but I knew him as a man who had been places and seen things and who knew things for, I guess, what they were.

And the drum ended, and the saxophone, too. Brigitte Bardoni proudly strutted her wondrous chest off the ramp. The bass drum began again, and our host introduced Alberta Einstein, the "dean of the scientific strip."

59

I lay there awake. The harder I concentrated on sleeping, the more impossible it became. Chris's smell lingered around me, and Bethany's face, now near the Seswan lunch table, glimmered under the fluorescent lights. About one-thirty I listened to my heart, moved it around in a sort of energy prayer, and slipped out of my sleeping bag. I packed my saddlebags tightly and quietly, stopping each time Chris or Rosie or Joanie stirred. I put the bags onto my bike, then used the men's room, and finally, around two-thirty, I called Norma. "It's two-thirty here, so it must be five-thirty there," I said when she picked me up on the second ring.

"Smithy," she said quietly, "wait a sec."

I waited for a minute or more. The phone bank was under a light at the corner of the tennis club. There was a frost on the ground. I had on my sweats and longjohn top, but I still jogged in place to stay warm.

"Okay," she said. "I had to splash water on my face."

"Sorry."

"Where?"

"Williams, Arizona."

"Wow!"

"I've been in a bicycle-club ride, but now I have to leave."

"Why?"

"I'm not sure. I think it's best, though. Are you all right?"

"Well, I guess, I'm tired a lot with this boat-design drafting. I mean, I have to keep all my other accounts going and not short-change them, but the Blount boat thing is the biggest job I've ever had. Also . . . I don't know. . . ."

"What?"

"Bea is sick again. She had a mastectomy about four years ago, and now she's sick again. I took her to the doctor, and he thinks she has to go into the hospital for more tests, but she's just so stubborn."

I'm on a bike, I thought to myself. I'm riding to God knows where, and nobody knows why, and Norma lives in real time and real things. I felt shamed and dark. I felt a shadow of a person. I let the phone pause fill it all up.

Finally Norma said, "Smithy?"

"I'm here."

"What?"

"Norma, I'm sorry. You got real things going on. Bea's sick. You're tired. I ought to be helping you, not calling you to help me."

"You wouldn't say that to me if I wasn't a damn cripple. Would you?"

The wind rushed out of me as surely as if I'd been punched in the chest. "Norma . . ."

"If I were a person who felt sorry for myself, I'd say that all the time. 'Poor me. Poor cripple.' It's ugly, isn't it? It's hateful. That's why I don't say it, and that's why I don't feel it. Okay, I'm tired. Okay, Bea's sick. That's life, Smithy, we can't get away from that. We have to go on and be strong, and the best way to be strong is to rely on people and be brave enough to trust them."

She stopped talking for a moment, and my silent admiration of this woman loaded the American countryside and flooded the cities.

"I'm . . . I'm not sure exactly where I'm supposed to go in Los Angeles. I lost the letter. It's a funeral home that gets paid by the city to keep the . . . bodies until someone comes."

"Okay," she said, all business now, "here's what we'll do. I'll make the necessary calls, and if you phone me tomorrow, I'll give you all the information."

"That would be wonderful, Norma."

Almost at once she said, "I dreamed we made love."

She stopped talking, and I saw Bethany watching from across the double-lane highway. She had her look of attention, as if something

296

very important had happened or would happen soon. She was still, but it was not the stillness of a pose.

After I'd stood a long time by the cold phone bank, Norma said, "Sorry. That's dumb."

I couldn't release myself from Bethany's stare. Looking at my sister, I said into the phone, "That's not dumb, Norma."

And in another moment, I said like a stupe, "We . . . the best way to be strong . . . is to rely on people."

"And . . . to trust them," she whispered.

The dry cold of Arizona took Bethany, and the stars twinkled down upon a fool.

"Call tomorrow, and I'll have the information."

More silence and stars.

"Bye, Smithy."

"Bye."

60

Count had slept for most of the ride to his house. He stretched out on the backseat of Pop's wagon and sawed logs. When we pulled into the driveway, he woke up immediately with a terrible headache.

It was late, and the night was wet and foggy. A true Rhode Island May had spread out from the Narragansett Bay and rolled in from the ocean. Aunt Paula switched on the light the instant we had turned into the drive, and she stood on the front steps, watching me and my pop coax Uncle Count out of the car and toward the house. Aunt Paula didn't say anything right then. It wasn't that she was angry as much as worried. Count had gone down hard with his heart for as long as I could remember, and Paula had always borne the brunt of his "dance with the Big Man," as Count referred to death.

The overload of cold beer and hot breasts had swelled my uncle to bursting. He held his head, and his bulging gray eyes pressed against their sockets.

"Looks like a migraine," said Paula, leading the way into their bedroom. We struggled on either side of my epic uncle. We could have steadied a mountain. We could have supported the Empire State Building. We sat him on one side of the double bed. I remember being astonished that another human being could share that space with the Count, but Aunt Paula was not just another human being. She was powerful and brilliant in the way a pilot fish is, or a kitten maybe. I realize that sounds stupid. She fit, is what it is.

"There's some ice already in the ice bag. It's in the big freezer in the garage."

I left Pop and Paula pulling off the moaning Count's pants and went through the kitchen into the connected garage. I had always thought it was the height of modern living to have your garage attached to your house. You had access. Our garage was a typical one-car structure that didn't seem functional. Especially in the winter.

Now here was a foggy, damp, dark Rhode Island night, and all I had to do was flip the switch.

I walked around Paula's Dodge Dart that Count liked to keep warm in the garage and over to the large white freezer. I opened it and scanned the top for the ice bag. Count and Paula had frozen dinners of every variety set neatly box to box on top. I began to rummage for the blue-and-silver ice bag. There was a large bag of turkey parts, and Paula had Scotch-taped a white piece of paper to it and written "Good for Soup." There was a paper bag of small, round things wrapped in aluminum foil, and on the bag Paula had written "Fresh Tomatoes. Good."

It was inevitable that the ice bag would be at the bottom of the freezer. I needed it, so it had to be in the very most inconvenient spot possible. Below the stacks of frozen juices, I saw the top of the ice bag. The silver screw top with the word THERMOS in black letters. I gave it a pull, but it seemed stuck to something. Probably a leak, condensation from when it was last put in, something.

"Great," I said, sourly and out loud. Already I had begun sharing my moods with nothing and no one.

I pulled again and felt the slightest give. Finally I yanked hard, and the rubber ice bag with the silver screw top loosened and rose heavily in my hand, and Wiggy rose, too, his icy mouth clamped desperately to the rubber bag under the hard frozen foods.

61

Twenty-four miles out of Williams, riding my bike in the truck night of Route 40, I pulled into Ash Fork. The dry cold had stiffened me up, and I could think of nothing except my warm sleeping bag spread out on the cot and Chris across the space of a whisper. My thinking made the cold worse. My feet numbed, and my ears ached even with the wool cap pulled tightly down over them. I was also feeling more stupid than usual, that phone conversation with Norma playing over in my head.

"Lips!" I shouted out loud. "Eyes!"

I shouted for no reason other than trying to shout out a bad feeling I had. A certain kind of lonely feeling. A feeling that embarrassed me.

I glided then into Ash Fork on the run. Chris, Norma, Little Bill, Carl, and Bethany glided, too, this time in the stars, twinkling on and off between me and God. I felt light-headed. I felt as if I could fall asleep balanced on my bike.

Passing several old gas stations and a small grouping of stores, all closed, I circled the rotary road until I spotted the blinking lights of Randy's 24-Hour Restaurant. I leaned my bike against the curbing and tried the door. Locked. All the lights were on, and I looked in. One old woman in a blue uniform and a white apron was laying out the silverware. Slowly. Table to table. I knocked on the glass. When she looked up to me, I smiled and waved through my chilly miserableness, and she came to the door.

"We're closed. Open in half an hour." She looked like Mrs. Santa Claus, and when she said she was closed, it was with a warmth and understanding you'd expect from Mrs. Claus, but I was cold and had lost understanding maybe seven or eight miles ago. I needed coffee. I needed a warm seat.

"But the sign says"—I pointed—"Randy's 24-Hour Restaurant."

"That's true, honey, but the sign's wrong. It's Randy's 23-Hour

Restaurant. I close between three and four in the morning so I can put a grand shine on everything."

She raised her watch hand up in a sweeping motion and announced the time. "It's three forty-five . . . forty-six now."

"Okay," I said.

Mrs. Claus closed the door and returned to her grandly shining silverware. I stood looking after her for a moment and then walked back to my bike. My legs were stiffening up, and my shoulders throbbed. It was unsettling to have begun aching again similar to that first bike week. I squatted and touched my toes, but the ache remained in an almost dizzying spray of needles and pins. I put my hands onto the main frame of the bike and pathetically laid my head on the leather seat. I closed my burning eyes. Bethany was singing a solo, in our church's choir. Her chin was softer than I imagined, and I couldn't recognize the song. It was a strange—I could call it light— dream, because it happened before I slept, but it was actually much clearer than a daydream. My daydreams have a soft edge, and the characters are in a kind of prearranged situation. People first and then the situation. I'm more or less in the daydream driver's seat. In a full dream, I'm not in command of events, but the events and people are specific, and they absolutely wouldn't sing a song I wasn't sure of, any more than they'd speak in a foreign language. Light dreams are problem dreams. There are no rules. With my head on the seat, my sister delicately sang, her head raised. She might have been calling birds—I'm not sure—but off to her side, in the empty soprano section, something moved, and it had the hands of a rake. It had the long fingers of the bamboo pieces of rake, and arms that could stretch around altars for what it wanted. And what it wanted, in the row, was my beautiful sister, her hand raised, her eyes somewhere off, looking into a mirror that wasn't there. I saw her clear, and the rake hands and fingers. I screamed, but the only words that came were "louder" and "Chevrolet." And then a great light turned on, and it made my head ache, and my eyes, already burning, burned in flames.

And it became dark again. And then the great light again, and . . . I opened my eyes. The light that was on and off continued. The light was no longer a part of my dream but a part of the restaurant's parking lot. I turned to it. Pulled into a far corner was an enormous freight truck, its lights on, then off, its engine growling. The great lights blinked on and off again. This time they remained off. I stood and faced the truck. Slowly, I pointed to myself.

"Me?" I asked softly, stupidly.

The lights blinked again, and I walked toward them. I circled to the driver's side of the cab and stopped as a deep, easy voice said, "There's some minutes left. Come around the passenger side. Heat's on."

I walked around the front of the truck and climbed high into the cab. Coffee and cigarettes drifted through the air. Warm. I smiled at the driver.

"Thanks," I said.

"Cold out there."

He handed me his coffee cup and poured the remaining coffee from his battered thermos into it.

"Warm you up nicely," he said.

It was a smooth, like I said, deep, honey sort of voice, and it fit him. A dark brown man, maybe sixty, with tufts of white hair underneath a round cap of brown-and-gold plaid. A neatly trimmed mustache played in his smile above heavy lips. Tired black eyes were set in a part of his face that seemed very young, almost as if the eyes and skin and bones around the eyes were new, some recent addition maybe.

"Good coffee," I said. "Thanks."

"Philip Wolsey," he said, offering his hand.

"Smithson Ide," I said. It was a bitter coffee, and I smiled over the taste of it. Mom would fill my pop's thermos every morning with a harsh and acidy blend. "That was real coffee," Pop said. Philip Wolsey had a thermos of the real thing, too. Wonderful aromas went with it. Toast. Bacon. This coffee was a feast of a memory. I smiled again, and my stomach growled.

"Good?"

"Oh, yes, sir. I need this."

"Real coffee. Call me Philip."

"My pop's coffee was exactly like this."

"What I do, you see, is instruct the counter worker to reboil my coffee before they fill the thermos. Trick is, you have to stop at the real places. No fast food."

I passed the cup back to Philip, who took a sip and handed it back.

"Finish it. Randy makes fine coffee. Five minutes."

Three more trucks pulled into the lot. A town police car. A small electrician's van. No one got out.

"Now, if I'm out of line, you must say so, but old Mr. Curiosity has got me. That's your bicycle?"

"Yes, sir," I said.

"Philip," he said.

"Philip, yes. Mine."

"And you are coming from somewhere. I know it."

"I'm coming from Rhode Island, Philip. I'm coming from East Providence, Rhode Island." I finished the last mouthful of coffee and passed the tin cup back to him. He shook it out the window and screwed it back onto the thermos. Whatever cloud cover there had been had miraculously blown off, seemingly in minutes, and the greatest starry sky of all time lit the space around Randy's diner.

Philip checked his watch, and a big grin spread across his wide face. "Ten, nine, eight, seven, six, five, four, three, two, and one."

Immediately the entrance lights popped on, and the old woman in the blue dress opened the door. The three truckers got out, and two policemen, and two men from the electrical van.

"Come on, young man. Breakfast is on Mr. Philip Wolsey of the Ames, Iowa, Wolseys."

303

I followed him into the warm restaurant and sat in a booth by the window.

"We'll order at the counter. Randy won't wait on tables between midnight and five. I haven't been through this particular route in maybe seven years, but I can't imagine it's any different."

We got up and ordered bacon and eggs and pancakes instead of toast. Orange juice and coffee, which we carried to our booth.

We sipped our coffee and our juice.

"Rhode Island. Nineteen sixty-three. I carted a freightload of semolina wheat, some exotic strain of wheat, from a Mr. Tamernack to Boston's Italian section. Brought back gourmet handmade fettuccini. Passed Providence on Route 95. Then passed it coming out. That's quite a distance."

"Pretty far." My eyes were still burning, and I still felt cold. I shivered a little. Philip reached across the table and put the back of his hand on my forehead. He left it there for about thirty seconds.

"Temperature. You're sick."

"I'll be fine."

"Excuse me."

Philip walked out to his truck. Our breakfast was ready, and I picked it up at the counter and brought it to the table. Philip returned and put two aspirin in front of me.

"Oh, I've got some in my saddlebags," I said.

"These are extra-strength. If you take them with food, they shouldn't upset your stomach."

I took them, and we ate. I could only finish about half of the food, although I was very hungry. I sat back and sipped my juice.

"So what you're saying is that you have ridden that bicycle from Rhode Island to Ash Fork, Arizona."

I hadn't been saying anything, but Philip was buying my breakfast.

"I changed bikes in Providence, Indiana. I had a Raleigh, and out there now is a Moto."

"Why?"

304

I thought for a second and stared at the juice in my hand.

"I think I'm on a quest. My friend Norma says I'm on a quest. I know it's strange. I used to be fat."

I don't have any idea why I said that last thing, except that, being sick, I was thinking differently.

"Don't look fat now," Philip said. "A quest. Don Quixote in America. But there's more."

Philip took both of our cups up to the counter, and Randy refilled them. He carried them back.

"There are people I've met," he said confidentially, "who swear that Randy never leaves. People who say they've never seen other help in here."

I looked over at the blue-and-white woman.

"Is that possible?" I said.

"All things, all things are possible. What do you think your bike ride says? People would say, 'Is that possible?' Of course you know it is, now."

"I guess."

"What's the quest?"

"That's the thing. Norma says it's that, but I don't know."

"Well," he said seriously, holding his coffee in both hands, "a quest could be someone seeking something, or pursuing something, or even an investigation of sorts. A personal investigation."

The black and twinkling sky had gotten red over a huge, distant bluff that I could see out the window. I told Philip what I knew. Bethany, Bill, Norma. I skipped a lot, I remembered a lot. When I finished, he said, "It's all of it, then, young man. I'm very fond of the way your Norma thinks. I'm going to Needles, in California, on Route 40, where I'll unload half of my freight. Dog food. Dry. Hundred-pound bags. Then I'll cut up to Vegas and deliver the rest. I'm going to highly recommend that we put that bike of yours in the truck and you hitch with me into Needles—if that's not cheating."

"That's not cheating," I said.

62

He came out hard, a white frosting over his black and brown and white beagle colors. I couldn't pry the thermos ice bag out of his mouth. Almost instantly his coat went damp, then soggy. I laid him on the Count's workbench. I never noticed how long Wiggy had been. He was always in some frenzy to eat, to be petted, to be played with. I rubbed him lightly from his ears to his tail.

"Wiggy," I said.

I walked back to Paula's kitchen and washed my hands in scalding water. Then I took one of her dish towels and emptied a tray of ice from her kitchen refrigerator into it.

"I couldn't find the ice bag, Aunt Paula. I did this."

"This will do," she said.

My pop was standing vigil, and Paula began applying the ice pack.

"I kind of left the frozen stuff all over the place. I'm just gonna put it back."

I don't lie very well. I don't lie very much. This was a good lie, I think, and I walked back to the garage. I bundled Wiggy up in a car blanket, grabbed a gardening shovel off the garage wall, and ran out through the backyard and around front. I crossed the street under a lamp, praying no one would see me. Shovel. Wiggy. Me. There was a vacant lot across the street, and behind that a small stream had created what could be called a little gulch. I used to play there when Paula and Count had baby-sat for me. The floor of the gulch was covered by generations of leaves, and the ground was spongy. I laid Wiggy down and began to dig. I worked frantically, and the labor made it seem less terrible. I pulled at rocks, I chopped roots. When the hole was deep enough that I had to be on my knees to work, I pulled Wiggy over by the blanket and set him down in the hole, wrapped in red plaid forever.

I haven't thought about God for a long time. I would say twenty-five years. People who think about God probably have a circle of friends and wonder and share things about God. Things like, is there one? I have thought about God recently. In the fields, in my tent, I think of God and me and the rest of it, but back then the last thing on my mind was God. Still, after I had filled in his hole and patted it down and even redistributed a layer of the oak and maple and birch leaves over that silly dog, I got onto my knees and said, "Dear God, please do something to make Wiggy happy. He was a nice dog, and now Count's sick." I kept my eyes tight for a moment, then ran like a madman back to my uncle's garage.

63

For fifteen minutes I followed the beat of my heart on its route to my feet. I imagined I was also moving the pieces of Philip Wolsey's extra-strength aspirin around. Doing for myself. Helping myself. I opened my eyes, and the burning had stopped, at least slowed down, and I didn't feel exhausted. I had progressed to tired.

The stars fell back, but the darkness had a clarity, and things around the highway seemed in shade rather than night. Philip sensed I was not sleeping.

"Sleep. Good for you."

"I'm fine. I feel a lot better. I do this thing with the beat of my heart. I move it. I mean, if I concentrate on it, I can move the beat around my body. When I get to my feet, I can send the beat right out the bottom."

"So you meditate, then."

"I guess I do."

"I ponder things," Philip said. "I ponder things and hope to one day understand."

I thought about this for a moment. "Understand what?"

"I'm not clear on the specifics, but I want to gain an understanding of the why. The why. I would like to go backward to the beginning. That's why I ponder."

We rode heavy and smooth. My bike wedged against dog food behind me. Philip Wolsey made sense to me.

"I would like to go backward, too," I said. "I think maybe that's part of the quest thing."

"Possibly." He nodded thoughtfully. "There's more, though."

"I guess," I said.

We climbed a small hill. I couldn't see morning, but I could feel it. Philip lit a cigarette. His cap furrowed down close to his eyes. He said, "What do you hope to accomplish at Bethany's rest home?"

For a second or two I had forgotten I'd told him some of Bethany at the diner. I simply shrugged.

We rode quietly. Philip took only a couple puffs of the smoke. Pondering.

"I am sixty years old," he said, his eyes tight on the highway.

"I'm forty-three," I said. "I used to weigh two hundred and seventy-nine pounds. I don't know, Philip. I just don't know."

Now there was the beginning of orange sun at the end of the desert, at the tip of the plateaus.

"Father was an Episcopal minister."

"I'm Episcopal. Kind of. I mean, I don't go or anything anymore. And . . . and, of course, I don't . . . believe."

"You don't believe?"

"No, I don't."

"Why?"

"It's like I said. I just don't know."

Philip nodded and cracked the window of the cab. Sage and pine smells. I thought that the desert smells an awful lot like Aunt Paula's turkey stuffing. "I was named for Sir Philip Sidney, the English adventurer and poet. My brother was named for Sir Walter Raleigh for similar reasons."

"I was named for the guy who turned the first official double play."

Philip smiled and pretended to catch a baseball. "Yes. We played baseball. All sports, really, that we could access in Ames. Our little Iowa town. The Wolsey boys. Walter was my senior by five years and some months. We attended St. Thomas Priory adjacent to Father's parish. A very liberal, a very leveling education. Classics and sciences. And most excellent people, too. Teachers, classmates. Walter and Philip Wolsey were the only colored children—the only children of African descent—yet we found a commonality with the others that served us powerfully for years.

"In 1943 Walter joined the army, of course. Turned eighteen and popped into the service like a weasel pops out of a box. We were all frightened, but Father explained about duty and honor and, in short, a kind of special American obligation to serve, to offer yourself to the common good. Want some coffee?"

"I'm fine," I said. "I offered myself, too. Drafted."

"As fate and luck had it, the war ended before he left the States, and before we knew it, he was out of the service and off to the University of Chicago. Father's alma mater. Legacy. Walter had distinguished himself in so very many areas of academia, he could have attended any school that accepted colored—African students."

"He was smart, huh?"

"Gifted. Intellectually superior, and I'm not a man who throws superlatives around. Gifted."

"That's great."

"*Who's Who on Campus*, 1946, 1947, 1948. Graduated in three years. I shall never forget . . ."

He lit another smoke against the wheel.

"I shall never forget driving up with Father for the graduation. Tall, flatheaded. Truly the features of an aristocracy that no longer has a place in our universe. That's my theory."

Philip took one puff and punched the cigarette out in the ashtray. We rode again in a shared quiet, and the sun came on, and the long, dry earth spread out.

"That's my theory," he said again, almost to himself.

"His degree was English literature with a special concentration on Thomas Hardy. Father assumed that Walter would teach, but our Walter surprised us all by applying for, and getting, a position on the *Chicago Times-Herald.*"

"That's great," I said.

"Journalism. We might have known. And there were books to be written. Wonderful novels somewhere. We knew that. We had always known that, really. In the meanwhile yours truly, Philip Wolsey, while not as brilliant a student, still, as now, I read voraciously and graduated from St. Thomas Priory in 1949."

"You speak great," I said, in a short and stupid and true compliment. Philip smiled.

"Sometimes, when one drives a truck, one speaks as a trucker. Sometimes one speaks as oneself."

"That's true," I said, but Philip had lost me on that one.

"I was to attend Chicago also. I would have loved to have read the law like Father's brother, Andrew, in Des Moines—who defended Bob Staghardt, the Tornado Rapist, and defended him successfully, too—but the Korean conflict began, and after another reminder of national obligation, I, too, went to war. Only mine happened."

This I understood completely.

"I went to war, too. Mine happened all over the place."

"The night before Father put me on the Des Moines train to Fort Bragg in North Carolina, Walter came home, and we had a wonderful dinner of steak and corn. Fresh sliced tomatoes. Melon. Mrs. Gautier was our cook and housekeeper. Mother, of course, had died of tuberculosis when I was just a baby. But Mrs. Gautier was a splendid and inventive cook. Catholic, though, but knew she was appreciated."

"That's sad about your mom."

"Well, yes, but I never knew her. It's in the knowing, isn't it?"

"It is."

"After dinner Walter regaled us with his electric accounts of working for the 'great paper,' as he called it. He was an assistant copy editor of the metropolitan room and occasionally covered sports and police."

"Cubbies?"

"Saw DiMaggio play the White Sox."

"Williams?"

"Saw him."

"Wow." My pop loved DiMaggio. You couldn't say a sour word about Joe DiMaggio, but he loved Teddy Williams more. I didn't know why I thought it just then, but I will always be surprised my pop never walked over to our Norma's house and picked her up and brought her to listen on the porch. Teddy Ballgame.

"And so I went to Korea and the hot gates and took the common duty," Philip said, another cigarette firing.

"That's the Mojave," he said, gesturing to the left of us. "Back in there. That's the Mother of Deserts."

"You wouldn't think so many things would grow on the desert," I said. "Flowers and things."

"Rain, rain's the ticket. October is a rainy time."

"I left Rhode Island August twenty-ninth."

Philip thought about this and then said, "Well, it's October sixteenth, so that would make this your forty-ninth day out."

I nodded and looked out at the Mojave. In October it just wasn't the desert I imagined it was. Flowers.

"October of 1951 I was returned stateside and reassigned to Petersburg, Virginia. Fort Lee. Quartermaster School, but really a place where those who had already fought waited for separation from the military. It was in Virginia that I first received word of the Chicago event."

Philip lit another cigarette. He took his two small puffs, held the smoke, then stubbed it out.

"What was the Chicago event?" I asked.

"Coming into Kingman, Arizona," he said, pointing straight ahead. "Now we'll roll, still on 40, down through a goodly slice of our Mojave to Yucca, and in no time at all we'll cross the Colorado into California."

"California, here I come," I said, and we both chuckled a comfortable chuckle, like two people who have known each other a long time. I felt that.

"Walter was not a copy editor for long. His compact prose made quite an impression on his employers at the Times-Herald, and of course one could not easily overlook this young colored man's access to sections of town and community not readily available to the paper's rank and file. In short order my brother secured his own beat and, within a year, a byline. Father had sent several of his articles to

312

me in Korea. Walter had a sense of person and place in relationship to the times he was writing in that was so utterly unique you felt you were virtually being taken into another's confidence and that the words were for only your ears.

"And such varied subjects. I remember one, listen: 'The Blues Are Looking Rosy.' That was the title of a piece on Ra Tanner, who played the twelve-string guitar and wrote songs only about a girl named Rose. There was 'Collards and Coloreds,' which got an inside look at the kitchen of Marie Bliss, who had the most successful Negro restaurant of all time. Later Mrs. Bliss used the title of Walter's article for her own cookbook."

A big smile played over Philip's face. But after a moment or two, his face flattened and his eyes seemed heavier.

"You okay, Philip?"

"I'm fine, young man. Thank you very much. He also began a series of stories about heroin and the jazz community, if 'community' is the word. Horn blowers. Brush drummers."

"My pop thought Errol Garner was a genius."

"Errol Garner had a vibrancy," he said, almost begrudgingly. Philip seemed angry, and his eyes narrowed onto the road.

"Personally, the deliberate distortion of pitch and timbre of sound into some polyphonic improvisation has left me cold, but I will admit to a certain coldness to many things I do not understand. And so my father sent on three articles in Walter's jazz-heroin series. Then the letters stopped. Abruptly. That was in Petersburg, 1951."

After a moment I said stupidly and forty years after the fact, "I hope nothing was wrong."

We drove on in silence. I saw a tall cactus and, behind it, peeking out, was my beautiful sister. I almost felt like waving to her, that's how real she seemed.

"Walter had been too . . . protected. In many ways Father's world was a difficult one to carry on into a cosmopolitan reality. Not, mind you, that Father was wrong in his insistence on duty and honor and belief. It's that for most people those things are much too difficult to incorporate into everyday life. And Walter could not. He fell hard, first into the propulsive, syncopated rhythms of jazz and then into its narcotic."

Heroin, I thought. Walter.

"I learned this later, and I think I have pieced the sequence of events correctly. But who knows? By the time I was informed of our predicament and returned home, it was finished."

Finished, I thought. Oh, God.

"I returned to Ames, and in the midst of my chaos, I determined this: Walter, as I said, fell hard. It doesn't take long with the horse. It offers euphoria but gives a horror. A horror. A few months and the wonderful byline gone. The job itself gone. Friends having to turn away. I tell you, they had no choice but to turn away from Walter, who in the snap of a finger became alone. He ran home. He left home. The days went on like years for Father. His superior boy, gifted boy, ruptured in the spirit. When Walter came home, he stole from Father. He became something adrift. Mrs. Gautier told me later that once he actually threatened her with violence if she would not give him money. Threatened our dear Mrs. Gautier while Father, overwhelmed, prayed in his study.

"One evening—Mrs. Gautier had by now left Father's employ because of fear of Walter—he fled Chicago again. He came home in that same hope of leaving his addiction in the city and being healed. But, of course, by the time he arrived home, he was nothing more than the beast who rummages for cash. This time Father had no illusion. Prayer had fortified him. It would require an almost superhuman strength of purpose, an absolute resolve, to save my brother from himself."

Philip smiled bitterly, a smile that goes inside and is really a crease across your face. He shook his head and seemed older than sixty. I had seen the downturn of his mouth on my father's face. I didn't want him to talk anymore. I thought I saw a woman, as thin as wire, old, in rags. I thought I saw her behind a small canyon we rolled through. I closed my eyes tight.

"Finally it's all a guess. A compilation of events. A personal belief, really, of events. Yet it was necessary, as I said, for myself, as a man and a son and a brother, to be clear. As clear as I possibly could be. As close to the actual truth as I could be. And so I re-created the evening as I feel it was, so that I might understand."

I opened my eyes, and the hag was not there, and we rolled out of the canyon back onto a desert flat. Philip's face was blank. Lightning flashed in the west, and five or six seconds later, thunder cracked over us.

"I can't be sure, of course," Philip said softly. "Maybe that's my cross to bear, but I will say that I'm personally satisfied with the conclusion I've drawn. Father confronted Walter in the rectory. It's my belief Walter was going to try to sell the communion vessels, which were quite authentic and had some value as antique and silver. Walter was no longer our Walter, and I'm certain Father understood this. Somehow, in the struggle for the vessels, Walter struck Father. Not a terrible blow. I'm absolutely certain it was not a blow designed to injure, to kill, a man as robust as Father. So no matter what the police findings, a more reasonable explanation was that the blow to Father simply loosed a preexisting condition—a clot, a weakness of the tissue around the cranium, something, as I said, preexisting."

"Walter killed . . ." The words just came, and I couldn't swallow them back.

"No, no, the essence . . . the essence is that Walter was only a catalyst. Walter loosed the malady. It was the malady itself, whatever it may have been, that took Father home. Now Walter, alone in the rectory, the room in shambles, the vessels strewn all over, realizes what has happened. Father lying there as if in a nightmare. As if Walter had awakened to an even worse horror. Father. Dear God."

Philip gripped the wheel and shook slightly. He reached for his cigarettes but could not get one out of the package. I took the pack, drew a smoke, and lit it. The first smoke I'd tasted since the wake. It tasted bad. I handed it to him. He took his small puff and held it against the wheel.

"Walter ran into the church, as I've re-created it, grabbed a cushion from one of the pews, and rushed back up the stairs to the rectory. The cushion was found lovingly under Father's head. That is an incontrovertible fact."

He puffed again with purpose.

"Cushion," he said with smoke.

Rain had begun to fall on us. A steady light rain. More thunder cracked above us, but I missed the sparks of lightning.

"Walter fled the church, ran across the open Iowa field, to our home. He ran to Father's study, tore the lock from the gun cabinet where the Wolsey men all kept their shotguns. Grouse and partridge. Pheasant, too. He frantically loaded his own, pressed both barrels against his eyes, and flew this world with Father."

Lightning flashed. This time I saw it. Philip stubbed out the smoke. He seemed embarrassed.

"I ponder, you see."

"That's so hard."

"Hard is this desert. Hard is this head here," he said, tapping the side of his head. "This old black head."

We rode on. We rode out of the rain and left the snap of thunder behind us. Ten miles later I said, "Bethany killed Uncle Count's dog, Wiggy. She grabbed that sweet thing and put him into a freezer."

Philip glanced over to me. "That's hard," he said.

"I never told anybody about that."

"Thank you," he said, "for telling me."

64

I couldn't sleep. I put on my clothes and went downstairs. I went through the small rooms and into our kitchen. Mom had left the oven light on. I got a beer from the refrigerator and drank it standing by the open fridge. Then I got out two more beers and sat at the kitchen table. Because this was the night before Bethany's marriage to Jeff Greene, Mom had wanted me to sleep in my old room.

"I don't know, Mom," I said. "I've got my own apartment and everything."

"Well, it would be just for tonight."

"I could come over first thing in the morning." Mom really wanted me to stay the night, though, and I admit I wanted that, too. It was going to be our last actual night as just the four of us. Also, I hated my apartment.

I drank the two beers quickly, then put the three cans into the trash. It was 3:40 in the morning. I made myself a screwdriver and stood in the low light by the sink window, sipping it. Bethany's wedding day was going to dawn wet and cold. I looked across to Norma Mulvey's window. There was a light coming out from behind the venetian blind, but no movement or shadows that I could see. I lit a cigarette and smoked it between sips of the screwdriver. I heard steps on our stairwell, so I emptied the screwdriver into the sink, swirled the glass, and filled it with water. Bethany entered the kitchen yawning. She went to the refrigerator and rummaged for food.

"You're up early," she said.

"Couldn't sleep."

"I figured."

"So you all excited and things?"

"I'm very happy."

"He's a great guy. Jeff is great."

"I don't like that a girl must change her name," Bethany said, pulling back from the fridge with mayonnaise, lettuce, and a tomato.

"I don't know." I shrugged. Now I was getting sleepy.

"Want one?" she asked me as she got a knife and some bread.

"I'm fine," I said. "Thank you."

"I mean, how would you like to have to give up your name?"

"I guess it'd be okay."

"That's because you don't have to."

"I meant, if I had to, it would be okay."

She finished putting the mayo and lettuce and tomato on Sunbeam bread, shook on some salt and pepper, and squeezed it shut with a top piece of bread.

"I don't like having to change my name. I might do something about that. Bethany Greene. Say it out loud for me."

It was the morning of her wedding day, and so I said it. "Bethany Greene."

"Again."

"Bethany Greene."

She took a little bite of sandwich. The lettuce crunched across the room. "I don't mind that, I guess."

"It's nice."

"I guess."

She ate a little more, and I listened to her lettuce.

"Is Norma watching?" she asked.

"I don't know."

"She watches you. You know that, don't you, Hook?"

I shrugged and sat at the table.

"She's coming to the wedding. I invited her. Will you dance with her?"

"Sure," I said.

"She's afraid, you know. She thinks you hate her because she's in a wheelchair."

"That's . . ."

"I'm not making it up. She thinks that's why you never see her and why you didn't write to her. After you were hurt, she came over like she does, rolled down the drive, and just sat out there crying. She'd read about it in the paper. When we heard her and went out, she stopped crying long enough to tell us that, no matter what, you'd still be Smithy and that bodies don't count."

"It's going to rain tomorrow," I said, looking out the window.

"Norma said it's what's in your spirit that's important. I thought that was amazing. Do you think I've stopped being crazy?"

I was feeling like I had to pee. Narragansett.

"Do you think, Hook?"

"C'mon, Bethany."

"*I* think I've stopped, is all. I really and truly don't believe I'm crazy anymore. I don't have a sense that something bad is going to happen. I talk easier, more honestly with the shrinks at Bradley. I talk to Jeff. I feel awfully confident. I'm confident things are going to be great. I think I'm going to be a good wife and a good mother."

"I think you'll be a great wife and a mother."

My sister's eyes were wide, and the water blue of them was light enough to be gray. I had never seen gray eyes before. She seemed smaller, also, than I had ever seen her. A dog barked in the backyard of one of the houses behind us. A yap of a bark.

"But I'm worried about you, Hook. I'm not worried that I'm crazy, that I'm going to be crazy. Now I'm worried about you."

I laughed.

"I'm serious," she said.

"Don't worry about me."

"Can I tell you something, Hook? Can I?"

"Sure."

"I think you're turning into a fucking fat-ass slob. Also, I think you're drunk a lot. I think you're drunk right now."

I looked out the window, and I was sorry I had thrown my screwdriver away. I thought to myself that tomorrow I would be an usher

319

at her wedding, under the direct command of Best Man Dave Stone, and my sister had just called me a fucking fat-ass slob. I got up.

"I'm tired."

"Now you're all mad."

"No I'm not."

"See, I'm not worried about me, I'm worried about you."

I thought her eyes had gone back to light blue, but maybe not. I sensed chemistry, though. I had this feeling of somewhere a mad scientist fooling around with his beakers and vials, and he had me strapped to a chair, and there was nothing I could do.

"Don't be mad."

"I'm not. I told you."

She took another bite of lettuce and tomato sandwich and spoke between chews. "I just love you and I think you're at an important crossroads in your life. I think you want to break out, get a better job, fall in love. I don't see you working on those things. I see you blowing up like a balloon and drinking, and you don't really have any friends. That's sad."

"I have friends. C'mon."

"Name one."

"C'mon."

I didn't want to stay in the kitchen and talk about myself, but we were all under one roof the way Mom wanted us, and that included kitchens, or at least that's the way I figured it. I lit a smoke.

"The rehearsal was nice, wasn't it?" she said.

We had a walk-through of the ceremony at church and then went over to Asquino's Restaurant for dinner. There were toasts and an accordion player and antipasto and spaghetti with sausage and peppers.

"It went great."

"I can't wait to see you in your tux."

"It will be a great wedding."

"What do you think of that guy Dave Stone? Jeff's best man? Sharon says he's a pig."

Sharon Thibodeau was Bethany's maid of honor. She was from Warwick, Rhode Island, and, like the rest of the girls in the wedding, was a friend from Grace Church. Except for some mild poses in church choir, my sister had never displayed to her church friends the horrible things the voice demanded. School was a different story. I liked the church girls better anyway.

"I don't know," I said.

"You always say that. 'I don't know. I don't know.' That's what I'm talking about. It's time you knew. Jesus Christ!"

"C'mon."

"He told Sharon a dirty joke. He told her a joke about two people fucking. It almost made Sharon cry."

"I don't . . . care about him. I'm only gonna see him one more time. Sharon's not gonna see him again. What's the big deal?"

"Norma loves you."

"Huh?"

"Norma Mulvey. That amazing person. That amazingly spectacular human being. Norma loves you. She's alone. What are you going to do? Are you going to be a pig? A big drunk slob? What? Are you going to love Norma?"

"What are you talking about? I haven't seen Norma. . . . She doesn't . . . stop, just stop."

"I asked her to be in my wedding, but she just cried and said she'd ruin it."

I turned away from her and looked out over the sink. I thought I saw the blind flicker on Norma's window. Bethany came from the corner of the table and put her arms around my shoulders and put her chin under my right ear.

"I just love you, Hook. I love you more than anything in the whole world. Even when I'm crazy, I think good things about you and hope good things happen to you. Remember how you'd look for me? Remember how you found me once under the water tower and you let me ride the bike back and you ran beside? That's why

I'm afraid. I'm afraid you've stopped running, and I don't want you to. I want you to stay a runner. I want you to remember running."

Norma's blinds opened, and suddenly she was there, sitting tall in a red flannel nightie. Bethany waved to her and blew her a big kiss, and then they were both crying, and then the rain fell.

65

Me: Hi.

Norma: Smithy! I love you.

Me: I had to leave the bike group. I took a ride from a truck driver whose brother killed his father, then killed himself.

Norma: What?!

Me: It's the kind of stuff I'd have to put in a letter or tell you, but the phone is hard. His name was Philip Wolsey. He said he liked the way you think.

Norma (happily): You told him about me?

Me: Well . . . you know . . . I told him some stuff.

Norma: Why did you have to leave the bike group?

Me: Well . . . I didn't really have to leave, but I just thought it would be best if I did.

Norma: Why?

(I will always be sorry I didn't tell Mom the truth about my pop when she was in the hospital. Who thinks like this at forty-three?)

Me: Well . . . there was a girl. . . . Chris . . . I mean . . .

(Now here is a pause that is not quiet. There is a change of wind across the country, and the wires whirl above the ground and below.)

She was with some friends, and they ride on weekends and stuff, and they run a day—

Norma: She's beautiful, right? Tall? Pretty? No, she's got to be better than pretty? Beautiful?

Me: I don't know. . . . She was pretty, I guess.

Norma: Hair?

Me: Uh . . .

Norma: Short? Long? Curly?

Me: Kind of up, you know . . . brown.

Norma: Brown? Great. Brown is wonderful for hair. And I'll bet her skin is all tanned from being outside and getting all that exercise. Right? Right?

Me: Her skin was white.

Norma: White? All-over white?

Me: Norma, I'm in Needles, California, and I was—

Norma: Was her neck white?

Me: Do you—

Norma: Huh? Was it?

Me: Yes.

Norma: Arms.

Me: Yes. Sure. She had white—

Norma: Tits?

(It's like the wires tighten. It's as if they could snap apart. We don't speak for a long time. Every now and then, I hear other voices crossing us, racing to other cities. I sit on the end of a bed and hold the phone with both hands. It is afternoon, but I have pulled the curtain tight, and the room is black. I have the chills. I shiver.)

Norma (softly): Did you say something?

Me: I shivered. I'm sick. I got a good old cold.

Norma: Did you take anything?

Me: I'm going to get stuff later.

Norma: Where are you?

Me: I'm at the Ramada Inn in Needles. California. The truck driver paid for my room, and I'm going to send him money. His name is Philip Wolsey. He's on his way to Las Vegas. Dog food.

Norma: Here's Needles. I'm looking at it. It's on the border of Arizona. You made love to Chris? Now you love Chris?

(I think, Jesus, I'm so sick. When I cough, the room shakes. But I didn't say it.)

Me: That's pretty stupid, Norma. I'm not mad or anything, but that is a pretty stupid thing to think. I'm forty-three.

Norma: I was . . . I was worried.

Me: Did you find anything out about—

Norma: I got it right here. Just a sec. I'm opening it. I folded it. Okay. What they do in Los Angeles is, when they have long-term, you know . . . bodies to take care of until people come for them, is, they subcontract them out to small funeral homes that have refrigerator systems that meet state and city specifications. I spoke to a woman in the coroner's office who explained that while the city maintains a potter's field—that's a special cemetery for . . . you know . . . indigents—because Pop had written to them, they try to accommodate the families as best they can. Bethany was subcontracted to the Cheng Ho Funeral Home in Venice, California. I called the funeral home, and the lady who answered the phone said it's almost on the water, where Winwood and Pacific come together. There's an old colonnade, and Cheng Ho's is directly behind the colonnade.

Me: Venice, California. I'm in California now.

(I cough. A deep cough and painful, but it loosens my chest even as it rocks the room.)

Norma: Oh, Smithy . . .

Me: I'm gonna go get some stuff. I owe Philip Wolsey fifty dollars on top of the room.

Norma: I would've sent . . .

Me: I know, Norma.

Norma: Get cough syrup. It will help you sleep. Don't be mad at me, Smithy. I know I don't have any right to tell you anything—just don't stop calling me. I love you. You don't have to love me. I think about you, I . . .

Me: I think about you, Norma. I'm sick.

Norma: I hate that you're sick. Don't be mad at me, okay?

Me: I'm not.

Norma: I just got scared when I thought you and Chris were in bed together.

(My sister sits at a small table across from the bed. She has on her Black Watch kilt and a white blouse. She is fourteen, and the cheeks of her pretty face are red. She looks at me so seriously.)

Me: Norma.

Norma: Yes, Smithy.

Me: Me and Chris . . .

Norma: What?

(My eyes burn hotter than the truth, and Bethany has flown.)

Me: Me and Chris were never, ever in bed. Okay?

Norma: Okay.

(I write down the address and phone number of Cheng Ho Fu-neral Home and shiver against a feeling that this ride has proved what I always knew. That I am a fool, a dog, a cat.)

66

Aunt Paula and Count drove over early, and Count brought two boxes of special doughnuts. Count looked great.

"That was a false alarm," he announced about the most recent striptease heart problem.

"Yeah, that wasn't what you call an actual attack. Doc called it one of my 'incidents.' I'm fine. Jelly doughnut?"

Upstairs Bethany and her attendants laughed and joked and squeezed into their wedding outfits—Bethany's gown and the maids' floor-length creamy brown dresses. They all wore gloves and wide, delicate straw hats. Bows were tied tightly under their chests, and Rebecca Coin looked particularly wonderful and full. Norma's mother had come over, but Bea came alone. These days she always seemed a little angry at me, but that might have just been my imagination.

"You look so handsome in your tuxedo," Bea said.

"Thanks," I said.

"Norma's being silly. Maybe you could talk her into coming over. For Bethany. Poor Bethany. She's going to be fine. I feel it. I'm very happy. Go get Norma."

I left Bea with Mom and Pop in the living room and walked into the kitchen. I got down my bottle of vodka and made a quick screwdriver. Then I made another quick screwdriver and walked next door and down the driveway to Norma's window.

"Hey, Norma," I said, tapping at the window.

Norma peeked through the blinds, then raised them and the window. I stepped back and put both hands in my pockets. She just looked at me. A fine, misty rain blew around.

"What?" she said.

"Bea told me to come and get you."

"Bea told you?"

"Yeah."

"Hey, if you don't want me to come, I'm not going to come!"

"Who said I didn't want you to come? I want you to come."

"All right, I'll come."

"I'll meet you on your porch."

"Why?"

"I'll just . . . you know . . ."

"What? Push? You gonna push the cripple? Bea tell you I can't come 'cause I'm a cripple?"

Norma slammed down the window. I stood in the rain. She opened the window again. "Okay, meet me on the porch."

I walked around to the back of the house. Bea and Norma had a long screened-in porch, connected by ramps to the driveway, and then to the house itself. I lit a smoke and waited. I had a feeling that I had better remember the way things look today. This included the arrangement of yards and rooms and porches. Then Norma came out, and the feeling went away.

How small and young in her wheelchair. She had made up her eyes and had put pink lipstick on. Her hair was short, and the way it was cut made her neck seem long and, I guess, elegant. Her dress was pink and satiny, and her white shoes shined out from the hem. It startled me how very perfect she looked. Enchanting, I would say if I could.

"You look very nice, Norma," I said.

"Push," she said. I stepped behind her, and we went down the ramp. I thought she said something.

"What?" I said.

"I said you look beautiful. I said I love you."

I pushed faster, out of the Mulvey drive and into the Ides'.

67

I had twenty-three dollars and some change. In a food shop inside a gas station, I bought cough medicine, spring water, orange juice, and four instant chicken-soup cups that you just add hot water to, and carried them back to my motel. I wanted to take a shower but didn't have the energy. I took three aspirin, two teaspoons of cough medicine, a huge drink of water, and sipped some of the chicken broth, even though I wasn't in the least bit hungry. I got into bed and was too sick and tired to sleep. This happens. So I opened *Suzanne of the Aspens* and read some more about her terrible first winter in the mountains.

One morning she looked out from her shelter and saw, walking across some newly fallen snow, two Indians. An old man and an old woman clutching each other against the cold. Naturally, being such a good woman and everything, Suzanne called to them and went out to help, but when they saw her, they started to run away. It was a confusing episode for her, but I fell asleep. That was about five in the afternoon. Needles, California.

I didn't even move until five the next morning, when I had to pee. I had more cough medicine, aspirin, and water and slept again until eleven, when the front desk called and reminded me that checkout was eleven-thirty. I showered, repacked my saddlebags, and went down to the lobby. My call to Norma was the only thing Philip Wolsey hadn't paid for. I walked out of the motel with $6.73. I felt a little hungry and pretty good.

I felt better once the rhythm of the bike and its pedals came back into me. I felt loose and fluid across the dry country. I stayed on the adjacent smaller roads off 40. Into Essex and then Amboy, where I spent the October 18 evening under a cactus, with my belly full of instant chicken noodle soup and stress vitamins and *Suzanne of the Aspens* moving slowly into spring.

The next day I reached Ludlow early and spent the last of my money on hot dogs and french fries. These are foods that do not have the right idea about them, especially if you're thinking about energy and goodness and healthfulness and that, but the feel of the food is important, too, and hot dogs and french fries have a very good feel. After food I cut down through the tip of Twenty-Nine Palms Marine Base, onto 247, then through Lucerne Valley to Victorville and Route 15. Outside of Apple Valley, I pitched my tent under an apple tree.

For some reason that night I was overwhelmed with a feeling of loneliness and sadness. I curled up in my bag, and a small rain cloud moved across the field and showered me, and I thought about big spaces and empty spaces. I wished my pop were in the tent with me so that I wouldn't be afraid, and then I wished I weren't afraid. I only know about America, and really not all that much, but I know it's not a place to let down in and be lonely in and, of course, frightened in. There is something about my country that never lets you be truly comfortable, really belong. At least for me. I thought of Tony Amaral, one of the guys at the lounge in East Providence. He was the nicest guy, but every now and then he'd get all tense and say, "What are you looking at?" or "What are you laughing at?" and you'd feel how threatening and how ugly he could be. I feel like that about my country sometimes. I really felt that under the apple tree. Also, I felt hungry.

I moved my heartbeat up to my shoulders, but it wouldn't listen to me. It's something that requires concentration, and I was feeling so hopeless that my hopelessness was all I could concentrate on. It's a big country and it's me. Maybe bicycles and men aren't good, even though most of the time it feels like a good combination. I curled lower into the bag, holding myself against my unhappy thoughts. Sorry to be alone, angry to have spent my fortune on hot dogs. My stomach rumbled, and I ran my fingers over the space where sixty or seventy pounds of guts used to rule. I was going back, I knew, and the swish of breeze through the apple boughs knew it, too. In the morning there would be Silverwood and Ontario and Pomona, and later in the day, right before dark, there would be Cheng Ho, on the Venice colonnade. But first this difficult night.

68

Bethany's marriage to Jeff Greene was a smooth example of how a wedding ought to be. Nothing went wrong. Dave Stone and his ushers kept the seating flowing, and the organ music that my sister had selected was perfect. "Love, Be in My Understanding" was—I'm not just saying this—magical. When Bethany walked down the aisle with my pop, I thought the Ides might burst. Sharon Thibodeau and her maids of honor were positively angelic. On the steps of Grace Episcopal after the ceremony, Byron Lapont, from Lapont Photography Studios in Barrington, took about two hundred shots. Bethany and Jeff. Bethany and Jeff and Dave and Sharon. Bethany and her maids. Jeff and his ushers. Me and Pop and Mom and Bethany and Jeff. They were wonderful pictures, and we would put them everywhere, and later Pop would spread them out and look for clues.

We left the church in a caravan, two limousines leading the way, and crossed the George Washington into East Providence, taking the Taunton Avenue exit to Agawam Hunt Country Club. In the Hole in One Room, Bethany and Jeff and their attendants were announced, and we ate from a huge buffet table set up by Shroeder's Delicatessen and danced to the rhythms of Armando's Hideaway, a six-piece band fronted by Tony Chambroni, who wasn't half bad.

Norma had driven Bea over. She got herself out of the van and wheeled to the stairs. One of the valet parkers, a nice old black guy, backed her up the stairs, and she came into the Hole in One. Bethany ran over and hugged her and twirled her around. Norma wasn't self-conscious or anything. All you had to do was look at the way she smiled at Bethany and you understood history. When she saw me watching her, she arranged herself taller in the chair and looked serious and tough. There was a bank of floor-to-ceiling mirrors behind the buffet table, where golfers could examine their swings. I examined my new belly, hard and round, and my ass and my snug tux. I undid my jacket button and had my fifth or sixth glass of sparkling wine.

Count squeezed in between Jeff and Dave and launched conspiratorially into one of the classics:

"Couple of Jews, by mistake, walk into St. Pat's. . . ."

"We're Jewish," snapped Dave.

Count looked at Dave, then Jeff. "Okay, couple of coons, by mistake, walk into St. Pat's. . . ."

Count finished the joke to chuckles from Jeff and cold stares from Dave and spotted Father Solving standing alone next to the gift table. Count was five feet away from him when he joyfully launched into it again.

"Couple of Jews, by mistake, walk into St. Pat's. . . ."

Like at the rehearsal dinner, there were toasts by everyone, and I thought it was terrific how people could come up with such meaningful and loving remarks of good luck and happy life, until Dave Stone quieted down the crowd by whistling.

"Ladies and gentlemen," he said, like a big-deal, in-charge kind of guy. "Ladies and gentlemen, if I can have your attention, please. As you all know, the wedding of the fabulously handsome Jeff Greene and the perfectly beautiful Bethany Ide was a harbinger of great things to come for these two terrific people. So before they change for their honeymoon . . ."

Oooohs and laughter from the crowd.

"I think it's appropriate to ask Bethany's brother and Jeff's brand-new brother-in-law, Smithy Ide, to offer the final toast."

Like in a movie, the group of people parted, and I stood alone next to the buffet table. At first I had forgotten I held two glasses of wine. I am a person who does not do well with anyone looking at me, let alone a roomful of people all wearing those goofy wedding grins. I put one of the wineglasses down on the buffet table and held the other glass with both hands.

"I hope," I said, "I . . . I hope that a whole lot of happiness and really good things happen for my sister."

I thought for a second or two.

". . . Oh, and Jeff, of course. Really, really good things."

Everybody laughed at my oversight, and their laughter turned into applause and Jeff and Bethany gave each other a little kiss and a click of their wineglasses. Mom and Pop kissed, too. Norma had wheeled close to me and stared at me. I wished I had clinked glasses with her then and kissed her, too. But I didn't. I finished my wine. Then I finished the other one, and then I had some more.

69

By the time a slice of orange sun was hitting me, I had ridden three hours. I had gotten myself too upset to sleep. Being hungry probably had a lot to do with it. I put this stretch of road into Los Angeles as my most unhappy. Doubt is terrible. Not that I had any doubt about my own stupidity, to do what I was doing. I was pretty confident I was in an idiot world of my own. But to have come to my middle age without any idea at all about anything . . . I tried to listen to my heart rhythms, to move them as I rode, but my brain was pedaling in another direction. Finally I settled on the road itself, and I followed my sister's flight over the San Gabriel Mountains.

I came out of the night and kept to the roads adjacent to the freeways. Here is another thing I find disturbing about how I look out at the world. I see the walled-in communities. I see parking lot freeways. I see a western city spread left to right and not up, and I say to myself, This is not Rhode Island. As if there is a common thing going here I cannot understand. I needed food. I was exhausted. I could no longer see my sister in the sky. Both of my tires blew out at the exact same time.

I walked backward for a hundred yards or so, trying to discover what could have ripped up my tires, but I couldn't find anything. I walked on until I came to a gas station. There was a woman filling up a car with gas.

"You work here?" I asked.

"Do I look like I work here?"

She topped off her tank and walked into the station. I followed her, waited while she paid, and then said to the teenage attendant, "Do you fix bike flats?"

"Bike flats? Uh-uh."

I could smell the coffee on the counter over the shelves of breakfast pastries. "Any bike places around?"

The kid got out a piece of paper and drew a map. "You're here. Okay? If you go right on Forest, past the cow place, about, uh . . . about seven or eight miles, there's Lippit Exxon station run by this guy, and he does bikes and boards and that shit. Okay?"

"Thanks."

I took the piece of paper. I started out, but the coffee and the doughnuts wanted me to look at them. "How much is the coffee and the pastries?"

"Dollar."

"Dollar?"

"Each."

"Any bananas?"

"Behind the chips. Apples. Oranges. Whole thing. What do you want?"

"I don't have any money. I was so stupid the other day, I spent all my money on hot dogs."

The kid stared at me like the bum I must have looked like. "I'm on a bike ride from Rhode Island. I'm not a bum or anything. Listen, I'll give you a lightweight blue tent with fiberglass poles and stakes and fly in perfect condition that a doctor in Indiana paid two hundred and seventy dollars for if you'll give me some doughnuts and bananas and spring water and maybe a couple of apples."

For a second the kid didn't say anything. I watched his face, and then I watched his pimply cheeks.

"Let me see the tent," he said.

70

Bethany and Jeff had talked around their honeymoon. Bahamas, Bermuda, even Europe. In the end they drove up to North Conway, New Hampshire, to the Level Wind Lodge, where they would hike and plan and get used to being married. I was relieved they chose to stay in New England. Bethany was a New Englander, and, really, Jeff was, too. It's just a feeling that you have a place to fit in, even if it's a little harsh in an accepting kind of way.

At the end of the reception, they both changed into regular clothes and kissed and hugged everyone and drove off from the front of the Agawam Hunt Country Club in Jeff's new Fairlane with cans tied to the back. I have never seen my pop so attentive to Mom as they watched the car roll onto Taunton Avenue and up to 195. He held her tight with his big pitching arm while he waved with his glove hand. He was crying. Hard.

I walked back into the club and had a screwdriver at the bar, and then I went out to Mom and Pop, who still stood there.

"They're gonna be great. I mean, I feel good," I said.

My pop squeezed Mom.

"Oh, yeah," he said.

71

My bananas and doughnuts kicked in after a few miles of my walk to Lippit, and I talked out loud to Norma, and to Mom and Pop and Bethany. There was a warm breeze and a salty kind of smell, and I could feel my sadness and, I guess, despair blowing off of me. People that you love can lift you and confuse you. Understanding them doesn't seem so important when they're inside your head. That's why love should be easy. I guess it is. I just don't know.

It was surprising how very clear Norma was to me. I mean, the physical Norma. I must have taken these snapshots in my head, because I could see her exactly how she was on my porch the night I left for Shad Factory. Her tight red hair, big round eyes. The way her smile was like cotton and how soft her face became when she spoke about Bethany. But I remembered the anger and the grip of her beautiful long fingers on her wheels.

"Norma," I said, and I smiled. "Hey, Norma," I said again to myself.

A small, hard, flat-faced Spanish man about my age was working on a car on the side of the Lippit Exxon station.

"Kid said I could get my tires fixed around here."

"*Sí,*" he said, not looking up from the engine.

"I got two flats." He didn't say anything. He grunted as he pulled up on his wrench.

"I don't have any money."

He looked up at me.

"I'm not a bum or anything. I'm on this trip from Rhode Island, and I spent all my money on hot dogs like a stupe, but I got this nice saddlebag and stuff, and I'll give it to you if you can fix my tires."

He raised his head and laid the wrench on a greasy towel draped on the car radiator. "That saddlebag?"

"Yes."

"What stuff?"

"I got a nice alpaca sweater and a pair of sneaks I've never used, and—"

"Size?"

"Ten."

"Ten?"

"Yes. And some pants and socks."

"C'mon," he said.

I followed him to the back of the station. He unhooked the saddlebags and handed them to me. Then he flipped my bike onto a long, waist-high vise. While he stripped off the ruined tires, I looked around his shop. Skateboards hung neatly against a plywood wall. Each one more colorful than the next, with peculiarly particular designs and angles. All of them said LUIS across the toe part. Most of the bikes were used, but they were polished and equipped with new wheels.

"I like your shop," I said.

"I like it, too," he said with no inflection.

"Are you Luis?"

"No."

He walked to a metal cabinet and pulled out two new racing tires, still in their plastic bags. He started on the back wheel. "Rhode Island, huh?"

"Yes."

"All the way?"

"I took some trains in New York and a truck a little in Arizona."

"Rhode Island," he said, shaking his head.

"Yes."

He moved to the front rim of my very beautiful bike. "That's not a real island, though, is it?"

"No," I said.

"This is a good bike. Kids like mountain bikes around here, but if you go on the roads . . . good, good bike. I'm gonna tune it up, too."

"Thanks."

He inflated both tires, then straightened the front wheel to line it up with the back. "This pull to the right?"

"A little, maybe."

"Won't now."

"Thanks."

He put a thin spread of clear jelly over the chain. "Teflon," he said.

"Wow."

"And graphite. They got everything. They got it all. You know, road dust won't even stick to it now."

He put a little drop of solvent on each brake mechanism and took my bicycle from the vise. "Like new. Better than new."

I handed him the saddlebag. He opened it up and took out the items one by one and laid them on the floor. Then he went to the metal cabinet and rummaged for a minute. He pulled out a dirty red saddlebag that had been patched with what looked like an old piece of blue jean. He brushed off the dust and tossed it to me.

"Just the new saddlebag. You keep the other shit. I got little feet."

I didn't know what to say, so I knelt down and started pushing my stuff into the new old saddlebag.

"Luis was my baby."

I stopped and looked up at him.

"Not, you know, baby. Thirteen. Big boy. On the back of a pickup fooling around, you know, thirteen. They weren't going fast or nothing, and they're good kids and Luis goes off the back. It's heads. You can't hit heads."

He shrugged and looked over my head and lit a cigarette. I would call him wiry and hard, but when I thought he was as old as me, I was wrong. Or maybe it was the bikes and the skateboards. He seemed young, hard face and all. A dry wind spurted onto us and stopped.

"My sister was named Bethany."

340

He looked down at me and didn't seem surprised.

"She was a beautiful girl. A woman. Only she—not all the time or anything, but sometimes—she heard this voice, and then it was awful."

The buttons on the old saddlebag were missing, so we tied it together and onto the bike with clothesline rope.

"I'm so sorry about Luis," I said, before I pedaled away.

"I'm sorry, too."

I nodded and left him walking toward the car engine. I checked my map and figured I was somewhere around Fontana. I would go down to Valley Boulevard, and fifty miles later I would pick my way into Venice. I looked over to the bike man and wanted to say something more about Luis and maybe make him feel better. I didn't, though. I guess you bump into people, and it's all about how they bounce off you.

I rode easy on my amazing bike, and without thinking I said, "Now I lay me down to sleep. I pray the Lord my soul to keep. And if I die before I wake, I pray the Lord my soul to take."

And then I said out loud, "I said that for Luis."

72

We knew this:

Mr. and Mrs. Jeff Greene drove up and around Boston, took the turnpike to Concord, New Hampshire. At Meredith they cut a corner of Lake Winnipesaukee and took 16 the rest of the way north to North Conway. The weather was "glorious" (Jeff's word). The Level Wind Lodge was perched on a ledge of granite overlooking Echo Lake. It was a Victorian house full of squares and points that a young couple had painted white and turned into a hotel. It was very homey, which was why Bethany had chosen it from the many brochures she had sent for. From the front porch, you could see Mount Washington, the highest peak east of the Mississippi and a mountain Jeff had hiked up with the Boy Scouts. All around the lodge were trails for exploring. The food was particularly excellent. Jeff has told us that Mrs. Thatcher, who was the owner along with her husband, Mr. Thatcher, cooked traditional New England Colonial style but added a special touch of European Nouveau. He has told us they both enjoyed Mrs. Thatcher's food very much. They had corned beef one night, with potatoes and cabbage and carrots, all boiled the way it's supposed to be, only it was served with a hot curry sauce and a cool chutney. That's what Jeff meant by the Nouveau touch. It was important for Jeff to tell us this, and so when he sat at our kitchen table and told us what he knew, we listened hard, because we knew it was important to him. Mom even wrote down a recipe that Jeff had on a piece of paper written by Mrs. Thatcher. I'm going to put it here because of Jeff. It's called:

Mrs. Thatcher's Pork Chops and Sweet Potatoes

(serves 4)

4 sweet potatoes

Flour

½ cup orange juice

4 pork chops

Lemon juice

Lemon rind (grated)

Butter

Dry mustard (tsp.)

½ cup currant jelly

Paprika (tsp.)

Heat the oven to 350°.

Boil the potatoes.

Dip the chops in flour and brown.

Arrange chops and potatoes in baking dish.

Cover with sauce made from boiling other ingredients.

Cook 15 minutes.

We never ate it, because Mom never cooked it, but it is a very special and clear memory that Jeff Greene had of his honeymoon.

On the third evening, after a dinner of haddock with cucumber mayonnaise, Jeff and Bethany sat on the porch and watched the first stars twinkle over the Presidential Mountain Range. They held hands, and Jeff felt a contentment he had never known. He was so happy to be on that porch with my wonderful sister that for the first time in a long time, he wasn't worried about the auto shop or his future. Bethany shivered a little, so Jeff went inside to get something to put around her shoulders. When he came back out on the porch, Bethany was gone.

"Just like that," he said, over and over, "just like that."

Jeff called for her, then looked around the lodge, and finally alerted the Thatchers to the possibility that Bethany was missing. By morning the police had been called, and around noon Jeff called my pop, who called me at Goddard.

"Hello?"

"Smithy?"

"Is it Bethany?"

"Come home."

Pop had gone to Woody's Gas Station and gotten a road map of New England. He had it spread across the kitchen table by the time I arrived from work.

"Your mother's by the phone in the den. Look here."

Pop took a red crayon and made a large circle around North Conway, New Hampshire. The red circle also took in parts of Maine. He looked up at me, standing there in my uniform jumpsuit.

"Are you thinking what I'm thinking?" he said.

"I was thinking about Bethany. What happened?"

"She walked off. It's got her again. Jeff called about twelve this afternoon. She walked off last night."

"From here?" I said, pointing inside Pop's circle.

"Look close here. Here's North Conway, East Conway, Kearsarge, and little tiny Echo Lake, where the Level Wind Lodge is. But look in Maine. Look how close Bridgton is. That's Highland Lake. That's our summer lake."

"You think she went to Bridgton, Pop?"

"I don't know, but it's a lead."

Mom packed us a lunch, and Pop threw some of his stuff into a small blue American Tourister suitcase. It was decided that Mom had better hold down the fort and be close to the phone. After stopping by my terrible apartment in Pawtucket for some clothing, we drove up to the Level Wind Lodge, alternating the driving duties.

Pop wasn't a small-talking kind of man, and so for the most part it was a quiet drive, except for a couple of minutes before we ate the lunch Mom had made for us, when my pop said, "You ask yourself . . . I mean, it's only natural, I guess, you grow older and wonder at the steps you took along the way. But your mother and I . . . so hard . . . what do you do? How . . . I don't know. How does a man know what to do? Your perfect daughter, beautiful, dear child, and then the years all pile up. I'll tell you this much that it took getting to be an old fart to learn, I'll tell you this much: It's been rain on the base paths. . . . It's been a headfirst dive into muddy second. I wish to Christ I never was born."

I was riding passenger, so I gave him half a bologna and cheese and coffee from the thermos. I ate the other half and shared the coffee. We took 495 around Boston, then 93 into New Hampshire. I switched to driver, and we shared another of Mom's bologna and cheeses.

"I didn't mean that about wishing I was never born. I wouldn't have had you guys then. You and Bethany."

"I know, Pop," I said. He didn't hear me. He turned his crying head to the side.

73

San Gabriel was hot. I was tuned for a different end of October, for some chill, for some damp. It was stale and windless and hot. I pulled off onto the sidewalk of Valley Boulevard and took off my sweats, down to a blue T-shirt and baggy running shorts. My socks felt wet, and I took them off, too, and aired out the dogs, I finished the last banana and bottled water. I sat on the curb between two cars and enjoyed the food.

When I rode again, I followed Valley into Mission Road and, like a miracle, came onto the fat beginning of Sunset Boulevard. Again, it's amazing to be a man doing a boy's ride or something. I only know there is no way on earth that Smithy Ide could go where he was going, to Venice, to Cheng Ho Funeral Home, any other way. The two thin tires took more than my disappearing body to Bethany. It took whatever me was. Not new or old, but just me. I knew I would be able to see her, and I knew she would let me.

At first my ride was easy and secure and reassured. I told myself over and over that there was no hurry. Starting so early had given me a jump, and even with the two flats, I could be in Venice by four or five. But my pace picked up when Bethany passed me on the back of a low and sleek Mercedes-Benz. She smiled and laughed and called my name.

"Hook's here!" I shouted, and pushed my bike harder onto the flat plain of Sunset at West Hollywood.

I ran a red light, another. I glided smoothly away from restaurants and office buildings, past huge homes and hotels. At the mouth of Coldwater Canyon, I heard brakes squeal in my wake. I was flying. Ahead, Bethany smiled and shouted and leaped in her wedding dress from car to car.

"Hook's here!" I screamed, the dry air pinching my hairy face.

I rode that last part of Sunset like a cartoon. I still imagine a line of fire behind me. Miles and miles of speed and shouts. And then I was standing against a rail, in a long, thin parking lot, looking out at the ocean. I had never seen a beach so wide and so empty. A tall man in a three-piece suit leaned stomach first against the rail and worked a kite out over the beach and over the highway. He worked it with string in both hands, and, really, you could say he was piloting it.

"Is that Venice?" I said, pointing down to the beach.

"That?"

"Yes."

"No."

The kite soared almost straight up, then stopped and swerved to the left. It was red, but it was so high I couldn't tell if there was a design on it.

"See that cement road on the beach?"

I looked. "Okay."

"Get on the road. It's a bike road. Joggers. Go left, and that goes into Venice."

In ten minutes I was walking my bike down the bike road. A cool breeze came off the Pacific. I didn't care. I took my T-shirt off and let the sun hit me. I had not walked on a beach since I could remember. I started an easy pedal.

I moved my heart around, because now I was afraid. Looking back, I was more than likely afraid of an ending, because an ending usually meant a beginning. But it was a real fear, and so I pedaled slow and moved my heartbeat as completely as I could.

I have never been in a place like where the bike road came to. I remember it, and I'm pretty sure most of what I remember was real. Of course, I understood my vision of Bethany for what it was. She was in Pop's baseball uniform and walked a little ahead of me, pointing with delicate fingers at the street bands and jugglers and mimes and dancers and speakers and weightlifters and people getting outdoor massages from a seven-foot blond man in a Superman suit. Behind a basketball court, I found a men's room. I looked at myself in the mirror. I needed a sink bath and to neaten my beard. I walked to my bike and took a towel and shaving supplies back into the bathroom. There is something so nice about water, that's all. I fixed myself, rolled the razor neatly in the towel, and walked back to my bike. Or where my bike had been.

"Hey!" I shouted. "Hey! My bike!" I looked around in every direction and ran to the main bike road.

"Anybody seen my bike?"

I waited as if somebody was going to say something, but nobody did. I saw a tall, thin black girl looking at me.

"Somebody . . . somebody stole my bike."

She smiled at me, and I guess I smiled at her. "Want your hair in a ponytail? Beads and wire?"

"A ponytail?"

"Free, 'cause somebody stole your bike."

Somebody steals bikes and there's ponytails. I don't get it.

"Okay," I said.

"Sit."

I sat in a short director's chair she had set on the sand just off the bike road. She combed my hair back.

"I . . . don't have a lot of hair."

I looked down. She had a hand-painted sign stuck in the sand. It said HAIR BEADS BY SHABBA.

"What color beads?" she asked.

"Red? You think?"

"Red's nice."

Shabba went to work and hummed a little song, and every now and then somebody went by and shouted to her and laughed, and she shouted, too, and laughed. In a few minutes, I had a small ponytail and red beads. She held a hand mirror off to the side so I could see.

"That's nice," I said.

" 'Cause somebody stole your bike. Lots of people, though. Most don't steal."

"Most people are really nice," I said.

"Most people are the best," she said, with a wonderful smile.

"Do you know where the colonnades are?"

She pointed. "You see the old tile roof?"

"Uh-huh."

"Colonnades."

I moved through the crowd and across a tiny walkway, and then I was standing in front of a circular roadway with the old building facing me. I pulled my T-shirt back on. I could smell chicken somewhere, and the chicken was frying. And then I could smell the Pacific Ocean and things that were in it. And then I walked across the roadway and behind the colonnade.

74

For a few years after the honeymoon, whenever we needed anything that Jeff's store carried, we'd drive out on a Saturday and visit and buy. Then one day Jeff told us that his feelings wouldn't be hurt if we wanted to buy from somewhere else. It all just got too hard for Jeff. He met another woman. It was very difficult, I know, with the Ides around, even though it was only out of our concern for him that we came to the store. So Jeff Greene drifted out of our lives, and Pop became a Bethany detective, and Mom sat by the phone, and I became a mountain. People separated by grief. Sharing the unshareable. But in the first days following her leaving of the Level Wind Lodge, what was shared was a hope.

Jeff was on the porch when we pulled up. He was sitting with a young Conway policeman and was angry. He met us at the steps.

"You will not believe what this guy is asking me," Jeff said, thumbing in the direction of the cop.

"Sir, I was only—"

"He asked me if we'd been fighting. God!"

"Sir, often in a domestic—"

"Domestic! God!"

Pop went past Jeff and took the officer aside.

"She just walked away," Jeff continued. "She just said good riddance and walked away. We were having a great time. The food . . . I mean . . . well, she planned it. Jesus! God!"

"It's the voice. We'll find her."

"She just walked away."

"It's not her, Jeff. I know that sounds stupid, but it's not Bethany. It's the voice."

"The Thatchers have a room for you and your father."

"We'll find her."

"I don't know. God."

I put our stuff in the room. Pop got all the dope from the cop. She'd been missing now for twenty-four hours. The Mountain Club had done a thorough search of White Horse Trail, which was connected up to the small path she must have taken off the porch. They had fanned out and covered Red Bridge Link Trail, White Horse Ledge Summit, Bryce Path Junction, Bryce Path Link Trail, and the Echo Lake parking area. The police were going to get their drag boat into the lake in the morning, but there were a lot of people around and nobody had seen anyone in the lake or even heard any splashing or anything, so Pop was assured that this was only precautionary.

The next morning we drove slowly for three or four hours, in and out of North Conway and Conway and the small, hilly roads around the town. In the afternoon we moved through Freyburg, over the viaduct at Moosepond, and into Bridgton, Maine, on Highland Lake, where the Ides vacationed until the car accident.

New buds came out late in Maine. New leaves were only now beginning to unravel. The lake looked ice cold. We untied the rope strung across the dirt road down to the cabin. The NO TRESPASSING sign clanged on the ground. "Pop, I don't know."

"See, she could have gotten a ride or something. You just don't know. We don't know."

We always came in August. Pop's friend rented it out June to August in two-week blocks. It looked sad and cold and lonely coming out of the winter. We got out of the car.

"Bethany!" Pop called.

"Bethany!" I called, too.

"Honey, it's me. It's Jeff."

We stood still and quiet and listened. It seemed very cold. Heavy, gray clouds passed over us. Pop walked down to the waterfront. Jeff followed him, and I walked around the cabin to the side door. It was open. Someone had smashed the bolt lock that was secured with a combination lock.

"Bethany?"

I walked into the kitchen and then the small living room.

"Hook's here," I said like a stupe, and walked into the first bedroom where Mom and Pop slept. The bed had a clear plastic covering to help keep out the moisture, and it smelled musty. I lit a smoke and looked into the bunk room.

"Smithy?"

"In here, Pop. Somebody banged off that lock."

"Nothing down at the waterfront."

"Nothing here either."

We closed the door behind us. Jeff found a sturdy stick that he propped under the knob, and we walked up the path to the car. When we heard the engine turn over, it froze us in our tracks. It revved loud and hot in the spring woods. High in the new branches, birds squawked.

We ran in a line onto the dirt road directly behind the wagon. It jerked forward. The driver scrunched down in the seat and revved hotter and hotter. We stepped to it, and it jerked forward again. We moved faster, its jerk faster and longer. Finally Jeff and I broke into a full run behind Pop's station wagon and were engulfed in a storm of tire-thrown rocks and dirt. The car roared up the camp road, past the rope fence and beyond. We stood again in our line, hearing Pop's car slice through the cold.

"Was that her, son?"

"Bethany?" Jeff asked. "My Bethany? Stealing a goddamn car? God! *No!*"

"Was it?"

"I don't think so, Pop," I said.

But I had heard it, if only between the revs, heard that scratch of a voice I had heard all my life. In the cold. Under the dangerous clouds.

75

The Cheng Ho Funeral Home was a two-story, square white stucco house with an orange tile roof. The front door faced a parking lot, which was chained off and empty. Lights were on in the second floor even though it wasn't dark yet. I stepped over the chain and walked up to the front door. There was a sign with an arrow taped under the bell that read OFFICE IN REAR. I walked around to the back of the building where the driveway was curved and where two limousines and a white hearse were parked. On the other side of an open garage, I could hear the crowd from the bike road. I listened for a second, and then I knocked on the office door.

A voice came over the intercom box. "Hello."

"Hello," I said, and waited.

"Yes?"

"Oh, uh, . . . I'm Smithy . . . Smithson Ide, and you've got my sister."

"One moment, please."

A balding, middle-aged Chinese man unlocked the door and let me in. "I'm very sorry. Mr. Ide. Yes?"

"Yes, I'm Smithson Ide."

"Yes, yes. We have the Linn funeral at six, and I thought the family might have arrived early. Sorry. I'm Larry Ho. Please follow me." Larry Ho wore blue suit slacks, a white shirt, and a deep maroon tie. I followed him down a narrow corridor into a bright, cheerful office.

"Sit, please."

He walked behind his desk. Before he sat, he took the blue suit jacket that hung behind his desk chair and slipped it on. He had a file on top of his desk.

"We received a call that you would be coming perhaps today," he said as he opened the folder.

I felt achy in my stomach. I tried to be calm myself.

"My brother Al," Larry said, "my partner, made the transfer quite a while ago. I think it's a lovely thing that you have made this journey. Often—"

"Somebody stole my bike," I said. Stupidness never lets up.

"Your bike?"

"See, I'm not a bum or anything. I've just been riding. I mean . . ."

"We never judge anyone," he said, with a serious smile that I could believe. "Often people make very general suppositions about Al and myself. Undertakers? Funeral directors? Ghoulish suppositions. We cannot live lives and worry what others think. Our father taught us that."

"Cheng Ho?" I asked.

"Archie."

"Oh."

"Cheng Ho was our granddad. Judge not, lest ye be judged. Good advice."

"Yes, sir."

Larry's smile left, and his eyes became pensive and even more serious. He stood and walked around the corner of his desk. His eyes narrowed on me. "Will you allow me to offer a thought?"

"Sure."

"I understand your sister was a street person."

I had never heard it. I had known it and dreamed it, but I had never heard another human say it.

"That it is a hard and unforgiving life is clear to you, I'm sure, but the aspect of physical deterioration is often alarming. Al has worked quite hard on Bethany, but I must tell you, Mr. Ide, the life of a street person is difficult."

I took a deep breath. The office smelled flowery and nice. "I know. I'm very thankful that you and your brother took care of my sister."

"The things that have driven her," he said, "we will probably never know."

"I know. It was a voice. It was a fucking voice that I would have liked to kill if it wasn't inside her."

He nodded. "We've moved her to a display coffin. The room is cold, of course. May I add something else?"

"Sure."

"Have you considered interment?"

"Where I'm going to bury her?"

"Yes."

"I'm going to put Bethany with my mom and pop."

"May I suggest, then, cremation. We could then forward the remains to your funeral home."

"I don't know. I mean . . . cremation."

"Well, I felt the option had to be extended. More and more people are embracing the return of the loved one to the elements."

"Can I think about it?"

"Of course. And now let's go downstairs."

I followed Larry to an elevator, and we rode one floor to the basement. It opened onto another pleasant corridor, similar to the one upstairs. We walked down to a locked heavy wooden door. Larry opened it and switched on several lights. The room was icy, and goose bumps jumped over my bare legs and arms. There were several stainless-steel tables on wheels, long and narrow, arranged in a neat row against the far wall. Opposite them a bank of eight sliding body vaults, closed and locked. The ceiling of the room was new, white perforated tiles. The floor and walls that were not stainless steel were also white. On a cart in a corner of the room rested a coffin with the half top raised, so that in order to see my sister, I would have to walk to it and around it. A folding chair was set up next to it.

Larry stood behind me and placed his hand on my shoulder. "Will you be too cold?"

I shook my head.

"Then I shall leave you. If you simply pick up this phone on the wall, I will return to you."

I nodded, and then I was alone in the room.

I stood very still. I could hear nothing. After a while I could hear the quiet itself. I walked on weary legs to the upturned coffin lid and stood again, quietly, looking at the wood and at the grain. I wondered if I had come close enough. On the other side of this wood was my sister. I had come this close. Was this close enough? And this is what I truly understand, now. You have to go all the way through. It's too hard any other way. I stepped around to my sister.

Not even her eyes. Not even the few patches of hair. Or the curve of her lips or the bones of her chin. Nothing linked to my memory. A tiny thing in death and sadness, and not at all my Bethany, except of course the few teeth that corresponded to the dental records Pop sent out. Is that all that ever remains, then? Teeth? Cavities and despair?

"Oh, Bethany," I whispered, brushing a few wisps of hair onto her pillow like I'd done with Mom in the hospital.

Larry and Al Ho had laid her in a pretty blue polka-dot dress that I knew couldn't have been hers. They had rouged her and arranged the weak hair to fall over the space where part of an ear was missing. Her eyebrows were penciled on. They didn't insult her with a smile. My sister looked stunned.

I put my face down close to hers, then laid my cheek against hers. She smelled like Mom's lilac soap. I was crying into her pillow, and it was a good cry, and it was for Mom and Pop and Norma, too.

"I'm so sorry I never came over, Norma," I said into the pillow. "I could spend the rest of my life being sorry for everything." But I was not sorry that Mom was not here. I was not sorry my pop was not. I heard a voice. A soft call.

"Smithy."

I thought I dreamed the voice, and I kept my face on Bethany's pillow.

"Smithy Ide," it said again.

I raised myself up and looked over the lid to the open doorway.

Larry Ho had brought Norma down to this room. She sat tall and alone in the corridor light. Across the cold room, I noticed that the white concrete floor glistened as if it were wet. We looked over the space at each other. She wore blue jeans and a green sweater. Her hair was short again. Her eyes glistened, too, only not hard like the floor. I tried to say her name, but I couldn't.

Finally she said, "I'm coming there, Smithy. I'm coming to you."

I looked at Bethany again and then at Norma.

"No. Please, Norma."

Norma took her hands off the wheels of her chair and put them in her lap. Then she said with all her defiance, "I'm staying. I'm staying right here."

I'm not sure about my face. What it does, I mean. Sometimes I feel a smile flip across it, but in a lot of ways it doesn't seem like a smile. I looked at her, then bent down to my sister.

"I love you, Bethany. Hook will always be here."

I kissed the stranger with my sister's teeth and closed the coffin lid. I walked slowly across the room to Norma, on unsteady legs. She didn't seem surprised that so much of me was gone or that I had a beard and beads hung off my head. I walked behind her and pulled her from the room. Larry Ho was waiting in the corridor. He switched off the lights, locked the door, and took us back in the elevator.

"Cremation is okay," I said.

"Yes," he said.

"I can call you with the information."

"Yes."

I pushed Norma out of the office and down a ramp. I pushed her back across the circular roadway and onto the bike path. I pushed her past the jugglers, and the vendors, and the muscle builders, and the basketball players, and the one-man bands. I pushed her fast, and then I was running. Over the beach, kites rose and soared side to side, and Bethany did, too, held only by string to the earth, and she dove and dipped and finally broke free of us, trailing the string behind. I stopped running and watched as my sister drifted up into a clear evening sky. Norma looked straight ahead, but her left hand flew over her right shoulder and held tight to my wrist. I looked down at the top of her head.

"I . . . love . . . you," she said.

I knelt on the bike road between Venice and Santa Monica, and I was not going to be sorry anymore. I turned her face to me and kissed her lips.

"I . . . love . . . you . . . too," I said.

And I said it again. And I did.